Anne Douglas, after a varied life spent elsewhere, has made her home in Edinburgh, a city she has known for many years. She very much enjoys life in the modern capital, but finds its ever-present history fascinating.

She has written a number of novels, including *Catherine's Land*, *As The Years Go By*, *Bridge of Hope*, *The Butterfly Girls*, *Ginger Street* and *A Highland Engagement* all published by Piatkus.

Also by Anne Douglas

Catherine's Land
As The Years Go By
Bridge of Hope
The Butterfly Girls
Ginger Street
A Highland Engagement
The Edinburgh Bride

The Road to the Sands

Anne Douglas

PIATKUS

PIATKUS

First published in Great Britain in 2006 by Piatkus
This paperback edition published in 2009 by Piatkus
Reprinted 2010

A CIP catalogue record for this book
is available from the British Library.

ISBN 978-0-7499-3729-4

Typeset in Times by
Action Publishing Technology Ltd, Gloucester
Printed and bound in Great Britain by
Clays Ltd, St Ives plc

Papers used by Piatkus are natural, renewable and
recyclable products sourced from well-managed forests and certified
in accordance with the rules of the Forest Stewardship Council.

Mixed Sources
Product group from well-managed
forests and other controlled sources
www.fsc.org Cert no. SGS-COC-004081
© 1996 Forest Stewardship Council

FSC

Piatkus
An imprint of
Little, Brown Book Group
100 Victoria Embankment
London EC4Y 0DY

An Hachette UK Company
www.hachette.co.uk

www.piatkus.co.uk

Author's Note

Once again, I should like to thank the staff of the City Library Edinburgh Room and the Scottish Library, for their willing and expert help in my research for this novel.

Of the books and papers consulted, I found the following particularly useful:

White, Dennis B. *Exploring Old Duddingston and Portobello*. Mainstream, 1990
Bonar, Ruth *The history of Portobello and Joppa as a holiday resort*. (Held in the Edinburgh Room collection).
Mullay, Sandy *The Edinburgh Encyclopedia*. Mainstream, 1996.

Although *The Road to the Sands* is set in the real Edinburgh district of Portobello, it is a work of the imagination, containing no real persons, firms or shops. The characters live in a road called the King George Road which has the same site as the real King's Road, but again this is purely fictional, as are all actions of the characters, though certain historical events, such as VE Day, feature in the story.

PART ONE

Chapter One

Dancing in the streets. That's what they'd be doing in Edinburgh, somebody told Tess Gillespie. She thought it sounded lovely. But would people be dancing where she lived, in Portobello? Maybe. Dear old Porty would be celebrating, anyway. The boys had been collecting wood for a bonfire for days, ever since they'd heard that Hitler was dead.

But now it was official. This day, in May 1945, had been declared VE Day, Victory in Europe Day, and the first of two public holidays. Tess, a tall, lanky thirteen year old, was still feeling a fool, because she'd gone to school that morning as usual and been sent home, with Erika her friend. Their mothers had gone to work too, and they'd also been sent home. It was nobody's fault really, there'd been a lot of confusion. For quite some time, folk hadn't known if they were celebrating or not. What did it matter, though? They were all so happy, anyway.

Now, Erika and Mrs Lange had gone to church to give thanks for victory, while Tess was taking her new flag to show her mother.

Flags were out all along the High Street as she approached her home, which was at the top of King George Road, the old road to the sands as it had once been known. That was in the days before it was a road at all really, just a track through furze and scrub, and long before there'd been a town called Portobello. Now, of course, there were houses everywhere, and a great power station with a chimney you could see for miles. Couldn't walk on the sands, though; they were shrouded in barbed wire.

Tess crossed the road and let herself into Number One, the house that had been her gran's and was now her mother's. Though it was as tall as the tenements that lined the rest of the street that sloped to the sea, it wasn't itself a tenement. No, a whole house. Tess felt quite proud of that, even if her mother had always had to let rooms to keep it going, Dad's job at the garage not bringing in much. He was at present a sergeant with a Scottish regiment in Europe. Would he soon be coming home for good? Tess's heart leaped at the thought.

Taking the stairs to the basement kitchen two at a time, she called out that she was back. Ma, having been given the holiday she hadn't expected, would be at home. Usually at this time she was over the road in what had been the ball-room of the Marine Gardens, helping to make landing craft. 'Would you credit it?' she would laugh. 'All us women making thae vehicles, where your dad and me used to go dancing?' But everything was different now, because of the war.

Yes, Ma was at home and waiting for Tess.

'Look who's here!' she cried, her eyes shining, and Tess stopped short. Her sister, Nola, twenty years old and in the WAAF, the women's air force, was standing in the middle of the long low kitchen. She must have wangled leave to come over from Drem, where she was stationed. And she'd be going dancing, thought Tess, if anyone would.

'Oh, Nola!' she cried, and the two sisters hugged each other, half laughing, half crying, with the emotion of the day.

'Am I no' the lucky one?' cried Nola, catching her breath. 'Got a public holiday, just like you. Well, a two-day pass, and it happens to be VE Day! I'm away to meet Clark in Princes Street soon as I've had a cup of tea. He's

4

got you some fresh eggs, Ma, so you can make us all a victory cake. They're in ma bag.'

'That Walters fellow?' Rena murmured, her face changing. 'Now where on earth would a flight sergeant get eggs, then?'

'Och, you know Clark! He can get anything.' Nola, plump and pretty in her uniform, her tunic unbuttoned, tossed aside her cap and pushed back her soft fair hair. 'Think he's pally with one o' the farmers round Drem. But, hey, Ma, never mind thae eggs and just give me a kiss. The war's over!'

Rena's expression softened, and as she went swiftly to embrace first Nola, then Tess, tears came to her narrow blue eyes. She was thirty-eight but looked older, because she was so thin, folk said, she should get some meat on her bones, so she should.

Aye, but she'd always been thin. Couldn't sit down, that was her trouble. Always on the go, but as she pointed out, that way she got things done. War work, queuing for everything under the sun, cooking, washing, mending, doing all her own repairs. But oh, how she was longing for her husband, Don, to come home, whether she could do things or not.

'Know what this means?' she asked, tucking her straight light hair into its roll around a ribbon. 'Your dad'll be safe. He'll be coming home.'

'We know that, Ma,' Nola said softly. 'We're waiting for him, same as you.'

Rena, blinking away tears, turned to look at her husband's photograph on the kitchen dresser. The eyes of her daughters followed. There he was, then, dear Don, dear Dad, in his army uniform, his forage cap at an angle on his dark curly hair, his grin lighting his face just as they remembered it. Five years he'd been away, with only occasional leaves home, when they could never be really happy because he was so soon to go away again. Now he would be coming home for good and as they dwelt on that, long sweet sighs escaped them.

'Ma, how do we know the Germans won't keep on shooting?' asked Tess, winding her long slender arms around Rena's waist. She had her father's looks, the curly hair, the wide smile, the clear grey eyes, but was as thin as her mother, much to Nola's despair.

'Of course they won't keep on shooting,' Rena told her. 'They'll want the war to end as much as us.'

'And do you think Hitler's really dead?

'Dead as a doornail in his bunker,' said Nola. 'No need to worry about him. Let's think about tea, eh? I'm no' wanting to be late for meeting Clark.'

Rena's face darkened as she moved to light the flame under the kettle on the gas cooker. 'You keep on calling him Clark. Thought his name was Ralph.'

'It's just that he looks like Clark Gable,' Nola answered defensively.

'Thinks he does,' said Tess, grinning.

'He does! He's got the dimples and the same sort of eyes. Everybody says he looks like Clark Gable when he was Rhett Butler in *Gone with the Wind*.'

'Ma wouldn't let me see that.'

'I should think I wouldn't!' cried Rena.

'Well, I'm meeting Clark whatever he looks like,' Nola declared. 'Tess, I see you got a flag. I got one, too. Want to put 'em in our window?'

'And if you're going upstairs, Tess, see if Mrs Lange's back from her church,' said Rena. 'She might like to come down for a cup o' tea – Erika as well.'

Mrs Lange and her daughter, who was Tess's best friend at school, were from Austria and the only ones left of the refugees billeted on Rena earlier in the war. Soon, Rena would have to think about taking in ordinary tenants again, but for the moment she was managing on what she earned from her war work and what Don could send her from his pay. And very nice it was, she often thought, not to be bothered with folk wanting to use her kitchen and taking over the bathroom.

'I'm just going to make a few sandwiches,' she added. 'Only got cheese, mind.'

But Tess, holding the flags, seemed to be hovering.

'What's up then?' asked Rena, beginning to slice the dreary national loaf everybody had to buy.

'If Nola's going into Edinburgh, Ma, can we go too? I mean, Erika and me?'

'Now, what d'you want to do that for? There'll be too many people up there.'

'Some o' the girls from school are going. Said it'd be exciting. Seeing the dancing, and that.'

'I think you'll be better off here, Tess. I'm no' keen on mixing with that crush.'

'But we could go with Nola.'

'Nola will be with that young man o' hers. And she'll be late back, and all. Too late for you girls.'

'I don't mind taking 'em,' Nola said gallantly.

'No, I've said, I think we'll be better off here. Mrs Lange and the girls and me will all go out together. Now, away with your flags, Tess. I'm waiting to make the tea.'

'You canna blame her for wanting to see what's going on in Edinburgh,' Nola murmured, as Tess went out with the flags.

'I ken what Tess wants, and I understand, but sometimes I have to lay down the law and there's only me to do it.'

'Now, when did Dad ever lay down the law?'

Rena, buttering bread, smiled slightly. 'Well, we always used to talk things over. If I was worried, I mean. Like I'm worried now.'

'Over Tess?'

'Over you. Don't get too close to that laddie you're seeing, eh? I've a feeling he's no' right for you.'

'You leave me to worry about that.' Nola rose and put her arm round her mother's bony shoulders. 'Come on, Ma, be happy. Just remember, Dad'll be coming home.'

'You don't think they might send him to the Far East? That war's still going on.'

7

'They've already said that men over twenty-five who've had long service won't get sent there. Dad's fought in Italy and right through to Germany.' Nola smiled. 'Before you know it, he'll be walking in the front door and it'll be like he's never been away.'

Rena's face relaxed into a smile that took the years from her face. 'Here comes Tess. I'll make the tea.'

'Mrs Lange and Erika aren't back yet,' Tess announced, as she took her place at the table. 'Do you think we should've gone to the kirk?'

'We can go on Sunday. There'll be a thanksgiving service, I expect.' Rena shook her head. 'To tell you the truth, I'm sending up thanks all the time, anyway.'

'Me, too,' said Nola. 'Tess, when we've had our tea, d'you want to come upstairs while I get ready?'

'Like the old days?' asked Tess. 'Oh, yes, please!'

8

Chapter Two

Tess, so much younger than her sister, had always liked watching Nola getting ready to go out. Before she joined the WAAF she'd had a job in the box office at one of the local cinemas, and on her night off had always gone out somewhere with one of her admirers. Maybe dancing, or to a show in Edinburgh. Something that involved changing her dress, anyway, and putting on fresh make-up and redoing her hair, and Tess had always been there, in the attic room the sisters shared, watching and helping.

How patient her sister had always been! For ever talking and laughing, as Tess handed the vanishing cream and watched her rub it in, or passed the combs she needed to do up her hair. Then there'd be the lipstick to apply, with Nola making her mouth into an 'O', and working in the bright red colour, pressing her lips together and smiling at herself in her mirror.

Oh, those had been good days when Nola'd still been at home! Take the times she'd let Tess and Erika sneak up the stairs into the four and sixpenny seats at the cinema, always swearing that it was quite all right, the manager didn't mind, and teasing Tess because she used to fly up to the circle as though the police were after her.

Never turned down the offer of a seat, though. Nor did Erika, even though she was a little nervous, too. 'These seats cost four and sixpence?' she would ask in her precise

English, as she and Tess sat together, eyeing the entwined girls and young men around them, not surprised at all that they would be kissing and such, but that they could afford to be there.

'Whatever would Ma say, if she knew you'd let us into thae seats?' Tess asked Nola once, but Nola only flung back her cloud of fair hair and promised faithfully that it was OK. One of the perks of her job, see? Like when girls who worked in sweet shops got given chocolates. Used to get given chocolates, she amended, for no one saw chocolates now. A bar of gritty 'Blended', if you'd any sweet ration left, was the best you could hope for.

All this excitement came to an end when Nola was called up and opted to join the WAAF. Very pretty she looked, too, in her air-force blue uniform, even if her tunic was always that bit tight and she was always threatening to go on a diet, but oh, what a miss she was to Rena and Tess.

It was at the time when most of the lodgers had departed, and the shabby old house seemed echoing and lonely, with only Mrs Lange and Erika on the first floor, Rena on the second, and Tess all by herself in the attic with no light because of the black out. She'd lie in her bed, hugging her old doll, Alice, and keep very still so that anything moving in the darkness wouldn't find her.

'Och, you're a big girl now to be frightened of the dark,' said Rena.

'I just miss Nola, Ma.'

'Aye, well, I miss her, too. And your dad.' Rena had given Tess a hug. 'Maybe I'll find a little nightlight for you, then. That'd never show, eh?'

'And there aren't any air raids now, even in Glasgow.'

'Got to be careful, though. Canna be sure of anything until the war's over.'

Well, the war was over now, or most of it, anyway, and here was Nola getting ready to go out again, and Tess watching her, just like in the old days.

10

'But can you no' wear one o' your dresses?' she asked her sister, when she returned from the one and only bathroom, buttoning on a clean uniform shirt.

'Got to wear our uniform as usual.' Nola sat down at the dressing table to begin the ritual of making up her face. 'Anyway, I want to wear it. Might as well let folk see I've done ma bit.'

In no time, she'd slapped on her cream and powder, smoothed vaseline over her eyelids, and applied her scarlet lipstick. Next came her hair. First the brushing, then the combing and pinning up with nimble fingers, finally the fluffing out into a pompadour style above her brow, in the fashion of her favourite film stars.

'How do I look?' she asked Tess, when she'd finished.

'Lovely.'

'Just give ma collar a brush, will you? Then I'll put ma tunic on. Oh, God, I swear it's shrunk. Now, I'm ready.'

'I bet you'll have a grand time, Nola.'

'Aye, but it'll be packed out in Edinburgh tonight, and Ma's right, it's no place for you. Don't wait up for me, eh? I'm sure to be late back.'

'Off to the celebrations?' Mrs Lange asked, coming in the front door with Erika, as Rena and Tess came to wave Nola off.

'Aye, painting the town red,' said Rena. 'Though why you need that much paint on your face as well, Nola, I canna imagine.'

'Come on, Ma, you use lipstick yourself,' Nola protested.

'No' so much to shame the pillarbox, though. Och, get along with you!' Rena gave Nola a kiss on her powdered cheek. 'Have a good time, eh? But take care, mind.'

'You've no need to worry, Ma, I can look after maself.'

'Such a lovely girl,' murmured Mrs Lange, a sweet-faced woman, who seemed to fade into the shadows as Nola, bright as a flame, passed her on her way out. 'And so happy.'

11

'We're all happy today, Mrs Lange,' said Rena, who never used her tenant's first name and would not have expected Mrs Lange to use hers. 'I was wondering if you'd like to take a walk out with Tess and me, to see the celebrations? Have a cup o' tea first, mebbe?'

Mrs Lange glanced at Erika, pale and dark haired like herself. 'Why, thank you, Mrs Gillespie. That would be very nice, wouldn't it, Erika?'

Erika, moving closer to Tess, nodded with enthusiasm.

'And I can let you have a couple of eggs, if you'd like 'em for later,' Rena went on, as she led the way along to the basement stairs. 'Nola brought some over from Drem.'

'Eggs for tea!' Mrs Lange's Viennese accent was pronounced as she thanked Rena. 'I think you are an angel in disguise, Mrs Gillespie.'

'Och, this laddie that's sweet on Nola got 'em for her. 'Course, there's nothing in it. Between him and her, I mean. Still, a nice fresh egg's a nice fresh egg, eh? Sit yourself down, Mrs Lange, and then we'll have our own little celebration.'

Rena took out a packet of cigarettes and offered it to her tenant. 'Like a Capstan? Nola let me have these. They get cigarettes at the base, you ken.'

Mrs Lange's dark eyes shone. She was a heavy smoker, as Rena knew, and always out of cigarettes.

'I still don't see why I couldn't have gone to Edinburgh,' Tess said in a low voice, as her mother lit her tenant's cigarette and her own.

'Now we've had all this out already, Tess. We're joining in with Porty folk, so make that do.'

'You can feel safe here,' Mrs Lange said quietly. 'Which is wonderful.'

Rena knew that Mrs Lange herself had found it difficult to feel safe, even in Porty. That wasn't surprising. Her husband had been killed in Vienna by the Nazis, for 'political reasons', and after she and Erika had managed to get to England, they'd had a difficult time, even though

12

they had not been actually interned. Eventually, Mrs Lange had been given a factory job that had proved too much for her, and it was only when she'd been found translation work at Edinburgh University that she'd begun to recover.

And now she could relax, thought Rena. Feel really safe, at last, and look forward to a new life for herself and Erika. The war was over.

Chapter Three

There was joy in the air in the town that spring evening, and yes, there were some people dancing. But everyone was smiling, everyone was sharing the same feelings. It was as though they were floating on clouds, aware even then that they might never feel quite so happy again, and that they must be sure to make the most of it. True, there was another war to be won and they were not forgetting it, but here and now they had their own victory and it was sweet.

Joining the people milling round one of the bonfires, Rena, wearing lipstick and with her hair now loose on her shoulders, was in her element, greeting everyone she knew, and looking suddenly so much younger that Tess was astonished.

So this was what being happy did for people, she thought, and looked with interest at other faces around her. Yes, it was true. Everyone looked younger, except perhaps Mrs Lange, but then you could tell that her happiness was mixed with sadness. She must be thinking of her husband who would never come back to her. It wasn't long, in fact, before she was whispering that she would like to go home.

'Has it been too much for you?' Rena asked sympathetically. 'Aye, it's grand there's no more need to worry, but there'll still be some folk feeling sad today. Victory won't bring back the ones that are gone.'

'That's true, but I've been very glad to be here. I've been glad to celebrate.' Mrs Lange put her hand on Rena's arm. 'I am a little weary, though. Don't worry, I can let myself in.'

'Well, you know I never look ma door,' Rena said with a laugh. 'If you don't mind, then, I'll just have a word with Vera MacFee over there. She'll be wanting me to help with the street party, if I know her.'

While Rena crossed to talk to her neighbour and Mrs Lange made her way home, Tess and Erika, allowed to stay out a while longer, left the bonfire that was dying down to see what was happening on the promenade.

Here was the most beautiful part of Portobello, the long golden beach that had brought it fame. Long ago, it had been fashionable as a watering place, a northern Brighton, with fine houses and bathing machines. Even when those days had passed and industry had become as important as visitors, it was still a holiday destination for Scottish folk.

Before the war the lovely sands would have been packed with holidaymakers. There would have been donkeys and people selling ice-cream and candy floss, children digging, their parents sunbathing, maybe moving on later to the funfair or the splendid art deco swimming pool.

Now the pool was under camouflage, and the beach, behind its screen of barbed wire, rolled away to the waters of the Forth, as quiet and lonely as when the area had been just a wilderness; a haunt of highwaymen waiting for travellers.

'The Figgate Whins it was called, then,' Tess had said to Erika when she'd first arrived, and had gone on to tell her the old story of how Portobello had got its name, as her father had told it to her.

There'd been a sailor who'd helped to capture the Spanish town of Puerto Bello many years before. When he retired, he'd built a little cottage by the sea and called it after the victory – Porto Bello. The name had taken

15

people's fancy, and when a town had gradually grown up, it had become known as Portobello. It was only many years later that it had become part of Edinburgh, and Porty folk still liked to think of themselves as separate anyway, in their own place with the beautiful name.

'Yes, Portobello is a beautiful name,' Erika had agreed, in halting English. 'And a beautiful place, too.'

'I think so,' said Tess. 'Even though some folk say there's too much industry. But I'd like to see your city, Erika. I'd like to see Vienna.'

A shadow had crossed Erika's small pointed face. 'Perhaps you will one day. But Mutti says we shall never go back to Vienna.'

Now, the two girls gazed again at the beach through the coils of wire that would at last be coming down, while people walked up and down the promenade, linking arms and laughing at nothing in particular, just happy that the European war was over.

'I don't know why Ma always treats me like a bairn,' Tess murmured. 'I am thirteen.'

'Not so very old,' commented Erika.

She was herself so small and slight, she apeared younger than thirteen, except for those great dark eyes, which were the eyes of someone who'd seen too much for a child of any age.

'Folk used to go to work at thirteen, Erika. Aye, they went into service, or did errands and that kind o' thing.' Tess shook her curly head. 'I'm no' saying I'd want to do that, mind. But I bet, if ma brother had been thirteen, Ma would've let him do anything he liked.'

'You think about your brother a lot, Tess, don't you? Though you never knew him.'

'I was only a baby when he died. He was the middle one. That's why there's a big gap between Nola and me.'

'It's so sad. Your poor mother.'

'Aye, Ma's never got over losing wee Rickie.'

16

'You still have Nola.'

'And she's ma best friend. Apart from you, Erika.'

Erika put a thin hand on Tess's arm. 'You've been very kind to me, Tess. I'll never forget it. When I first went to the school and the girls thought me so strange, I think I should have done badly without you.'

'They didn't mean anything. They're just like that with anybody different.'

'You weren't like that.'

Tess grinned. 'Och, no! I like folk to be different. And I loved to hear you talk.'

Erika flushed. 'My terrible English. I think I have improved, though?'

'You'll soon be sounding a proper Scot.' Tess laughed. 'Let's walk on, eh? It's no' time to go back yet.'

Their way took them past the great skeleton of the funfair's figure-of-eight railway, and the shuttered little shops that had once sold ice-cream, seaside rock and souvenirs, all remembered fondly by Tess.

'We used to have such good times when I was a wee girl,' she murmured. 'Going to Fun City, and having ice-cream at the Italian shop, and all o' that. When Dad had the money, I mean. Sometimes, we'd go on the donkeys. I can remember falling off!' She laughed. 'You should have heard me bawl!'

'Those good times will come back,' said Erika firmly. 'We can be sure of that now, you know.'

'Aye, but when you look around, you canna believe it, can you?'

Moving on, they passed some of the grander buildings of the promenade. Elegant flats, and the Portobello Sea Water Baths establishment; large houses with front gardens. But everything looked deserted, the owners of the houses long gone for the 'duration', the baths closed. It seemed as though all the properties were sleeping, waiting their turn to be used again. Surely now, that would be soon?

17

'There's ma favourite house,' Tess whispered, standing at the entrance to the driveway of a stone-built house, with a portico and gables and rows of rounded Victorian windows. It had been a fine residence once, and with attention could be again, but now like its neighbours, it was a house in waiting. There were no longer any gates – probably they had been of wrought iron and removed to aid the war effort – but there was a name on the stone pillar where the gates had once hung, which read 'Pax House'.

'It is beautiful,' Erika murmured.

'Really grand, eh?' Tess's grey eyes shone as they rested on the house she so much admired. 'Ma knew the housekeeper here before the war. She said the man who owned it had a mint o' money, but soon as the war started, he went off to Edinburgh. Said he wasn't going to wait here to be invaded.'

'People thought they might be?'

'Yes. What did you think the barbed wire was for? Loads o' folk went away, but the Germans never came.'

'Thank God,' whispered Erika.

'Better go back,' said Tess, after a pause. 'Or Ma'll be after us.'

The sky was still light over the sea, as they turned in to their road from the promenade; the wonderful day was not yet over.

'Mutti said she never thought she'd see the day the Germans were defeated,' Erika said, as they moved homewards. 'But, you see, it has come.'

'Aye, and this'll be the road to the sands again. I told you it was once called that?'

'Before King George came here, you said. But you have a King George now.' Erika frowned. 'That is confusing.'

'This was an earlier King George.' Tess laughed. 'They'd have had the flags out then, an' all. Can you see mine and Nola's?'

They looked up towards Rena's house and saw Tess's

18

Union Jack and Nola's Scottish flag bravely flying from the window where Tess had clamped them.

'It was ma dad told me about King George's visit to Scotland,' Tess went on. 'He's the one knows all the old stories. Sometimes, when Ma was busy with the dinner on a Sunday, he'd take me and Nola out and we'd go round the town and he'd tell us about the early days.' She shook her head. 'I do miss him, Erika.'

'Well, he will soon be back,' Erika reminded her comfortingly. 'And you'll go out with him again. Round the town, or on the sands.'

'And there'll be no more barbed wire.' Tess halted at the steps of her mother's house and looked back down the street to the closed beach and the sea. 'What a grand day this has been,' she said quietly.

Chapter Four

Although she tried hard to keep awake, Tess was asleep before Nola came home. In the morning, though, when she sprang up, as alert as though she'd never been to bed, there was her sister, fast asleep, in the opposite bed, her uniform jacket and skirt draped around a chair, her shoes just dropped where she'd taken them off.

So she did come home, thought Tess, who'd wondered if celebrations in Edinburgh might have gone on all night. But Ma would have had something to say if Nola had stayed out. And Ma would not have been asleep before she came in.

Though Tess didn't have to go to school, she was hungry and got up anyway, trying not to wake her sister as she padded around, finding her clothes, finally creeping out to get ready in the bathroom.

'Tess!' came her mother's voice up the stairs. 'That you up?'

'Yes, Ma!' sang Tess. 'Coming, Ma.'

'Oh, God,' murmured Nola, opening her eyes with difficulty as Tess came back. 'Oh, Tess, is it morning already? I didn't get to bed till four.'

'Nola! How d'you get back?'

'Taxi.'

'Taxi?' Tess's eyes widened. 'Who paid?'

'Clark, if you're interested.'

'Did Ma no' kill you when you got in?'

'Never appeared.' Nola struggled up against her pillows, pulling the straps of her nightdress over her plump shoulders, throwing back her hair and coughing. 'Too many cigs last night,' she said huskily. 'No' to mention drinks. Had a grand time though.'

'Were you dancing?'

'You bet. We were on the Mound and round the Ross bandstand, hundreds of us. Folk said it was quiet to begin with, but by the time we got there, it was hopping, I can tell you. There were Yanks and Poles and Free French and everybody you could think of, and folks climbing the statues and handing out coppers to bairns. Och, what a night!'

'Bairns?' Tess frowned. 'I knew there'd be plenty o' children there. I could've gone.'

'No, no, I'm glad you didn't, Tess. We all went drinking in the end. It'd never have done for you.'

'I wonder why Ma didn't come out and blow you up, though? I'll bet she heard you come in.'

'It was VE Night. She must've let me off.' Nola lit a cigarette and lay back, still coughing. 'Get us a cup of tea, eh, Tess? My throat's like – well, I'll no' say what. Go on, it'll only take you a minute.'

'I've no' had ma breakfast yet.'

'Ah, come on, I'll soon be away, you ken.'

'OK. You still want sugar?'

'Aye, two, please.'

'I'll no' dare tell Ma about you using the ration like that.'

'I'm giving it up tomorrow. Cigarettes, as well.'

Rena was standing at the gas cooker stirring porridge, her hair bundled into a turban, her eyes watchful as Tess poured a cup of tea.

'That for Nola? Och, what a devil that girl is, then. Coming in at all hours!'

'You never told her off, Ma.'

Rena shrugged. 'She'll no' be here long. And it was a special occasion. Be quick, now, and take that up, I'm going to put out your porridge.'

'Oh, what a sweetheart you are!' cried Nola, when Tess took up her tea. 'How's Ma looking then? Like a thundercloud?'

'She's all right. Said you were a devil, coming in so late, but it was a special occasion.'

'That's a relief. Tell her Clark's coming round this afternoon, will you? Just to prepare the ground.'

'Clark?' Tess, in the doorway, stared. 'Why's he coming here?'

'Why shouldn't he? He's to be back on duty this evening, so I said he could look in and say hello before he went.'

'Ma might be a thundercloud after all, then.'

Nola drew her fair brows together. 'I wish I knew what she's got against him.' She sipped her tea. 'Well, tell her anyway that he's coming, OK?'

'OK,' Tess agreed reluctantly.

Sitting at the scrubbed wooden table, in the kitchen that was filled with shadows even on a bright spring morning, Tess ate her porridge and gave her mother the message. As she had predicted, Rena's brow darkened.

'Clark's coming here? And will be expecting his tea, I suppose?'

'Nola never said anything about tea.'

'Looks like I'll have to find something for sandwiches, though.' Rena chewed her lip. 'He'll be sure to want a bite before he goes back.'

'Can I have some toast, Ma?'

'Och, that grill burns everything. Just have a bit o' bread and butter, and be quick or you'll be late for school and getting the belt.'

'Girls of my age don't get the belt,' Tess said loftily. 'And do you no' remember – it's another holiday today.'

'Oh, so it is!' Rena put her hand to her brow and laughed a little. 'And here's me getting ready for work again just like yesterday! No need to worry about that, then.' She took out one of her Capstans and lit it. 'Aye, but will the shops be open? Might have to open a tin.'

What boring lives grown-ups had to lead, thought Tess, spreading jam on another slice of bread and butter. Always worrying about what was in the shops, for instance. Surely, now the war was over, Ma could stop thinking about what to get to eat?

'I needn't go for the messages, need I?' she asked. 'I mean, even if the shops are open?'

'I'd better go out maself this morning,' her mother told her. 'See what I can find.'

Some time later, after Tess had gone up to see Erika, Nola, in a faded pink dressing gown, came drifting into the kitchen, carefully avoiding her mother's eye.

'Four o'clock,' Rena said shortly. 'That's when you got in, Nola.'

'I'm a big girl now, Ma.'

'If you're under ma roof, I'm responsible for you. What did you get up to, then?'

'Och, just dancing and that.'

'Till four o'clock?'

'Somebody had a party going. Over at Toll Cross.' Nola poured herself tea and bravely met her mother's gaze. 'Just dancing to records and a few drinks. No beds available.'

'Folk don't always need beds for what I'm thinking about.'

'Well, you've no need to think about it. I told you, I can take care of maself.'

'And I'm telling you, I'm no' keen for a grandchild till you've got a ring on your finger.'

'There won't be a grandchild. Till I'm wed.'

Rena was silent for a moment. 'Is it going to be him, then?' she asked at last, slicing bread. 'This Clark fella?'

23

'No, it isn't.' Nola got up and lit the grill on the gas cooker. 'Well, let's just say I've no plans to wed anybody at the moment.' She took the bread Rena had sliced and put it under the flame. 'I'm pretty young yet, you ken.'

'Older than me when I had you.' Rena sniffed. 'That grill's sure to burn your toast, Nola.'

'I'll watch it. Just stop fussing, Ma.'

Chapter Five

Tess and Erika were coming back from the High Street, where they'd been window-shopping with girls from school, when Clark Walters roared up the Edinburgh road on a motorbike.

'Nola's young man,' Tess whispered as they watched him leap off and wheel the bike to the side of Rena's front-door steps. He was wearing a raincoat over his uniform, which he stopped to take off, and when he saw the girls by the power station, waved and grinned.

'He is the one who looks like a film star?' Erika asked dubiously.

'Sort of. He's got the dimples.'

'Hello, Tess!' cried Clark, as they joined him on the steps. 'This your friend?'

'This is Erika. She stays here, with her ma.'

Clark favoured Erika with his Gable smile, and asked Tess if he could put his bike round the back somewhere. It belonged to a pal of his and he didn't want it pinched.

'Folk round here don't pinch things, but you can put it in the yard if you like.'

'Everything gets pinched in the barracks. Borrowed, is the word, but not much comes back. You going to let me in the house?'

'Door's no' locked. I told you, folk round here don't pinch stuff. Come on in.'

Tess led the way into the hall and called to Nola, who came running.

'Clark, you're here! Oh, that's grand!'

Tess and Erika watched closely as the young couple hugged and kissed, amazed that the lovely Nola should appear to care for Clark as much as he cared for her. Maybe he did look rather like Gable, but that meant little to them and they certainly couldn't imagine kissing him.

Yet he was kind. That very afternoon, for instance, he produced two bars of American chocolate, and gave one to Tess and one to Erika.

'Chocolate?' Erika cried. 'That is so lovely. Thank you.'

'Thanks,' said Tess. 'Where'd you get it, then?'

'From some Yanks last night. They were handing out everything like it was Christmas – chocolate, nylons, chewing gum.' Clark laughed. 'I was expecting coffee and doughnuts any minute.'

'Oh, Lord, I left ma new nylons at the party!' Nola exclaimed. 'Oh, trust me, eh?'

'Got 'em here,' Clark told her, taking out a shiny package from his pocket and enjoying Nola's shriek of delight. 'Found 'em when I went back after taking you home. What'd you do without me, eh?'

As they went off together to move his bike, Tess and Erika again exchanged glances.

'He's very generous,' Erika said after a pause. 'Why don't you like him?'

Tess looked around the shabby hallway that hadn't been painted since before the war. There had once been coloured glass in the front door, but it had long been replaced with plain, and latterly two broken squares had had to be repaired with brown paper. The hall stand that held a variety of coats and old mackintoshes needed a new mirror, and the carpet that matched the stairs was so faded you could no longer see the pattern.

But none of this depressed Tess; she was used to it. Besides, now that the war was over, somebody might wave

26

a magic wand and make everything look like new. All that depressed her was the thought of Nola and Clark together.

'I didn't say I didn't like him,' she said carefully.

'Tess, it is not necessary to say. I see it in your eyes.'

'At least he gave us the chocolate,' Tess said after a pause.

'I'm going to give some of mine to Mutti,' said Erika, and climbed the stairs to her mother's room.

Tea went off as well as could be expected, with Clark working hard to charm, Rena and Tess being polite, and Nola's blue eyes darting from face to face.

'Very kind of you to give me tea, Mrs Gillespie,' said Clark, starting on another sandwich. 'I don't like taking your rations.'

'Och, what's a bit o' corned beef? And you gave me thae eggs. And that American chocolate.'

'When are you going to make the victory cake, Ma?' asked Nola.

'Tonight. It'll be for the street party. I managed to get some dried fruit from the grocer's, but he'd no icing sugar.'

'Icing sugar?' Clark shook his head. 'That's something I don't think I can find, I'm afraid.' He smiled. 'I'm not usually stumped, but that's beyond me.'

Rena stared at him. 'You must be a handy laddie when you're at home, Mr Walters. I bet your ma looks forward to you coming back on leave. Did you say she lived in Leeds?'

'That's right, but I wish you'd call me Clark – everybody does, except my mother. My folks are Scottish, really. Come from Galashiels, but my Dad went in with his brother in a cycle firm down there.'

'They'll no' be selling many bikes at the moment.'

'No, closed for the duration. Both in munitions.'

'But if they open up after the war, would you be joining 'em?' Rena passed a plate of scones, still keeping her eyes on Clark.

27

'Are these home made? My, what a treat. No, I think I'll probably do something else.'

'What sort o' thing?'

'Ma,' Nola murmured, twisting in her chair. 'D'you have to ask all these questions?'

'Just interested, you ken.'

'It's OK.' Clark flashed his smile. 'Mothers like to know things. Mine's the same.' He bit into his scone. 'I'm thinking of going on the road.'

'The road?'

'Travelling. Selling. I'd be good at that.'

You would, thought Rena. Good at selling yourself, and all. Refusing to look at Nola, she rose to make more tea.

When Clark said he had to go, Nola, with some relief, said she'd see him out to collect his motorbike, but he stopped to look at Don Gillespie's photograph on the dresser.

'Nice looking fella, your dad,' he observed. 'You'll be looking forward to seeing him home, eh?'

'How soon do you think he'll come?' asked Tess quickly.

'Ah, can't be sure. Some of the guys over fifty might be out by June, but there's still the other war to finish, you see.'

'You think Don'll have to wait for that? He's no' forty yet.' Rena's look was desolate. 'They say the Japanese'll never give in.'

'If they're defeated, they'll have to. Look on the bright side, Mrs Gillespie. We are going to win that war and then everybody'll be home. I bet, sooner than you think.'

At Clark's words of comfort, Rena's face softened. He did try hard, you had to give him that. Maybe he wasn't so bad after all. But she didn't put her thin cheek forward for a farewell peck, only shook his hand instead, and when he'd left by the back door with Nola, stood waiting until she heard the roar of the motorbike. Then she looked at Tess.

'He's gone. I'll clear the table.'

Tess began to stack the dishes on the wooden draining board, aware of her mother nervously hovering as she waited for Nola, who, when she came back, slammed the door.

'No need for temper,' Rena murmured.

'Who's in a temper? I'm just fed up with the way you treat Clark, Ma. Asking him all thae questions, as though he was my intended, and I told you he wasn't.'

'I ken what you told me.'

'It's true! Honestly, I didn't know where to look.'

'I thought I'd just let him see you've got somebody to look out for you, even if your dad's away.'

'I don't need anybody to look out for me!' Nola snatched up a tea towel as Tess began on the washing up. 'Clark's just somebody I'm going out with, that's all.'

'I'd like to think so.'

Nola gave an exasperated sigh. 'Just what have you got against him, Ma? He's always polite to you, he's kind and generous, I don't know what more you want.'

Rena folded the tablecloth and shrugged. 'I canna say. All I know is, Nola, he's no' what I want for you.'

There was a silence as Tess finished washing the dishes, Nola finished drying them and Rena put them away. Suddenly Rena glanced at the kitchen clock.

'Listen, I think we should all go to the pictures. Take us out of ourselves, eh?'

'Oh, Ma!' Tess hugged her. 'But will there be anything open?'

'Sure to be,' answered Nola. 'They might've closed yesterday, but no' today. Oh, I wish I could've got us free seats, like I used to, but it'll be grand to go out anyway. Just what we need.'

They were ready in five minutes and out of the house and into a cinema that was indeed open, where Rena bought them seats in the one and ninepennies. And as the lights went down and the opening titles of the 'big picture' appeared, even Nola quite forgot Clark Walters.

Chapter Six

As the year advanced, the Gillespies' hopes faded for Don's early arrival home. It had to be accepted that troops were still needed in Europe anyway. And then there was the war with the Japanese looking like it would never be over, in spite of Clark's optimism. The euphoria of VE Day was fast beginning to be only a memory.

Don, in Germany, wrote home regularly, as he had always done, and in July, with the general election approaching, reported that he and most of the troops would be voting Labour. It was time for the nation to change, try someone new, even if it meant saying goodbye to Churchill. Nola, now twenty-one and voting for the first time, agreed, and so did Rena, who went canvassing for her Labour candidate while Tess delivered leaflets.

'I will not help you, if you don't mind,' Erika told her. 'Mutti says we must not get involved in politics.'

'Well, she doesn't have a vote, does she? No' being British.'

'Mutti is going to apply for naturalisation, though. Then she will be British and when I'm old enough I will be, too. I want to be able to go to university.' Erika looked down modestly. 'If I am clever enough, I mean.'

'Och, you're clever enough!' cried Tess. 'That's really grand news, Erika. I never knew you could change like that.'

'Oh yes, we do not wish to be Austrian any more. I told you, didn't I, that we would never go back to Vienna.'

How strange that must be, thought Tess. Never to want to go back to your real home. She couldn't imagine ever living away from Scotland, though of course, if the government had killed her dad, she'd have felt the same as Erika.

As she looked into Erika's tragic eyes it came to her again how hard life had been for her friend and her mother, how close they had perhaps been to perishing in the concentration camps everyone was beginning to learn about.

Neither Tess nor Erika had been allowed to see the news-reel pictures of the camps that had been shown at the cinemas, but they knew about them and had talked about them in whispers at school. And then girls who'd always looked at Erika strangely now treated her as something of a heroine, to have been so close to horror and escaped.

'Oh, you should go to university!' Tess told Erika warmly. 'You deserve to. What'd you do? I mean, what would you study?'

'Medicine. Like my father.'

'Oh yes, your dad was a doctor, eh?' Tess murmured with awe. 'He must have been clever. And you're clever, too.'

'And you, Tess. You could stay on at school, you could try for university.'

Tess shook her head. 'No. I'm what they call bright, but it's no' the way you're bright, Erika. I think I'm more practical.'

'What would you like to do, then?'

'Nobody'll let me do what I'd like to do.' Tess laughed. 'I fancy working with cars, same as Dad.'

'Well, why shouldn't you?'

'Och, you know why. I'm a girl. You're lucky, Erika, you know where you're going, and folk'll no' stop you.'

'I still have to get there,' said Erika.

The result of the July election was a Labour landslide. Mr

31

Churchill, who had led the country to its European victory, was deeply shocked and wounded, but the majority of voters were pleased they'd been given a fresh start. If it was time for change, change had come. Not that much could be done until they were really at peace, and when would that be? The war with the Japanese dragged on.

'They think it's shameful to surrender,' Rena told Tess. 'That means they'll fight to the last man.'

'But Clark said we'd beat them in the end.'

'Aye, but how many of our chaps'll be killed first?'

These were grim thoughts and Tess often lay awake at night, still clutching Alice, and remembering how happy they'd been on VE Day and how VJ Day seemed as far away as ever.

Then something happened that no ordinary person could have foreseen. On 6 August, the Allies dropped an atomic bomb on the Japanese city of Hiroshima, with appalling results – 66,000 people were killed instantly, and a further 69,000 died or were injured later. Three days later a second bomb, even more powerful than the first, was dropped on Nagasaki with such horrendous consequences the Japanese did the unthinkable and surrendered.

At first, all that seemed to matter was that the Second World War was over. VJ Day had arrived. No more troops would be killed, no more prisoners would suffer under the Japanese. It took a little while to realise that the world, after the dropping of those bombs, was never going to be the same again.

'All thae folk dead,' Rena murmured, as she cut sandwiches for another street party. 'Canna bear to think about it.'

'Plenty died in the war, Ma,' Nola replied.

'Aye, but there seems something worse about this, eh? They weren't soldiers who died.'

Nola, still in uniform, helped to pile the sandwiches on makeshift plates cut out from cereal boxes. 'There were thousands of civilians killed in other air raids. I mean, that's what happens in war. Civilians get killed, too.'

'But if someone else gets this new kind o' bomb, they could drop it on us, Nola.'

'Who'd you mean by someone else?'

'Some other country.' Rena lowered her voice. 'Russia.'

'Russia? They're on our side.'

'Were. Now they're on their own side. The papers say we should watch out.'

'Never believe what you read in the papers, Ma. All I'm thinking about now is that I'll soon be out of the WAAF and Dad'll soon be coming home.'

'Now where have I heard that before?' Rena asked, a little bitterly. 'I'll believe it when I see him. Walking in the front door, as you said.'

'He will be doing that. Just you wait and see.'

'Like in that song Vera Lynn used to sing?' Rena smiled. 'Bluebirds over the white cliffs of Dover? Just you wait and see? When did you last see any bluebirds, Nola?'

Chapter Seven

The bluebirds came though. Almost when they'd given up hope, a letter arrived from Don one Saturday morning in November. Tess picked it up from the mat in the hall and went racing downstairs with it, anxious to please her mother, who had been despondent of late. Don wasn't out of the army, Nola wasn't out of the WAAF, yet Clark Walters, would you credit it, was back in Leeds, demobbed, suited up, and job hunting!

'While our dad is still in Germany,' Rena had complained fretfully. 'Is it fair? It's a piece o' nonsense, that's what it is.'

Then there were the new tenants in the bedsits, all causing difficulties of one sort or another, and expecting miracles in the matter of bathroom accommodation, fresh decoration, new furniture, none of which was forthcoming at present, nor likely to be in the future.

'Och, they get on ma nerves,' Rena would groan, but then everything got on her nerves just then, as the lines on her brow and by her mouth grew deeper.

'This'll cheer her up,' thought Tess that Saturday morning, skidding to a halt in front of her mother and waving the envelope in front of her eyes. 'Ma, a letter from Dad!'

'Tess, give it here!' Rena's face was alight. She snatched a knife from the table drawer and slit the letter open. 'This could be good news, eh?'

As Tess watched closely, Rena's eyes darted along the lines of Don's handwriting. The letter seemed shorter than usual. Was that good or bad?

It was good. Oh, thank God, it was good. Don was coming home. He'd got the date. By next week, he'd be back in his own country, going through the motions of getting himself demobbed. Within a couple of days after that, he'd be wearing his new suit, he'd be walking in the front door, just as Nola had said he'd do, just as they'd all waited for him to do, all this time.

'Oh, Ma!' cried Tess, hugging her mother's thin frame to her and bursting into tears.

'Oh, Tess.' Rena pulled herself away, dabbing at her eyes. 'I canna believe it. I just canna believe it, that's the thing. When you wait for something so long, you think it'll never come, and when it does, you don't know what to do. How we'll get through the next couple o' weeks, then?'

'Let's write to Nola,' said Tess. 'Maybe she can get some leave?'

'Leave? She should be out o' the WAAF altogether. She should be a civilian. But I will write, soon as we've done the messages, eh?' Rena shook her head. 'Whatever happens in this world, you've got to eat. So we'd best do the messages first.'

Tess stood in the baker's queue, with her instructions to get a large loaf, two teacakes, and, if possible, a couple of small fruit pies. The fruit couldn't be identified and the pastry was like cardboard, but they'd be something for pudding and Rena had no lard left to make pastry herself.

Och, it was no wonder everyone in the queue was complaining. They'd won the war but there was no sign of any improvement in the rations. In fact, some items had even been reduced, and there were rumours that things like bread, never rationed during the war, might have to be put on a points system.

'Aye, things are worse since we won, eh?' the voices

moaned. 'And when'll we ever see an orange again? Or a banana?'

It was the same in Rena's queue at the butcher's, with tired women asking for joints that weren't there, or maybe ham shanks.

'Are you joking?' asked Will Hawkins, the butcher.

Or a bit o' liver, then? Yes, he'd that, and a few chops for those at the head of the queue.

'Two chops, please,' said Rena dreamily. 'And see what you can do for me when ma man comes home, Mr Hawkins, eh?'

'Don's coming home? That's grand!'

'Don's coming home, Rena?' The women in the queue were smiling at her, except for those still waiting for their husbands to be demobbed. 'You'll have to find him something good, eh? For a celebration?'

'If Don's back in his own home, that'll be enough celebration for him,' said old Hawkins, wrapping up two small chops for Rena. 'I remember how it was when I come back after the Armistice. Never thought about food. Well, no' for a day or two!'

Early that afternoon, Tess and Erika, their chores done, went walking on the sands. They would not have long, for November days were short and the light was already fading. Still, they'd get the fresh air, said Rena approvingly, and she'd get on with her letter to Nola if her tenants would leave her alone.

'What's the betting that one of 'em will be sidling in here, wanting me to cook something for 'em? But as I tell 'em all, when they first come, I don't cook for folk. They are welcome to use ma gas stove if I don't need it, otherwise they can use their gas ring. This house is no' a guest house.'

Rubbing ink from her forefinger, Rena looked across at Erika, who was standing with Tess, patiently listening. Poor plain little thing, she thought. It's a good job she's

36

clever, like Tess says, for I canna see her ever finding a man when she's grown.

'Course I'm no' talking about your mother, Erika,' she told her kindly. 'Your ma's never a bit o' trouble, and neither are you.'

'Bye, Ma!' cried Tess cheerfully, and the two girls thankfully ran up the stairs and out of the house, Tess apologising for her mother's 'going on', as they went.

'She'll be better when ma dad's back,' she added, her eyes resting on Erika's face for a moment and moving away. 'And guess what, he is coming back. We got word today.'

'Tess, you never said!' cried Erika. 'Why didn't you tell me?'

'I am telling you.'

'I mean, earlier.'

'Well – I didn't like.' Tess looked down the road towards the Forth in the distance. 'With you losing your dad, and everything.'

'Oh come, Tess, you should not be thinking of me.' Erika put back her blowing dark hair. 'I'm only happy that your father is coming home. It's what Mutti and I want for you. When will he arrive?'

'Next week, maybe. Ma's writing to Nola now, to tell her.'

Erika squeezed Tess's arm. 'That is wonderful. Really wonderful.'

The two girls looked at each other for a moment, then both began to run down the road to the sands, revelling in their youth and freedom, knowing that the barbed wire had gone and that there was no longer anything to fear. There weren't even any people on the beach, this being November, except for one man in the distance exercising a young honey-coloured labrador, no more than a puppy from the look of its plump little body.

'Never seen that fella before,' commented Tess, screwing up her eyes against the wind. 'Or that bonnie dog. Must be from one o' the big houses.'

The houses along the promenade were gradually being refurbished, some of the larger ones having already opened for visitors, but as yet the girls had seen no activity at Pax House. Always, when she walked on the sands, Tess's eyes would stray up towards her favourite house, but never was there a window opened, or smoke from the chimneys, or any sign of life. Now, however, as she moved her gaze from the distant man and the dog, she gave a little cry.

'Erika, look! There's a car in the drive of Pax House!'

'Why, it's huge,' said Erika. 'I have never seen such a big car.'

'Wonder if it's a Rolls Royce?'

It was already dusk as the two girls moved up from the beach, and the lights were coming on all along the promenade. Yes, in Pax House too, and the smoke was rising from its chimneys, grey against the darker sky. So the rich man who had moved to Edinburgh was back?

Shivering in the November chill, they decided they'd better not venture into the drive to look at the long black car, but stayed at the gate, just gazing in at the lighted house. It seemed another wonderful sign that the bad times were over, to see all those windows lit again. Another sign that the world was at peace, and as Erika said, peace was the name of this house where the rich man had returned to live.

'Pax House,' she said softly. 'Pax means peace, you know.'

'Och, it's lovely,' murmured Tess, and would have lingered, still looking in, but the cold of the evening seemed to be entering their bones. It was time to go home.

Turning once again to look back, they were excited to see, by the light of the street lamps, that the honey-coloured puppy they had seen on the sands was now bounding into the driveway of Pax House, followed by the man who had been exercising it.

'Think that's the owner?' asked Tess.

'No, I think he is wearing some sort of uniform.'

'So he is. Maybe he's the chauffeur for that grand car.'

'But petrol is rationed. He won't be able to drive it much.'

'Rich folk can get anything,' Tess said sagely. 'I'll bet the fella who lives in Pax House can get all the petrol he wants.'

'Aye, that'll be Mr Seton back,' Rena said, when Tess told of seeing the lights in Pax House. 'Taken his time, eh? Wanted to make sure he'd have no problems opening up again.'

'We saw a dog running in to the drive, with a man who might have been a chauffeur.'

'Always had a chauffeur, Mr Seton. And old Mrs Fleck for housekeeper and three or four maids.' Rena laughed scornfully. 'All for one man!'

'Is he no' married, then?'

'Wife died before the war. Had a daughter, but she went to America. I'll tell you this, he might no' find it so easy to get staff now. Mrs Fleck's retired for a start, and women are no' keen to do domestic work since they've done other things.' Rena began to scrape carrots with her usual energy. 'I wish I could've kept ma job at the plant but of course they're no' wanting landing craft any more. I've plenty to do here, but I might still look round for something else.'

'I think women should have jobs,' said Tess. 'Even when they're married.'

'End up working twice as hard as men.' Ren shrugged. 'But most of 'em do, anyway.' She plunged the vegetables into cold water. 'What do you fancy doing, then?'

'My teacher says I should do something technical. She says that's where ma talents lie.'

'Technical? That could mean a lot o' things.'

'Well, I've decided I'd like to work with cars. In a garage, like Dad.'

'Just because he used to take you to Todd's when you

were little?' Rena shook her head. 'Women do a lot o' things, Tess, but they don't work in garages. They're no' mechanics.'

'In the war, they were. And you made landing craft over the road.'

'That was factory work. We just put things together.'

'Well, I saw a photo once of Princess Elizabeth working on an engine.'

'Hm?' Rena looked sceptical. 'I'd say women drove cars, no' repaired 'em.'

'I want to learn to drive, anyway, when I'm grown.'

'A car like Mr Seton's, I suppose?' asked Rena.

The possibility of Tess's ever driving a car like Mr Seton's was so remote they couldn't help laughing. But then both grew silent, thinking how things like cars were so very unimportant, compared with a man's coming home from the war.

Chapter Eight

How the days dragged as they waited for Don's arrival!
Every morning Tess ran to look for the post, and every
morning ran downstairs to the kitchen, shaking her head.

'Nothing from Dad, Ma.'

'You'd think there'd be a postcard or something by
now,' Rena would say, stirring the porridge as though she
were punishing it. 'Och, this waiting's getting me down.
Never could stand waiting.'

'No news?' Erika would ask Tess sympathetically on the
way to school.

No news. No news. Then, suddenly, news they hadn't
expected. Nola was demobbed.

'Aye, happened all out o' the blue!' she cried, dashing in
with her suitcase and haversack one grey afternoon, when
foghorns were sounding over the Forth and the gulls were
wheeling and crying across the sands. 'I knew I was due for
getting out, but I thought they'd put me back till after
Christmas. You could've knocked me down with a feather
when I saw ma number on the board! I didn't need telling
twice, eh?'

'Oh, Nola, I canna believe it, you're home!' cried Rena.
'Did you get ma letter, telling you about your dad?'

'I did.' Nola kissed her mother and flung her arms round
Tess, just in from school. 'Never had time to reply, but I
was thinking he might be here before me. I was thinking he

might be here in the kitchen, waiting.'

'We've no' even had a postcard,' sighed Rena. 'These days of waiting have been like weeks, so they have.'

'Don't they say the longest mile is the last mile home? But what d'you think of ma new suit?'

Nola walked up and down the kitchen pretending to be a model, holding out her arms, drawing them in, smiling and posturing, as Rena and Tess admired her new tweed coat and skirt. 'Nice, eh?'

'Is it a demob suit?' asked Tess. 'Did they give it to you?'

'No, they gave me fifty-six clothing coupons and some money, and I bought it before I handed everything else in. It was goodbye to ma tunic, ma skirt, ma shirts – pretty well everything.' Nola laughed. 'Except ma underwear, of course.'

'I should think they'd let you keep that!' cried Rena. 'But why'd they no' give you a suit like the men?'

'Must've known women would rather have the coupons and make their own choice.'

Rena fingered the tweed of the new coat sleeve. 'Well, that's a nice piece o' stuff, Nola. Seems you got something out o' the forces, after all.'

'Certainly did. A gratuity and all, even if it is less than the men's.' Nola hesitated. 'But I don't regret it, Ma. Being in the forces, I mean. It'll be something to tell folk, eh? I did what I had to do.'

'That's right, you did.'

'And I met all different sorts of people and did different jobs, and all o' that. If I hadn't joined up, I suppose I'd've still been in the box office at the picture house.' Nola laughed. 'Well, that's what I'll be going back to, anyway. They say you should take your old job back, so that's me. All fixed up.'

Rena and Tess exchanged glances. So far Nola hadn't mentioned Clark Walters. What had happened to him then? Might it all be OFF?

Then Nola said, casually, 'No letters for me, are there? Clark said he'd write. I rang him at his dad's shop to tell him I was out.'

'No letters,' Rena said firmly. 'No letters for anybody.'

The sisters, shivering in the chill of it, were up in their attic room again, with Nola humming cheerfully as she unpacked and put her things away, while Tess watched from her bed.

'Och, it's grand to be back,' Nola sighed. 'Back for good. No' just on leave, when you always knew you couldn't stay.'

'You said you didn't regret it though. Being in the WAAF.'

'Sort o' thing you say when it's over.' Nola laughed, and threw herself onto her bed. 'Thing is, you can do what you like at home.'

'First I've heard of it.'

'Ah, Ma's no' so bad, Tess. Compared with some o' the dragons I met, I can tell you she's an angel with wings.' Nola leaped up again and walked to the window to look out at the lights of the power station across the way. 'It's just so nice to be home, that's all. Like I say, for good.'

For good? Still watching her sister, Tess picked up Alice and smoothed her hair. How long would that be though? With Nola waiting for a call from Clark Walters?

'You still got that dear old doll?' asked Nola quickly, perhaps sensing Tess's unspoken thoughts and hoping to divert her. 'Whatever happened to ma Gloria, then?'

'Gloria?'

'That doll I had, Tess. She was made of stuffed velveteen and had little bits of blond hair under a velveteen hat.'

'Oh Lord, d'you no' remember? I washed her.' Tess began to laugh. 'It was awful. She sort of shrank. Sort of flopped to nothing. I was so scared of what you'd say.'

'And I didn't care, did I? All I wanted then was a Shirley Temple doll with Shirley Temple boots.' Nola was laughing too. 'But thae dolls cost a pound. Would you credit it?

A whole pound. Needless to say, I never got one.'

The sisters were running downstairs, still smiling over the old days, when someone knocked at the front door.

'One o' Ma's awful tenants?' asked Nola. 'Don't they know the door's never locked?'

She went to open it and Tess, swinging from the newel post at the bottom of the stairs, heard a man's voice ask huskily, 'Does anybody call Gillespie live here?'

'Oh, God!' cried Nola. 'Oh, I canna believe it!'

'Who is it?' called Tess, standing very still.

'Who is it?' called Rena from the basement door.

'It's Dad!' shrieked Nola. 'Oh, heavens, it's Dad!'

Don Gillespie had come home at last.

Chapter Nine

He seeemed a stranger at first, but that was only because of the new raincoat. And the trilby hat. They'd never seen him in such a hat before, and the way he was wearing it, pulled down over his brow, made him look like one of those fellows in the films, handsome, but from a different world, no one they knew. Then, of course, as they were still standing transfixed, he took off the hat and sent it twirling towards the coat stand, laughing as he missed a peg, and he was their Don again, their dad, and they all tried to hug him at once, crying his name.

'Oh, Don,' whispered Rena, still trembling with joyful shock. 'Oh, Don, are you really here?'

'Looks like it.' He held his daughters close, then kissed Rena long and tenderly.

'Why did you no' let us know when you were coming?' she cried. 'I was going to try to get something special for your tea—'

'As though I care about ma tea. I'm home, that's all that matters.'

'And I'm home, too,' said Nola. 'D'you realise that, Dad? I came back today an' all.' She laughed, throwing an arm around her mother's shoulders. 'So, where's ma special tea, then?'

'Oh, Nola, I don't know whether I'm on ma head or ma heels. Let's all go downstairs, eh? Tess, pet, run and put the kettle on. I'm that wound up, I feel I canna do a thing.'

'That'll be the day,' said Nola, and took her father's arm, hurrying him down to the kitchen, where he took off his smart raincoat and revealed himself in his equally smart demob suit, turning slowly round and grinning as they admired him.

'Well, isn't that grand?' cried Rena, giving the lie to her weakness as she ran to and fro, opening up the range, taking out cups and saucers, turning up the gas under the kettle. 'Did they give you a whole outfit, then?'

'Aye, the lot. Three-piece suit, raincoat, hat, shoes, everything. Gratuity, an' all.' Don's grin faded. 'Farewell presents from a grateful country.'

'Well, that's true, eh? The country is grateful.'

'There's plenty o' lads they won't need to be grateful to, if you remember. Plenty no' needing demob suits, because they won't be coming back. What the rest of us are wondering is, how far will the gratitude go? Will it be like it was after the Great War?' Don shook his head. 'All smiles and cheers, then men selling matches and bootlaces to try to make a living?'

'Things'll be different this time, Dad,' Nola said quickly. 'There's plenty o' jobs and money about now.'

'Aye, now.'

'Och, we'll no' see the thirties back again!' cried Rena. 'What's the matter, Don? It's no' like you to look on the black side.'

'No.' His face relaxed, his grin returned and the atmosphere lightened. 'Let me look at ma girls, then. Let me look at this bonnie Nola, and this great tall Tess. How come you shot up behind ma back, Tessie? Where's that little girl I used to take around the town?'

'Still here, Dad,' whispered Tess, hanging on to his arm.

'And we'll go round the town again, eh?'

'Of course we will.' The two faces, so much alike, were equally radiant, yet just for a moment something flickered in Don's grey eyes, or Tess thought it did. There, it had gone. Had it been there at all? A look of weariness was replacing her father's radiance, anyway, and he sank onto a chair by the table.

'Could do with that tea,' he murmured and Rena flew to give him his cup, with just the amount of milk he liked and the one sugar, and two of the biscuits she'd made from oats and precious butter.

'You're worn out,' she said softly. 'You look as though you've had no sleep.'

'Aye, well it all happened in such a rush, you ken. I didn't have time to let you know what was happening, and then I thought I'd send a card from the depot, but I didn't have to go to the depot. I got ma marching orders in Edinburgh, no trouble at all.' Don stirred his tea and sighed deeply. 'So, here I am then.'

'Thank God,' Rena said simply, while Nola poured tea for everyone else, and Tess, crunching a biscuit, kept her eyes on her father, keeping guard, as though if she didn't he might not be there.

'Think I'll go up and unpack ma bag and get out o' this good suit,' he said, after a second cup of tea. 'I'll feel more like maself, then.'

'I'll come up with you,' Rena said swiftly, at which Tess's face crumpled a little and she would have protested that she should go up with her dad, only Nola knocked her arm.

'Let 'em be on their own,' she whispered, as their parents left them. 'We'll see what there is for tea.'

'No' much,' sighed Tess. 'Wish Ma really had got something special for you and Dad.'

'If Clark had been here, he'd have managed it. Ma can say what she likes, but he could usually find whatever you wanted.'

'Do you miss him, Nola?'

'Yes, I do, but I expect I'll be seeing him soon.'

'When?'

'Christmas, maybe. Or, Hogmanay. He's asked me to go down to Leeds. Come on, let's do these cups.'

'Same room?' asked Don, pausing on the second floor, but Rena put her hand on his back and told him to keep going.

'We're one floor up,' she told him. 'I gave our room to Miss Denny. She works for an insurance firm.'

'Why'd you do that? You always liked our room.'

'Aye, well, I thought she should have the space, you ken.' Rena laughed a little. 'Got to keep the tenants happy. They pay rent.'

Don said no more as he followed her into their new room on the second floor and threw his bag onto the double bed.

'We've still got that,' she said tremulously, snapping on the light.

'Aye. And the wardrobe. Somewhere to hang ma suit.' He walked to the window and pulled aside the curtains. 'Same view o' the power station.'

'No blackout.'

'No blackout. The war's well and truly over.'

'Now you've come home.'

He turned to face her and began unbuttoning his jacket. 'Better get out o' this, eh? Where's ma things, then?'

'Hanging up. I've put everything away for you.' Rena began helping him out of the suit, though her hands were trembling and she was slower at undoing the buttons than he. At last he was in his shirt and looking for something to wear in the wardrobe, when she caught him to her and leaned against him, crying softly as he held her.

'Hey, hey, what's all this, Rena? I'm home. No need to cry.'

'I'm just so happy, Don.' She looked up at him with swimming eyes. 'It's been so long, eh? Since you were on leave. Since we – you know ...' She looked sideways at the bed. 'Oh, do you no' wish we could go to bed now, Don? Never mind the tea, or anything, just be together?'

'Aye, I do.' He stroked her arms, put back her hair and kissed her. 'But there's the girls, you ken. I mean, they'll be downstairs, waiting.'

'I know, I know. And if there's any tenants about, they'll be listening.' She tried to smile. 'No' much privacy now, Don.'

'We'll have to wait for the night.'

She gave a shuddering sigh and again sank against him, letting her hands move over his body. 'You're awful thin,' she murmured. 'See, I can feel your ribs. Have they no' been feeding you in that army?'

'Talk about the pot calling the kettle black! Who's thinner than you, Rena?'

'You think I'm too thin?'

'No, no. Just right.' As she slowly released herself, he kissed her. 'Look, I'll get changed and come down. Got a few presents, you ken. No' much, mind.'

'Presents? The girls will like presents,' she said softly. 'I only need you.'

Chapter Ten

There was a lace-trimmed tablecloth and nylons for Rena, nylons for Nola, a silky scarf for Tess, and pretty necklaces for all three.

'Wherever did you get them, Dad?' cried Tess, smiling with delight. 'I never thought you'd find presents in the war!'

'Och, you'd be surprised what you could get, if you'd cigarettes or a packet o' coffee to barter with,' Don told her. 'Folk'd sell their souls for coffee, you ken. I was lucky to win some from a guy in a poker game. He'd got it from a Yank, the nylons and all.'

'Poker?' cried Rena. 'You were playing poker, Don! Whatever would your old dad have said, him being that anti-gambling!'

'Had to have some relaxation, Rena.'

'Aye. Well, I suppose I don't know much about what it was like for you fellas over there.'

'No,' he answered evenly. 'You don't.'

After a little silence, Rena leaped up and said she'd better get on with the tea. It'd just be fish cakes and chips, and maybe peas, if she still had a tin. No' much of a celebration, eh? She felt that bad.

'It'll be fine, Ma,' said Nola, rising to help. 'Who cares what we eat? We're all together, and Dad and me needn't go away again, that's all that matters.'

'Thought you were going away at Christmas?' asked Tess, admiring herself in her new scarf and necklace before the kitchen mirror.

'Christmas?' Rena swung round from the stove. 'Why, where are you going at Christmas, Nola?'

'Oh, Tess,' Nola said reproachfully. 'Nothing's fixed up. You shouldn't have said anything.'

'You never told me it was a secret,' cried Tess, turning red. 'How was I to know?'

'What are we talking about?' asked Don. 'I feel I'm missing something.'

'It's Rena's young man, Clark Walters,' said Rena. 'You remember, I mentioned him in ma letters? The one that was in the RAF?'

'Ah,' murmured Don. 'That one.'

'I didn't say for sure when I would see him,' Nola said in a low voice. 'But when he got demobbed, he said he'd like me to go down some time and suggested Christmas, but I didn't promise, because I thought you'd want me here.'

'Thought you'd want to be here yourself,' cried Rena. 'With your dad just back an' all.'

'Now, don't go on at the lassie, Rena,' Don said mildly. 'She's just trying to please everybody.'

Rena gave a sudden quick smile. 'Like you, eh?'

He looked away. 'Wouldn't say that.'

'Mebbe Clark could come here for Hogmanay?' asked Nola, taking a pan from a cupboard by the gas cooker. 'I want you to meet him, Dad. I think you'll like him.'

Rena, slicing potatoes, flung back her hair and sniffed. 'If you want him to come, Nola, ask him. It'll be better than you going down there anyway.'

'Thanks, Ma,' Nola answered, with a placatory smile, and peace descended on Don's first evening home.

Over the meal, he asked about the tenants. He'd have to meet them all, so might as well be forearmed.

'They're no' so bad,' Rena answered. 'But I think I'd be

51

better off with students if this lot go. Less trouble.'

'Students less trouble?' Don stared. 'How d'you work that out?'

'Well, they get their meals at college, eh? They're happy with just a gas ring and a kettle, but Miss Denny, now, she's for ever hinting that I could put something in to cook for her, and the young couple, the Wights – they got thrown out by her mother, you ken – they're always wanting extras, new this, new that, as though I was made o' money. And old Mr Crombie, he's got this terrible old pipe and never opens a window – you could choke to death just passing his room, I'm no' joking.'

'All right, all right, think I've heard enough,' Don said with a grin. 'But students drink, you ken, and throw parties, so I've heard.'

'No' in this house,' Rena said firmly. 'Och, I'll have to leave it for the time being anyway. But the only tenant who's really no trouble is Mrs Lange. She smokes, it's true, but she always airs her room, and her Erika is good as gold.'

'Ma friend, Dad, remember?' asked Tess. 'You met her when you came on leave. And her mother.'

'I do remember. Nice woman, nice lassie. Sad looking, eh?'

'Aye. Dr Lange was killed by the Nazis before the war. When I think o' what that poor woman's been through – well, I feel I shouldn't complain.' Looking round at the faces of her family, Rena's eyes stung with tears. 'Who wants some pie, then? It's only the grocer's, mind. But I'm going to make you some proper pastry tomorrow, Don, come what may.'

'If that's what you want,' he said with an indulgent smile. 'But you know I don't care what I eat. To tell you the truth, I don't feel hungry tonight. Just tired.'

They were all tired, in fact. Perhaps their joy had exhausted them, and Don and Nola had been travelling too. Whatever

52

the reason, as soon as the meal was over and the dishes washed and put away, first Tess went up to bed, then Nola, and after they'd smoked cigarettes together by the stove, Rena and Don followed.

'So much noise,' Don murmured, as they climbed the stairs. 'All your tenants, eh? Humming and rattling and stepping around. You can feel 'em, even if you canna see 'em.'

'That's what it's like, letting rooms,' Rena told him. 'Do you no' remember?'

'Doesn't bother me. When you've lived for years with a battalion, you never expect peace and quiet again.'

'It does quieten down, you ken.' Her eyes met his and slid away. 'At night.'

'Aye.' He raised his eyes to the stairs to the floor above. 'Think I'll just say goodnight to the girls.'

'They'd like that.'

Oh yes, their eyes lit up when their father looked in on them, both hugging sheets to their chins, for the attic room was bitterly cold as it usually was at that time of year.

'All right?' he asked softly. 'No' got your light out yet?'

'Think we're six years old?' laughed Nola. 'I was just going to read a bit. Settle ma mind, I'm that excited, you ken.'

'Been an exciting day, you could say.'

'It's all right for you folk,' said Tess. 'But I've got to go to school tomorrow. I wish I could've been on leave, like you.'

'But then we'll have to go back to work soon.' Don sat on her bed and touched her cold cheek. 'Nola and me'll have to go back to our old jobs.'

'The cinema for me,' said Nola, with a groan.

'And the garage for me.' Don grinned. 'At least there'll soon be cars around again, now that things are getting back to normal.'

'I wouldn't mind working in a garage,' said Tess. 'But when I say that, everybody laughs. See, you're laughing too.'

'No, no,' said Don, his mouth twitching. He stood up, yawning and stretching. 'But I'd better get to ma bed, I canna keep ma eyes open. See you in the morning, girls.' He kissed them both and moved to the door. 'You still want this light on, Nola?'

'Please Dad. Just for a bit.'

He hesitated. 'Goodnight again, then.'

'Goodnight, Dad.'

'It's lovely to have you back,' called Tess.

'Grand to be back,' he answered quietly, and left them.

Neither of the girls spoke as they listened to his step going down the stairs. He was going to their mother; she would be waiting for him. Would they make love? The thought would not be put into words. No one ever thought of their parents making love. Didn't seem right, did it? Parents weren't like other folk. Only they were, of course.

'Where's that Agatha Christie book I had?' Nola murmured, at last.

Tess was already deep in *Jane Eyre*, her icy fingers turning the icy pages.

In their room on the floor below, Rena was locked in her husband's arms.

'Thought I'd forgotten what to do,' she said with a shaky laugh, as they drew apart. 'It's been so long.'

'Ma last leave.'

'Aye, long ago. Seems like it, anyway.'

She lay against Don's chest, smiling now, so happy she almost didn't dare to breathe, as though breathing might bring her back to reality, puncture her dream. But this was no dream. Don was here. She held him and he held her, just as they'd held each other on that last leave, but this time there would be no going away. Oh God, that was best of all. No more going away.

Gradually, her arms around him slackened and sleep enfolded her, but Don lay for a long time, staring into the darkness of the unfamiliar room, his eyes seeming to start from his head, his whole body crying out for the rest that would not come. Finally, he crept from the bed and fumbled for his cigarettes on the dressing table. Where was his lighter? He drew aside the curtain and quickly dropped it again, for fear the still burning lights of the power station would wake Rena. But she was deep in tranquil sleep.

Everyone in the house was asleep, he supposed, as he let himself out onto the landing and lit a cigarette with the lighter he'd finally managed to put his hand on. Oh, thank God! Thank God for a smoke. He'd feel better soon, able to go back and get some sleep himself maybe. Get away from the air that was chilling him to the bone.

Rena made no sound as he at last slid in beside her, but then her stick-like arms wound round him and in a voice thick with sleep she whispered his name.

'Don?'

'It's all right, Rena. I'm here.'

Chapter Eleven

The dark days before Christmas seemed full of light to Tess because her father had come home. And Nola was home, too, of course, but Tess felt she couldn't be sure of Nola. Clark Walters was coming for Hogmanay; they'd have to see what happened then.

But her dad was really back and part of her life again, just as he used to be, and at weekends they did go walking round the town as he'd promised they would, and sometimes Erika came too. Both she and her mother had said they found Mr Gillespie very kind, very charming, and they weren't alone in that.

Tess had seen how the large and bosomy Miss Denny from the insurance office lay in wait for him, listing all the little jobs he might do for her, and telling him, as she told everybody, that she was only in a bedsit because her previous landlord had taken back her flat and she hadn't been able to find another. Oh, the housing shortage in Edinburgh and everywhere else was terrible, and this Labour government had so far done nothing to help, had it? Didn't Mr Gillespie agree?

'Got to give 'em time,' he told her. 'We've just come through a war, remember.'

'Yes, but they need to bring in legislation to protect tenants, then I wouldn't be in this position, you see, of having to cook on a gas ring! I am not a gas ring sort of person, you understand.'

'I'm sure they will bring in legislation,' said Don, sidling away. 'They're very keen to help ordinary folk, you ken.'

Ordinary? From the look on Miss Denny's face, that was not the word she would have chosen to describe herself.

As for poor old Mr Crombie, all he wanted was for Mr Gillespie to put a few shelves up in his room to hold his Wild West paperbacks. Sort of thing he'd had in his last place, before he'd been asked to leave just for smoking his pipe. Would you credit it?

And then there was young, blonde, Polly Wight, who'd been thrown out by her mother for marrying 'layabout' Kennie, who was very keen to get Don to make Mrs Gillespie put in a second bathroom. It was true, every tenant had a washbasin, but well, one bathroom! It was a piece o' nonsense, eh? For all thae tenants! What would Mr Gillespie do about it, then?

'No' much,' Don answered cheerfully, and explained that even if his wife could afford to put in another bathroom, there wasn't a plumber who could do it at the present time. No materials, eh? There had been a war, after all.

'That's what everybody says,' sighed Polly. 'Seemingly, nobody can do anything, because there's been a war on.' But she gave Don a wide smile anyway, because he was such a lovely fellow, a lot sweeter than his wife, who was as tart as a cooking apple, so she was.

'Aye, you're the popular one, Don,' Tess once heard her mother tell her father. 'But leave the tenants to me, eh?'

'Gladly,' Don had replied. 'Just wish they'd leave me alone, an' all.'

At least he seemed not to mind being back at Todd's garage, unlike Nola, who said she was bored to tears at the cinema box office. But that was only because she no longer took any interest in the young men buying tickets and smiling at her, now that she had Clark Walters to think about. It was still Tess's secret hope that some really nice, handsome guy would sweep Nola off her feet and make her forget Clark, but she knew the hope was forlorn. Nola saw something in him that nobody else saw, and that was love, Tess supposed. Nothing she could do about it.

One Sunday morning, when a pale December sun was shining over the Forth, Tess and Erika walked down the road to the sands with Don and saw Mr Seton's chauffeur in the distance, exercising the dog as usual.

'Grand to see the beach without the barbed wire,' Don murmured, clapping his arms with his gloved hands, for the wind was chill. He was wearing his demob raincoat and his trilby hat, but they no longer stopped him looking like himself. Nothing could do that now.

'And empty,' said Erika.

'At its best in the winter, I always think.' Don narrowed his eyes at the figure of the chauffeur. 'Who's that, then? Got a lovely dog.'

'That's the chauffeur from Pax House,' Tess told him. 'He drives Mr Seton's Daimler, and that's Mr Seton's dog he takes out.'

'Daimler, eh? Very nice, too.'

'Tess thought it might be a Rolls-Royce at first,' said Erika. 'But then she saw it in the street and she said it was a Daimler.'

Don smiled. 'And Tess would know.'

'I'm interested in cars,' Tess said proudly. 'I know the makes.'

'Let's walk up and have a word with that fella. I'd be interested to know how he finds the Daimler. And which garage he uses.'

The chauffeur seemed pleased when Don, followed by the girls, came up to speak to him. He was perhaps in his fifties, a small man, rather worn looking, with straggling grey hair showing beneath his cap. Not an ex-military man, that was for sure. When they joined him, he was throwing sticks for the young Labrador that was exuberantly fetching them, but when he saw that Don wanted to stop, he wiped his hands on his handkerchief and left the girls to throw the sticks.

'Oh, she is so lovely!' cried Erika, patting the dog as she came racing back to her. 'Please, what is her name?'

'What you might guess,' the chauffeur answered with a grin. 'Honey.' He glanced at Don. 'Nice morning.'

'Grand.' Don put out his hand. 'Don Gillespie. Haven't seen you before, but I'm just back from the war. Hear you drive for Mr Seton of Pax House?'

'That's right. The name's Arthur Beith.'

'Nice to meet you. That's ma daughter, Tess, and her friend, Erika. We live at the top o' the King George Road.'

'Just demobbed, eh? I was over age to go, you ken. Wouldnae have minded going, as a matter o' fact. How you finding Civvy Street, then?'

'No' so bad. Got ma old job back, at Todd's garage.' Don looked out across the steel grey waters of the Forth, then back to the chauffeur. 'The Daimler still doing well, then?'

'Aye. Up on blocks for the duration, but never took no harm. Made 'em good and strong in the old days, eh?'

'You've no' thought of trying Todd's for servicing, I suppose?'

Arthur Beith shook his head. 'Sorry, the boss has got a contract with an Edinburgh firm. Been with 'em for years. I could have a word, but I dinna think he'll change.'

'Thanks, anyway. You walking back?'

'Think I will. I'm ready for ma Sunday dinner now.'

'Us, too.' Don smiled and touched his hat. 'Might see you in the pub for a jar one night, eh?'

'Look forward to it.' The chauffeur put his fingers in his mouth and let out a shrill whistle, at which Honey left the girls and came skidding back along the sand. 'Nice seeing you, Mr Gillespie. And you lassies, too, though I've seen you before, eh?'

'We like to walk here,' said Tess. 'And we like to look at your house.'

59

'My house?' The chauffeur laughed. 'I'd be a lucky fella if Pax House was mine.'

'You would,' agreed Tess. 'I'd like it to be mine, one day.'

'Come on,' her father said fondly. 'Better no' be late when your ma's cooking for us.'

Chapter Twelve

'Tell you what I don't like about Sundays,' Nola remarked, when they were at the table. 'No post.'

'I know what you mean,' said Don.

'Why, when do you expect letters?' asked Rena, smiling.

He looked down at his plate, a sudden colour on his cheekbones. 'Some o' the lads write to me. We like to keep in touch.'

'That why you always collect the post?' asked Tess. 'I used to do that, didn't I, Ma? See if there was anything from you, Dad.'

'I wrote pretty regular, eh? Canna complain about that.'

'Who's complaining?' asked Rena. 'I was always very grateful, to hear from you. Some o' the lassies I worked with, their men never put pen to paper, from one year to the next.'

'Aye, some fellas are like that.'

'But no' your friends?' As Don made no reply, Rena began to stack the plates. 'Fancy you picking up the post, then. Never used to bother.'

'I'm usually around when it comes.' Suddenly, Don's eyes blazed. 'What the hell does it matter, anyway?'

There was a stunned silence. Nola and Tess looked at each other, amazed, while Rena stared at Don until he dropped his gaze and put his hand to his face where the colour was deepening.

'I'll get our pudding,' Rena said tightly.

'Sorry.' He looked up. 'Didn't mean to snap.'

'That's all right.'

'I'm just a bit out o' sorts.'

'I said, it was all right.'

But the pudding was eaten in silence, and though Don offered to help with the washing up, something he was never expected to do, Rena said the girls would do it, and swiftly left the kitchen. After a moment or two, Don, followed, and Nola's eyes went to Tess's.

'Well, what a fuss about nothing!' she exclaimed. 'Just because Dad never snaps and never swears, when he does for once, he gets stick. I mean, you ken what some men are like, eh? The air's blue wherever they are. And they don't just snap, they belt you one. I often think how lucky we are to have a father like ours.'

'I know some girls are afraid o' their dads,' Tess said in a small voice.

'They are, and we're not. Och, that's what you get for being nice, I suppose. People expect you to be always the same.'

'But why was he cross, Nola? I mean, he'd no reason.'

'I daresay he's feeling a bit mixed up.' Nola began to stack the dishes on the draining board. 'They say a lot o' men are not managing well, being at home again, it's all too different from the forces. I can understand, I sometimes feel mixed up maself.'

'I never knew that.'

'Och, it's just that you're all keyed up to want to come home, and then when you are home, it's no' quite what you expected. Like Christmas – it's sometimes a bit of a let down.'

'I thought you were so happy, Nola, and Dad, too.'

'I am happy, really. And so is Dad, I'm sure. Though, sometimes I've thought—' Nola stopped and began to run water into a washing-up bowl.

'Thought what?'

'Nothing.' Nola gave a brilliant smile. 'Hey, talking of Christmas, we should get some post soon. Christmas cards, eh? You'd better get making yours, Tess.'

'This year, Erika and me are going to Woolworth's. I'm too old to make Christmas cards anymore.'

Don found Rena in the hall, putting on her coat, tying a scarf over her hair. He took her in his arms and put his face against hers, but she did not respond.

'Look, you're no' mad at me, are you? I said I was sorry.'

'I was just that surprised, the way you spoke to me, Don. You never snap, it's no' like you.'

'A fella can snap once in a while. It doesn't mean anything.'

'But why did you? I canna understand it.'

'It's like I said, I'm out o' sorts.'

'Being home, you mean?'

'No. Och, I canna put it into words. I think a lot o' guys feel like me.'

'Let down?' she asked coldly. 'Disappointed?'

'No!' He held her close again. 'No, no. Oh, let's forget all this, eh? Let's no' have bad feeling?'

She let him kiss her and after some moments, kissed him back, but then she held herself a little away.

'Why do you want to collect the post, though? What's so important about letters from old mates.'

'It's the guys who are important. We went through a lot together.' He smiled. 'But I don't care who picks up the post. Why should I?'

She looked at him for a long moment, as she pulled on her woollen gloves. 'OK, let's forget about this. I'm going out now for a breath of air. I've been in all morning.'

'I'll come with you. Wait while I get ma coat.'

'Tell the girls we won't be long.'

'They're friends again,' Nola murmured. 'Thank the Lord

for that. But what was it all about, then? Just a storm in a teacup.'

Still a storm, thought Tess.

Chapter Thirteen

After that little skirmish, it became Tess's job to pick up the post again, which she was delighted to do, especially as the Christmas cards were beginning to arrive. She laid them all out for the tenants on the side table near the hall stand, noting that the Wights and Miss Denny got the most, Mrs Lange very few, and Mr Crombie least of all.

Poor old thing, Tess thought, and decided to send him a card herself; maybe, just for him, a hand–drawn one, with cowboys and Indians, same as on the covers of the books he liked. She needn't make one for Mrs Lange, because she'd already bought her a pretty one with snow and candles that Erika had said was very Austrian. They'd had such lovely Christmases in Austria before the war, she'd told Tess. How glad she was that she could just remember them.

But Tess was wondering – where was all the post her father had been expecting? He didn't seem to get much at all, apart from household bills and Christmas cards that were addressed to her mother as well. He must have made a mistake about those old mates of his wanting to keep in touch. Perhaps he realised that already, for he never asked Tess if there were any letters for him.

And then, some days before Christmas, one came. It wasn't big enough to contain a card, so must be a proper letter, Tess decided, and was addressed in small, neat hand-writing just to her father. Feeling guiltily nosy, she tried to read the postmark but couldn't make it out. Wasn't from abroad, anyway.

'Dad! Dad! A letter for you!' she cried up the stairs, and down he came at once, dressed in his work clothes.

'Thanks, Tess.' In a flash, he'd taken it from her hand and put it in his breast pocket. 'I'll read it later – have to hurry.'

'Are you no' going to have your breakfast?'

'No time, we've a rush job on. Tell your ma, I'll get something at work.'

'If Ma's made your porridge, you'll be in trouble!' she called after him, as he put on his old jacket and let himself out of the front door. He didn't seem to hear.

In the kitchen, Nola, who had mornings off, was having an early breakfast because she was going shopping, while Rena was indeed stirring porridge.

'More cards, Ma,' said Tess. 'I think it's nice there's plenty of cards, eh? At least they're no' rationed.'

'Rationed Christmas cards? What an idea!' cried Nola. 'But the paper's awful thin. No letter for me, then?'

'Sorry, Nola.'

'You got one on Saturday,' her mother said, serving out Tess's porridge. 'Tess, better eat this quick. Time's getting on.'

'My last day,' said Tess cheerfully. 'Break up tomorrow, you ken. Canna wait!'

'Where's your dad, then?' Rena had his bowl ready. 'He's going to be late an' all, at this rate.'

'He's already gone,' Tess told her. 'Said they'd a rush job on and he'd get something to eat at the garage.'

'A rush job?' Rena stared. 'He never mentioned it. Now all his porridge'll be wasted!'

'You can eat it, Ma,' said Nola, jumping up from the table and stopping at the mirror by the door to study her hair. 'You could do with fattening up.'

66

'You ken fine I canna eat two lots o' porridge.' Rena sat down at the table and poured herself a cup of tea, frowning. 'He might have told me he didn't want his breakfast.'

'Och, he was all in a rush,' said Tess. She was about to add that her father had had a letter, when something, she didn't know what, made her hold her tongue. Maybe the letter was a secret. But why would it be? Dad hadn't said so. It was just the way he'd snatched it from her and immediately put it away made her think so. Anyway, she said nothing, and was soon on her way upstairs to collect Erika for their last day of term. Oh joy, holidays! The thought of her father's letter went completely from her mind.

It was sleeting when Don came home in the evening, and at first he looked wonderfully rosy from the cold. Soon, however, his colour faded and he seemed weary as he sat by the kitchen range and put his slippers on.

'Had a hard day?' asked Rena.

'Aye. Had a big job on for a guy who wanted his car in a hurry.'

'That's why you'd to go in early, without your breakfast? You should have come home at dinner time, had something hot.'

'No, Mabel Dixon from the office had laid on soup and sandwiches. We were all right.' Don lay back in his chair and closed his eyes for a moment, then sat up, yawning. 'Did Tess tell you I had a letter?'

'No, I didn't,' called Tess from the table where a quick rush of relief ran through her as she worked on finishing Mr Crombie's Christmas card. So the letter wasn't a secret. Why'd she ever thought it was?

'Aye, it was from Bob MacEwan, one o' my mates I told you about. He's back in Glasgow.'

'How's he getting on, then?' asked Rena.

'Finding it a bit hard to settle.'

'I see. Another one.'

'How d'you mean?'

'Did you no' say you felt like that?'

'I said I felt a bit out o' sorts.'

Rena shrugged. 'You going to meet him?'

'Maybe after Christmas.'

'You could ask him over with his wife, eh?'

Don hesitated. 'He's no married.'

'Foot loose and fancy free?' Rena laughed. 'Tess, come on now, I'll be needing that table. Hurry up.'

'Finished,' said Tess, holding up her card. 'What d'you think? I've put two cowboys and one Indian. They're supposed to be in the desert.'

'Is that a Christmas tree in the corner?' asked Don. 'Should've been a cactus.'

'I had to make it look Christmassy, Dad. Anyway, I think Mr Crombie will like it.'

'Of course he will,' said Rena. 'I think it's a very kind thought, pet. Poor old chap, eh?'

'Is he going to be on his own for Christmas?' asked Tess. 'Should we ask him down for his dinner?' But Rena, breathing a sigh of relief, shook her head.

'Thank the Lord, that son of his in Trinity has asked him round – just for once, you ken. I did invite Mrs Lange and Erika, but they're going to some friends, so there'll just be ourselves. I've a nice piece o' pork promised, anyway.'

'Ooh, pork crackling, I love it!' cried Tess, clearing away her drawing materials. 'And Christmas!'

Some Scots took very little notice of it, she knew, preferring to celebrate at Hogmanay, but Tess was always glad that her family celebrated both. And this Christmas was going to be very special, the first since the war had ended. They'd be able to enjoy it without worrying.

'Don't you, Dad?' she asked, coming to sit near him.

'Don't I what?'

'You've no' been listening. Don't you love Christmas?'

He slowly withdrew his gaze from something distant and smiled. 'Sure, I do.'

Chapter Fourteen

As she was now on holiday, Tess thought it would be a good idea to ask her father if he would take her again to the garage.

'I mean, it'd interesting,' she told him at breakfast the following morning. 'You used to take me when I was little.'

Don swallowed some tea and stood up, shaking his head. 'Aye, if we weren't busy, but we've a lot on at the moment. Sorry, pet, you'd be in the way.'

'I wouldn't. I'd just watch. Nobody'd know I was there.'

'Think Mr Todd wouldn't notice a lassie standing round?' Don quickly kissed Tess's cheek. 'If you'd been a boy, now, I might've taken you in for an hour or two, but you canna work in a garage, pet, and that's all there is to it.'

'I say the same thing,' Rena put in. 'But she'll no' listen to me.'

'Tess, if you'd seen the WAAFs working on engines during the war, you'd soon have changed your mind about garage work,' Nola said with a laugh. 'Och, you should've watched 'em trying to get clean.'

'Dad gets clean,' Tess muttered.

'Well, maybe I'll try to take you in some time after Christmas,' Don said, from the door. 'But it's just no' convenient today. Now – I've got to go.'

'Cheer up, Tess,' Nola said, clearing away the breakfast dishes. 'You can come Christmas shopping with me instead.'

'You went shopping yesterday,' cried Rena. 'What on earth are you buying?'

'Ask no questions, you'll be told no lies, Ma. But I am looking for something and I'm no' telling you what.'

'Ah, like that is it?' Rena smiled self-consciously. 'Just don't go spending all your money, though, that's my advice.'

'Want to come then, Tess?' asked Nola, and Tess's face brightened.

'Yes please, I'd like to.'

'Want to ask Erika?'

'She's got to go to the dentist's.'

'Oh, don't speak of it!' Nola shuddered. 'Wonder how much that'll set her mother back then. Canna wait for this national health service, eh?'

'Supposed to be starting next year, but I'll believe it when I see it,' said Rena. 'Now, are you two lassies going out, or not? I've the sheets to do this morning; want to get them out the way before Christmas.'

'Shall we stay and give you a hand then?' asked Nola.

'No, I'll manage better on ma own. You do your shopping.' Rena laughed. 'I know it's going between you and your wits.'

'It's Ma I'm stuck for,' Nola told Tess on the tram. 'I've got Dad a scarf – one o' thae spotted ones with tassels – and I've got Clark a cigarette case – nothing expensive, you ken – and I've got something for you—'

'Oh, what?'

'As though I'd tell you! But I canna think of anything for Ma. What have you bought her?'

'Lavender bags and hankies. I got 'em at the Store. You don't think they'll be too boring?'

'Och, no, she'll love 'em. Anyway, what choice is there?

70

You need coupons for clothes, and there's no boxes o' chocolates, canna afford scent – I'm stumped.'

'What'll you do then?'

'Somebody at work said there was a wee shop at the back o' the station where they sold vases and things. Might try there.'

'Could be expensive.'

'I can just look, eh? I tell you, I'm desperate.'

In fact, the wares of the little shop behind Waverley were quite reasonable in price. Nola, with Tess's help, spent a happy time browsing among vases, paperweights, teapots, miniature elephants and artificial flowers, finally settling on a blue jug she thought would appeal to Rena.

'This is all new stock just in,' the owner told her, as she wrapped up the jug. 'First we've had since the war, and it's all going like hot cakes. Och, it's that grand, getting back to normal, eh? Still got rationing, o' course.'

'Might have that for some time.'

'Ah, dinna spoil ma day!'

'What a relief,' said Nola, when they were out of the shop. 'Now I can relax. How about a cup o' tea at the station buffet? That'd be nice and quick before I have to get back for the box office.'

'Can we have something to eat? I'm starving.'

'Aye, if you don't mind Waverley rock cakes!'

They had almost finished their pale tea and solid rock cakes, and Nola was checking the clock over the buffet counter to make sure she wasn't running late for work, when Tess clutched her arm.

'Nola, look!'

A tall man wearing a raincoat and trilby hat had come through the buffet door and was holding it open for a young woman in a navy coat and navy beret.

'Dad?' whispered Nola. 'Is that Dad? Oh, yes. Yes, it is. But what's he doing here?'

'And who's that with him?' asked Tess.

'Is she with him? He's just holding the door for her.'

'She's with him.'

'Keep your head down then. Don't let him see you.'

Both sisters bent their heads, only looking up after a few moments had passed, when they saw that their father and the young woman had taken seats at a table some way from their own. There seemed no danger of their father's seeing them, however, for his eyes never left the heart-shaped face of his companion, who now loosened her coat and pulled off her beret, revealing bright red hair. After a moment or two, during which they stared silently at each other, Don Gillespie got up and went to the counter.

'Head down,' said Nola again.

'He's getting two teas,' whispered Tess. 'Oh Nola, who's that girl?'

'Some friend's daughter, I expect.'

'Whose?'

'I don't know, do I? Maybe he was asked to meet her from a train.'

As their father carried a tray of tea across to the redheaded girl, the sisters raised their heads again and snatched covert glances at the pair across the room.

'She doesn't look like anybody's daughter,' said Tess, and Nola took her meaning. No, she wasn't the daughter of anyone their dad knew. She might be a number of years younger than he was, but she wasn't looking at him as though he were a different generation. Nor was he looking at her as though he'd just met her from a train to do somebody a favour. In fact, Nola didn't want to describe, even to herself, just how her father was looking at the young redhead.

'She's no' happy,' Tess murmured. 'I think she's crying.'

'Tess, we've got to go,' Nola said with a groan. 'Quick, before he sees us.'

'Can't we speak to him?'

'No! For God's sake, Tess, turn your face away and let's get out o' here!'

In the tram going home the sisters sat in silence, staring straight ahead as they lumbered along the familiar route, oblivious of passengers' chatter around them and the usual rattles that accompanied tram travel. It was only when they were outside their own front door that Nola turned and spoke to Tess.

'We'll keep this quiet, eh? We'll no' say anything.'

'But who do you think that girl is, Nola? Don't say she's somebody's daughter.'

'No, I think she's somebody Dad met in the war. An ATS girl, or a nurse, maybe.'

'He's never said anything about her. Never said he was going to see her today.'

'No, well, we don't know why he did, do we?'

Tess's eyes met Nola's, then fell.

'That's why we shouldn't say anything,' Nola murmured. 'Till we know.'

'How will we know if we don't say anything?'

'Look, I say we leave it all till after Christmas and Hogmanay. Clark's coming at Hogmanay. I don't want trouble.'

Tess caught her breath. 'You think there'll be trouble?'

'I don't know, I don't know. Just don't say anything to Ma, eh?'

'I'd never say anything to Ma.'

'Or, Dad.'

Tess was silent. She couldn't imagine what she would say or do when she saw her father again.

The long afternoon was spent with Erika, who reported that her visit to the dentist had not been too bad. She'd only had one filling and had not required an injection.

'No injection?' cried Tess, stirred from her anxieties by the thought. 'Oh, Erika, you're brave!'

'I am not, I just hate needles.'

But Erika, in Tess's view, was as brave as she was

clever. How would she cope if she were Tess, though, having to face her father when she'd caught him seeing a woman who was not her mother? For though Tess might have asked her sister more than once who that redheaded girl might be, she didn't really need to be told. She'd seen enough films, read enough books, heard enough gossip from folk at school, to know, anyway. And she'd seen the girl's tears, seen the way she'd looked at her dad, and the way he'd looked at her.

But how was Tess going to look at him? When he came in from work that evening – if he had been to work, and that wasn't certain – she didn't, in fact, look at him at all.

Chapter Fifteen

'Tell you what, Tess,' Rena said after tea, 'you can put the decorations up now if you like. I've got the box out ready, and your dad'll give you a hand.'

Tess raised her eyes to her mother. Rena'd been working hard, trying to get the washing done before Christmas as she'd said, and that was a big job, with the gas wash-boiler to heat in the back room, and all the clothes to agitate round in it, then put through the wringing machine. No wonder she looked so tired, so worn, her face pale and shiny, her hair escaping from the ribbon where she'd wound it. Tess's heart seemed to swell to fill her chest, so she could scarcely breathe, as sympathy and anger consumed her. She pushed back her chair.

'Nola can help me,' she said tightly.

'You know I've got to go back to work.'

Nola, who had to snatch her tea between shifts at the box office, was already rising from the table. Like Tess and their father, she'd left all talking during the meal to their mother, who had appeared not to notice that she was the only one with anything to say.

'I meant, we could put the decorations up tomorrow,' said Tess.

'No, I want to get the box away,' her mother told her. 'And your dad'd like to help. First Christmas since the war, you ken. Don, you'll help Tess, eh?'

'What?'

'Och, where are you? Woolgathering? I said you'd like to help to put the Christmas decorations up, wouldn't you? And maybe tomorrow you could cut us some holly from the top of the railway line. There's a nice bush up there.'

'All right, fine,' said Don. 'Tess, get the box then.'

'No, I don't want to! I don't want to do the decorations! I'm going upstairs.'

Pushing past her startled sister, Tess, scarlet-faced, ran from the room.

'Well!' Rena was staring at the door, as though unable to believe that Tess had gone through it. 'Whatever's got into her then?'

'Maybe she feels sick,' Nola said uncertainly.

'Why, what could have made her feel sick? Did you have anything when you were out? Some o' thae awful fizzy drinks, or something?'

'No, we just had a bun and a cup o' tea at Waverley,' Nola replied, then put her hand to her lips as a deep wave of colour rose to her brow.

Don, his eyes fixed on Nola, got to his feet, but he said nothing.

'Waverley?' cried Rena. 'Whatever were you doing at the station?'

'We were looking in the shops and it was handy, you ken, just to – have tea in the buffet.'

'I'll go to Tess, I'll see what's wrong,' said Rena, hurrying out, while Nola, her colour dying away, faced her father.

'You saw me?' Don asked quietly.

'Yes.'

'With Valerie?'

Nola shrugged. 'Don't know her name.'

'I didn't think anyone I knew would see us there,' he said in a low voice. 'She'd just come over from Berwick. The buffet seemed the place to go.' He laughed briefly. 'Fancy you being there, Nola. And Tess. That's why you've no' been speaking to me?'

76

'You noticed?'

'Nola, I want you to understand. I want you both, to try to understand—'

'I've got to go to work, Dad.'

'I have to talk to you. I have to explain.'

'I canna be late. I have to go.'

'I'll walk with you—'

'No. I'm away.'

'Nola!' Don grasped her arm. 'You'll no' say anything to your mother, eh? Promise me you won't.'

She shook herself free. 'You needn't worry. I don't want to upset Ma.'

'What about Tess?'

'Tess feels the same.'

Don turned aside, his face grey. 'Thanks, then. Thanks to you both. I'm going to speak to your mother maself, you see.'

Something cold clutched Nola inside. 'Do you have to?' she whispered.

'Aye, I do.'

'When? When will you speak to her?'

'After the holidays. After Hogmanay.'

For a long moment, Nola stared at her father. 'Don't say anything to Tess without me then. Don't say a word.'

'Oh, I'm no' going to say anything to Tess,' he answered, with a shuddering sigh. 'I wanted to talk to her, I wanted to talk to both o' you, but I can see there'd be no point. No point. You could never understand.' He swept his hand through his curly hair. 'But why in God's name, Nola, did you have to go to Waverley today?'

It wasn't long before Rena was back with Tess, pale now, and looking chilled, but no longer rebellious. It had come to her upstairs that she would do her mother no good by making it plain she was upset with her father. Nola had said they should say nothing, and that's what she, Tess, had better do. She still didn't look at Don.

77

'Tess is all right now,' Rena was saying cheerfully. 'Just felt a wee bit under the weather, the way girls sometimes do, you ken. She'll help with the decorations, Don.'

'That's good.'

'We're going to light the fire in the front room – we can spare a bit o' coal – and get it all looking nice. I'll put the cards up and come Christmas Eve, you can get the tree, Don.'

'We should've had the tree by now,' Tess muttered. 'Why do we always have to wait till the last minute?'

'Because they're cheaper at the last minute. Come on then, let's get started.'

The front room in Rena's house was rarely used. Even before the war, it had mainly been a shrine to the three-piece suite, the large tinted oleograph pictures and family photographs; kept brushed and dusted but not sat in except on special occasions. With the coming of the war and coal-rationing, the special occasions had wound down to Christmas and Hogmanay, and even then, if Don had not been able to come home on leave, Rena and the girls had celebrated in the kitchen.

This year, however, was going to be different. This year, they were all set to enjoy the first post-war Christmas, and putting up the decorations was the start. Don did use the precious coal ration to make a good fire, and when he and Tess had hung the silver bells over the mirror, strung up the paper chains, the imitation lanterns and the amazing coloured balls that opened out when you undid the clips, even Tess's spirits rose.

She'd always loved this room, finding it a never-failing source of interest. The pictures, the ornaments, the photographs, the Turkey carpet that had not been new in her grandma's day – all of these were a part of her. She knew them as well as her own face.

The photograph of Ada Mackie, her mother's mother, showed a formidable little woman wearing a long dress and

78

a large hat, taken against the background of a battleship.

'Why a battleship?' Tess had asked, and had been told photographers liked unusual backdrops – ships, or palm trees, temples – anything like that. And Don might have said that a picture of a battleship would have suited his mother-in-law, for she was a tough one all right. Yet they owed her quite a debt of gratitude, for it was she who'd had the forethought to take out a mortgage with her dead husband's insurance money, to buy the house that Rena had inherited. And how many folk at that time would have thought of that?

Aye, you had to admire Grandma Mackie, the only woman of property that anybody knew, before Rena became one too.

The pictures in the front room were as interesting as the photographs. Rural scenes of girls in sunbonnets tending cows – Tess knew every face, every animal. Beautiful sunsets over rolling waves – Tess thought it wonderful that you could make paint look like waves. And then a great, heavily framed portrait of a lovely woman in black velvet, surrounded by weeping attendants, and entitled 'Mary, Queen of Scots, on her Way to Execution'.

Her mother had explained to Tess who Mary, Queen of Scots was, and what had happened to her.

'Did she really have her head cut off, Ma? No, it was a story, eh?'

'It really happened, Tess. Very sad, I'm sure, but then she was a troublemaker, so they say. Troublemakers come to sticky ends, you ken.'

These were words that had sunk well into Tess's consciousness. Cause trouble and you knew what you'd get. She'd better always be careful to watch her step.

When the decorations were up, Tess and her parents sat down and watched the flames of the fire for a while. It was so warm and comfortable, so very peaceful, it seemed to Tess that nothing much had changed; there couldn't really

79

be anything to worry about. The heart-shaped face of the girl with the red hair wasn't real, just something she'd dreamed, and her Dad hadn't been in the Waverley buffet, buying that girl tea, looking into her eyes. Not this dad here, stretching out his long legs, staring into the fire with thoughtful eyes. Not Tess's dad.

But then Nola came home, having closed up the cinema box office, and the feeling of peace was shattered. Not because she caused any commotion, but because somehow she seemed to bring reality with her. As she stood in the doorway and looked in at them around the fire, she was a reminder to Tess of what they'd seen together and she knew she couldn't fool herself. Everything might seem just the same. In fact, she knew, and Nola knew, that nothing was ever going to be the same again. Their dad must have known that all along, and had borne his secret alone. Now there were three of them sharing it, and only Rena, jumping up to put the kettle on, was still happy.

Chapter Sixteen

According to Nola, the only way to get through this crisis was to put it right out of your mind. For the time being, just forget all about it.

'We canna do that!' Tess cried. 'It's no' possible.'

'I tell you, it's the only way. Otherwise, we spoil Christmas and Hogmanay and everything.'

'They're spoiled already.'

'No, we've Ma to think of, remember.' Nola hesitated. 'And there's Clark coming.'

'But how long do we have to go on, pretending everything's all right?'

Nola shook her head, as though she couldn't say, yet Tess caught a caginess in her eye that made her wonder if her sister knew something she wasn't telling her. Had Dad said anything?

'Just let's get through till the New Year,' Nola murmured, putting her arm round Tess's shoulders. 'It's no' so long, eh? And then I think all this will have sorted itself out.'

That was the way they left things, and it did seem to be the best plan, for gradually, in spite of Tess's worries, the spell of Christmas began to work and there was so much to do she did manage to put the girl with the red hair to the back of her mind. Except at night, of course, when she lay awake and listened to Nola's regular breathing, and knew that she was putting on a good act and was in fact as wide awake as Tess herself. Everything had worked forward to the front of her mind by then and had to be put back when morning came.

On Christmas Eve, Don brought in a pretty little tree from the market, which they dressed with the old ornaments that came out year after year, and because the paper fairy had finally fallen apart, put a silver star, made by Tess, on the top.

'Does that no' look grand?' cried Rena, and invited Mrs Lange and Erika down to see it, after which Mrs Lange invited them all up to her room for coffee and Christmas biscuits.

'Real coffee?' Nola exclaimed. 'Wherever did you get it then?'

'Logie's,' Mrs Lange told her, naming Edinburgh's most expensive department store. 'I was told by a friend that they had small supplies of ground coffee newly arrived. I did not waste much time in joining the queue, I can assure you!'

'The Austrians have always liked their coffee, eh?' asked Don, who was looking well, apart from his eyes, but his daughters could only hope that no one was noticing that his usually cheerful grey eyes now seemed quite different. Couldn't say how, they just were. Thank God, Ma was so absorbed in the little presents they were all exchanging, she wasn't looking at Dad.

'It is the Continental custom to exchange gifts on Christmas Eve, rather than Christmas Day,' Mrs Lange was explaining. 'Then we go to Midnight Mass, usually in the snow.'

'Makes me feel guilty,' said Rena, smelling the soap she had received. 'Mebbe I'll get to the kirk tomorrow.'

'Got to cook the pork,' Nola reminded her, laughing. 'We canna do without our crackling! Shame you're no' joining us, Mrs Lange.'

'We shall look forward to seeing you on Boxing Day,'

82

said Mrs Lange. 'But why can nobody ever tell me what Boxing Day means?'

As everyone laughed, Tess and Erika hugged each other and admired again their presents to each other. Tess had given Erika a second-hand copy of *A Christmas Carol*, found in an Edinburgh market, while Erika's gift to Tess was a tiny wooden doll she had dressed herself in Austrian costume.

'Och, it's one o' the prettiest things I've ever had,' Tess exclaimed. 'See the wee apron and the bodice, and the feather in her hat!'

'From Mutti's eiderdown,' Erika told her, smiling. 'What shall you call her then?'

'I don't know. What's an Austrian name?'

'Heidi, as in the story?'

'Heidi, yes. That'd be perfect.'

'I hope she will cheer you up, Tess,' Erika said quietly. 'Make you happy again.'

'Why, Erika, I am happy!' Tess cried, flushing. 'I'm just the same as always.'

'Yes, of course, I am sorry,' Erika said quickly. 'I do not wish to pry.'

'No, it's OK, it's OK.'

But Tess's eyes did not meet Erika's, so full of wondering sympathy. Clever Erika. Was she sharper than Rena then, in seeing things folk wanted hidden? Tess couldn't really believe it.

Chapter Seventeen

They got through Christmas, the three with the secret. Had the roast pork and crackling, the bought pudding that wasn't too bad, the cake that was excellent, and then there was just the New Year to face. After that, who knew what would happen? Maybe something worse? First, there was Clark's visit, though, to make Nola, at least, feel better.

He arrived on the day before New Year's Eve, loaded with presents, including a bottle of whisky for Don and a beautiful ham for Rena.

'Whisky?' murmured Don, looking dazed, for whisky was like gold dust to find, even in Scotland. 'I canna believe ma eyes.'

'Hope it's not coals to Newcastle,' Clark said modestly. 'I know it isn't malt, but maybe it'll do.'

'Do? I'll say. We'll have a dram tonight, eh?'

'I could do with one now,' said Rena, staring wide-eyed at the ham. 'I mean, I've never seen anything like this since before the war, Clark. Where'd you get it then?'

'Got my contacts.' He smiled. 'And I wanted only the best for Nola's folks, you understand?'

'You've done us proud,' Nola told him. 'What with scent for me—'

'And sweeties for me,' cried Tess.

'It's like Christmas all over again, that's what it is.'

'I'm sorry we've no' got so much for you,' Rena said awkwardly. 'Just a book on Scotland.'

'Mrs Gillespie, please don't apologise. You've invited me to stay for your very special holiday, you've invited me to spend it with Nola, and I couldn't be more grateful.'

'What a charmer,' said Don, as Nola took Clark off to show him where he was to sleep, which was as far away from her own room as possible. (Trust Ma, Nola had said, with a laugh.) 'I can see why Nola's smitten.'

'Who says she's smitten?' asked Rena. 'There's nothing definite between 'em.'

'How would you feel if there was?'

'No' very happy. I want a different sort o' fellow for Nola.'

'Girls don't always have the same ideas as their folks.'

'Well, if he says anything to you, you tell him she's too young.'

Don gave a weary smile. 'He'll be more likely to say something to Nola, and then she'll tell us what she's decided.'

'A fat lot o' help you are,' Rena snapped. 'I was relying on you to put him off.' She stared at Don for a moment, then her face softened. 'Are you no' well, Don? You look exhausted.'

'Just under the weather.'

'Like Tess the other day? It'll be Nola next, I suppose. But she's looking fine since Clark turned up, of course.'

'Hey, your dad's good-looking, isn't he?' Clark remarked, unpacking in his tiny room that wasn't big enough for letting, holding as it did only a single bed and a chest of drawers. 'Just like his photo. Bet he was a heart-throb, eh?'

'Heart-throb?' Nola repeated coldly.

'I mean, before he married your mum.'

'Ma had plenty of admirers too, you ken.'

'Sure.' Clark laughed and pulled Nola to him. 'Handsome family, aren't you? Young Tess'll be a heart breaker too, before long, if I'm not mistaken.'

'There's nothing to be proud of in that.' Nola moved from Clark's arms. 'Breaking hearts.'

He stared at her, frowning.

'Why, what's got into you then? There's no need to pick me up before I've fallen down, as they say. I was only meaning that Tess was a pretty girl. Like her sister.'

Nola smiled and she leaned forward to kiss Clark gently on the lips, at which he kissed her back, strongly, and would have continued kissing her, except that she pulled away again and said they'd better go down.

'Ah, Nola, I haven't seen you for weeks and you don't want to kiss me?'

'I do, but Ma and Dad'll be waiting for us. There'll be plenty of time for us to be on our own.'

'When?'

'We can go out somewhere this evening. And if we hurry, we could have a cup o' tea now and go walking on the beach before it gets dark.'

'Can't see us cuddling on Portobello beach,' he said wryly. 'Not in December.'

'Well, come on, let's put your things away and go down. I'm sorry there's no wardrobe. Could you hang your coat on the door?'

'Nola, will you listen a minute?' Clark took a package from his pocket. 'I didn't just bring you scent, you know. There's this, as well.'

Her face was wary as she unwrapped a small box. 'What's this, Clark?'

'I'm sure you can guess. It's a ring.'

'A ring? You've bought me a ring? Clark, you never said you'd do that. You never said you wanted to marry me!'

'Thought it was obvious. I mean, what am I doing here? Aren't I on approval?'

'No, no, I never said – I didn't know – what you had in mind.'

'You did know, you must've known.'

86

'I wasn't sure.'

'Nola, dearest, you can be sure now. Look at the ring. See if it fits.'

She slowly opened the box and swallowed hard as she looked at the diamond hoop glittering up at her. Clark, watching her, grinned.

'Go on then, put it on. It's yours. I know we should speak to your folks first, but you could just try it on, couldn't you?'

'I canna think how you afforded it,' she murmured, sliding the ring onto her finger where it fitted comfortably. 'It must have cost the earth.'

'I'd my gratuity, don't forget.'

Bright colour flooded Nola's face and she pulled the ring from her finger. 'Oh, you never went and spent all that on a ring for me!' she cried. 'I've no' even said yes!'

'But you will!'

'No.' She put the ring back in its box and pushed it into his pocket. 'I'm sorry, Clark, but I'm no' ready. I thought I was, but – well, there's been a few problems here – I'm a bit mixed up, to tell you the truth.'

His face was stricken. 'You've met somebody else?'

'No, no. It's nothing like that, honest. It's just that I canna think straight at the moment. I need some time, that's all, Clark. More time.'

'I see.' He turned away from her. 'Well, I can wait. Take all the time you want.'

'I'm sorry.'

'What do they say up here?' He turned back to her with a crooked smile. 'Nae bother? Nae bother, Nola. Shall we go down?'

'Oh, Clark . . .'

Her eyes filled with tears and she would have kissed him, but he put her aside and opened the door.

'Think I'll go down and have a word with your dad. Don't worry, only about the war. You can tell he had a tough one, he looks that tired.'

Chapter Eighteen

Suddenly, it was 1946. When she was younger, Tess had been fascinated by the way one night could seem as long as a whole year, but that was because she'd gone to bed in one year and woken up in another. Now that she was allowed to stay up to see the New Year in, it was still strange to find herself in another time, just because the clock had struck twelve.

What would 1946 bring? When everyone around her was kissing and raising their glasses, her main thought was that this was Hogmanay over and that something might happen now, but of course she didn't know what. She longed for the comfort of Nola's presence, for Nola was the only one she could talk to about her fears. But her sister had gone with Clark and a bunch of friends to see in the New Year outside the Tron Kirk, the traditional meeting place for revellers.

Poor old Clark had been looking very glum. Tess had heard her mother commenting on it to her father; she'd been wondering if Nola had turned him down and hoping she had. Her father had said nothing, but then he'd been very quiet for days. Surely her mother had noticed? She'd that ham to cook for New Year's Day, though, and the thought of it was taking all her attention. The tenants had been invited, and some of the neighbours, and though she didn't care much for Clark, she was certainly giving him credit for being a kind, generous lad.

'He is that,' agreed Don, who would have been thinking of the whisky.

The first day of 1946 went off well, mainly because everyone felt so satisfied after the superb meal, something they weren't used to and could only marvel at.

'Is it no' terrible, the way we talk about food all the time?' asked Vera MacFee, Rena's friend, who was large enough for folk to think she always ate meals to match her size, but had to manage on the rations the same as everyone else. 'I feel that ashamed, sometimes, but what can you do? You have tae eat, you have tae keep finding what you can.'

'Queuing,' sighed Miss Denny.

'I remember reading that thae explorers used to imagine food,' Mr Crombie remarked. 'Captain Scott and such. Used to dream up Christmas dinners, you ken, then open another tin.'

'Poor fellows,' said Mrs Lange. 'But there has been nothing imaginary about this meal, Mrs Gillespie. We must all give you our thanks.'

'And Clark, here,' Rena said, flushing a little. 'He's the one to thank, eh?'

Clark flashed his famous smile and Nola, Tess noticed, pressed his hand. She was really looking after him, wasn't she? As though he were an invalid. She must have turned him down then. Tess felt relieved, yet at the same time sorry for Clark.

What tangles folk got into over love! Look at Polly Wight there, still at odds with her mother, because of that long drink of water, Kennie. Look at Dad. Tess slid her eyes to her father, who was being talked at by Miss Denny as usual, and at once stopped her thoughts as though she'd met some impenetrable fence. She didn't want to think of her father in connection with love, and when Erika asked her how little Heidi was getting on with Alice, was glad to laugh and be silly for once. Later, they did Erika's

89

Christmas jigsaw up in Mrs Lange's immaculate room, and had more of the special biscuits that were a Christmas treat.

The following morning Clark departed. Don shook his hand before going into work, and Rena felt willing to give him a smacking kiss, because it looked as though there were no plans for him to be her son-in-law. Nola went with him to the station, as she didn't have to be at the cinema until the afternoon, and on her return Tess had the nerve to ask her what she'd said to him.

'Honestly, Tess, that's my business, eh?'

'I bet he did ask you to marry him, didn't he? And you said no?'

'As a matter o' fact, I told him I'd think about it.'

'Oh.' Tess's face fell. 'You're going to think about it? But you canna be as keen as you were, else you'd have said yes.'

'I don't know what I feel at the moment. To tell you the truth, I'll be glad to get back to work and no' have to think about maself at all.'

Or Dad, thought Tess.

But Hogmanay was over and nothing had happened yet. Perhaps everything was going to be all right after all? Tess went to bed early and read one of the Chalet School series she'd borrowed from the library. It was not so exciting as *Jane Eyre*, but less worrying, and quite interesting really. Imagine going to school in Switzerland. Bet nobody got the belt there, eh?

When Nola came to bed, she said she felt tired and would put the light out, if Tess didn't mind.

'Had a good Hogmanay?' she asked, her eyes meeting Tess's, before she switched off the light.

'Aye. Nothing's happened, has it?'

'Who said anything was going to happen?'

'Well, you said we'd to get through Christmas and New Year, didn't you?'

Nola snapped off the light. 'I don't remember what I said exactly. Let's get some sleep, eh?'

She had been asleep only for a little while when something woke Tess. A door banging? Or voices?

'What was that?' she whispered to Nola, who was sitting up in bed, listening.

'One o' the tenants coming in late?'

'Must be after midnight.'

'Aye, well, they're always banging doors, eh? Better get back to sleep.'

'Should we see what it was?' Tess was shivering. 'Mebbe somebody's broken in?'

'Who on earth'd do that? We've nothing to steal.' Nola got out of bed and put her thin dressing gown around her shoulders. 'Och, I'm freezing! But I'll go down and have a look. Keep you happy, Tess.'

'Shall I come?'

'No, you stay where you are. I'll no' be long.' Nola took the pocket torch she kept by her bed and glided away, leaving Tess humped under her bed clothes, her cold nose coming up for air from time to time.

All doors were shut as Nola passed by, and all was quiet, but she went on down the stairs to the ground floor. All quiet still, but the door to the front room was open and she was sure she remembered it being closed when she went up to bed. That was funny, eh? No lights on in the room, though. Surely nobody there.

But there was someone there. Looking cautiously round the door, her torch casting a little pool of light, Nola made out someone sitting very still in one of the armchairs, and caught her breath.

'Dad?'

He was wearing a coat over his pyjamas, and did not look up when she said his name.

'Dad, what are you doing here? You'll catch your death.'

91

'Couldn't sleep,' he said after a pause.

'Why didn't you go to the kitchen? It'd be warmer there.'

'I'm all right here.'

'Want me to make you a cup o' tea?'

'No thanks. You go back to bed.'

'Something's up, Dad. I'm no' leaving you like this.'

'I tell you, I'm all right. Go back to bed. We'll talk in the morning.'

'At least let me get you a blanket.'

'I'll get one maself, I'll get a bit o' sleep on the settee.'

'Goodnight then,' Nola said, turning reluctantly to go. 'Like ma torch?'

'No.' He stirred and gave a deep, wrenching sigh. 'Nola, please, do me a favour. Just go to bed, eh?'

She went, her heart so heavy it seemed almost to prevent her climbing the long flights of stairs to the top floor.

'Is everything all right?' asked Tess, starting up from her nest of blankets.

'Aye, fine.'

Nola, shuddering with the cold, took off her wrap and flung herself into her own bed, which by now had lost all its warmth. Why tell Tess yet about their dad sitting down there alone? As he'd said, they could talk in the morning. Oh, and they would. Nola, shuddering still, was sure of it.

Chapter Nineteen

There had been talk earlier that night. Between Don and Rena after they'd gone to bed.

When Don had come in from the bathroom, already in his pyjamas – new that Christmas, from Rena – he'd found her waiting for him, wearing her best nightdress, and smiling. And he had known, as he got into bed, that he wanted them to make love that night.

'You've left the light on,' she whispered.

'Och, yes.' He began to get out of bed.

'I don't mind, if you don't.'

'No, no, I'll put it off.'

'Should have some bedside lamps. When things come back into the shops, I'll get some. If they're no' too dear.'

Don grunted a little, as though already feeling ready for sleep, but Rena's arms were around him.

'You know what I've been thinking, Don? We might try for another baby. I'm no' too old, you ken. Plenty women my age have bairns.' She lay against him, her head on his chest. 'We might have another boy. Another Rickie, Don. Think o' that.'

He lay very still. So still she was alerted, and drew away.

'Don, what's wrong?'

It was his cue to say, 'Nothing,' and take her into his arms, but he knew the time he'd been dreading for so long had come. He was going to have to speak. But he couldn't find the words.

Rena raised herself against her pillow. 'What's wrong?' she asked again. 'Don, what is it?'

In a voice he didn't recognise as his own, he told her.

'Rena, I – I've met someone else.'

She was to say afterwards that those words were the worst anyone could hear, worse even than the announcement of a death, because they spelled out not only loss but rejection. At the time, however, she could scarcely take them in. It was as though Don was a foreigner, speaking to her in a language she didn't understand.

'Someone else?' she asked at last, with dry lips. 'What are you talking about? Who? Who have you met?

'She's called Valerie Arnold. She was in the ATS. I met her in Germany.'

After a long terrible silence, Rena got out of bed and put on the light. For some moments she stared down at Don, who met her gaze unflinchingly, for so much he knew he owed her – not to turn away.

'Is this the one who wrote you that letter before Christmas?' she asked, her voice trembling. 'Was she the pal who lived in Glasgow, who wasn't married?'

'She lives on a farm near Berwick on Tweed.' He swung himself out of bed and stood beside it, his back ramrod straight, as though he were a soldier again, ready to be inspected. 'Yes, she wrote that letter. She wanted to see me.'

'And you wanted to see her too?'

'Had to see her.' He faltered a little, putting one hand to his brow. 'Had to, Rena.'

'Had to,' she repeated contemptuously.

'Listen, I ken I've no excuse for this, no excuse at all, but what's happened, it's like an illness. It's a sickness.'

He knew he could never explain to her how he felt, how he'd always felt since he'd first seen Val Arnold, sitting with a crowd of girls in the canteen. That blaze of hair, the

94

eyes she'd turned on him, the lovely mouth that trembled into smiles.

He'd never felt before as he did then, not even for Rena, who'd been so pretty when she was young. But his feelings for Rena had been right. Normal. The sort any man might feel when he'd found a nice girl and wanted to get wed. But Val had taken possession of him, that was the only way to put it. Once he'd met her, this scene with Rena had been inevitable. He'd known it, though he'd fought against it. Now he couldn't fight any more.

'I canna fight it, Rena,' he said in a low voice. 'I've tried. You may no' believe me, but I've been trying ever since I came back. The thing is, it's no good, I canna do it. I canna give her up.'

'That's silly talk, Don!' Rena, who had no dressing gown, took down a coat that was hanging on the back of the door and shrugged herself into it. 'That's nonsense! You've a wife and family and your whole life here, and you talk about no' fighting this? All right, it's a sickness, I'll believe it, but if it's a sickness, it'll pass. You'll get better.'

He shook his head. 'No, that won't happen.'

'Yes, it will. Remember hearing about ma cousin Nora in the Borders? Same thing happened to her man, Bernie Howat. He fell for a girl that served in the paper shop. Used to sell him his paper every day. He was all for leaving home, couldn't think of anything else, but Nora wouldn't let him go and it all died away. The girl married someone else and Bernie never even cared. Och, don't talk to me about no' fighting this, Don! We'll fight it together!'

'Rena,' he said, in a voice she could barely hear. 'There's a baby on the way.'

Sitting in the cold darkness of the front room, Don relived that moment when he had mortally wounded his dear, loyal Rena. Put the knife in, as surely as if he'd had a real blade to slip into her heart. How was he ever going to live with himself again? He didn't know.

95

He'd tried to explain to her that he still loved her, still loved his girls, only wanted to be with them, yet he was being pulled in two, drawn apart by what he felt for his family and what he felt for Val. But Rena had laughed in his face and he couldn't blame her.

When she'd walked to the door and opened it for him, he'd walked through it. When she'd banged it behind him, he'd felt glad, that she was letting him see what she thought of him. Tomorrow, she'd said, he could move out. Get himself a room. Go to Berwick.

'I canna go to Berwick, Rena, there's her family to think of. And then there's ma job here.'

'Too bad. You'll have to find somewhere else then.'

Rena, now ashen pale, was very close to the edge, but keeping going on her spirit, drawing on all her resources, to fight back from the wound he had given her. 'There'll be no divorce, of course. No' because I want to hang on to you. I don't. If you don't want me, I don't want you. But divorce costs money and we've none. None to spare anyhow. Will you spend the rest o' the night downstairs then?'

And there he stayed, wearing his coat from the hall, huddled under a rug on the settee after Nola had left him, until it was morning. When he would have to face Rena again, and Nola. And Tess.

Chapter Twenty

It had come then, whatever they'd been dreading. Tess knew, as soon as she opened her eyes, that a blow had fallen because there was Nola, who liked her lie-in and her cup of tea in bed, already up and dressed and with her hair done. As Tess gazed at her with wide, fearful eyes, her sister told her to hurry up and get ready, they'd go down together.

'What's up, Nola? What's happened?'

'I think Dad has told Ma.'

Tess's hand flew to her lips. 'Oh no!' But understanding slowly came into her eyes. 'Did he say he would? Did he tell you?'

'He said he'd have to.'

'After Hogmanay? He said he'd tell Ma about that girl after Hogmanay? That's what we've been waiting for?'

'You knew that, didn't you?'

Tess was silent, hurrying into her clothes. Yes, she'd known, without ever putting it into words. She'd known their dad was going to ruin everything, and now it seemed he had. So Nola said, but how could she be sure? There might still be a little hope.

'I saw Dad last night,' Nola told her, as though she knew what Tess was thinking and was telling her not to think it. She put her arm through Tess's. 'Let's go down then.'

*

When they went into the kitchen, Tess knew that Nola had been right and hope was dead. Her mother, her face quite white, her eyes blank, was sitting at the table, stirring tea, the spoon going round and round, round and round, as though it would never stop. Her father, in his work clothes, a plaster over a shaving cut on his cheek, was standing in the middle of the room, his arms folded over his chest, his eyes cast down. They were like strangers. Strange to their daughters, strange to each other.

'There you are,' Rena murmured, and now she did stop stirring her tea, but made no move to drink it. 'Your father has something to say to you.'

He raised his eyes and lowered them. 'You tell them, Rena,' he said hoarsely.

'It's no' my job to tell them. Be man enough to tell 'em yourself.'

'Don't worry,' said Nola. 'We know already.'

Rena shot to her feet, her face mottling with colour. 'You know? How? How d'you know?'

'We saw Dad with that girl, Valerie. At Waverley.'

'Waverley?' Rena sank back on her chair. 'Oh, God, I remember. I remember that day. I couldn't understand why he was looking at you the way he did. Nola, why did you no' tell me?'

'We'd never have told you, Ma.'

'No need, anyway.' Rena, pale again, took a cigarette from a packet on the table and lit it with shaking fingers. 'He told me himself last night. He's leaving us, girls. Canna give the young woman up, seemingly. She is young, eh? How old is she, Don?'

'Twenty-three,' he whispered.

'Twenty-three? Young enough to be your daughter.' Rena laughed. 'Have you ever heard of a man leaving home for somebody old enough to be his mother? That'd be something new.'

'Rena, for God's sake!' Don shook his head. 'I know you can none o' you understand, but I have to do this, I canna do anything else. I don't want to do it – I'm being torn in pieces – but I canna help maself. These things happen. It doesn't mean I don't still love you!'

Tess, bursting into tears, ran from the room followed by Nola, while Rena, grinding out her cigarette, stood up.

'Just go, Don,' she said evenly. 'Pack up your stuff and go. There's no more for us to say.'

'There's the girls,' he said doggedly. 'I'll still want to see them.'

'They'll no' want to see you.'

'You don't know that.'

'Ask 'em, and see.'

'Well, we've things to discuss. I canna just walk out, Rena. There's – there's money, you ken. I'll no' leave you short, I'll pay ma whack—'

'You can give me something for Tess, but Nola's working and I've got ma house. We don't need anything.'

'Your house,' he said shortly. 'Yes, you've always had that.'

Rena raised her eyebrows. 'Always rankled, eh? I was the one with the property?'

'I was never the true provider,' Don said quietly. 'Things were always the wrong way round.'

There was a silence, during which they could hear the sounds of the morning. Tenants moving about, steps on the stairs, voices calling. Rena, her shoulders drooping, turned away.

'Are you going then?' she asked, not looking round. 'You'd better take your ration book. It's in the dresser drawer.'

'I canna just go like this. I'll be back. We'll sort things out.'

'For God's sake, just go now then.'

She closed her eyes until she heard his steps receding, then the front door bang. For long moments, she stood, sagging, tears filling her eyes, but then she brushed them away and went to find her daughters.

Chapter Twenty-One

The girls had been made to come back, sit down at the kitchen table, have some breakfast. Rena was already getting the porridge started and slicing bread. Things would be just the same as usual. It was not the end of the world that their father had gone.

'It is,' said Tess thickly. 'It is the end o' the world. I don't want any breakfast.'

'Now look.' Rena turned round from the stove. 'I'm going to say something. What's happened has happened, we canna change it. But I'm no' going to let it spoil our lives, yours or mine. We're going to weather this and come through. We're going to be happy again. Understand?'

'Ma, don't try too hard,' Nola said gently.

'What do you mean?'

'I mean, we canna just pretend that things can be the same.'

'Nola, I'm saying we won't let what's happened ruin our lives.'

'We have to have time, though. To get over it.'

Rena began to ladle out the porridge. 'There'll be time, all right.'

Tess stared down into the bowl her mother put in front of her. 'I'll never forgive Dad,' she said slowly. 'I'll never forgive him for leaving you, Ma. Or, me and Nola.'

'He says it's an illness he's got. A sickness.' Rena, her

own porridge in front of her, made no move to pick up her spoon. 'Funny kind o' sickness, eh? When it's other folk get the pain?'

'I think Dad is suffering,' Nola said quietly. 'I don't think he wanted to leave us.'

'Oh? Why did he then?'

'That girl's got her hooks into him. He canna get free.'

'Nola, folk do what they want to do. If there's one thing I've learned in ma life, it's that.' Rena took a few mouthfuls of porridge, then leaped up and put her bowl in the sink. 'But there's something I haven't told you. Made him choose her anyway,'

'What?' asked Nola, her tone wary. She glanced quickly at Tess, whose eyes were wide on her mother's face. Rena looked away.

'The girl's expecting,' she said in a low voice.

There was a stunned silence. Tess had flushed crimson. Nola's hand was holding her brow. Rena came back to the table.

'I didn't want you to know.' She put her arm round Tess's shoulders. 'But you'd have heard anyway. It's best to come from me.'

After a moment, during which Tess caught at her hand, Rena moved to her chair and sat down.

'You want a cigarette, Nola?'

'Aye,' Nola answered hoarsely. 'Please.'

No one made a pretence of eating any more breakfast. Rena and Nola smoked their cigarettes. Tess sat with her eyes cast down. She was thinking that she would tell Erika about her dad, but not about the baby. The baby that would be her half-sister or brother. Her dad's child. She knew that neither she, nor her mother, nor her sister, would ever talk to anyone about that.

Erika's large dark eyes were full of compassion, as she walked with Tess on the wintry sands and listened to her story.

101

'Your poor mother,' she whispered. 'How could this have happened?'

Tess shrugged, staring ahead at the low sky and the scudding clouds with eyes as bleak as the sea.

'I knew there was something wrong,' Erika went on. 'You were brave, you kept it from me, but all the time you were worrying that your father might go. That must have been terrible, Tess.'

'Aye, it was terrible, but we'd seen him with that girl, you ken, and Nola said there'd be trouble. We were just waiting for it. Now it's come, it's worse than we ever thought.'

As she turned to look at Erika, the wind tugged at her woollen beret, tore it off and let her dark hair blow free, as though its wildness suited her spirit and all that she was feeling.

'I'll never forgive him,' she said harshly. 'Never. He was ma dad, he was special. And we waited all thae years during the war for him to come back, and when he did, we were so happy.' She took out a hankie and wiped the trails of tears on her face. 'No· for long, eh? It's Ma I'm sorry for, though. She says it's worse than if he was dead.'

'Oh, no, no, Tess. Death is so final. With death, there is no hope.'

'There's no hope now, Erika.'

'But your father might come back.'

'No.' Tess set her mouth in a hard little line. 'We don't want him back, you see.'

They walked on in silence.

'I know how hurt you must be, Tess,' Erika said at last. 'What has happened has been so cruel. But one day you might feel better, you know.'

'Better? I don't see how. Nothing's going to change.'

'You might change, Tess. Feel less bitter.'

'I bet you've never felt less bitter, Erika. About your dad.'

Erika hesitated. 'It would not be good to be like Mutti

and me. We can't forget, you see.'

'We'll no' forget, either. But Dad'll no' come back to us, anyway. That's for sure.'

In the winter twilight, however, Tess saw him again. He was standing outside Rena's house, waiting for her.

'Tess!' he whispered urgently, and she stopped as though shot.

'Good afternoon, Mr Gillespie,' Erika said politely, and glanced swiftly at Tess. 'I will see you later, Tess.'

As Erika slipped with some relief into the house, Don took Tess's hand in his.

'Don't!' She pulled her hand away.

'I had to say goodbye to you, Tess. Because you're still ma Tess, you ken. You always will be. And Nola's still ma Nola.'

'I canna talk to you, Dad. After what you've done.'

'Look, pet, I know how things must seem to you, but I'm no' as bad as you think. Believe me, that's true. One day you'll understand. And we'll meet sometime, eh? You'd be willing, you and Nola? I'll fix it with your Ma—'

'No, no, don't fix anything. We don't want to meet you, Dad. We don't want to see you. We don't want to see you ever again.'

He took the words as blows, wincing at their pain, but Tess did not see their effect. She was running up the steps and into the house, slamming the door behind her before he could call her name. And then, with the good solid door between him and her, it was too late.

Chapter Twenty-Two

Once the news of Don's departure broke, the atmosphere in Rena's house became hushed, the tenants moving soft-footedly, as though there had indeed been a death, all expressing sympathy for poor Mrs Gillespie and the girls.

Who'd have thought Mr Gillespie would go off like that then? Such a nice guy, eh? So helpful, so friendly!

'Too friendly, seemingly,' said Kennie Wight, with a grin.

'Aye, but such a grand fella,' moaned Mr Crombie. 'Nothing too much trouble. A shelf here, a bit of oil there. He's going to be missed, that's for sure.'

'Mind you, I'm not really surprised,' Miss Denny remarked to Polly. 'Mrs Gillespie can be – shall we say – a little sharp? Maybe Mr Gillespie got tired of dancing to her tune?'

'Mrs Gillespie is sharp, all right, but she's been very kind to us,' Polly replied. 'I'm just that sorry for her, you ken.'

'Oh, we are all sorry for her!' cried Miss Denny, with perfect truth.

This Rena knew, and while acknowledging that folk meant well, hated their sympathy. Hated being in a position of seeming to need it, because she'd become a woman whose husband had left her for someone younger and prettier.

Even from Vera she found it hard to take, though Vera was so good-natured and had only Rena's welfare at heart. But she was happily married herself – her Phil had never looked at another woman. How could she possibly understand?

Only Mrs Lange's understated feeling for her brought Rena balm. When she first heard the news, the Austrian tenant did not immediately rush round, as Miss Denny and Polly had done, anxious for all the details. She let a day or two go by before coming to take Rena's hand, letting her know she was thinking of her, but assuring her that she needn't talk. Needn't tell her anything. She understood, anyway.

But now Rena wanted to talk.

'I was such a fool,' she murmured, offering Mrs Lange her cigarettes. 'I couldn't see what was under ma nose, could I?'

'Why should you ever have suspected?'

'Well, I don't know. Looking back, I think I did have some idea. I think there was something I could never put ma finger on. Never wanted to, you ken.'

'That would be understandable.'

'Aye, when he came back from the war, he'd talk and laugh, just like he used to do. It was only now and again, I'd see him sitting by himself, looking at nothing, and I'd think, that's new, that's no' like Don. But then he'd smile and be just as usual, and I'd wonder what I was on about.'

Rena lit a cigarette and watched its smoke rise.

'Once, he fired up, shouted at me, for no reason, or so I thought. Maybe I knew then. Like I say, I'd no let maself see.'

'He must have been under a great strain,' Mrs Lange said quietly. 'I have no sympathy for him, you understand, but it may have been that he was trying to forget the young woman.'

'Twenty-three, she is,' said Rena flatly. 'And with lovely red hair, so Nola tells me. No' much chance for me, eh?'

'Don't say that, my dear. You have been a wonderful

105

wife to him, and my guess is your husband will soon regret what he has done. Before you know it, he will come hurrying home.'

'If he does, he'll find the door locked.' Rena flung back her head and straightened her shoulders. 'I'm going to make maself a new life, Mrs Lange. I'm going to make sure I don't need Don any more.'

'Where is he now?' Mrs Lange asked delicately, after a pause.

'Staying with a friend from the garage.' Rena's tone was curt, as though she was not in the least interested where Don might be. 'But of course he'll be looking round for something to share with the girl. It'll no' be easy to find.'

'The housing shortage is terrible,' Mrs Lange agreed. 'Maybe they will have to move away from Edinburgh.'

'Suits me,' said Rena.

In fact, Don was lucky. He not only found a job at another garage in Edinburgh's Old Town, he was also able to rent a small flat over the premises. Rena was sent the address.

'No mention of the girl, of course,' she told her daughters when Tess brought the letter down to the kitchen.

'I believe she's moved in,' said Nola. 'I saw Mr Todd the other day. He thought she had.'

'Didn't mind telling you, eh?' Rena murmured.

'It was what we expected, Ma.'

'I bet she's wearing a wedding ring, an' all.'

Nola was silent for a moment or two. 'Talking of wedding rings,' she said at last. 'I might be getting one.'

Tess's head shot up, while Rena turned pale.

'Oh Nola, you're never going to take him on?' she cried. 'You're never going to marry Clark?'

'He has asked me, Ma. He had the engagement ring ready at Hogmanay, but I told him I'd to make up ma mind.'

'And now you have?' Rena sat down desolately, and Tess put her hand on her shoulder. 'Nola, I canna understand

106

you. After what's happened to us, how can you think about marrying Clark Walters?'

'What's Clark got to do with what happened to us?'

'Surely you won't be ready to trust him?'

'Ma, you have to trust somebody. You canna go through life thinking you'll be cheated all the time. At least, I canna do that.'

'I thought you might've wanted to stay with Tess and me for a bit,' Rena said quietly, and Nola, flushing, lowered her eyes.

'I do want to stay with you and Tess, Ma. Be some support. But it's no' fair to keep Clark hanging on, eh? If we get engaged, we needn't get married till the summer. Just as long as we know what we're doing.'

'If you're sure you do know what you're doing, Nola. All I want is for you to be happy.' Rena's voice was low. 'You and Tess.'

'I know, I know, but I've been going out with Clark for a long time. I think I should know ma own mind by now.'

'Why didn't you say yes straight away then?' asked Tess.

Nola drew her brows together. 'I've said yes now, and that's all there is to it. You'll get to like Clark, Tess, I promise you. He's always been very nice to us all. Isn't that right, Ma.'

'I suppose so,' Rena agreed without warmth. 'I certainly hope you'll be happy. So when do we start planning the wedding then?'

'A register office wedding will do. We don't want any fuss.'

'A register office? When you'd make such a lovely bride, Nola? And there's Tess, she could be bridesmaid.'

'I wouldn't mind,' Tess admitted graciously.

'You can still be my attendant, Tess, if you want. But these big weddings are all a waste o' money, you ken, and we haven't got it to spare.'

'If your dad had been here, you'd have wanted a nice wedding.' Rena's eyes were moody. 'It's because of all the trouble he's caused that you just want to run out the door and get wed.'

'You think about what we'll save, Ma, and that'll cheer you up,' said Nola.

'Well, there is that, I suppose. We've no' got your dad's money now, except for what he lets me have for Tess.'

'You were a fool to let him off sending money to you, Ma. Why should you go short?'

'I don't want his money, Nola.'

'And neither do I,' said Tess.'

'What he sends you is going into the post office,' her mother told her. 'I'm putting it by to pay for secretarial training for you later on. No more talk of working in a garage, eh?'

Secretarial training? Tess's heart sank. But it was still a long time before she need worry about it, and if Ma was happy about the idea, let her be happy. Just as Ma wanted happiness for her girls, so all Tess wanted was to see her mother smile again.

Chapter Twenty-Three

Clark's parents came up for the wedding that was arranged for late June, accompanied by his father's brother and his aunt. As Rena's house was full they stayed in a reopened guesthouse on the promenade, expressing themselves amazed at the number of people on the beach – the first post-war visitors – but thought Portobello a very good place for a holiday. Not the size of Scarborough, of course, or Blackpool, but who'd have thought you'd get the seaside as part of Edinburgh?

Clark's father and uncle were tall, colourless men, quite unlike Clark himself. As Rena pointed out, you had to go to his mother, Connie, to see where his looks came from. It was she who had the glossy dark hair, the dimples, the engaging smile. And what a talker, eh? Just like him. His Auntie Edie never got a word in; nor did Ray, his dad, nor Percy, his uncle. Only Clark could override her, for she would always give way to him. It was clear her Ralph, as she called him, was her pride and joy.

'Better watch out,' Rena warned Nola. 'Mrs Walters is never going to think you're good enough for her boy. Try to keep your distance, eh?'

'No' easy, when we're sharing the flat over the cycle shop,' Nola replied. 'Seemingly, the housing shortage is just as bad in Leeds as everywhere else.'

'Aye, it's a difficult time to be getting married. No'

much better than the war, eh? Fancy them putting bread on the ration!' Rena shook her head. 'And thae Russians are up to no good. Did you see what Mr Churchill said about the Iron Curtain between them and us?'

'Well, if they stay behind it, we needn't worry,' said Nola tartly. 'Honestly, Ma, you're a wee bit depressing, eh?'

'Och, I'm sorry!' Rena flung her arms round Nola and hugged her. 'I'm an old misery, so I am, but I don't want to be. Things'll work out for you two – of course they will! Who cares about bread rationing?'

'Not me,' Nola replied. 'As long as we can scrape the coupons together to get our wedding clothes.'

For the short ceremony at the register office, Nola found the clothing coupons and the money for a pale-blue suit from John Johnson's, and Tess wore a cream-coloured dress Rena had made for her. Rena herself made a real effort to look her best, with a new outfit, new hat, new hair-do, and plenty of make-up. Folk would not be able to say she'd let herself go just because Don had left her, she told her girls on the morning of the wedding, and was rewarded by their approving smiles.

In fact, when the wedding party came out into the June sunshine, all sorrows and troubles were temporarily forgotten. This was a truly happy day, with Clark in his dark demob suit hardly able to take his eyes off Nola, so pretty in her blue, with a hat of flower petals and bouquet of white carnations. Who wouldn't wish them well? Even the two mothers were kissing and laughing and flinging confetti, along with everyone else.

Then Rena's eye went to a tall man in a trilby hat standing at the back of the little crowd outside the register office, and all the colour drained from her face, leaving the rouge standing like paint flung at her cheekbones.

'He's never come!' she whispered. 'He's never had the nerve?'

110

But he had. Don Gillespie was there, an onlooker at his daughter's happiness, though there was no happiness to be seen in his own face.

'Is that Dad?' asked Nola. 'Oh, God, how come he's here? Who told him about the wedding?'

Tess, who had taken one look at her father and turned away, was hurrying towards the wedding cars.

'Aren't we going back home?' she cried. 'Ma, let's go home.'

Back at Rena's house, a cold buffet had been laid out in the front room, together with the wedding cake, made to the best of his ability by the local baker with half the dried fruit he needed and imitation almond paste. There was beer, and even wine, provided by the Walters family, and if folk wondered where the wine had come from, well, Clark had had his contacts as usual.

'There's not a thing my boy can't get,' his mother declared proudly. 'He's not like his father, I can tell you. Poor old Ray's always at the back of the queue.'

As soon as she'd seen her guests happily piling up their plates, Rena caught at Nola's arm.

'Nola, did you tell your dad you were getting married today?' she asked in a whisper.

'Of course I didn't tell Dad.' Nola whispered back. 'I never see him anyway.

'Well, who did tell him then? It wasn't in the paper.'

'It was me told him,' said Clark, coming up to give Rena an apologetic smile. 'I'm sorry if I did the wrong thing, Mrs Gillespie, but I thought Nola's dad ought to see her on her wedding day.'

Rena's eyes flashed. 'Oh, did you? When we're trying to manage our lives without Don, you have to go and bring him in, spoiling everything! I suppose you never bothered to think what I might want. Or Nola?'

'You didn't mind seeing him, did you?' Clark asked Nola, who looked down and said nothing. 'He didn't stay

111

long anyway, but I think it meant a lot to him.'

'And how did you find out his address?' asked Rena, 'You didn't dare ask me.'

'I asked the garage where he used to work. They told me. And they told me something else.' Clark hesitated, looking back at the guests milling round the table. He leaned forward and lowered his voice. 'Mrs Gillespie, the baby died.'

She stepped back, sharply drawing in her breath, and put her hand to her lips. 'When? When did the baby die?'

'Some time in May, they said. Was a little girl. Died when she was born. Terrible, isn't it?'

'Terrible,' whispered Nola. 'Wouldn't wish that on 'em.'

'Never,' said Rena. 'No, whatever they've done, I'd never wish that.'

'You've upset Ma, telling her that,' Nola told Clark.

'No, it's all right,' her mother said quickly. 'We had to know. I think I won't tell Tess just now though. She's upset enough already, seeing her dad.'

'The people at Todd's said Mr Gillespie was thinking of moving away,' said Clark quietly. 'Somewhere down south. Seems the girl doesn't want to stay in Edinburgh now.'

Rena and Nola exchanged glances.

'Let's say no more about this,' Rena murmured. 'It's your wedding day, Nola. Be happy.'

'Ma, I'm thinking of you,' said Nola.

'Well, don't. I'm all right.' Rena summoned up a smile. 'Go on, now, talk to the guests, eh?'

112

Chapter Twenty-Four

For the honeymoon, Clark had borrowed a friend's car – a pre-war Ford that still ran very well – and somehow, of course, had managed to get petrol coupons. Still, they wouldn't be able to go too far, only over the Borders into Northumberland, where they'd do some touring. Oh, weren't they lucky, everyone cried, for nobody'd had proper holidays for years and very few had ever done any touring.

'Yes, I am lucky,' Nola agreed, kissing her mother when the time came for the going away. 'I'm so happy, Ma, so happy. Just wish I didn't have to leave you though.'

'I've told you. No need to worry about me, pet. And I've got Tess, remember.'

'You do look better, Ma.'

'Aye, I'm coming through. Just like I said.'

But the news of Don's dead child had shaken Rena, bringing back the time when her little boy had died and Don had been comforting her and not another woman. And if the other woman in his life had had a healthy son, how would Rena have felt about that?

All she knew was that she must put her remembered pain aside, along with the new pain of seeing Don, and wave goodbye to Nola, who was so radiant as she ran through the well-wishers to the waiting car, so sure that everything was going to be wonderful. Of course it would be a sad bride who didn't think that on her wedding day. Please, God, Nola was right then.

'Take care of her!' Rena cried to Clark, who leaped out of the driving seat to run back and kiss her on the cheek.

'I will, Mrs Gillespie, or can I call you Ma, now?'

'Och, go along with you,' she said, embarrassed.

'Am I forgiven for telling Nola's dad about the wedding? I only did it for the best, you know.'

How many people had said that before they caused disaster? wondered Rena. And wasn't it remarkable that this new son-in-law of hers should not only be able to get folks anything they wanted, but information they might not want as well?

'Hasn't this been a splendid day?' Erika asked Tess, when they had waved the honeymooners away. 'I thought everyone cried at weddings, but people here seem so happy.'

'Ma and me wanted Nola to wear a white dress and a veil,' Tess muttered. 'She'd have looked lovely.'

'I thought she looked lovely anyway.'

'If our dad had been a proper dad, she would have had a proper wedding,' Tess went on, not listening. 'But he only came and stood outside.'

'He came to the register office?'

'Aye, we saw him.'

Erika put her hand on Tess's arm. 'You were upset to see him?'

'A bit. I was just getting used to not seeing him, and then there he was.'

'It shows he cares. He still wants to be part of the family.'

'Canna be that now.'

The girls were silent, as the guests around them laughed and talked and finished up the drinks and sandwiches.

'Talking of white weddings,' said Erika, 'perhaps you will have one, Tess, when the time comes, and please your mother.'

'Me?' Tess shook her head. 'I'll never get wed, Erika.'

'Oh, come, why do you say such a thing?

'I'd never trust anyone enough, that's why.'

Erika's eyes were full of compassion. 'You have to trust somebody,' she said gently.

'That's what Nola says. But Ma trusted Dad, didn't she?'

'It wouldn't be fair to think everyone would let you down.'

'No, well, I suppose I'd trust ma friends. But getting married – that'd be different.'

'I think you'll change your mind if you meet the right person.'

'And you'll get married, too, will you, if you meet the right person?' Tess laughed a little.

'Oh, no,' Erika answered seriously. 'I shall have my career to think about.'

The guests were finally leaving the reception, hugging brave Rena and pretty Tess, murmuring encouraging words about Nola, who wasn't going so very far, eh? Och, Leeds was no' distance at all, then, and it was true what folk said, a daughter was a daughter all her life. She'd always be coming home for a visit, or else Rena and Tess would be going down south to see her. And it'd been a lovely wedding, so it had.

'Can we no' help you clear up then?' asked Polly Wight, who had recently made up her quarrel with her mother and might be leaving Rena's, but wasn't sure.

'Aye, we'll give you a hand!' cried Vera,

'Please allow me,' said Mrs Lange.

But Rena shooed them all from the door, with thanks and smiles. She and Tess would soon buzz through the dishes, put the bottles out and sweep up the crumbs, nae bother.

'Oh, but we feel bad, leaving you!' Connie Walters exclaimed. 'Now why don't you let us help and then come back with us to the guesthouse for a chat and a cup of coffee?'

115

Her eyes, so like her son's, were friendly; her voice, still Scottish in accent rather than Yorkshire, was persuasive. Yet Rena stayed firm. She and Tess would just like to get to their beds early, thanks all the same. Maybe the Walters family would look in tomorrow, before they left for the train? They would? Well, that'd be grand. They'd see each other tomorrow, then.

And the front door was closed.

Rena and Tess looked at each other.

'Best get out o' that dress, pet, if we're going to do the washing up,' said Rena. 'And I'll change, too.'

'I'm glad they've all gone,' Tess murmured. 'We can get on better.'

'That's a lesson learned. Folk are very kind, but they just get in the way. Don't know where anything goes, or how you like to do things. Come on, we'll soon be finished and have everything shipshape.'

'I know what you'll do then, Ma.'

'What?'

'Make another cup of tea.'

Chapter Twenty-Five

And so they did, when all the work was done and the kitchen tidy again. Dishes away, rubbish out, tea towels in to soak, ready for boiling next day.

'Want anything to eat?' asked Rena.

'Oh, no thanks, I couldn't eat any more. '

'Well, it was a good spread, if I say so maself.'

'It was lovely. They all said so.'

'And I suppose I did save a bit. Thae formal receptions set you back a bonnie penny.'

'I think Nola was happy, anyway, Ma. She looked happy, didn't she?'

'I suppose she did. Got the one she wants, so she must be happy.'

Rena, suddenly weary, lit a cigarette when she had drunk her tea, and looked up at the narrow kitchen windows. Time for this day to end, she thought, seeing that the evening sky was darkening at last. Thank the Lord for that. Sometimes, it seemed as though the June light would never fade, but maybe now they could go to bed and not be kept awake. Well, not by the light, at least.

'Tess, did Nola tell you your dad might be moving south?' she asked suddenly.

'No. Why? Why's he moving?'

Rena studied her cigarette. 'I didn't want to say so before, but that girl's lost her baby. She doesn't want to stay in Edinburgh.'

'Oh.' Tess looked away.

'I'm sorry, of course. Anybody'd be sorry, eh? But if your dad takes her away, it'll be easier for us.'

'Will it?'

'Yes. They'll be right out of our lives and we can really start again.'

'I see what you mean. Yes, it'll be easier.' Tess turned her gaze on her mother. 'Did Dad tell you all this?'

'No, it was Clark.'

'Clark? How did he know?

Rena smiled wryly. 'Clark knows everything.' She stubbed out her cigarette and jumped up. 'Time for bed, Tess. It's been a long day.'

They went up the stairs together, Rena accompanying Tess to the attic room, which was hers alone now.

'You'll no' mind being on your own this time?' Rena asked. 'Remember how you used to want a night light?'

'I'm older now, I don't mind being on ma own.'

Not true, of course, for Tess could scarcely look at Nola's bed stripped of sheets. And the empty dressing table. The empty wardrobe. There wasn't a thing lying about. Except for the lingering smell of her face powder and the scent Clark had given her last Christmas, Nola seemed to have left scarcely a trace of her old self.

'Now there's just the two of us again,' her mother murmured, watching Tess's expression. 'Just like in the war.'

Not quite like in the war. This time, no one was coming back.

'Nola will be coming home, you ken,' Rena went on, perhaps reading Tess's mind. 'Often, she says.'

'Oh, yes, I know.' But not to stay.

Tess suddenly moved to her mother and flung her arms around her. 'We'll be all right, Ma. I'll take care of you.'

Rena laughed, a sweet, genuine laugh, that made some-

118

thing in Tess rise and seem to sing.

'Of course you will, and I'll take care of you. As long as there's the two of us, we'll get by. Goodnight, pet.'

'Goodnight, Ma.'

When her mother had left her, Tess sat for a while on her bed. Dad had gone, Nola had gone, but she still had Ma. Still had Erika. And Alice, and Heidi. She flicked the feather in Heidi's hat and settled Alice on her pillow. Time to get ready for bed then, though it wasn't even now completely dark. See the streaks of light in the sky framed by the window? No need to be afraid of the night.

She'd thought she'd never sleep. Had thought all the excitement of the wedding, and then the misery of seeing Dad again, would go round and round in her mind the whole night through. The next thing she knew, however, was the warm touch of sunlight streaming in on her face, and she realised it was morning.

Sunday morning, too. No school. Her heart lightened. Maybe, when Erika came back from early church, they'd run down the road to the sands together. The holidaymakers would still be having breakfast in their lodgings; the beach would be empty, except perhaps for Mr Beith and Honey. They'd throw sticks for the dear, friendly dog, and then, if the water wasn't too cold, maybe even splash their feet in the sea.

Och, things weren't so bad, eh? As she leaped out of bed, revelling in the warmth of the morning, Tess felt she was ready to start the new life her mother was always talking about. Or at least, not think too much about the old one.

119

PART TWO

PART TWO

Chapter Twenty-Six

Tess and Nola were sitting together by the side of Portobello's vast, open-air swimming pool. The day was sunny and warm, just as on Nola's wedding day, but this was September 1951 and she had been married more than five years. Five years, and no bairns! was the thought always in her mother's mind, but never expressed. Certainly not when Nola was home from Leeds on a visit, and without Clark as well. Nobody was going to spoil that!

Tess, nineteen and slim as a reed in a blue one-piece swimming costume, was waiting for the pool's wave machine to start. Still with the look of her father, though her mother and sister didn't care to dwell on that, she had changed of course since 1946. Lost the rough edges of the adolescent, become a poised and vividly attractive young woman. As was proved by the glances from young men that followed her at the pool, and elsewhere. But Tess was good at avoiding those.

Nola, pulling her towel over her shoulders, had scarcely changed at all since her wedding day, for she had been plump and pretty then, and was plump and pretty now. Only her hair was different, being short and permed instead of elaborately dressed, forties style, but suited her just as well, everybody said. Oh yes, she attracted attention too, and if Tess didn't care to notice admiring glances, Nola only took as her due those that came her way.

'Soon be time for the wave machine,' said Tess, checking the pool clock. 'Watch everybody scatter when that siren sounds!'

'Aye, like at the opening ceremony.' Nola laughed. 'Remember Ma telling us how all the grand folk got wet? The Lord Provost an' all?'

'The waves were stronger than they expected – always are. Och, I love 'em! Canna wait for the machine to start.'

'I can.' Nola shivered and drew her towel closer. 'Och, it's freezing in there, Tess. I'd no' go in for all the tea in China!'

'Come on, it's warm. They heat it from the power station.'

Nola cast a glance up at the great chimney of the power station that always cast its shadow over the pool, and made a face.

'Might have done that one time, I'm no' so sure it works any more. You go in, Tess, and I'll watch you.' She laughed. 'Along with half Porty, eh?'

It was said that the spectators' stands of the fine art deco pool could hold as many as 6,000 people, and if that figure seemed hard to believe, you only had to look around on a fine summer's day to accept it. The pool itself could take over a thousand bathers, and had cost, back in 1936, the amazing sum of £90,000. But worth every penny, declared Porty folk. Who else could boast a pool like theirs?

'You could swim if you liked,' Tess said, not yet prepared to give up on Nola. 'You did pay to swim, remember.'

'Should have paid just to watch. Shame Erika couldn't have come, eh?'

'Aye, she's no' as lucky as me. At least I get Saturday afternoons off at Appleton's.'

'At least?' Nola raised her eyebrows. She'd thought, as her mother thought, that Tess was well suited working as a secretary for an Edinburgh accountancy firm. 'Is that all that's good about Appleton's then? Are you no' happy there?'

'It was Ma wanted me to work for them.' Tess looked furtively over her shoulder, as though her mother might be listening. 'Good firm and all that. Thing is, I've applied for something else. Haven't told her yet.'

'No' mending cars, is it?' Nola laughed, and Tess laughed with her.

'How'd you guess? No, I'm joking. But it is in a garage. Office work – typing, sending out bills, that sort o' thing.'

'And you haven't told Ma?' Nola's eyes narrowed. 'This garage – is it Todd's by any chance? Oh Tess, it is! It's Todd's! Whatever are you thinking of, applying for a job at Dad's old place? Ma will be upset, yes, she will. It'll bring it all back.'

'I don't see why. It's years since Dad left. It's nothing to do with him where I work.' Tess's tone was spirited, but her eyes were troubled. 'Anyway, I haven't got the job yet. I just happened to meet Mr Todd in the High Street the other day, and he asked me if I'd be interested. Seemingly it was in the paper, but I never saw it.'

'Sounds as though he'd like to give it to you.'

'Don't know about that. I've to see him on Tuesday.'

'Better tell Ma before that, then.'

'Aye, when you're here. You can support me.'

Nola sighed. 'What a pair we are, eh? I don't like my job, either. I thought it'd be a step up, working for a building society, but – och – I'm so bored! Don't get me on to that though. I'm on holiday, remember?'

'I just wish I was Erika,' said Tess thoughtfully. 'She's going to get what she wants.'

'Doesn't get Saturday afternoons off.'

'That's only while she's working at the chemist's. When she's of age, she's going to apply to be British, then she'll go to university and end up a doctor. Which is what she wants.'

'Clever folk usually do get what they want, so I've noticed.'

'There's the siren!' cried Tess, springing up and pulling

125

on her bathing cap, as the wailing of the warning siren filled the air. 'I'm going in. Watch me, Nola!'

Away she ran, leaping into the water with a satisfying splash, as the engineers' grills opened at the deep end of the pool and the famed waves began to roll. Nola, moving well out of the way, looked on with a smile as Tess jumped and shrieked with those around her, seeming, in her blue cap and suit, like some sort of exotic bird, hovering. But then she dived under the manufactured breakers and came up again, thin hands fluttering, the water on her skin glistening in the sun, and laughed aloud as the next wave came.

Oh Lord, she's so slim, thought Nola. Why can I no' be like her?

But some things didn't change.

Chapter Twenty-Seven

On the other hand, every time she came home Nola found something different. Changes in her mother's house, or in her mother herself, for Rena'd had her hair cut too, and sometimes it made her look young and fashionable, and sometimes, Nola thought, not like Ma at all.

Sometimes the news was of buildings knocked down in the town, or maybe built up, or it might be that Tess and Erika had grown another inch, or somebody had unfortunately 'passed on'. This last time it had been poor old Mr Crombie, who'd died from a heart attack. Aye, and hadn't his son thrown out all his beloved Wild West stories before he was even cold? Now, wouldn't you think he'd have kept 'em in memory of his dad? But some folk had no idea of what was right, said Rena.

But there had been a special improvement for Nola to see when she arrived for her September holiday. Not the telephone – Rena was on a waiting list for that – but, guess what, the second bathroom! Money had been saved, a plumber had found a suite, and there it was, installed, Rena's pride and joy. What a shame Polly Wight wasn't there to see it, then. But Polly and Kennie were long gone, and so was Miss Denny, who had finally, triumphantly, found a flat of her own. In fact, the only remaining tenants known to Nola were Mrs Lange and Erika, though they now had two rooms instead of one.

'Aye, I've got mostly students now,' Rena had announced with relief. 'Makes a quick turnover because they're always on the move, but that suits me. The longer folk stay, the more they want, except for Mrs Lange, of course. But I've given Erika a room of her own – that little one I gave your Clark, you remember – and she was that thrilled, poor girl.'

'You ought to let summer lodgings, Ma,' said Nola. 'That's where the money is, with this place bursting at the seams in the season. I mean, Porty gets Edinburgh trades holiday folk, and Glasgow folk, and people from the Borders. You could advertise and charge the earth, I'm telling you.'

'Oh, so easy, eh? And if I did get summer bookings, what'd I do in the winter?' Rena shook her head. 'Thae holiday folk want meals, you ken, and that's me then, working like a slave for the whole o' the season. No thanks, I'll stick to ma bedsits and ma work at the pottery.'

And there, of course, was another change – Rena's working part-time at Harebell Pottery, something she said she really enjoyed, though she wasn't doing anything artistic.

'Aye, it's just routine stuff for me, you ken,' she told Nola, who was interested, even so.

'Who does the artistic work, then?'

'Och, the designers and such. Some create the shapes and patterns and that, and some decorate. It's all skilled work.'

'Wouldn't mind having a go,' Nola said thoughtfully. 'I've done a bit o' painting and pottery work at evening classes, you ken. Made some jugs and things on the wheel.'

'Now, I never knew that!' cried Rena. 'Since when did you get arty? It was always Tess who made the Christmas cards.'

Nola shrugged. 'Makes a change from the building society. Och, every time folk bring in their books and I have to make them up or do their withdrawals, I could scream.'

'Why'd you do it then?' her mother asked, after a pause. 'Clark earns enough, eh? He's got a good job?'

But Nola, always vague on what Clark did, said they needed the money to pay the mortgage on the semi they'd bought on the outskirts of Leeds. Aye, they'd finally got out of the flat over the cycle shop, and not a moment too soon, for Nola had found that living with her in-laws was another thing that made her scream. Life was much easier now.

'I'm glad to hear it,' said Rena, her blue gaze meeting Nola's which did not waver. It was clear no confidences were to be made at that time, and Rena had to retire, defeated.

'Oh, that was grand!' cried Tess, shaking herself by Nola's side and spraying her with a good quantity of pool water, when the wave-making session ended. 'Nola, you should've come in.'

'Don't feel I need to, now you've given me a shower bath!' cried Nola, laughing. 'Och, where's your towel then? You're turning as blue as your costume.'

'I'll soon get warm in the sun, then we can go and change. Listen, shall we walk along and look at Pax House? It looks so lovely now it's all been done up.'

'Coffee first,' said Nola, thinking how pretty Tess was, even though she was so like their father, whose photograph had long gone from the kitchen dresser but whose face remained in his daughters' minds. Nola kept her thoughts on Tess. Why no young man then?

'Why no young man?' she asked aloud, as they made their way to the changing rooms.

'What young man?'

'Yours, of course. Come on, Tess, there must be someone.'

'No one special.'

'Safety in numbers, eh?'

'Do we have to talk about this now?' Tess had found an empty cubicle.

'Just curious, that's all.'

'I'm no' interested,' called Tess, slamming the door of the cubicle shut and fastening its bolt. 'Satisfied?'

'No,' called back Nola. 'Not at all.'

Chapter Twenty-Eight

'Sorry if I spoke out o' turn,' Nola said, when they had changed into cotton dresses and cardigans and were drinking coffee at the pool café, their towels and costumes stuffed into a canvas bag.

'That's all right,' said Tess coolly.

'I know it's nothing to do with me who you go out with.'

'No.'

'But I just want to say, you shouldn't let what Dad did damage your life.'

'Damage.' Tess stared down at her coffee. 'That's a good word.'

Nola heaved a long sigh. 'Remember what I told you once? You have to trust somebody?'

'I remember.'

'Well, it's still true.'

Tess fixed her sister with her large grey eyes. 'True for you?'

'For everybody. But I'm thinking of you.'

'You never talk much about Clark these days. We don't often see him.'

'He's busy, he's all over the place.'

'Still a commercial traveller?'

'No.' Nola finished her coffee. 'He's got his own business now.'

'See? You never told us.'

'Look, can we drop this, Tess?'

'If you leave me alone too.'

'All right, I've said I'm sorry. I just don't want to see you shutting yourself off from happiness.'

'And I just don't want to get hurt.'

The sisters were silent for a moment, until Nola, after looking longingly at the café's ice-cream menu, said she would settle for a cigarette.

'How about one for me?' asked Tess.

'I don't like to see you smoking, Tess.'

'Come on, everybody does. Seems it's OK for you.'

Nola hesitated, then laughed and shook her head. 'All right, I'll no' say a word. Here – take ma lighter.'

They left the pool and began to stroll down the promenade, passing the crowded fun fair, pausing occasionally to look in at one of the little knick-knack shops, sidestepping small children and wandering dogs. Though it was almost the end of the season, every space on the beach seemed to have been taken, with towels spread out, spades at work in the sand, queues gathering at the ice-cream sellers, while in the distance, the waters of the Forth glittered under the sun.

'Oh Porty, why are you so popular?' Nola murmured. 'Remember how Dad used to say he liked it best in the winter?'

'I don't think about Dad much,' said Tess.

'Has he been in touch lately? I never like to ask Ma.'

'No, we haven't heard from him. No' since he stopped sending money for me.'

'He did write then, though.'

'Aye, said he wanted to keep it going, but Ma wrote back and said he needn't bother.'

'I've only heard from him once,' Nola said, after a pause. 'He sent me a birthday card from Oxfordshire. Said he was working for Morris cars. Think he's still there?'

'Don't really know.'

And don't care, thought Nola. Or pretends not to care.

For herself, there was still a hole in her life left by her father's betrayal, a hole that nothing would fill, and she was sure, however much Tess shrugged and looked away when his name was mentioned, it was the same for her. Yet Nola wasn't so sure about Ma, who seemed remarkably at ease with herself considering what had happened. Had five years healed the wounds for her? Or, was she putting on a very good act? Och, it was never easy to understand Ma.

'Here it is, then,' said Tess, brightening as they approached Pax House. 'Doesn't it look grand?'

'Spells money,' Nola murmured, looking in at Tess's favourite house, now well awakened from its wartime sleep and returned to pre-war perfection. Oh yes, money radiated from the glossy paintwork and plastered stone, from the rebuilt chimneys and perfect roof, the climbing roses, the closely cut lawn, the sweep of gravel without a single weed.

'The fellow who owns that must be rolling,' Nola commented. 'Has he still got the chauffeur?'

'Oh yes, and the lovely dog.' Tess stood still, just looking in at the new wrought-iron gates. 'The car's no' there. Mr Seton must be out.'

'Making more money, I expect.'

'No, he's retired.'

'Getting old, is he?'

'I've never seen him, but the way Ma talks, you'd think he'd never been young.'

'Doesn't need to be young if he's rich.'

'Bet you don't think that, really.'

'No, being young's best. Only you don't stay young, and you might stay rich.' Nola took Tess's arm and turned her round to face home. 'Better get back, eh? Got to wash our towels and costumes out.'

'Your towel and costume never even got wet,' said Tess, laughing, and Nola put her finger to her lips.

'Needn't tell Ma.'

Chapter Twenty-Nine

When Tess and Nola came home, they found their mother in the hall talking to two young men, one with a thatch of rough brown hair, the other blond. Students, obviously, come to look at a couple of rooms that were vacant. As Rena had told Nola, there were always students coming and going, looking at rooms, moving in, moving out.

'My daughters,' Rena said now. 'Mrs Walters, who's on a visit, and—'

'Tess,' put in Tess quickly, in case her mother should introduce her as Miss Gillespie, which would sound ridiculous.

'Simon Maitland,' drawled the blond young man, whose nose was a beak and whose smile was cool.

'Toby Dene,' said the brown-haired young man, whose nose was straight and whose smile was distinctly warm. As were his brown eyes, resting on Tess.

'Mr Maitland and Mr Dene have taken ma vacant rooms,' Rena announced. 'For October.'

'We're medical students,' said Toby.

'About to begin second year,' put in Simon.

Like Toby, he had an English accent, and an easy manner that indicated money somewhere in the background. Probably there'd been private school and no shortage of the good things in life. Even so, thought the sisters, smiling politely, finding a place to live in Edinburgh in 1951 would not be easy.

'I hope you'll be happy here,' said Nola. 'You're a bit far out, but there's the train, and plenty of trams and buses.'

'Thank you, I'll probably be using my car,' Simon told her.

'And I'll be cadging a lift,' said Toby, grinning.

'What sort is it?' asked Tess, looking at Simon.

'I beg your pardon?'

She blushed a little. 'I was just asking – what sort of car?'

'An MG,' he told her. As though she wouldn't know, he added kindly, 'that's a sports car.'

'You'll have to park it on the street, whatever it is, Mr Maitland,' said Rena 'I've no garage.'

'That will be quite all right.' He slightly inclined his head and put out his hand to shake Rena's. 'Thank you so much, Mrs Gillespie. We'll see you in October then.'

Toby also made his goodbyes, his eyes following Tess, who was turning to go down the hall. 'Till October, Mrs Gillespie.'

When the front door had closed on the two young men, Rena gave a wry smile.

'They'll no' stay long. I can always tell.'

'How?' asked Tess.

'Och, I know the type. They'll want something more their style. Well that fair chap will. You should've seen him look down his nose when I showed him his room, the one Miss Denny used to have. And he's got plenty o' nose to look down, too, though I shouldn't be rude about it.'

'Think he's only taken it while he looks round?' asked Nola.

'Aye, that's what some of thae students do. Grab something for the new term, then move on.' Rena tossed her head. 'Doesn't bother me – they've paid in advance, anyway.'

'Think Mr Dene'll move on too?' asked Tess.

'Sure he will, he'll go with his pal. But he was nice

135

enough, I'll have to say, when I showed him Mr Crombie's old room. Mind you, the two laddies who had that before him liked it fine, so why shouldn't he? Did you have a good swim then? Are you ready for your tea?'

'Nice, eh?' Nola whispered to Tess, as they followed their mother down to the kitchen.

'Who?'

'Mr Dene. You liked him, didn't you?'

'Nola, I've just met the guy.'

'I think you liked him.'

'I wish you'd stop trying to find me some young man, Nola. You know I'm no' interested.'

'Well, just remember what I told you, eh?'

'You tell me so much,' sighed Tess.

'That's what elder sisters are for.' Nola smiled and turned her head, raising her voice. 'Ma, what can we do to help then?'

Chapter Thirty

The evening was passing, and still Tess hadn't told her mother about the job at Todd's. She wanted to tell her, that was the truth of it, even though Nola might not believe it, but whenever she opened her mouth to speak, something else came out.

And then Ma was whizzing about as usual, never sitting still until almost bedtime when she opened the evening paper and began musing on televisions. They were a terrible price, eh? But there was a Co-op advert in the paper giving good terms for HP. Should she go in for one?

'Do you want one?' asked Nola.

'That's the thing, I'm no' sure. I mean, what are they like?'

'Well, the sets are awful big and the picture's awful small. But if you want one, Clark could probably get you a better deal than at the stores.'

Rena lowered her paper and stared at Nola. 'I thought he was a commercial traveller.'

'Got his own business now.'

'What sort o' business?'

'Oh – supplies, and that.' At the mention of Clark's business affairs, Nola's expression had taken on its usual vagueness. 'Imports and exports sort o' thing.'

'Fancy. You might have said.'

Nola was silent, and Tess, clearing her throat, said, 'Ma—'

Has Clark got you a set, then?' Rena asked Nola, not listening to Tess.

'We're thinking about it. Tell you the truth, I'd rather go out than stay at home watching a box.'

'Aye, I think you're right. I mean, what can you see on a telly that you canna see at the pictures? I'll no' get one just yet. Tess, make us some cocoa, eh?'

But Tess said desperately, 'Ma, I'm thinking o' changing ma job.'

Rena lowered her paper and stared at Tess over the top of it. 'You're what?'

'I want to leave Appleton's.'

'Oh, my God!' Rena put a hand to her lips. 'You've no done something wrong, Tess? Been given the sack?'

'No, no, nothing like that.' Tess gave a wavering smile. 'I just want to try something else.'

'Now don't tell me you're giving up secretarial? After all your training? All the money we spent?'

'For goodness' sake, Tess, spit it out,' cried Nola. 'Tell Ma you want to move to Todd's!'

'Todd's?' Rena crumpled her paper and threw it to one side. Her blue eyes were incredulous, her colour high. 'Am I hearing right, Tess? Whatever would you want to be doing at Todd's?'

'Running the office,' Tess replied, glancing furiously at Nola. 'I met Mr Todd the other day. He asked me to apply for Mrs Dixon's job. She's retiring.'

'Mabel Dixon? Well, I don't know what to say. This is something out o' the blue, eh?'

'I'd still do letters and that. I could maybe still use ma shorthand.'

'How's the pay compare with Appleton's?' asked Nola.

Tess hesitated. 'It's a bit less,' she admitted.

'There's more things than money to think about, anyway,' Rena said coldly.

'I know.' Tess lowered her eyes. 'I know it might be upsetting for you, Ma, if I work where Dad worked. That's why I didn't say anything before.'

Rena shrugged. 'It's your decision, nothing to do with me.'

'It is to do with you. If you're unhappy, I won't apply. I mightn't get it, anyway. Mr Todd said he'd advertised, so I won't be the only one in for it.'

'Anybody'd think it was a wonderful job.'

'He asked me to see him on Tuesday,' Tess said patiently. 'So I'll try for it, shall I? If you don't mind?'

'Listen, didn't I once say that we'd to live our own lives, whatever your dad had done? If you want to work where he worked, you do it. Now, is one o' you going to make the cocoa?'

But as Tess set the mugs of cocoa on the kitchen table, and Nola began searching in the biscuit tin, Rena's smile was wry.

'Beats me, Tess, why you want to work in a garage at all. But you were always hankering for it. You're like your dad, you ken, in more ways than one.'

'I'm no' like him at all, Ma,' Tess answered quietly. 'Whatever I look like.'

'Same old room,' sighed Nola, padding round their attic in a flowing nightdress. 'Nothing ever changes here, thank God.'

She picked up Alice, who was on Tess's pillow as always, then laid her back reverently and put a varnished fingernail on Heidi's little hat.

'Ooh, Tess, Heidi's hat's all dusty! You're neglecting her!'

Tess, her eyes flashing, swept Heidi away from her sister's outstretched hand and set her back on the bedside table.

'Hey, what's all this?' Nola asked indulgently. 'In a temper? Just because I got you to tell Ma what you were on about?'

'I was preparing her,' Tess said frostily. 'I didn't just want to blurt it out.'

'Och, you'd have got there in a month o' Sundays! Poor Ma was beginning to think you'd had your finger in the till at Appleton's, the way you were rambling on. If you've got something to say, it's better to come out with it, that's my advice.'

'Always know best, eh?'

'Sometimes, yes I do.' Nola turned aside and began to comb her short, fluffy hair. 'Still, I'll say this – Ma didn't seem to mind you trying for Todd's, did she? I was wrong about that.'

'I don't think you were wrong,' said Tess, climbing into bed. 'She minded all right.'

Nola laid down her comb. 'You think she still minds about Dad?'

'No, it's no' that. She's managing fine without him. She just doesn't think working for Todd's is as good as working for Appleton's. Maybe I shouldn't go.'

'No, Tess, no. It's right what Ma says, you mustn't let him spoil things. You've to live your own life, do what you want to do.'

'It's Ma I'm thinking about.'

'She said, if you want to work at Todd's you work at Todd's.'

'OK, I'll apply. See how I get on. You going to read?'

'No.' Nola yawned. 'I'm tired tonight. Must be all that fresh air by the pool. I'll put the light out, shall I?'

'I will.' Tess laughed. 'Have you forgotten we've got a bedside lamp now?'

'That's what I call progress,' said Nola.

For some time, they lay awake in the darkness without speaking.

'Sorry I was snappy,' Tess said, at last. 'Just a bit worked up, you ken.'

'Och, nae bother. We're all a bit on edge.'

There was another silence.

'Nola?' came Tess's voice again.

'Yes?'

'Mind if I ask – are you happy?'

'What a question!' Nola turned over and thumped her pillow, then lay back with a thud. When she made no further answer, Tess tried again.

'Are you though?'

'Yes, of course I am. Don't I seem happy?'

'Sort o' different. From when you were first wed.'

'Oh, well, five years is five years.' Nola's tone was light. 'You're no' still on honeymoon, obviously. When you get married, you'll understand.'

Not that again, thought Tess. WHEN you get married, folk said, as if everybody got married. As if everybody wanted to get married.

'Sorry again,' she said aloud. 'I mean, I told you to leave me alone, and here's me being nosey.'

'It's OK. I know you're thinking o' me. But I'm all right. No need to worry.'

'And Clark's all right?'

'Clark?' Nola's little laugh came through the darkness. 'Clark's always all right. 'Night, Tess. Get your beauty sleep, eh?'

Tess closed her eyes and hoped she would sleep. Hoped she wouldn't lie awake thinking about Todd's, and whether she was doing the right thing. Hoped her mother wasn't upset and that Nola was truly happy. Wondered vaguely if the fellow with the brown eyes was as nice as he looked. As though it mattered.

Chapter Thirty-One

For her meeting with Mr Todd, Tess had decided to wear her best outfit, a grey suit, which was New Look in style with nipped-in jacket and long pleated skirt. She wasn't too happy about the matching hat with its strip of veiling, and sure enough, when she put it on, Nola asked her if she was going to a wedding.

'You think it's too smart?' Tess stood frowning at herself before the hall mirror.

'Well, more Appleton's than Todd's.'

'Now, why'd you say that?' asked Rena, coming downstairs dressed to go to Glasgow with Nola, for she'd taken a few days' holiday from the pottery. 'Tess doesn't have to dress like a mechanic to work at Todd's, you ken.'

'I suppose I needn't wear the hat,' Tess said doubtfully.

'Aye, might be best. But that grey's a nice suit, anyway, even if it is that daft New Look style; no' so new now, anyway, is it? Been out a few years.'

'Since 1947.' said Nola. She was herself wearing a tightly fitted jacket that was causing her some suffering and was wondering whether she'd have enough breath to get herself to Glasgow. Maybe if she tried undoing the buttons? Wouldn't look the same, of course.

'We were all knocked for six, I remember,' she added, undoing a couple of buttons anyway. Oh, the relief!

'Knocked for six?' Rena cried. 'We thought it was a

piece o' nonsense! All that material wasted in thae trailing skirts and such, when you still needed coupons to get anything to wear!'

'Calm down, Ma,' said Nola. 'At least clothes are off the ration now.'

'Aye, well, food isn't.' Rena clicked her tongue. 'Did we ever think we'd still be rationed all these years after the war?'

'Never mind the rations, Ma.' Nola touched her sister's shoulder. 'You look lovely, Tess, with or without the hat. Mr Todd'll give you the job soon as he sees you.'

'If you want it,' Rena picked up her bag and umbrella. 'Now, we're away for the train. We'll be thinking of you, pet.' She kissed Tess's cheek. 'Good luck then.'

'I tell you, you'll walk it,' said Nola, giving her sister a hug. 'And by the time we come back, it'll all be over.'

'Wish I was going to Glasgow,' sighed Tess. 'I hate interviews.'

Not that a chat with Mr Todd was to be compared with the formal interview she'd had at Appleton's, when she'd been so petrified she could hardly hold her pencil for the short-hand test. Yet she'd done well. Both Mr Reginald Appleton and Mr Frederick Appleton, who was Mr Reginald's nephew, had expressed themselves pleased with her. Well, they'd given her the job, hadn't they? And her ma had been so proud. Secretary at Appleton's. Now that was something to tell everyone they knew! There was to be no boring factory job or dreary shop assistant's work for Tess Gillespie, even if her dad had walked out on her.

Oh, I feel so bad, thought Tess, running up the stairs to the attic after her mother and Nola had left. I've disappointed Ma, I've let her down. Why am I doing this?

Because she wanted to, that was all she could say. She wanted to do it, wanted to get away from Appleton's, come closer to something that mattered to her, even if she did disappoint her ma. 'You've to live your own life,' Nola had

143

told her. 'Do what you want to do.' And that was true.

As she put on a little lipstick, she thought how strange it was that she'd come round again to the idea of working with cars. After her dad had left, she'd deliberately put them out of her mind. He'd worked with cars, she no longer wanted to; no longer wanted to be like him, or share his interests in any way. And then, gradually, over the years, the fascination had come back. It would not be true to say that the image of her father had receded, but somehow it no longer came between her and what she wanted to do. Her old interest came to the foreground again, right through the time at the secretarial college, right through the time at Appleton's, until now, when she was applying for this job at Todd's.

Am I a freak, she wondered, to exchange a job at gentlemanly Appleton's for work in a noisy garage that smelled of oil and petrol? It wasn't as if she'd actually be working with cars even; she'd still be in an office of sorts. So? She shrugged her shoulders. Freak or no freak, she was going to apply for the job. Maybe, she wouldn't even get it. But she would at least try.

Would have to look right, though, so as to feel right, and she didn't feel right in her smart grey suit. She kicked off her high heels, took off the suit and dressed instead in navy slacks, navy woollen jacket, flat-heeled shoes, and a little red scarf to add a bit of colour. When she looked in the mirror again, she gave a sigh of relief. She looked right, she looked at ease. She was ready to do the best she could.

Chapter Thirty-Two

Todd's garage, in a narrow side street, was large, draughty and noisy, its double doors that were always open in daytime bearing the faded sign 'Motor Engineers – John Todd, Proprietor'.

Though she hadn't seen it for years, Tess remembered it from her childhood, and for a moment, as she stepped through its doors again, felt a certain misgiving. But not for long. After all, she'd prepared heself well, and when a middle-aged mechanic came up and asked if he could help, she straightened her shoulders and smiled.

'May I see Mr Todd, please? He's expecting me.'

'Is it wee Tess then?' The mechanic grinned. 'D'you no' remember me? Alf Bennie? Knew your dad way back. This way then; Mr Todd's in his office. Mind yourself, eh? Plenty o' things to fall over here.'

Thank God I didn't wear ma suit and heels, thought Tess, following Alf through a maze of vehicles and machinery, avoiding wrenches, spanners and piles of tyres, as well as a large inspection pit in the centre of the floor.

Passing the mechanics, who were giving her friendly grins, she noticed one who was familiar. He was easy to notice anyway, being well over six feet tall, with hair the colour of a ginger biscuit, and as he smiled and nodded to her she suddenly remembered his name.

Ginger Moffat. Yes. He was the 'gentle giant' who was

the older brother of Joey Moffat, who'd been in her class at school, and an easy-going fellow everyone liked. How nice to see him here, thought Tess, though if she didn't get the job it wouldn't matter where he was, would it?

'Tess, come away in,' said Mr Todd, appearing at the door of his little office, and Tess, nerves returning, went away in.

John Todd was short and middle-aged, with fading grey hair and a long sagacious upper lip that made him look like a lawyer in dungarees. As long as Tess had known him, he'd looked the same; she supposed he always would.

'You know Mabel?' he asked, waving to the office assistant who was leaving him, and Mabel Dixon's soft, freckled hand closed on Tess's. She was a pretty woman, some years older than Rena, with wobbling double chins and bright blue eyes that reminded Tess of the eyes of Alice, her doll.

'Och, Tess knows me!' she cried. 'Me and her ma have been pals for years. Lost touch a bit lately. How is your ma then, Tess? Keeping well?'

'She's very well, thank you, Mrs Dixon.'

'Mabel, dear, call me Mabel. I wish I could say I was well maself, but I've got a little trouble with ma ticker.' She patted her large bosom. 'The doctor says to me, "Mrs Dixon, you'll have to give up work, you ken, it's a case of your money or your life." And I says, "You sound like one o' thae highwayman that used to go riding through the figgate whins." He did laugh!' Mabel laughed herself as Mr Todd waited patiently to put in a word.

'So, that's me, dear,' Mabel finished. 'Going to be spending time with ma grandchildren and very nice too, eh? Now I'll go and make us a cup o' tea and let you and Mr Todd have your talk.'

'Take a seat, Tess, if you can find one,' said Mr Todd, when Mabel had bustled away. 'Move thae papers, eh? That's right. Now – I'm very glad you came, you ken.

146

Wasn't so sure you would. With your good job, an' all.'

'I'm interested in this job, Mr Todd.'

'Aye, but you might have got to thinking.' He rolled a pencil between grease-stained fingers. 'About your dad.'

'Dad?'

'Bit of awkwardness there, maybe?'

'I did talk to Ma about it.'

'She was upset?'

'Said I should do what I want to do.'

'And you want to work here?' He gave a wry smile. 'What's wrong with Appleton's then?'

'Nothing. It's just that – well, I like cars.'

'Like cars?' His smile broadened. 'Fancy you saying that. Thing is, Tess, you'd no' be working on the cars.' She could tell he found the idea of that quite extraordinary. 'Just running the office.'

'Oh, I know. But I think I'd be happier here than at Appleton's.'

'You're sure? The money's less, you ken.'

'There's no' much in it.'

'But then you've good qualifications. Better than the other lassies I've interviewed.'

Tess tried to appear unconcerned. She cleared her throat. 'I thought there'd be other folk applying.'

'Aye, three. Saw 'em yesterday.'

'Oh.' Tess took up her bag. 'I brought ma references, Mr Todd, if you'd like to see them. There's one from the secretarial school and one from Appleton's.'

He put on a pair of horn-rimmed glasses. 'Suppose I should just have a look.' There was silence for a while as he scanned the typewritten pages, then he put them aside.

'Seems Appleton's dinna want to lose you, Tess, and I don't blame 'em. So let's get to the point.'

She waited, trying to appear calm, though her hands kept moving on her lap quite against her will.

'You might've guessed I've already made up ma mind,' Mr Todd said quietly. 'Well, I did ask you to apply, didn't

147

I?' He grinned. 'I knew you'd be right. If you want the job, it's yours.'

Tess's hands stopped moving. 'Mr Todd – I don't know what to say.'

'Needn't accept now. Wait till Mabel's shown you round. Maybe discuss it with your ma.'

'No, I'd like to accept now,' she said firmly. 'Ma said she'd leave it to me. It's ma own decision.'

He gave her back her references and stood up. 'Then I'll just say, welcome, Tess. Ma hand's a wee bit greasy, but if you dinna mind—'

She shook his hand gladly. 'Mr Todd, if I minded grease, I'd no' be here.'

He gave a gratified smile. 'So, when can you start?'

After she'd been given tea and shown round by Mabel, privately thinking that she'd have a field day with Mabel's unique filing system, Tess was introduced by Mr Todd to the mechanics. The older ones said they remembered her, but were tactful in not mentioning her father, while towering Ginger Moffat and a thin fellow called Norrie Smith were obviously too young to have known him. And Norrie, said Mabel, would be glad to see another young face about at Todd's.

'Aye, he's a devil, he is!' she added with a laugh. 'Better watch out for him, Tess.'

'Mabel, how can you take ma character away?' he cried, hugging her. 'When you ken fine you're the one for me?'

'Och, will you get away then?'

As Mabel blushed and laughed again, Tess smiled at Joey's brother.

'Ginger, I think you remember me?'
His good-natured face darkened a little.

'I'm always called Luke now,' he told her diffidently.

'I'm sorry, I didn't know.'

'Aye, well you wouldn't, but I never liked folk at school taking the mickey about ma hair. Ginger, Copper-knob,

148

Carrots – they'd call me anything but ma name.'

'Never mind your hair, Luke,' said Mr Todd. 'Just give the lassie a word o' welcome, eh?'

'Hope you'll be happy here, Tess,' Luke responded hastily. 'I do remember you and I'm glad you're coming.'

'Me too,' said Norrie. 'When d'you start?'

'Two weeks on Monday,' said Tess, herself amazed.

Walking back down the High Street, she found it hard to believe the speed with which events had happened. Only a couple of hours ago she was an Appleton's secretary. Now she was an Appleton's secretary who would be working her notice. From Appleton's to Todd's, in so short a time, she couldn't seem to take it in; her head was whirling. Had she done the right thing? She had, hadn't she? Without a doubt she had. Yet she wasn't looking forward to telling Mr Frederick that she was on her way. Or Ma, come to that. But Ma and Nola might not be back yet from Glasgow.

They were back from Glasgow. As soon as Tess reached the top of the stairs to the kitchen, her mother appeared at the foot with Nola at her shoulder.

'How did you get on then?' cried Rena.

'Did you get it?' asked Nola.

'Aye, I got it.' Tess, feeling acutely self-conscious under her mother's and sister's scrutiny, moved slowly down the stairs and into the kitchen. 'I start a fortnight on Monday.'

'Well done, you!' said Nola beaming, but Tess could see her mother's shoulders droop and her blue eyes flicker.

'Did I no' say you'd get it?' she asked, turning away. 'I knew John Todd would give it to you. Now you'll have to explain it to thae Appletons, eh? Explain why you're leaving a grand place like theirs to work in a garage. Whatever will they say?'

Chapter Thirty-Three

Of course, they said exactly what Tess had expected them
to say. That they were surprised and disappointed. Baffled,
in fact, that Miss Gillespie should consider leaving
Appleton's for a garage. A small garage, too, where she
would scarcely be able to use her skills or build on her
experience.

Mr Frederick, who had given her such an excellent refer-
ence, confessed that he'd never thought she would actually
take the job at Todd's, and it seemed to be beyond Tess's
capabilities to make him understand why. How could she
say 'I like cars'? He would think her mad. She settled for
saying she just wanted a change.

'Change, change! That's all you young people think
about!' Mr Frederick groaned, but he and Mr Reginald
shook her hand and wished her luck, and all the staff
clubbed together to give her a leather writing case as a
leaving present which made her feel rather bad.

'Come in and see us – don't lose touch!' everyone said,
and of course she said she would, but somehow didn't see
herself going back. She'd taken a different path and mustn't
risk regrets.

But what was she thinking about? There would be no
regrets anyway.

Brave words. No regrets.

'No regrets. If I say it often enough, it'll be true,' she told Nola when she saw her off at Waverley station. Nola's holiday had come to an end; she was going home to Clark.

'It's true anyway,' said Nola. 'You've done the right thing and don't you forget it.'

'I hope so.' Tess's eyes were on the guard with his flag. 'Nola, you'll take care, eh? You'll let us know if there's ever – anything we can do.' As she stumbled a little with what she wanted to say, Nola's blue eyes glinted.

'Ever anything? What sort o' thing? I'm no' sure what you're on about.'

'I'm no' sure maself.' As the guard took his last look up and down the platform, Tess flung her arms around her sister. 'It's just, I want you to remember, that Ma and me – we're always there. If you need us.'

Nola's expression softened. 'Same goes for me. Come and see me, eh? When you get a holiday?'

'A holiday?' Tess laughed. I've no' even started in the job! Oh, Lord, you'd better get in, Nola. The guard's got the flag ready.'

'Let me know how things go!' Nola cried as she climbed nimbly into her compartment. 'Write, Tess!'

'I will!'

The guard's flag was down, the train was moving and for a few minutes Tess ran beside it, feeling strange desolation at the departure of her sister. Nola was only going home – there was no need to feel so sad. No need to feel sorry for her. Why, if Nola thought anyone was feeling sorry for her, she'd be furious, eh?

The train was gathering speed and Tess had to fall back, watching, until it was out of sight, her sister's hand waving. Then she turned away.

No regrets. The amazing thing was that she'd been right. There were none. From the moment she moved into the garage office on that first Monday morning and hung up her coat, she was happy.

She had her own little empire, her enclave, and beyond it was the world of the cars of which she also felt herself a part. That it was a man's world, full of noise and talk and the 'bad language' Mabel had in hushed tones warned her about didn't bother her at all. As she remarked, she didn't expect the fellows to sound like the ladies of Morningside, eh?

'That's all right then, pet,' said Mabel with relief. 'You being a young lassie, I was a wee bit worried, you ken. And that Norrie, he's a devil for putting up thae awful calendars wi' naked women, you ken. Take no notice, eh?'

'I'll sort Norrie out,' said Tess. 'How'd he like it if I put up pictures of naked young men?'

'Tess, you'd niver!' cried Mabel, but Tess only laughed. She was thinking of her plans to reorganize the office.

Chapter Thirty-Four

Good-natured Mabel didn't object at all to Tess's changes when she 'dropped in', as she called it, to see how things were going. Now, she wasn't planning to come poking her nose in all the time, she explained, no need to worry about that, she just thought she'd see if Tess needed any more help. But as Tess showed her round, revealing the apple-pie order that had been achieved, Mabel's doll's blue eyes widened.

'Tess, you're a marvel!' she cried. 'Och, will you look at thae files then! And all the bills and receipts in order, and everything out o' the way. Now, I'll be the first to admit, ma filing system was all ma own.' She gave a peal of laughter. 'And how you've sorted it out I'll niver know, but it's all credit to you, eh?'

And as John Todd looked in to say hello, she told him too, that all credit was due to Tess.

'Aye, that's right,' agreed Mr Todd. 'But you did good work an' all, Mabel. Dinna forget that.'

'You did,' said Tess swiftly. 'All I've done is tidy up a bit.'

'Just as long as you dinna follow Mabel and leave us, now you've done it,' said Mr Todd, at which Tess smiled.

'No chance o' that,' she told him.

Whenever she could find the time, she studied Mr Todd's car

manuals that lined the office, and sometimes on her way through the garage she'd stop beside men working on vehicles and exchange a few words. They were always pleased to have 'a bit crack' with her, and if she asked them something about their work, they'd tell her, but lost no time warning her not to come too close. Wouldn't want to get herself dirty, eh?

'I'd no' mind at all,' she once told Luke when he said something of the sort, and he straightened up his big frame and looked at her with an indulgent smile.

'First lassie I've heard say that.'

'Well, how many lassies come in here anyway?'

'Och, we get plenty ladies coming in with their cars. Niver want to touch the engine, I can tell you.' He laughed. 'Some of 'em dinna ken where the engine is.'

'When I have a car, I'll know where the engine is, I can tell *you*!' Tess retorted.

Luke stared. 'You're going to get a car?'

She relaxed, laughing. 'One day.'

'Me too.'

'Bet you can drive though?'

'Canna work in a garage without driving, Tess. I learned in the war. Now some lads learn doing national service, but you don't have to do that, eh?'

'I'd have done it like a shot if they'd taught me to drive.'

He looked at her with his head on one side. 'You're awful different from most lassies, Tess. Ken that?'

'Whenever a girl wants to do what men can do, they say she's a funny sort of girl, eh?'

'Very pretty girl anyway.'

'Watch yourself, Luke!' cried Norrie Smith, joining them. 'Old Todd'll have his eye on you, flirting wi' the office staff! You'd better get on.'

'You're just jealous,' Luke said with a grin. 'Tess and me've been having an interesting talk, and you've been in the yard, smoking. Better get back to work yourself.'

'I'm on ma way. But dinna worry, I'll no' tell Lorna about Tess.' Norrie slapped Luke on the shoulder and went off, laughing. 'Mum's the word, eh?'

'Who's Lorna?' asked Tess, thinking that these two young men were like a couple of puppies scuffling and scrapping together.

'Ma young lady,' said Luke, colouring. 'D'you no' remember her, Tess? Lorna Allardyce, from school? About your age?'

'Oh, Lorna *Allardyce*! Of course I remember her. Tall girl, with plaits? Ma friend, Erika, and me used to play peevies with her.'

'No plaits now. Got a perm.' A look of tenderness swept over Luke's still blushing face, and his eyes were bright. 'Works in Logie's in soft furnishings. Very grand, eh? Norrie's going out with a girl from the same department. Lorna introduced them.'

'Fancy.' Tess, anxious not to be caught gossiping by Mr Todd, said perhaps they should get back to work.

'Aye.' But Luke hesitated. 'How about you, Tess?'

'Me?'

'Got anybody special?'

'No. Nobody special.'

'That's a mystery. For a girl like you.'

'Thought we were getting back to work, Luke.'

'Aye,' he said again, and returned to his engine.

Tess, back in the office, sat down at her typewriter. She felt a little unsettled. Sort of – she struggled to define it – out of step. With Luke and Norrie? Och, what a piece of nonsense! Just because they had their 'young ladies', and she didn't have her 'young man'? Didn't want one, did she?

Yet, as she rolled paper into her machine, she couldn't help remembering the look on Luke's face as he spoke of Lorna Allardyce. If anyone were to look like that over her, how would it be? She killed the thought immediately. Looks like that didn't last. As she rattled away typing up Mr Todd's letters, Norrie Smith, going whistling by, wondered how that machine of Tess's stood the strain. Certainly gave it some stick, didn't she?

155

Chapter Thirty-Five

One Sunday in October, Rena asked Mrs Lange and Erika down to share the joint of beef the butcher had managed to find for her.

'Aye, Will Hawkins has always been very good to me,' she told her guests over the meal, 'but I still say it's shocking we're no' finished with rationing, eh? Will was telling me yesterday that meat'd be the last to go. Would you credit it? What do they do with it, I want to know?'

'This is really delicious,' Mrs Lange remarked. 'Such a treat.'

'Wish you'd take a bit more of it then. You don't eat enough to feed a sparrow.'

'Exactly what I tell her,' said Erika quietly.

Her dark eyes on her mother seemed too large for her face. Though she had grown tall, her features and her bones were as delicate as ever, and if she was not the little waif she had once appeared, she was still fragile. Not as fragile as her mother, however, who was now very thin, with a cough that never went away.

'I am well enough,' Mrs Lange murmured. 'I smoke too much, that is all.'

'Your cough is a sign of that, Mutti.'

'A smoker's cough. Sounds worse than it is.'

'Should let the doctor see you,' said Rena. 'Just for a check, eh?'

'Something else I tell her,' said Erika.

Mrs Lange shrugged and said she would like another of the splendid Yorkshire puddings, if there should be one left.

'Plenty left!' cried Rena. 'Now you're pleasing us, eh?'

'Which was her intention,' Erika said in a low voice to Tess. 'Mutti is good at switching attention from her health.'

As a a special treat, Rena had lit the fire in the front room, and when she and Mrs Lange had retired there, Tess and Erika tackled the washing up. Afterwards, Tess asked Erika if she'd help her to make the coffee.

'I got some proper ground stuff; I know your ma likes it.'

'Oh, she does! That's so kind of you, Tess. Of course I'll help. I'll make it for you.'

As she busied herself with the coffee-making, Erika's face brightened a little, but not for long. 'There is an old lady comes into the shop,' she said quietly. 'Her name is Mrs MacRoy. You might know her?'

'I think Ma knows her daughter. Worked at the aero-engine plant with her.'

'Yes, well, Mrs MacRoy has a cough like Mutti's and comes in regularly to buy cough mixture. Every time I see her I tell her to go to the doctor's, and every time she says, "Hen, I'm no' going to the doctor's, he'll send me to the Infirmary and they'll start poking roond and that'll be the end o' me."'

'Poor old soul,' murmured Tess. 'You've got her voice off to a T, Erika.'

'My point is that Mutti is the same as Mrs MacRoy. She thinks by keeping quiet about it, her cough will go away.'

'Might no' be anything to worry about, you ken.'

'How can we know until she gets it checked?'

Tess put cups on a tray. 'You don't think maybe all the medical books you read might make you believe the worst?'

Erika, straining the grounds from the coffee, gave a slight smile. 'You could be right, Tess. I might be worrying about nothing. Anyway, let's talk about you. How is the new job going then?'

'New? I feel as though I've been there for years. I'm very happy, Erika. I truly am.'

'You look happy,' said Erika. 'And therefore pretty. Happy people are always good-looking people.'

'I'll pour the coffee,' Tess said awkwardly. What could she say to Erika, who was obviously not happy, and not usually considered pretty either, even though in Tess's eyes she was attractive?

'You always look nice yourself,' she said hurriedly, and Erika smiled.

'Tactful Tess. Let us take the coffee in then. Such a treat for Mutti!'

When Mrs Lange had gone back to her room to rest, and Rena had said she must get on, she'd a load of things to do, Tess and Erika went for a brisk walk on the sands.

The season was over now, with most of the holiday-makers gone, but there were still people about, facing the October wind, walking by the edge of the water, throwing sticks for dogs. There was no sign, however, of Mr Beith with Honey.

'Poor Mr Beith,' Tess murmured. 'I think he's getting old.'

'All have to come to that,' said Erika. 'Until the doctors discover something amazing.'

'I suppose we're like cars. Need replacing after a few years.'

'Some people can't be replaced,' said Erika.

They didn't stay out long. Erika wanted to work on her textbooks and Tess thought she should offer to help her mother, whose new tenants would be arriving soon. But when they arrived back at the house, a red two-seater sports car was standing at the door. It seemed the medical students had already arrived.

158

Chapter Thirty-Six

'Ships that pass on the stairs' was how Nola had once described her mother's tenants, and it was true that the students seemed to be always on the move. Either running out of the house, or running back in, but certainly never stopping long enough in one place to have a conversation.

But who wanted conversations with the students? In Tess's experience they only led to complaints about the hot water system, or the lateness of the post, or the noise from the power station, or whatever else came to the young people's distracted minds. And as complaints always had to be passed on to her mother, Tess was skilful at avoiding anyone who might make them, particularly Simon Maitland.

Oh, how she longed for him to give in his notice and depart, so that she might never again see that nose of his, lifted like an eagle's beak, as he tramped the landing, flinging his towel around his neck and complaining about the coldness of his morning bath! But so far it appeared he'd found nowhere else to go.

And what of Toby Dene? He never complained. Only gave Tess a rueful smile if they met in the bathroom queue when Simon was sounding off. Would he go if Simon went? Tess was always a little surprised to find herself hoping he would not. It was not as though she wanted to get to know him. Why should she? He was just another ship that passed on the stairs. Those brown eyes of his were kind though. Or seemed so.

Seemed. That was the word of anxiety. Things weren't what they seemed. People weren't what they seemed. Tess was sure she would never trust the kindness of Toby Dene's brown eyes.

When those same eyes smiled at her one Saturday afternoon, however, she couldn't resist smiling back.

Toby was on the promenade close to Pax House. Tess was walking out for a breath of air in her time off from the garage. It was December and chill; she'd been shopping and felt tired and jaded, but now, in the wind that was blowing her dark hair and freshening her cheeks, she felt exhilarated. Even more so, perhaps, when she saw Toby smiling at her.

'I've never seen you out here before,' she told him. 'I didn't think you spent time in Porty.'

'Shame! I'm very fond of Porty.' His face, too, was reddened by the wind, though he wore a tweed cap over his unruly hair. He looked well and happy, and it came into her mind that he might not, after all, want to leave with Simon Maitland. 'Don't get much time to see it, that's the problem. Work, work, work, you know.'

'But here you are today.'

'Yes, today I thought what the hell – get out there, Dene, and fill your lungs with some good Scottish air.' He grinned. 'You doing the same?'

'I often walk here or on the sands. I like to look at that house there. It's ma favourite.'

'"Pax House".' Toby read the name on the gates aloud. 'Yes, it's splendid, isn't it?' His eyes travelled over the fine façade and returned to Tess who had been watching him. 'Who owns it?'

'Mr Seton. We know his chauffeur, and his dog. But they don't seem to be around today.'

'Mind if I walk with you?' Toby suddenly put her arm

in his. 'We could face the wind together.'

'We'd better no' go too far, it'll be dark soon.' She sounded calm, yet was secretly amazed that her arm should be resting so naturally in his, as though they'd walked together many times before. Did he feel that? His face below the tweed cap was relaxed, his eyes, no longer on her, were looking ahead at the long empty promenade. She still had the impression that he was content. Happy, in fact, to be walking with her.

'Don't worry,' he said comfortably. 'We can always go and have tea somewhere.'

Tess took him to Bridie's, a little tea shop well away from the High Street, where she might have met people she knew. The season being over, it was half empty and they were able to take a corner table where they ordered girdle scones with butter and jam and a pot of tea for two.

'Thank God for butter again,' said Toby, biting into his scone with pleasure. 'Things are getting easier at last.'

'We're still rationed though. Folk used to blame the Labour government.'

'And now the Tories are in, they blame the Tories.' Toby stirred his tea. 'I don't have time to think about politics, but once I'm working for the health service, I suppose I'll be involved.' He grinned. 'Listen to me, talking as though I'm qualified already, when I've years to go.'

'You'll qualify. I know, I can tell, you'll be a good doctor.'

'A GP do you think?' he asked, still smiling.

'Yes, you're good with people.'

'And Simon?'

'A specialist,' she answered promptly. 'He'd no' be one for ordinary ailments, eh?'

'My father was a GP. What they used to call a panel doctor, in Durham. Never liked charging anybody, poor old Dad.' Toby shook his head. 'Died when he was fifty, worn out. I was fifteen at the time and my brother ten.'

161

'I'm very sorry.'

'Yes, it was tough. Particularly on Mother. She had quite a struggle.'

'I know about struggle,' Tess said quietly. 'But I never thought, somehow, that you would.'

'Saw me as another Simon? I'm afraid I'm not in his league. But he's not too bad, you know. He'll care about his patients, I promise you.'

They ordered more tea and some 'fancy' cakes, which were not particularly fancy, but which Toby enjoyed anyway as he said he was always hungry. While he ate and Tess poured the fresh tea, she told him her friend, Erika, who was also a tenant at Number One and wanted to train as a doctor.

'Erika? Do I know her?'

'Yes, you must have seen her. Tall and slim, with dark hair. Works in the chemist's in the High Street.'

'And she wants to be a doctor?' Toby smiled indulgently. 'Not so easy for an assistant in a chemist's shop.'

'Her father was a doctor in Vienna before the war.'

'Ah, well then, she might make it. But listen, we've talked about your friend and we've talked about me, yet not a word's been said about you. Tell me about yourself, Tess.' He raised his hand. 'And don't say there's nothing to tell.'

She flushed and looked down at her plate. 'There's plenty to tell, only I don't like telling it.'

'I'm sorry.' He grew serious at once. 'I don't want to intrude. Let's just finish our tea.'

'I have finished.' She looked up, her eyes very bright. 'Truth is – ma father left us.'

'Oh.' He reached out to touch her hand. 'Tess, I'm sorry. Listen, I've said I don't want to intrude – you don't have to tell me about this.'

'No, I want to tell you.' She gave an uncertain smile. 'You must be easy to talk to, I think.'

'People say I'm good at listening.'

'So you'll be a good doctor. Well, like I say, ma dad left us. Walked out five years ago for a young ATS girl. Didn't want to go, he said. Still went.'

'I can't believe it. I know it happens, still can't understand how a guy can do it.' Toby shook his head. 'Your poor mother.'

'It's OK. She's over it. We all are. We don't need him any more.'

'That's good. That's very good.'

She picked up on his careful tone. 'Don't you believe me?'

'Yes, of course I believe you. People do get over things, I know that. Wounds heal. Then you can forget them.'

'I said we were over it. I didn't say we'd forgotten.'

Again, he touched her hand. 'As long as you don't let it spoil things for you, Tess.'

She shrugged. 'Everybody says that. I never know what they mean.'

'I suppose, they mean you mustn't be afraid.'

Tess was silent. She knew, and didn't try to pretend otherwise, what he meant by that. For some time Toby was silent too, only keeping his compassionate gaze on her face.

'I still feel bad,' he said at last. 'Making you talk to me. I mean, you don't even know me.'

'I told you, I wanted to talk to you. And I feel as though I do know you.'

'That's funny. I feel the same about you.'

Suddenly, the sun seemed to come out from behind clouds as they exchanged wide, genuine smiles

'Hang on, I'll just get the bill,' Toby said, rising to catch the waitress's eye. 'Shall we walk back along the sands?'

163

Chapter Thirty-Seven

Outside, it was much colder and already dark, the street lamps shining through little pockets of mist. Turning up their coat collars and shivering, they looked at each other for a moment, then Toby again put Tess's arm in his and they turned to make their way down to the beach.

'What sort of work d'you do then?' asked Toby. 'Secretarial, did I hear?'

'I was with an accountancy firm, but I changed to Todd's. That's a garage.'

'A garage?' In spite of his polite tone, she recognised his surprise. 'You like it there?'

'I do. I run the office, but I wouldn't mind having a go at the cars.'

'A go at the cars?' He burst into laughter. 'I must tell Simon to take in the MG. He's looking for a good garage.'

'Todd's will be good enough, even for Simon,' said Tess.

Down on the beach the wind seemed wilder and stronger, and they had to hold each other tightly as they tried to walk where the sand was firmest, laughing at their own foolishness for choosing this way home.

'My shoes'll be in a state,' cried Tess.

'Who cares?' asked Toby. 'We'll feel the better for all this fresh air.'

'If you say so, Dr Dene.'

It was a relief, all the same, to reach the lights of their own road, to be out of the darkness, the whipping wind and the blowing sand.

'Thank heavens,' Tess murmured. 'We'll soon be back at Number One.'

'But then we have to say goodbye,' said Toby.

'We see each other every day,' said Tess.

Back at the house, she loosed her arm from his and was about to open the door when he put his hand over hers.

'Tess, would you like to go out with me? I mean, to the cinema or something?'

She stared into his eyes that seemed black in the pale blur of his face. 'Go out? How could you find the time? I thought you said it was work, work, work, for you.'

'Ah, look, I need some time off, don't I? Just one evening a week? Or am I speaking out of turn?'

'What do you mean?'

'Well, I never thought to ask if you have someone else to see.'

'There's no one else.'

'So would you like to go out with me? Next Saturday afternoon, maybe? We could go into Edinburgh and you could take me sightseeing.'

'Sightseeing, when you've been in Edinburgh a year?'

'Well, we could just look around, maybe have a meal? What do you think?'

'I think I'd like that.'

'That's arranged, then. We'll leave at two, so as to get the daylight for my tour.' He looked down at her and in the darkness she could just see his smile. 'Now you can open the door.'

'Aren't you a bit late?' her mother asked, when Tess, cold and rosy, came into the warmth of the kitchen, carrying her sandy shoes. 'Whatever have you been doing then?'

'Window shopping.' Tess set her shoes on a piece of

165

newspaper. 'Will you look at these? I'll have to clean 'em later.'

'Window shopping on the beach?' asked Rena, staring at the sand on the shoes.

'Well, afterwards I went along the prom for a breath of air and bumped into Toby Dene. We had tea at Bridie's and walked back along the sands.'

'Mr Dene?' Rena stared. 'Fancy him asking you then.'

'I don't see why he shouldn't.' Tess put her hands to her scarlet cheeks. 'As a matter of fact, he's asked me out next Saturday. I said I'd go.'

'Oh, Tess!'

'What do you mean – "oh, Tess"?'

'I'm no' sure it's a good idea, going out with the tenants. I do want you to have a young man, it's time you had, but tenants never stay, you ken.'

'This isn't the start of anything permanent, Ma.'

'Once you start something, you canna say how it'll finish.'

Tess sighed. 'I'll away upstairs to get tidied up.'

'I'm cooking haddock. Don't be too long.'

In the chill of her attic room, Tess tried to feel calm. But as she combed her hair and looked at herself in her mirror, the rosy-cheeked girl she saw was all at sea.

Only a few hours before, she'd had no problems. Toby Dene had been just a nice young man with kind brown eyes, and no more than that. She had been very sure she wouldn't trust him, because she never trusted anyone, but she would have been sorry if he'd left. Now – and she still couldn't believe it – she'd walked with him, arm in arm, she'd told him things she preferred to keep to herself, and she'd agreed to go out with him next Saturday.

Just what are you playing at, Teresa Gillespie? she asked herself, putting down her comb. Toby Dene isn't your young man and you don't want him to be, so why are you going out with him?

166

'You mustn't be afraid,' he had told her. Afraid of life, he meant. Afraid of love. He didn't understand that to be afraid, not to be involved, was what she wanted. That way she wouldn't get hurt. But surely she wouldn't be hurt by Toby Dene? There was no doubt that her mother was right – he wouldn't be staying. In spite of her mistrust, even of his kind eyes, she was sure she would be safe. And she would be very, very careful.

Chapter Thirty-Eight

The following Saturday, when Tess took Toby on his 'tour', it was a perfect winter's day, with diamond-hard frost and gun-metal sky, and the air of 'Auld Reekie' seeming as fresh as in the Alps.

Tess's coat was long and black, and with it she wore a fake fur hat that made her look, Toby said, like a heroine from a Russian novel. But when Tess said she'd never read any Russian novels, he confessed that he hadn't either, and would she settle for being Snow White?

'Oh, honestly!' she laughed, as they sat together in the tram. 'You do talk nonsense, Toby.'

'Well, you've got the dark hair and the pink cheeks. Wasn't that Snow White? Or was it the Snow Queen? I get these stories muddled up.' Toby frowned in concentration. 'Wait a bit – didn't the Snow Queen have ice in her heart?'

Tess hesitated. 'I think that was the little boy she took away.'

'The boy had ice in his heart? Oh no, that must be wrong. Much more likely it was the Queen.' Toby was smiling as he folded Tess's hand into his. 'Much more likely to be a woman with an icy heart.'

'No more teasing,' said Tess. 'Where do you want to go first?'

They took another tram up the Mound to the Old Town,

where Toby maintained that he knew only the university and a few pubs.

'You've never been down the Royal Mile, or looked at Holyrood?'

'Not really.'

'What about Saint Giles's?'

'Never been inside.'

'The Castle? You must have seen the Castle?'

'Yes, thank God, I can say I've seen the Castle. Went up with a crowd at the beginning of my first year.'

'What a relief,' said Tess. 'We need only see everything else then.'

In fact, they just wandered where their fancy took them, stepping gingerly through the icy streets, staring up at ancient tenements and the famous old buildings of the High Street and the Canongate, avoiding Christmas shoppers who were milling everywhere. They had tea at a little café near the Palace of Holyroodhouse, then braved the cold of Arthur's Seat, before walking briskly back to find a central restaurant.

'This is so grand,' murmured Tess, admiring the décor, though not daring to look at the waiters. There were marble floors and potted palms, and the leather-bound menus were enormous.

'Yes, but what's the food like?'

It was better than they'd expected, for restrictions on what could be provided had been lifted, and though meat was still rationed, nobody had to accept spam fritters any more – certainly not in the sort of restaurant Toby had selected. Tess, making mental notes of the menu to tell her mother, grew anxious when she read the prices.

'I hope you'll let me pay ma share,' she told Toby, as their steaks arrived.

'As though I would!'

'Well, it's a piece of nonsense, really, that men always have to pay for women. I mean, the fellows I know don't have much more than the girls, yet they're supposed to

169

shell out every time.' Tess smiled a little. 'Don't always do it, as a matter of fact. Some'll say, "Let's go to the pictures – see you inside."'

'They actually say that?' Toby shook his head. 'Poor lads, must be hard for them. But please don't worry about paying, Tess. I'm not actually stony; I can afford to take you out to dinner.'

And Tess, looking at him thoughtfully, believed him. There might have been struggle in his family, but it was not the same as poor folk knew, and even if he was not in Simon's 'league', he was certainly out of hers.

They moved from the restaurant into a splendid starlit night, and stood for a moment in the frosty air, looking up at the heavens, looking down at each other.

'Better get back, I suppose,' Toby said quietly. 'Though it's not late.'

'No,' agreed Tess. 'Quite early.'

'Your mother will be pleased with me, not keeping you out late.'

'I'm no' exactly Cinderella.'

He laughed and drew her arm in his. 'I was thinking we might have walked up Calton Hill, looked at the view by night. But we'd better get back.'

Tess pictured herself and Toby walking up Calton Hill, high above Princes Street, looking at the view. And then what? Trouble was, she had no idea what Toby wanted. Or what she wanted herself.

'Better go back,' she said with decision, and they set off for the tram.

There they were, outside Number One again, the lights from the power station on them and the traffic zooming past.

'I've had a wonderful time, Toby,' Tess told him, as he held her hands and looked into her face. 'Canna tell you how much I enjoyed it.'

'So did I.'

'I just want to say thank you. I wish you'd have let me pay something.'

'No more of that.' He put his fingers against her lips. 'Thing is, would you like to come out with me again?' As she hesitated, he brought his face closer to hers. 'You did say you'd enjoyed being with me.'

'Oh, I did!'

'Well, then?'

'I'd like to, Toby. If it's what you want.'

'What I want? What about you?'

'You've got your studying, and that. Maybe you shouldn't be going out with anybody.'

'One night off a week, I'm allowing myself, as I said. And I'll be working like the devil all the Christmas vacation, starting from next week. We leave on Wednesday.'

'Oh? That seems early.'

'It's the end of term. But you should see the ton of books I'm taking home. Simon's giving me a lift to Durham. Don't know if he'll fit 'em all in, considering he's got his own as well.'

Tess gazed beyond Toby's shadowed face to the power station, with its smoke rising to the stars. 'I hope you have a good Christmas then. In between working.'

'Never mind Christmas. Think about January when I'll be back.'

For how long, wondered Tess. How long before he and Simon found a new place and moved on?

'We'd better go in, Toby,' she said quietly. 'Or Ma will be coming out.'

'Wait, Tess, wait.' He drew her into his arms, hesitated a moment, then kissed her, long and tenderly. When he let her go, he looked at her apologetically. 'Sorry, I've been wanting to do that all day. You don't mind?'

'No,' she said huskily. 'I don't mind.'

And suddenly, as though she had stepped out of her own personality and become someone she didn't know, she kissed him back.

'Why, Tess—' he began delightedly, but she had already opened the front door.

'Goodnight, Toby,' she whispered from the hall.

'Had a good time?' asked her mother, who was of course waiting up for her.

'Lovely. We had a very good meal at Franklin's restaurant. Want to know what we had?

'Not just now.' Rena's eyes were fastened on Tess's face. 'Listen, pet, I'm worried about you. I think you're making a big mistake going out with Mr Dene. He's no' for you.'

'Ma, we've only been out once.'

'I'll bet you're going out with him again though?'

'He's going home for Christmas on Wednesday.'

'I know when he's going home. What happens when he comes back?'

'He might no' even stay. You keep saying he'll find somewhere else with Simon Maitland.'

'Tess, this is the first time you've ever been interested in anybody. I'm your mother, I can tell you're getting keen. Look me in the eye and say you're not.'

Tess kept her eyes down. She did not reply.

'He's going to be a doctor, you ken,' her mother went on. 'He's got years of studying ahead of him; there's no place in his life for you.'

Tess leaped to her feet. 'Ma, will you just leave me alone? I have to run ma own life.'

'But can you no' see what's in ma mind, Tess?' Rena put her hand to her narrow brow, as though her head had begun to ache. 'I don't want to see you get hurt, you ken. Like me.'

But Tess, upstairs in her attic bed, for the first time in years had gone beyond caring about hurt. The ice in her heart was melting. She was ready for love.

Chapter Thirty-Nine

'You're looking awful happy these days, Tess,' Luke Moffat told her one dreary afternoon in February. He had come into the office, a mug of tea in his hand, and was gazing at her with frank interest. 'What's up? Have you come into money?'

'That'll be the day!' Tess's smile was radiant, but she let it fade. 'Shouldn't be looking happy, eh? With the King dead, an' all?'

George the Sixth had died in his sleep a few nights before, and the country, still shocked, was trying to come to terms with the new order his death had brought. They were to have a lassie for a monarch now, eh? And she only twenty-five? Well, they'd have to see how she got on. As long as she didn't try to call herself Queen Elizabeth the Second in Scotland, where there'd never been a Queen Elizabeth the First.

Luke shrugged and drank his tea. 'Aye, very sad, eh? But life goes on. Did you hear I'd got a car?'

'Luke, no! When? Oh, I'm green with envy!'

'Och, it's only an old banger. Pre-war Morris Eight. I knew the fella who was selling it and he didnae want much for it, so I borrowed the money from ma dad and took it.'

Tess's eyes were shining. 'I'm really pleased for you, Luke. Imagine, having a car of your own to tinker about with!'

'Aye. Well, I just thought I'd ask if you'd like me to teach you to drive? I taught ma brother, you ken, when he bought an old Austin. Did the car up for him, gave him a few lessons, and now he's a rep in Glasgow, driving everywhere.'

'Luke, are you serious?' Tess leaped up from her desk. 'I canna believe it. I'd love to learn to drive. Would you really let me drive your Morris?'

'Sure I would. It's an easy car. You'll be through the test in no time.'

'But when, Luke? I mean, when could you teach me?'

'I canna get away on a Saturday, and the evenings are still dark. Think it'll have to be Sunday.'

'But doesn't Lorna want to see you on Sundays?'

Luke set down his mug and looked away from Tess's eager eyes. 'It's all off with Lorna,' he said, after a pause.

'What do you mean, all off?'

'She's found somebody else. A white-collar guy. Works for one o' the breweries. Och, yes.' Luke's face twisted. 'Trainee manager, would you credit it?'

Tess went white, as though Luke's news had been a personal blow. At one time it would have come as no surprise. You gave your heart and someone broke it. What did you expect? But for some weeks now she had been floating on a cloud of shared love. She no longer expected the worst, only the best, and here was Luke reminding her that the worst was still a threat.

'Oh, Luke, I'm so sorry,' she said quietly. 'I know how much Lorna meant to you. Maybe it'll only be a temporary thing. She's got carried away or something.'

'Carried away? Well, she can damned well stay away, that's what I say. I dinna want her back, I'll niver want her back.' He looked down at Tess. 'Think about the driving then, Tess. Get yourself a provisional licence.'

'I will,' she said with dry lips. 'And thanks, Luke, thanks very much.'

'And when we go out, you can tell me what's making

174

you so happy,' he said with an attempt at a grin. 'Give me the secret, eh?'

All the rest of that day, the thought of Luke's misery over Lorna's betrayal kept coming between Tess and her work, and by the time she left for home, her head was throbbing. She longed to see Toby, but knew he wouldn't be back until late. Since Simon had moved out in January he'd had to come home by tram, and in any case often had work to do, but as soon as he came in she promised herself she would see him. Not bother him, or disturb him – this was not, after all, Saturday, their day for going out – but just kiss him and hold him for a moment or two, and reassure herself he was still hers.

She made tea and took two aspirins for her headache, then, as her mother wasn't home yet to disapprove, lit a cigarette. How strange it was, she thought, the way things had worked out between herself and Toby. Who would have thought that he would really care for her, and that she, after all her declared intentions to keep herself aloof, should fall in love with him?

She had been so anxious when she'd waved him away in Simon's car before Christmas, thinking she'd never see him again. And even when he'd returned in January, she was still unsure of him, for Simon was clearly champing at the bit, always going off to look at flats and studying details. And if he went, wouldn't Toby go with him?

When Simon came in with the news that he'd finally found the perfect place, she'd been on a knife edge, until Toby asssured her he had no intention of moving.

'Now why would I do that, dear Tess? Share again with Simon? I'd be crazy.'

'But it's a flat, you'd have plenty of room and it'd be grander than here.'

'And it'd have Simon instead of you.' Toby had shaken his head. 'I'm afraid you're stuck with me.'

'There, you see!' Tess had cried triumphantly to her

mother. 'Toby's not moving out with Simon Maitland, he wants to stay here.'

'Wants to stay here,' Rena had repeated, looking at Tess. 'Well.'

Both had watched Toby help Simon load up his car on the day he moved out, and had not missed Simon's sigh of exasperation as Toby had shaken his hand and wished him well.

'You're a perfect idiot,' they'd heard Simon say. 'I think you're stark, staring mad, but if you should ever change your mind, I might still be able to fit you in, you know. I've got three bedrooms and I'm only subletting one.'

'Thanks, I'll be OK,' Toby had murmured, and away Simon had driven with a roar from the MG's engine.

And oh, it's grand without him, Tess thought now, drawing on her cigarette, for the young man who'd taken Simon's room knew nothing of Toby, which made Toby seem more her own. There was no Simon to give disapproving glances any more when she and Toby laughed together in the bathroom queue, or raise his eyebrows when he saw them going out on Saturdays, arms already entwined.

No one, either, to talk against her behind her back, as she'd always been afraid Simon might do, though Toby said he never would and she'd got him all wrong. Whether she had or not, he'd gone, and she could breathe more freely. Except for Ma's watchful blue eyes, of course, and her frequent warnings over Toby.

It still seemed a matter of wonder to Tess that she and Toby had only been seeing each other for a couple of months, for the time seemed so much longer. Yet she'd heard of folk getting engaged in less than a fortnight, having fallen in love at first sight. It hadn't been quite love at first sight for her, though she'd always been attracted to Toby's brown eyes, but now her love for him couldn't have been stronger. If he'd asked her to marry him tomorrow, she knew she'd do it, but of course she also knew he had his studies to think of. They'd have to wait and she wouldn't mind that. Wouldn't mind how long she waited, as long as they were together in the end.

It was nine o'clock before he came in and Tess, who'd been waiting for his step, flew down the stairs to greet him. He looked pale, his skin shiny with sweat and said he was exhausted.

'Spent the whole day with a skeleton – what a treat!' he said with a grin, struggling up to his room with an armful of books that Tess tried to take from him. 'No, honestly, I'm worn out. Can't wait to put that kettle on the gas ring. Just hope I've got a shilling for the meter.'

'I've got a shilling,' said Tess. 'And I'll come in and make your coffee. You sit down and rest.'

'Tess, you know your mother doesn't like you to come to my room. It's sweet of you to help me, but I don't want to be thrown out on my ear.'

'It's all right, Ma's gone to a whist drive with Mrs MacFee. Come on now, sit down and I'll get the kettle on.'

'What would I do without you?' Toby flung himself into his armchair and stretched out his legs. 'But better not stay too long. I really have to get to bed.'

They looked at his bed that he had roughly made that morning, then turned their eyes away. Much as they took pleasure in kissing and caressing, sleeping together was not something to be considered. Toby would never have asked it of Tess, and though she had thrown aside caution in falling in love, she was glad he hadn't. For what would she have done? You were supposed to wait until you were married, although she wasn't at all sure that she'd have wanted to wait at all. But it would have been a terrible risk, not to wait. And difficult to find a place or a time. Her mother was not often out at whist drives.

'I was a bit upset today,' Tess told Toby as she made the coffee. 'One of the fellows at the garage has been let down. His girl's left him for someone else.'

177

'Oh, that's a shame.' Toby yawned. 'Taken it badly, has he?'

'Of course.' Tess frowned. 'He really loved her.'

'Seems she didn't love him.'

'Och, she thinks she's found someone better. A trainee manager at the brewery.'

'Sounds like she's not worth worrying over then. He should just forget her.'

'You make it sound so easy.'

'No, I know it's not, but it's what he'll have to do. Is that my coffee? Thank God. You're an angel, Tess.'

She watched him as he drank the coffee and lit a cigarette, shaking her head when he offered her his case and saying she wouldn't stay for coffee, either.

'I'd better go. You need to sleep, Toby.'

'You do sound down, poor Tess. Are you worrying about this chap? There's nothing you can do, unfortunately.'

'He's offered to teach me to drive.'

'Has he? Well, that's good. Should take his mind off his troubles for a while. Though I can't think of anything more nerve-racking than teaching a learner driver.'

'I'll be going out on Sundays.'

'As long as it's not on our Saturdays.'

She ran to him and knelt beside his chair. 'You do still want to go out with me, Toby? I've been so miserable, thinking how I'd feel if you didn't want to see me any more, like Luke's girl.'

Toby set down his mug and pulled Tess on his knee. 'Of course I want to see you! You make my life bearable at the moment. You know that.'

'Yes, but you know what I used to think – how you could never be sure of anyone.'

'Well, you can be sure I want to see you, dear Tess.' Toby held her close. 'Now, I think maybe you'd better sidle out, just in case your ma comes back and reads the Riot Act.'

Tess swung from his knee, then stooped and kissed him passionately on the mouth. 'I don't know what I'd do if you stopped loving me,' she said in a low voice.

Toby, rising, gently put her aside and went to his door. 'I'll see if the coast's clear,' he said over his shoulder. 'Yes, it's OK. No one about.'

'See you in the morning then,' Tess whispered, sliding past him, just managing to touch his hand as she went.

'In the morning,' he agreed.

Chapter Forty

It seemed a long wait until Saturday, but Tess somehow put the time in. One evening she went to the pictures with her mother and Vera MacFee, though what she saw she couldn't afterwards remember, except for the newsreel that showed the new Queen, solemn faced, in the first days of her reign.

'Oh, the poor lassie!' whispered Rena. 'Looks that young, eh? To be queen?'

'Expect she'll have a lot o' help,' said Vera. 'Folk giving her advice, and that.'

'Still lost her dad though. And she's got the funeral to get through tomorrow, with her poor mother.'

'Aye, loss comes to us all, eh? High or low.'

Tess, scarcely listening, was trying to control the apprehension that had gripped her ever since she'd talked to Toby in his room. She didn't want to face it. Didn't want to go into what had or hadn't been said. All she could do was look forward to Saturday. Everything would be made clear then, and things would be as they'd been before. She clung on to that.

It didn't seem appropriate, when Saturday evening came round, to do more than go for a quiet supper in a little café in Porty. After the King's state funeral, the mood of the city was subdued. Like mine, thought Tess, but could not decide what Toby was thinking.

She kept her eyes on his face throughout the meal, seeking clues to his thoughts in his expression, but he was giving nothing away. How calm he was! How natural was his gaze as it rested on her. Perhaps she was imagining the strain she felt beneath the surface. She would have given a great deal for that to have been the case.

'Let's walk a bit,' he suggested, when they came out of the café. 'Needn't go in yet.'

A February night was not the ideal time for walking, but Tess at once slipped her arm in his and agreed.

'Maybe no' the beach though,' she murmured. 'Let's stick to the promenade.'

There were lights on the prom and a few people also out walking, some with dogs. One was Arthur Beith, limping along with Honey towards Pax House, and Tess called 'Good evening' as they overtook him.

'Evening!' he answered, though she guessed he didn't know who she was in the darkness.

'That's Mr Seton's chauffeur,' she whispered to Toby.

'Think we've seen him before, haven't we? Looks as though he's getting on a bit.'

'I expect he'll be retiring soon.'

It almost made her smile, the way they sounded as though they were so interested in Mr Seton's chauffeur, but her arm in Toby's was trembling.

They came to a glass-walled shelter, and Toby said they might sit down for a little while. It was certainly cold, but they sat close and looked out over the dark waters of the Forth. After they had been sitting together for some moments, Tess turned her head to look into his face. For the first time that she could remember, his eyes failed to meet hers.

'Tess, can we talk?' he asked quietly.

'If you want.'

'Well – I've been thinking–' He stopped, took off his cap

181

and ran his hand through his hair. 'Oh, God, this is so hard!' He put his cap on again. 'The thing is, I've been thinking, it might be best if we didn't see each other for a while.'

Tess sat very still. She took a deep breath, drawing on courage she wasn't even sure she had, not to cry in front of him.

'Why? Only the other day, you said you still wanted to see me. "You can be sure I want to see you, dear Tess," you said. I remember the exact words.'

'I did say that, Tess, and it was true. I did want to see you. I still do. But it might not be for the best. That's what I'm thinking now.'

'No' best for you or me?'

'For both of us.' He took her hands and gently held them. 'Look, you don't know how bad I feel about this. I've no excuses, I'm to blame. I knew how vulnerable you were, I knew I shouldn't get involved. But you were so pretty.' His voice faltered. 'And I was so attracted . . . I just wanted to be with you. That's the way it was, Tess.' He shook his head, staring down at her hands still in his. 'I didn't stop to think how it would seem to you.'

'So how did it seem to me then?'

At last he raised his eyes to hers, those eyes that had always been so kind, and now were filled with contrition.

'I suppose you might have thought – must have thought – I wanted more than I did.'

'Marriage, you mean?'

'And love.'

'You don't want us to love each other?' she whispered.

'The time is wrong. You're very young, but you're ready to be married. I'm nearly twenty-three, but I'm not even halfway through my studies. It'll be years before I'm able to take on commitment to a wife.' Toby gave a deep wrenching sigh. 'That was what I forgot. That you'd be wanting something different from me. I know you'll never forgive me, Tess. But I'll never forgive myself.'

The wind from the Forth was blowing in cold around them, chilling their bodies that were still close, though in spirit they had already drawn far apart. Tess took her hands from Toby's and rubbed them together, over and over.

'All this,' she murmured. 'Because I said I didn't know what I'd do if you stopped loving me. That's what frightened you, eh?'

'Don't say frightened. That's the wrong word.'

'What's the right one then?'

'I don't know, I don't know. Maybe it made me see ... what I hadn't seen before.'

'I trusted you, Toby. That's what you taught me. How to trust.' Tess stood up. 'What a joke, eh?'

She turned and ran from the shelter, ran down the promenade with Toby following, calling her name above the wind, begging her to wait. But she didn't wait. Knew she would never wait for him again. And when she reached her mother's door, she threw it open and almost fell across the threshold.

'Oh, Tess, thank God you're back!' came Erika's voice from the stairs. 'Oh, please, please, will you run to the phone box? Mutti's had a haemorrhage. She's unconscious. We must phone the hospital.'

'Let me see her,' said Toby, arriving, gasping for breath in the hall. 'Please, I might be able to help. Tess, phone for an ambulance. Tell them it's an emergency, a patient haemorrhaging. Make sure they understand. Miss Lange, show me where to go.'

Chapter Forty-One

The ambulance, its lights flashing, was at the door, and Mrs Lange, waxen pale and unmoving on her stretcher, had been placed inside. Now one of the attendants looked at Erika.

'You coming, miss?'

'Oh, yes! Yes, please!' Erika, who was almost as white as her mother and whose great eyes were stricken, leaped up into the ambulance followed by Toby.

'Couldn't I come?' cried Tess, looking beyond his anguished face to Erika, but the ambulance driver was already closing the doors.

'Got to go, miss. Stand back, please.'

'Where are you going? Which hospital?'

'The Royal,' called Toby, just before the doors closed. 'Don't worry, Tess. Leave things to us.'

'Come back, pet,' whispered Rena, shivering under a coat thrown round her shoulders. She put her arm round Tess, as the ambulance sped away up the Edinburgh road. 'We'll follow them, eh? We'll get the tram.'

'Is it no' too late?'

'Too late? It's only a few minutes after ten. Wait while I get ma bag.'

'I thought it was much later,' Tess said dazedly. 'Seems like midnight.'

'Och, you're in a state. So am I. Oh, poor Herta, eh? Oh, poor woman!'

And as they hurried towards the tram stop, nothing marked the shock of that evening for Tess as much as her mother's suddenly calling Mrs Lange by her first name.

In the tram, Rena, clutching the strap of her handbag as though it was a lifeline, kept looking at Tess and sighing.

'Do you think it's TB?' she whispered. 'That's the way thae chest cases go, you ken – suddenly sort of burst. Cousin Freda, she went like that.'

'Mrs Lange hasn't died, Ma,' said Tess. 'They'll be able to help her at the Royal.'

'She's been ill a long time, eh? And wouldn't see the doctor. Ma heart goes out to Erika. What'll she do if she's left?'

'She won't be left. Try no' to think the worst, Ma.'

But Tess herself was thinking the worst, and ashamed that sorrow for herself was mixed with her fears for Erika's mother. How could she be letting herself care about Toby Dene, when real tragedy was staring her in the face? Death should take precedence over betrayal. Only Toby's betrayal was a death of sorts – the death of love.

No. She shook her head. That wasn't true. Toby Dene's love for her had not died; it had never been there. She realised that now. And her love for him wasn't dead either. If only it were! But she was going to do her best to forget him. Oh yes, she was going to put Toby right out of her mind. She glanced at her mother.

'Ma, I don't know if I should tell you this now, but I think you'd better be prepared to let Mr Dene's room pretty soon.'

'Mr Dene's room?' Rena's hands still gripped her bag. 'What d'you mean? He's giving notice?'

'Aye, he'll be giving notice.'

Rena's eyes rested on Tess's face. 'You've split up?' she asked.

'We've split up.'

'When? Tonight? Did you have a row, or what?'

'No, there was no row.' Tess folded and refolded her tram ticket. 'Seems you were right and I was wrong. He doesn't want to be involved.'

'The devil!' cried Rena. 'Och, I knew, I always knew no good would come of it. Did I no' say? He's thinking of his career, he's no' interested in marrying? Then he has the cheek to take you out and make you think he's serious!'

'Ma, I was a fool. Just leave it, eh? I don't want to talk about it.'

'Oh, pet, I'm that sorry.' Rena touched Tess's hand. 'Just try to forget him, eh? He's no' worth worrying about.'

Exactly the advice that Toby had given to Luke, thought Tess grimly. Well, it was good advice, and she was going to take it. But when would the pain stop?

'I feel bad, thinking about maself, when Mrs Lange's so ill,' she murmured. 'It's just happened, you see, it's all still in ma mind.'

'Of course it is, Tess. And it's like an illness anyway, that sort of grief. You'll have to take each day as it comes, until it goes away.'

Poor Ma, thought Tess, holding tight to her mother's hand. She knows what she's talking about. I wish she didn't.

At the Casualty Department of the Royal Infirmary, they were told that Mrs Lange was with the doctors. Rena and Tess were welcome to wait for information if they wished.

'Where's Mrs Lange's daughter?' asked Rena. 'Could we wait with her?'

The nurse said that Miss Lange was waiting elsewhere with Mr Dene, and it seemed to Tess from her manner that Toby had already told her he was a medical student. Of course he'd try to get specialised information, to be of help to Erika, which was good. Even so, Tess's lips tightened at the sound of his name.

'Wonder if we can get any tea?' Rena murmured,

186

looking round the department at the other people waiting: men who looked as though they'd been in fights; women who looked as though they'd been beaten up; a couple of children, screaming. 'Och, what a place! Saturday night, eh? You have to hand it to the folk who work here, specially when the pubs turn out.'

'Sorry, the canteen's closed,' a nursing orderly told them. 'There's a machine, if you want to try it. Doesn't always work.'

'I'll bet it doesn't,' Rena muttered. 'Still, we might have to have a go. Och, I'm just so worried about poor Herta, you ken. She looked that bad, eh?'

'Nothing we can do except wait,' said Tess. 'Shall I try to get us some of that machine tea?'

Time passed. Somebody took away the crying children. The men who'd been fighting and the battered women were called for treatment. Drunks came in, singing and swearing, and an old lady, wrapped in layers of shawls, sat next to Rena and asked her for a cigarette.

'No smoking,' said Rena coldly.

'Och, come away, hen, ye can spare one or two, eh? And is this your lassie then? Is she no' bonnie? Gie us a cuppa tea, pet, eh?'

'We'll have to go,' Rena whispered to Tess. 'We'll no' be able to get home at this rate.'

'They're here!' cried Tess, starting up from her chair. 'Erika and—'

And Toby Dene, whose hand was under Erika's arm supporting her, for she had become a waif again; so pale and fragile, she looked ready to collapse. But she managed a smile when she saw Rena and Tess, and ran to them and held them.

'Mutti's condition is stable,' she whispered. 'They've given her medication and they want her to sleep. In the morning, she must have the X-rays, but she is not strong enough tonight.'

'Oh, the poor thing, the poor thing.' Rena hugged Erika again. 'Did you see her? Did she know you?'

'I saw her for a minute or two and I think she knew me, but she is so weak.' Erika's voice trembled. 'But it's so good of you, Mrs Gillespie, and you, Tess, to wait like this. You are so kind. You've all been so kind – Mr Dene, too. I want to thank you all.'

Toby's eyes were on Tess, but she was resolutely not meeting them. To look into those brown eyes she had thought so kind – no, she wouldn't do it. Anyway, she had to think of her friend.

'Are you coming home now?' she asked Erika. 'If your mother's sleeping, you should try to get some sleep too.'

'I wanted to stay, but they told me it would be safe for me to go home.' Erika swayed a little and Toby quickly took her arm again. 'I'm to come back tomorrow, at lunchtime. Then I can bring Mutti's things.'

'What'll we do then?' asked Rena. 'We'll have missed the last tram now, but I think there's a later bus, or maybe a train. Shall we get a taxi to the station?'

'A taxi all the way home,' Toby said firmly. 'Erika is in no state to go for a train. Don't worry about it, I'll pay.'

'Who's worrying?' Rena's eyes flashed. 'We'll pay for ourselves, Mr Dene, thank you very much.'

'I'll ring for one now,' he told her quietly. 'Erika, would you like to sit down?'

'Lassie, you look like deeth!' cried the old lady, wrapped in shawls, who had been taking a keen interest in their conversation. 'You sit doon before you fall doon, eh? Why's nobody got the nurse? Nurse, nurse! Fetch this lassie a cuppa tea! Or, mebbe a wee dram! Can naebody spare me a smoke then? Jist one or two, eh?'

'Oh, Lord,' groaned Rena, holding Erika's white hand. 'Where's that taxi?'

No one spoke during the long drive back to Portobello, and even the driver, perhaps aware of the tension among his passengers, offered no conversation. When they arrived at Number One, Toby attempted to be first out, but Rena was before him, paying the fare herself, and scornfully refusing to take the ten-shilling note he was trying to push into her hand.

'All I want from you, Mr Dene,' she said in a harsh whisper, as Tess and Erika went into the house, 'is one week's notice, starting from today. Is that understood?'

'Perfectly,' he answered, flinching under her gaze. 'In fact, I will pay you what I owe you and leave tomorrow, Mrs Gillespie. If that's all right?'

'That's fine with me. Now, I'm going up to see to Erika.'

Toby, overcome with sudden weariness in the hall, sagged and would have taken a chair, but Tess was coming silently down the stairs and he tried to catch at her hand.

'Tess, for God's sake, will you look at me? I'm leaving tomorrow, you needn't see me again, but please just look at me and say you'll try to understand.'

'How can you talk to me,' she whispered angrily, 'when there's poor Erika up there?'

'I haven't forgotten her, or her mother, but I'm leaving and I can't bear to go, thinking you hate me. You must believe I never meant to hurt you, Tess.'

'I wonder why you think that makes everything all right?' Tess began to walk away from him, then suddenly came back. 'About Mrs Lange – can you tell me if she's going to be all right?'

'I don't know. Her condition is serious.'

'Is it TB?'

'I don't think so.'

'That's good then?'

He hesitated. 'Let's wait for the X-rays, Tess.'

'There's something you're no' saying, isn't there?'

'Take care of Erika,' he said quietly. 'She needs friends.'

With a last, long look at Tess, he made his way up the stairs, while she stood without moving, her face blank as a statue's, scarcely realising he had gone.

Chapter Forty-Two

Another taxi arrived at Number One on Sunday, the following day, and into it Toby piled his bags and books, his golf clubs, tennis rackets and squash rackets that he had scarcely used, and one pot plant bequeathed to him by Simon. He had already settled his bill with Rena, who had not spoken to him, except to thank him with icy politeness, and now he was ready to go. He stood by the open taxi door, looking back at the windows of the house that had been his home, not expecting to see Tess, of course, but hoping she might just say goodbye. Let him off the hook. Wish him well.

But it was Erika, not Tess, who came down the steps of the house, still looking pale in a long black coat and carrying a small suitcase.

'Erika! You're on your way to the Royal?'

'Toby? Yes, I am going for the tram.'

'Give me that case, then, and jump in. I'll drop you off. Driver, there's another passenger.

'As long as you're ready to go sometime, sir,' muttered the driver, while Erika stood gazing at Toby's belongings in the taxi.

'Why, what's happened, Toby? You are leaving?'

'I'm afraid so. But do get in, Erika. It'll be no trouble to take you to the Royal. In fact, I'll be going there myself, soon as I've taken my stuff to Simon's.'

'If you're sure?'

'I'm sure.'

Tess, watching from behind an upstairs curtain, saw them both climb into the taxi, which then drove off at speed.

'That's it then, he's gone,' she told her mother when she joined her in the kitchen. 'Gave Erika a lift in the taxi, an' all.'

'Well, that was nice anyway. I have to say, he's been very kind to that poor girl.' Rena finished basting their small joint of beef and put it back in the oven. 'I wanted her to have her dinner with us, but of course, she's to get to the hospital. We can go this afternoon, eh?'

'Don't be disappointed if you canna see Mrs Lange, Ma. She's very ill.'

Rena gave Tess a sharp look. 'Did you ask Toby Dene about her?'

Tess nodded. 'He said he didn't think it was TB.'

'What then?'

'He wouldn't say, but I got the impression – well, it was serious.'

Rena caught her breath. 'Oh, Tess, it's no' the other thing, eh? Don't say it!'

'We'll just have to wait for the X-rays.' Tess put her arm round her mother's shoulders. 'They might be OK, you never know.'

'Aye, but I feel in ma bones they won't be. She's no' going to last, Tess. Got that look. I've seen it before.' Rena dabbed at her eyes. 'Well, better get on with the dinner, I suppose. It's always the same, eh? Whatever happens, you've got to eat.'

They were ready to leave for the tram when a heavy knock sounded at the front door and Rena cried out.

'Does that no' sound like bad news, Tess? Quick, quick, see who it is!'

But it was only Luke Moffat, wearing his Sunday suit and with his ginger hair well plastered down.

'Hello, Tess! No' too early, am I?'

'Too early?' She stared at him. 'What for?'

His face fell. 'Why, your lesson, of course! Mean to say you've forgotten?'

'Oh, Luke!' Tess's hand flew to her lips. 'Oh, I'm so sorry, I canna go out today. The thing is, Erika's mother's been taken ill and she's in the Royal. We're just going to see her, Ma and me.'

'Erika? Oh yes, the one you knew at school. Well, I'm very sorry to hear about her mother, but I'm disappointed about no' seeing you, Tess. I was looking forward to taking you driving.'

'I know, Luke, so am I disappointed, but there'll be next Sunday. I'll be sure to come next Sunday.'

'Aye.' He turned away, then back again, his face brightening. 'If you're going to the Royal, I could give you a lift. Then you could see ma car.' He pointed to a small black car parked at the kerb. 'There it is, ma wee beauty. Spent all morning cleaning it.'

'Luke, it looks lovely. Will you really take us to the hospital? I'll tell Ma.'

So Toby Dene was not the only one who could give lifts, thought Tess, hurrying to fetch her mother, who came up from the kichen, breathing fast.

'Was that you knocking at ma door like you were the Last Trump, Luke Moffat? Heavens, you've got a heavy hand. This your car then? Why, what a grand little motor!'

'Just what I say,' said Luke happily. 'Right, in you get, ladies. Next week, Tess, it'll be you in the driving seat, remember.'

'What's that?' asked Rena.

'I don't think I said,' Tess answered. 'Luke's going to teach me to drive.'

Rena's eyes flashed with interest. 'Fancy. Well, I think that's a grand idea. Yes, that'll do you good, Tess.'

Oh, Ma, thought Tess, looking out from the car at quiet Sunday Edinburgh. Don't try too hard, eh? Swapping Toby

Dene for driving lessons with Luke Moffat isn't going to do the trick for me.

The first person Tess and Rena saw outside Mrs Lange's ward was Erika. She gave them a sweet, unsteady smile but looked no better. How could she? It was clear she'd had no good news.

'I am so sorry,' she murmured. 'They will not let you see Mutti today. She needs absolute rest, you see. Even Toby was not allowed in.'

'Toby?' Tess repeated sharply.

'He came along to see how Mutti was. He has been talking to the doctors.'

'And where's he now?' asked Rena.

Erika looked back. 'He is just coming. We thought we might have coffee in the cafeteria.'

'Oh, well then, Tess and me'll be going, eh, Tess?'

'Yes, we'll go,' Tess agreed, ashamed that a part of her still wanted to see Toby again, determined that she wouldn't look at him anyway.

'Perhaps we could all have coffee together?' suggested Erika, but even before Tess could refuse, Toby had seen her and her mother and was making his excuses. He had to seec a friend, collect some books, Erika would understand; he would try to see Mrs Lange tomorrow. Politely inclining his head, he made his farewells and departed down the corridor as fast as he could decently go.

'That's all right then,' said Rena, with some relief. 'Now I'll take us all to the canteen, and Erika, you can tell us about your ma.'

It seemed it was very probable now that Mrs Lange would have to have what the doctors described as a lung resection.

Rena, resignedly drinking her weak hospital tea, raised her eyebrows.

'A lung resection? Is that no' what the King had then?'

'He got better from that, Ma,' Tess said quickly and

193

gave her mother a meaningful frown. 'That was last year, eh?'

'It's all right, Tess.' Erika studied her coffee. 'No one has told me, but I know enough to know the truth.' She raised her dark eyes. 'Mutti has lung cancer.'

'Oh, no!' cried Rena. 'Lassie, don't be saying that! You canna be sure – your ma's no' even had the operation yet.'

'There is no point in trying to keep these things a secret. I would rather face what I have to face. That's the way to find strength.'

'Your mother – she doesn't know?' asked Tess in a whisper.

'I am sure she's known for months. That's why she wouldn't go to the doctor.'

'But why? Why no' try to get better? For your sake, Erika.'

'I think she was just tired. Too tired to fight.' Erika's eyes slowly filled with tears. 'Life has been hard for her, you know? I think now she wants to join my father.'

They were silent, as the noise of the cafeteria echoed around them, unheeded. Then Rena asked if Erika's mother would agree to the operation.

'Oh yes, she will do what the doctors advise, now that she is here. But afterwards?' Erika shrugged. 'I don't know.'

'Erika, if there's anything we can do, you'll tell us, eh? Cooking for you, or helping with your ma's washing – anything.'

'Thank you, thank you, that is so kind. You have all been such wonderful friends, I'll never forget you. And Toby, he has been kind, too. So strange, he doesn't even know me.'

'Mr Dene can be very kind, when it suits him,' Rena said, sorting out coins for the tram fare home, while Tess looked away.

Later that evening, when Tess was leaving Erika, having

194

kept her company for a little while, Erika touched her hand.

'I was so sorry, Tess, to hear about you and Toby.'

'What did he tell you?' Tess asked fiercely.

'Only that you weren't seeing each other any more.'

'Canna think why he should talk about us, when you're so worried about your ma.'

'I suppose he knows we are friends, and that I would care about you.'

'I was going to tell you maself later.'

'You were so happy, Tess. What went wrong?'

Tess hesitated. 'Seems I wanted too much from him. He wasn't ready for love from me.'

'Oh, Tess! Oh, I'm so sorry!'

'Och, these things happen. I'll get over it.'

'You will, you will,' Erika agreed warmly. 'Maybe he wasn't right for you anyway.'

'Maybe. Don't you go worrying over me anyway, Erika. You've enough to worry about.'

'Of course I will worry about my friend.' Erika put her arms round Tess and hugged her. 'I hope with all my heart that you will soon be happy again.'

'I'll be thinking of you and your ma,' Tess answered. 'Let us know how things go.'

'I will. Goodnight, Tess.'

'Goodnight, Erika.'

On her way downstairs, Tess paused at the door of Toby's old room. Someone else would soon be moving in here, taking his chair, hanging things in his wardrobe, sleeping in his bed. Just as well. A new tenant would make the break even more permanent, and she wouldn't find herself standing at this door thinking of what might have been.

Plenty of good fish in the sea as ever came out of it, her mother was always telling her.

If only I wanted them, thought Tess.

Chapter Forty-Three

The anxious days passed. Erika went every day to see her mother, sometimes in the afternoons when Mr Meldrum kindly gave her time off, but mostly in the evenings. Rena and Tess were allowed to visit once or twice, but Mrs Lange was so frail, so ghost-like, they rather wished they hadn't.

'I'll be surprised if she ever has that operation,' Rena said to Tess. 'She's no' up to it.'

And, in fact, the operation was postponed, to allow Mrs Lange to build up her strength, and eventually she was moved to a different ward.

For Tess, there was at least the new interest of her driving lessons. Luke was a good teacher – calm, patient, steady as a rock – and soon had her forgetting her nerves as she made her first attempts at getting a car along. 'Nerve-racking,' was her own comment. 'Fine,' was Luke's.

'Aye, you're a natural,' he told her on their third Sunday out, when they'd parked for a while on the nice straight road by the golf course. 'Strange for a lassie, eh?'

'Oh, Luke, women can drive as well as men! Fly aeroplanes, too. Think of Amy Johnson! The first woman to fly alone to Australia.'

'I'm no saying women canna do that sort o' thing. I'm just saying it's unusual.'

'Folk don't expect the same from women as they do from men, that's the difference. Men don't expect it, I should say.'

'Canna say what I expected of you, Tess, but you're doing very well.' Luke gave her a sideways glance. 'Though you're no' the happy lassie you were a while back, eh? Mind if I say that?'

'You've said it anyway,' Tess retorted.

'Sorry.' Luke's cheeks flamed.

'No, it's OK. Didn't mean to snap.'

'Is it Erika's ma you're worrying about?' he asked after a pause. 'I know she's pretty bad.'

'Partly that.' Tess ran her hands down the steering wheel. 'But mostly because I – well, I made a mistake about somebody.'

'That medical student? Stays at your ma's?'

'How did you know?' cried Tess.

'Och, word gets about. Canna keep secrets, you ken. There's always somebody to see.'

An image of herself and Nola, watching their father and the girl in the station buffet, came into Tess's mind. 'You're right,' she said quietly. 'Well, it's no secret that we've split up, Toby Dene and me.'

'If he gave you up, he must be crazy,' Luke stoutly declared.

'And so must Lorna be, to give you up,' Tess answered with a smile.

'Aye, they're a couple o' daft ones, that's for sure.'

'Suppose we'd better get on? What d'you want me to do then?'

'Just make a nice smooth start, then we'll find a corner and try a reverse. Come on then, good look round, mirror, signal, and away you go. Very nice, Tess, very nice indeed.'

One Sunday evening towards the end of March, Tess had returned from her lesson and was studying the Highway

Code, while her mother was covertly studying her.

'How's it going then?' she asked casually.

'Very well. Luke thinks I ought to book a few lessons with a driving school now. For polish, you ken.'

'Polish? I thought he was doing the teaching?'

'Aye, but the schools take you round the test route and all that sort o' thing.'

'You're ready for the test? So soon?'

Tess shook her head. 'Och no, I need plenty more practice, but Luke says we can go out in the evenings now they're getting lighter. Meantime, I should get an idea of what the test'll be like.'

'Driving school lessons will be awful dear, Tess.'

'I know. I'll have to take something out of the Post Office.'

'I'll help. I've a bit put by, you ken. And this driving means a lot to you, eh?'

Tess reached out and pressed her mother's hand.

'I know you think it's making me forget Toby,' she said quietly. 'Maybe it will one day. But you've spent enough on me, Ma. I can manage.'

'Well, ask me if you need any help.' Rena stood up, yawning. 'And tell that Luke Moffat from me he's been a good lad to help you like he has. Don't suppose he minds spending time with you though?'

'Ma, he's still carrying a torch for Lorna Allardyce. He's no interested in me.'

Just like I'm no' interested in him, thought Tess, as her mother asked whatever did carrying a torch mean? Couldn't Tess speak so's folk could understand then?

'Och, there's the front door! Who's that coming in, Tess?'

'Not being able to see up the stairs and into the hall, I'll have to guess it's one of your tenants, Ma.'

'Oh, so sharp! You'll cut yourself one day, Tess. Why, it's Erika!'

'Oh, God, what is it?' cried Tess, taking one look at

198

Erika's face and knowing the answer.

'Oh, pet, sit down, sit down!' said Rena, taking Erika's arm. 'What's happened?'

'Mutti's dead,' Erika whispered. 'She died this afternoon. Very quietly. No pain, no fuss, just the way she wanted it. Oh, Mrs Gillespie, I'm so glad I was there!'

And as Tess and Rena folded her into their arms, the tears came.

Chapter Forty-Four

As soon as the first shock was over, Rena offered to help Erika to arrange the funeral.

'Poor, orphaned lassie, we're all she's got for family, you ken,' she told Vera MacFee. 'I says to her, you leave it to me, pet, I've had plenty practice. Too much, you might say, with all our folks and ma own wee laddie. Anyway, she said she'd be glad if I could give her a hand with the refreshments, but she'd have to arrange the service herself, seeing as it'd be Catholic, you ken.'

'She's being awful brave, eh?' Vera commented. 'Looks like a puff o' wind'd carry her away, but she's stronger than you think.'

'Aye, she's had the training. Losing her dad, and being a refugee, and all that.' Rena shook her head sadly. 'And now she's on her own. We must do what we can.' She suddenly put her handkerchief to her eyes. 'Oh, but I do miss Herta, you ken. She was brave as well. Brave, and kind, and good. A truly good woman, Vera. Ma house'll no' be the same without her.'

Tess agreed. There was just something missing now from Number One, without the sweet-faced Mrs Lange, brewing up her coffee, smoking her cigarettes, always looking a little away from this new life she had found for herself in Portobello.

How would Erika manage without her? People kept

expecting her to give way under the strain, but it was true
what Vera has said of her, she was stronger than she
appeared. She was taking one day at a time, she told Tess
that was the only thing to do. And Tess, who was doing the
same, again felt a little ashamed that she should compare
her grief for the end of love with Erika's grief for her
mother.

Two days before the funeral, Nola arrived, bringing a blaze
of vitality into the subdued atmosphere of her mother's
house.

'Oh, Nola!' Rena cried. 'You're a tonic, you are! It does
me good to see you.'

'And me,' added Tess, flinging her arms round her
sister. 'Oh, it's been so awful, Nola, you canna even
guess.'

'Poor Mrs Lange, I remember her when she first
arrived,' said Nola. 'She was so thin – do you remember,
Ma? All eyes. And wee Erika was the same. And when
they talked English, they still sounded German. Och, I
thought they'd never settle.'

'They did, though, and in no time their English was
grand,' said Rena. 'Though Mrs Lange never lost her
accent. Canna believe I'll never hear her voice again.'

'Come and help me unpack,' Nola whispered to Tess as
Rena dashed away tears. 'You'll no' mind having me back
in your room?'

'Are you joking? I'm over the moon to see you, Nola.
It's true what Ma says, you're a tonic.'

'Well, I don't like to say so, but you look as if you need
one. That'll be the fault of Mister Brown-eyes, is it?'

'You mean Toby Dene?'

'Well, he's no' Mister Long-Nose, is he?' Nola, opening
up her case, began to unpack. 'What happened to him?'

'Simon Maitland? He found a flat. That's where Toby is
now. Ma threw him out, but he'd have gone anyway.'

'Ah, Tess, I'm so sorry.' Nola held her close. 'I could

201

tell you were taken with him, right from the start, and I was sure he felt the same.'

'So was I. Look, it's over, let's just forget it. I've cleared these drawers for you, Nola, and there's a bit o' space in the wardrobe.'

But Nola wasn't prepared to let the matter drop.

'Listen, Tess, I've been thinking, is it no' possible you've got this all wrong? Maybe Toby does care for you, but just doesn't want to get married. He's young, you ken, and's got his career to think about.'

Tess's eyes were large on her sister's face. 'I'd like to think that that was true, but if he'd really cared for me, he'd have asked me to wait. I wasn't the one, that's all there is to it.'

Nola was silent for a moment, then picked up a black dress and held it against her. 'What do you think of this, Tess? I thought I'd wear it for the funeral with ma black coat. Might make me look a bit slimmer. But I've lost two pounds this week, you ken.' She put a hand to her scarlet mouth. 'Oh, will you listen to me? Talking about ma weight when I should be thinking about Mrs Lange.'

'You are thinking about Mrs Lange,' Tess said warmly. 'You've come all this way to the funeral.'

'I do want to go to the funeral, I do want to help Erika.' Nola hung the black dress on a hanger in the wardrobe. 'But I wanted to come home as well. Haven't seen you folks for a long time, have I?'

'Is everything all right?' asked Tess, looking at her sister's averted face.

'You're always asking me that,' Nola answered, with a shrug. 'Everything's fine.'

Chapter Forty-Five

The Requiem Mass for Herta Annaliese Lange was held in the local Catholic church where she had always worshipped. There was a good turnout of mourners, Rena was glad to see. All Mrs Lange's colleagues from the university came, as well as friends from the church, Mr Meldrum from the chemist's, some of the tenants, and even Miss Denny, with Polly and Kennie Wight, from the old days. Yes, they'd seen the notice in the paper, and wouldn't miss the chance to pay their respects to dear Mrs Lange. Such a kind, sweet lady, eh?

There was also Toby Dene, standing at the door of the church, looking, in black suit and tie, like a member of the family Erika didn't have. As soon as she arrived – a forlorn figure, accompanied by the Gillespies – he went forward, ready to take her hand, but at a look from Rena turned aside and allowed her to pass before him into the church.

Tess, keeping her shoulders back and her head high, gave no sign that she had seen him as she walked slowly with her mother and Nola to the front pew, where Erika had asked them to sit.

'You are the nearest thing I have to a family,' she'd told them. 'I'd like you to be with me.'

And as Mrs Lange's coffin was borne up the aisle and the solemn Requiem Mass began, Tess concentrated on thinking only of her.

*

She couldn't escape seeing Toby Dene again though, for when the mourners reached the cemetery for the committal, he was already at the graveside. He must have taken a taxi, she decided, to have arrived so quickly, and wondered at his taking so much trouble for someone he hardly knew. Erika herself had said that his kindness to her was strange.

Strange. As she stood with her family, buffeted by the chill March wind, something colder than the wind entered Tess's heart. Perhaps it wasn't strange at all. Perhaps all his kindness and his trouble added up to just one thing. And as she watched him give his arm to the weeping Erika and saw his face as he looked down at her, Tess knew that she was right. Toby Dene, who had been her beloved, was in love with Erika, her best friend.

Of course, Erika didn't know. It was obvious – she had no idea why he was always with her, always taking her arm, always giving her his support. Her only care at this time was for her mother. All her feelings, her whole being, were centred on her dear Mutti who'd been taken from her. Everyone else, including Toby, would be shadows; only kind, sympathetic shadows. But she was not a shadow to him.

Thank God, he did not come back to Number One for the refreshments Rena had provided after the funeral was over. Tess, who was finding the afternoon hard enough to endure, didn't think she could have borne that.

'Are you all right?' Nola asked her, carrying in a tray of cups. 'You're awful pale.'

'I'm OK. It's been a bit of a strain.'

'You can say that again. Poor Erika looks ready to call it a day. Give us a hand with these, will you?'

It was a relief to have something to do. Pour the tea, hand the sandwiches, mingle with the neighbours, hear about Miss Denny's bridge games, Polly Wight's children, a tenant's engineering course at the university.

And then it was all over. People were thanking Rena and shaking Erika's hand, saying, now, if there was anything they could do, she'd only to let them know. Soon, only Tess, Nola and her mother were left, looking at Erika visibly wilting on her feet.

'Up you go to your bed, pet,' Rena ordered. 'You're fit to drop, anybody can see. Tess, you go with Erika. Give her a hand.'

'No, Tess, it's all right.' Erika managed a smile. 'I can manage.'

'I'm coming anyway,' said Tess.

But Erika was murmuring her thanks again, saying she couldn't have done without them. Mrs Gillespie had been so kind, had done so much, they'd all done so much, and now there was all this clearing up to do, she felt she should help.

'Just take Erika upstairs, Tess,' ordered Nola. 'Tell her there's no need to worry about the washing up. Ma and I will get through it in no time, nae bother.'

'Come on,' said Tess, holding the door.

Mrs Lange's room was as neat as it had always been – Erika had seen to that. As the two young women stood looking round at her chair and work-table, her divan bed with scattered cushions, her coffee pot on its tray, they melted into tears and clung together.

'Oh, Erika,' Tess whispered. 'I'm so sorry, I'm so sorry. Do you want me to stay?'

'I must manage myself, Tess, thank you all the same. Thank you for everything.'

Tess, looking into Erika's drenched dark eyes, knew she could say nothing about Toby. She might have almost felt sorry for him, loving someone so far from reach as Erika, but he'd hurt her too much. It wasn't possible for her to feel sorry for Toby Dene.

She hugged her poor friend again and said goodnight, then ran downstairs, her heart aching, and was glad to be handed a tea towel by Nola so that she could get on with the drying up and need say nothing.

It seemed it was Nola who had something to say, for when everything was tidy again she set three cups of tea on the kitchen table and cleared her throat.

'Making a speech?' asked Rena.

'No, just an announcement.'

Tess and her mother exchanged glances.

'Sounds formal,' said Tess.

'No, it's pretty informal.' Nola took a sip of tea and set down her cup. She seemed strange, rather ill at ease. Not their usual Nola, that was for sure.

'Fact is,' she said slowly, 'I'm here to stay. If it's OK with you. Ma.'

'Stay?' Rena's eyes narrowed. 'What do you mean?

'I mean, I'm no' going back to Leeds. I've left Clark.' Nola gave a short laugh. 'Seemingly, we're all in the same boat then. Three women without men. Who cares?'

Chapter Forty-Six

'Another woman, is it?' asked Rena.

She seemed tired, slumped in her chair. Defeated, at the end of a long, sad day by a crisis that seemed all too familiar.

'What?' Nola was taking out her cigarettes, her blue eyes a little glassy with emotion as she stared at her mother.

'Clark's found someone else. Is that what's wrong?'

'There's no other woman, Ma. Never has been. Clark thinks the world o' me.'

Rena glanced at Tess, who had defiantly lit one of Nola's Craven A's. Och, the silly girl, thought her mother, there she is, smoking again, just because we do. How often had she been told never to get into that habit? But now was not the time to tell her again.

'What's happened then?' Rena asked, turning to Nola. 'What's Clark done?'

Nola hesitated. She lit her own cigarette and blew smoke. 'It's more the way he is.'

'The way he is? How d'you mean?'

'He's no' straight. He's just no' straight.'

There was a silence as Rena and Tess took this in.

'Some sort o' crook?' Rena asked at last.

'Canna believe that,' said Tess. 'Come on, Nola!'

'OK, he doesn't go round wearing a mask, with a bag marked swag,' Nola said impatiently. 'But he's always on the fiddle. It's his way of life. Do you no' remember the eggs he used to bring, Ma? And the chocolate? The whisky for Dad when nobody could get whisky?'

Rena pursed her lips. 'I did have ma doubts,' she admitted.

'More than I did.' Nola's smile was grim. 'Och, I was such a fool. So green! I used to think he was so clever, but all the time he was just a spiv. Dealing with the American GIs, or locals, making money on the black market.'

'That's what he was up to?'

'Aye. Then and now. Well, no' so much now with the black market, because that's faded out, but shady deals. Government surplus fiddles, you ken. Cigarette fiddles, housing fiddles – all that kind o' thing.'

'And when did you find out what was going on?'

'After a couple o' years.' Nola lowered her eyes. 'Should've walked out then, eh?'

'It's no' easy to break up a marriage, Nola,' Rena said uneasily. 'Clark's your husband.'

'I know. I did try to tell him what was in ma mind, but he could never understand what I was on about. According to him, everybody was on the fiddle. What was wrong in making a few quid, same as everybody else?'

'He made more than a few quid though? Got you a nice house?'

'Oh, don't. Don't remind me.' Nola bent her head. 'The one thing I was glad about was that we never had any bairns, and I could get maself a job. Meant I could pay ma own way.'

'Bairns might've helped.'

'No, they wouldn't have helped. With me trying to change their dad and their dad saying no?'

'His folks – were they like him?' asked Tess.

'No, nothing like him. And they never had a clue about him either. Even now they think he's wonderful, especially his ma.' Nola rolled her eyes. 'Oh, her Ralph is just the sweetest, most generous lad in the world! And it's true, he

208

is generous. He likes to please. Brings presents and flowers, gets us anything we want.'

'Always the charmer,' commented Rena.

'Aye.' Nola's eyes suddenly filled with tears. 'He could always get round me. That's why it was so hard – making the break.'

'How did he take it?'

'Oh, he couldn't believe it. Couldn't believe I wasn't happy, with everything he'd given me. After all I'd said, he still couldn't see what was wrong.'

'Did you tell his folks why you wanted to leave?'

'No, I didn't have the nerve. Just made out Clark and me weren't suited. So of course they think I'm crazy. But Clark is sure I'll go back, you ken, once I've tried being away.' Nola gave a faint smile. 'He's got another think coming. I'll never go back.'

They made some cocoa and tried to finish up the sandwiches that were left from the funeral gathering, but the strain of the day was taking its toll and they were too tired to eat.

'You think I've done the right thing, Ma?' asked Nola, looking despondent.

'Sure you have! So don't you go having second thoughts about it.'

'For better, for worse. That's marriage, eh? And I haven't put up with the worse.'

'You gave him more than five years o' your life, and he never deserved it,' Rena told her. 'You've no call to feel bad. I never trusted him anyway.'

'Well, it's done now. I've left him and that's that.' Nola looked into her mother's concerned face. 'If you're sure it's all right for me to stay here for a bit? Till I get a job? Then I could look round for a bedsit, or something.'

'Don't talk so daft! You can have a bedsit here. Soon as one o' the tenants moves out, you can take over. Pay me a bit o' rent, and there you are.'

'Ma, that'd be grand.' Nola touched her mother's hand, then glanced across at her sister. 'In the meantime, Tess, it'll be you and me sharing the attic again, but no' just for me visiting. You won't mind?'

'I'll say what Ma said. Don't talk so daft! Of course I won't mind.'

Nola took a deep breath and stood up. 'So now all I need is a job. Listen, Ma, do you think they'd take me on at the pottery? You know I did some classes in Leeds? I really fancy doing that kind o' work.'

'We'll ask on Monday.' Rena took her key to lock the back door. 'Now, I don't know about you girls, but I'm away to ma bed. It's been a long, weary day.'

'Sorry I had to spring all ma troubles onto you, Ma,' Nola murmured, suddenly putting her arm round her mother's shoulders. 'I know what it's like for you just now, thinking of Mrs Lange.'

'Aye, she's in ma mind. I've lost a good friend and I'll never forget her. Always hang on to your friends, girls, while you can. Now, let's away.'

210

Chapter Forty-Seven

Upstairs in their attic, the two sisters, almost ready for bed, looked at each other a little self-consciously. Things seemed so much the same, yet after the evening's revelations, so subtly different. Nola was still the big sister, the one to lean on, but now, it seemed, vulnerable. Just as vulnerable, perhaps, as Tess.

'Here I am then,' Nola said lightly. 'Back again. For a while anyway, till I get one o' Ma's bedsits.'

'Funny to think o' you as a tenant,' Tess murmured. 'But I don't mind you sharing again, honest.'

'Thing is, everybody likes their own room, and you've had this to yourself for years.'

'I like you being here, Nola, I really do. So move ma stuff up in the wardrobe if you want more space. Though you don't seem to have much with you.'

'I've a trunk coming. Sent it by rail.' Nola laughed. 'Don't worry, I've no' left ma clothes for Clark to sell.'

'Nola! Even Clark wouldn't sell your clothes!'

'No, that's a joke. But he'd sell most things.'

Nola began to brush her hair at the dressing table, while Tess, in her pyjamas, sat on her bed and picked up the little wooden doll Erika had given her for Christmas all those years before.

'Always hang on to your friends,' poor Ma, grieving for her own friend, had told them. 'While you can.'

At least, thought Tess, she still had Erika.

After a moment she returned the Austrian doll to the table by her bed and lay back against her pillow, watching Nola cleaning her face with cold cream. How often she had watched her sister in the past, doing her face, doing her hair, chattering about where she was going, or the fellow she'd be seeing ... The hands of the clock seemed to be turning back fast, but Tess knew it wasn't really so. They weren't the same people, she and Nola, as those two girls of years gone by. Still sisters though.

'Lovely girl, Erika,' Nola was murmuring. 'Even today, when she was crying, she still looked good, eh?'

'She did,' Tess agreed.

'Remember how we used to think her a plain little thing? You'd never say that now.'

'No, we wouldn't.'

'She's so upset about her ma, poor girl, you wonder how she'll ever get over it. But folk do get over things, you ken.' Nola swung round. 'And you'll get over Toby Dene, Tess, and pretty soon too. I guarantee it.'

'I know I will. Just wish I could be over him this minute.'

'Takes time,' Nola said flatly. 'And I need time too, to get over what's happened to me. Or what I made happen, I suppose.' She returned to the mirror, picked up her brush and laid it down. 'Maybe I'll feel better when I get another job. I've great hopes of the pottery.'

'Maybe I'll feel better when I get back to driving,' said Tess. 'Didn't tell you, I've been having driving lessons with a laddie from the garage. Do you remember Ginger Moffat? Likes to be called Luke now.'

'Ginger Moffat.' Nola smiled. 'I remember him. Red hair and freckles. Fancy him teaching you to drive! I'll bet you're a natural.'

'Just what he said. But I still don't fancy taking the test.'

'I passed first time. Clark gave me some lessons, then I went to a school. Always had good cars, Clark, as you might guess.'

212

'Nola, you're talking an awful lot about Clark,' whispered Tess, quietly leaving her bed and padding over to her sister.

'I know, but it hurts, you see, leaving ma home, and even him. I'm glad to be back, I've done the right thing, but I canna help missing what I used to have.' Nola leaned against Tess and let a few large tears slide down her cheeks. 'It's true Clark's no good, but we were happy once. Whatever he's done, we had some wonderful times.'

'It's a shame, the way things've worked out for you,' Tess said soothingly. 'But you'll feel better when you've got used to be being back. You'll slip back into your old life and it'll be grand.'

Nola blew her nose and managed a smile. 'I'm supposed to be cheering you, Tess, and here you are, talking to me like Ma at her best!'

'I don't need cheering. I know I've just got to get through the bad days, and I'll be OK.'

'And you won't say no to chances because of Toby Dene.'

'Chances? What chances?'

'I mean, if you meet someone else, you won't let what happened with Toby put you off?'

'Three women without men, you called us, and that suits me.'

'I'm sorry now I made that joke.'

'Was it a joke then?'

Nola gave Tess a last hug and moved to her bed. 'Maybe no' for Ma and me – I think we'll be happy on our own. But someone'll come along for you, Tess. Just don't turn him away.'

'For now, I'm only taking one day at a time.' Tess jumped into bed and shuddered into her cold sheets. 'That's Ma's advice.'

'Ma at her best again. Tess, it's Sunday tomorrow, you don't have to go to work. Shall we go walking on the sands?'

213

'Yes, that'd be nice. Shame it's no' warm enough yet for the pool.'

'You just want to make me try that wave machine, don't you?'

They laughed, and found it good to feel light-hearted again for a little while. The day had been so hard, so long, it was difficult to think past their troubles. But they would come through, Nola thought, yes they would, she'd make it happen. Things would be all right again for all of them, Ma – herself and Tess, with or without men.

'Tess?' she whispered, wanting to tell her, wanting to make sure she'd something to look forward to in the days ahead.

But Tess made no answer. Though once again she had expected to lie awake all night, she had in fact already drifted into sleep.

PART THREE

PART THREE

Chapter Forty-Eight

One day at a time, that was the way to take things, Rena had advised. And that was how Tess, Erika and Nola were facing what they had to face, as the spring and summer of 1952 went by.

It wasn't easy. Erika, always pale, always dressed in black, seemed to have retreated into a protective shell of work and study, while Nola, now training as a decorator at the pottery, had to cope with visits from Clark. He would arrive with flowers, or chocolates, or expensive scent, anything he could think of to please her, and though he never got anywhere, she knew he wouldn't give up trying. Meanwhile, Tess wondered, in spite of herself, how Toby Dene was faring. Had he got over Erika? As she, Tess, was still trying to get over him?

At least she had some good news. She passed her test first time. Of course it was only to be expected, everyone said, but as her mother pointed out, it was sometimes harder to do what folk expected than surprise them.

Anyway, there'd been quite a celebration when she returned to the garage without her 'L' plates. Cheers had gone up, cakes had been brought in, and when Tess kissed Luke on the cheek and made him blush, even Mr Todd had smiled, and Norrie Smith had asked could he be next in the queue?

'Get away with you, Norrie,' Luke had muttered and had

given Tess a special grin. She'd been a little worried at one time, in case he might have been considering her as a substitute for Lorna, but luckily that hadn't happened. When she bought him a tankard as a thank-you present, he'd only given her a friendly hug, which had been a relief. Yet she was truly grateful to him.

'Luke, you're a good friend,' she'd told him. 'And if I ever have enough money to buy a second-hand car, will you vet it for me?'

'You bet!' said Luke.

Autumn arrived. The holidaymakers departed, and the people of Porty could see the colour of their sands again and find a place to sit on the promenade if they didn't mind the chill. They were already talking about next season, which would be Coronation year, when the young queen would likely visit Scotland and that'd bring in the celebrations and a bit of cheer, eh?

And with conflicts still going on in Korea and elsewhere, British lads fighting, Russia plotting behind the Iron Curtain and rationing still in force, they could do with a bit of cheer. Och, they'd surely get back to normal one of these days, but it seemed a long time since the end of the war when they'd thought it would be tomorrow.

Still, the Gillespie girls were beginning to feel better; Erika, too. Time had done its work, Rena said. Always did.

'I do feel happier,' Nola admitted. 'But then Clark's agreed to a trial separation.' She smiled a little. 'About time, too.'

'I don't know that I feel happier,' Tess murmured. 'I've got used to what happened. That's all I dare to say.'

'And Erika's getting used to losing her mother. Have you noticed how much better she's looking these days? Since she gave up wearing her black?'

Yes, it was true. Even if she was smiling only rarely, Erika was, day by day, looking more her old self; particularly, as Nola had said, since she'd given up her mourning. She was even willing to meet Tess occasionally for a light lunch, or to go walking at the weekends.

On a blustery day in late October, Tess went to Meldrum's in her lunch hour to call for Erika. They had arranged to go to Bridie's for something on toast, now that Tess no longer minded going to to the café where she'd first had tea with Toby. Sometimes she still thought of the happy, naïve girl she'd been that day, so unaware of what lay ahead, and when she did think of her, always made a little promise to herself that she would never again be like her.

The chemist's shop was in the High Street, an old-fashioned-looking establishment that still had the coloured medicinal bottles in its window, and yet, according to Erika, was very up to date and efficiently run by Mr Meldrum. Tess knew that he thought most highly of Erika and had been very kind to her, especially in his encourage-ment of her ambitions to enter medicine. But who wouldn't think highly of Erika? You only had to look at her to see that she was clever. Practically a doctor already, in Tess's view.

She tried the shop door, thinking it might be locked, for Mr Meldrum always closed for lunch between twelve and one, but the door was open and, as she entered, she heard its bell ring. The only customer heard it too, and leaped away from the assistant he had been kissing. But there was really no point in Toby Dene's doing that, was there? When Tess had already seen him. And had seen Erika, too.

'Oh, Tess,' whispered Erika, breaking the long, long silence that had held the three of them fast. Her dark eyes were enormous, her face as white as her overall which she had not yet removed. No doubt Toby had arrived unex-pectedly, for she would never have let him come to the shop when Tess was due. But there'd been nothing unex-pected about that kiss.

219

'Tess—' began Toby, taking a step towards her, and she saw that his brown eyes were full of that compassion she so much resented. 'Tess, please try to understand.'

'I've only been seeing Toby lately,' Erika said quickly. 'Only for a few weeks, that's all.'

'You never told me.'

'Yes, but I was going to tell you. I mean, we didn't want to have any secrets. It was just that we didn't want to hurt you.'

'These things happen,' Toby murmured.

'Happened a long time ago for you,' said Tess. 'Back at the hospital when Mrs Lange was ill, wasn't it?'

A flush rose to his cheekbones. 'Yes, that's true. I did fall in love with Erika then. But I didn't say anything. How could I? Erika was grieving for her mother, I couldn't intrude.'

'Until lately.' Tess turned her eyes on Erika. 'When you gave up your black, was it, Erika? When you started to look better?'

'Tess, I was still thinking of Mutti. I shall always think of her. But Toby came to me and asked me if he could help me – with my studies, you understand – and then, we went out and—'

'You don't need to say any more,' Tess interrupted sharply. 'I'm just wondering why you didn't tell me all this right from the start. I'd guessed how Toby felt about you, but I never dreamed you felt the same for him. Because you never said a word, did you? And you were ma friend.'

'I'm still your friend!' cried Erika. 'Oh, Tess, please don't let this come between us! Oh, I couldn't bear to lose you, I couldn't.'

Tess stood very still for a moment or two, looking from Erika's pleading face, to Toby's sorrowful brown eyes.

'I think I'll be on ma way,' she said at last. 'Never did fancy playing gooseberry.'

As she opened the shop door, the bell rang again, and she turned to look back.

'Should've locked the door, Erika. Would've saved a lot o' trouble.'

She went walking, didn't know where, until she found herself on the beach, the wind tearing at her hair. Everything was grey. Grey water, grey sky, grey silhouettes of industrial workings in the distance. And grey were the thoughts that churned in her mind, as her feet churned through the clogging sand.

All right, Toby had fallen in love with Erika, and though she didn't care for him now as she once had, that still hurt, of course it did. But not as much as knowing that Erika had betrayed her. Erika, her friend, her best friend, who'd been seeing the man she'd loved and never told her.

It had only been lately, for the last few weeks, Erika had protested, as though that made everything all right. As though a few weeks with a lover couldn't be a lifetime. As though Tess herself had had more.

Of course it was probably true that Erika hadn't wanted to hurt Tess. But was that a good enough excuse for acting out a lie?

No! cried Tess, digging her hands in her pockets, still trudging through the sand. No, because she must have known it would all come out one day, and that Tess would then be hurt even more. Which was exactly what had happened.

I can never forgive her, thought Tess. Never. She will never be the same to me, as she once was. So I've lost the man I loved and the friend I cared for. And there was nothing she could do about it. Nothing.

'Good afternoon,' said a young man passing by with a dog.

'Afternoon,' she answered mechanically, not recognising him, but thinking the dog looked like Honey. Couldn't be Honey, because the man wasn't Mr Beith, and soon, anyway, he had thrown a stick for the dog and both were lost in the distance. There were lots of labradors about, of course. It was a very popular breed of dog.

*

After a while, she left the beach and turned towards home. She had no watch, but guessed there was not much left of her lunch hour. Maybe she'd telephone to say she wasn't coming back, didn't feel well. And maybe she wouldn't. To stay away from work, to wallow in her misery, would be to admit that the blow Erika had dealt her was too much for her to take, and she wasn't prepared to do that.

No, she'd go home and ring the garage to say she'd be late. Have a cup of tea and something to eat, if she could swallow it, and carry on as normal. Keep what had happened entirely to herself. Except for Ma and Nola. She would have to tell them, for they'd eventually see Erika with Toby. Everyone would eventually see Erika with Toby, and at that thought Tess gave a sob, but stifled it. The last thing she was going to do was cry.

Ma and Nola still being at work, there'd be no one at home, which would give her a little time to make some tea and pull herself together before she faced the lads at the garage. Oh God, please let Norrie be out somewhere this afternoon, she prayed, letting herself into the house, or at least not making jokes. And please let Luke not ask me if I'm all right, because I might just break down.

Suddenly, on the kitchen stairs, she stopped. She had a sixth sense that someone was there, waiting for her. Ma? Nola? No. They'd have called to her. But someone was there, she knew it.

Very quietly, she pushed open the kitchen door and stopped again. A man was sitting by the table, smoking a cigarette. A man with dark curly hair turning grey at the temples, and bright eyes fixed on her. A man who leaped up, threw away his cigarette and took her in his arms before she could say no.

'Tess,' said her father. 'Oh God, Tess, is it really you?'

Chapter Forty-Nine

Tess pulled herself free and stood staring at Don Gillespie, breathing hard.

'How did you get in?' she asked, at last.

He gave a brief smile. 'I kept ma key. Is this ma welcome then?'

'Welcome?' She sat down, unbuttoning her coat. 'You expect a welcome, Dad?'

'No.' His eyes were fixed on her face, taking in every detail, as though memorising it. 'You've turned into a lovely girl, Tess. Beautiful, in fact.'

'Oh, don't say things like that. Don't bother.'

'I mean what I say.' He suddenly reached out and touched her cheek. 'But are you all right? You seem – I canna say exactly – upset. Have you been crying?'

'No, and I'm fine.' She rose and filled the kettle, glancing at the kitchen clock with sinking heart. 'What are you doing here, Dad? Ma's at work. So's Nola.'

'Nola's here? Is she no' in Leeds?'

'She's split up from Clark and working at the pottery with Ma. Got one of Ma's bedsits as well.'

'Never did like that fella she married,' Don muttered. 'Och, it's no surprise she's left him.'

'So why are you here?' pressed Tess, as the kettle sang.

'I've things to discuss with your mother. I'll just wait till she comes in.'

'Want some tea then?'

'Please.' He lit another cigarette. 'And what are you doing now, Tess? Still the secretarial work?'

She gave him a wry smile. 'I'm in the office at Todd's, as a matter o' fact.'

'Todd's!' Don's eyes widened. 'Why, I was planning to look in there tomorrow! Fancy you being there then!'

'I've got to ring them now. I'm going to be late back from lunch.' Tess made the tea, set out cups and saucers, poured milk into a jug. 'If you don't mind, I'd rather you didn't go to Todd's when I was there.'

'Too embarrassing for you?' he asked grimly.

'Something like that.' She poured the tea and passed him his cup. 'Wait while I telephone.'

'Grand, eh? Your ma getting the phone in?' Don sipped his tea. 'When'd she get that then?'

'April, I think. She'd to wait ages.'

'Changes everywhere.'

'That's right.'

When Tess came back from the phone, she announced that she'd been given the rest of the day off.

'When I told Mr Todd you'd arrived, he said I needn't come back.'

Their grey eyes met and Don's were the first to fall.

'I suppose he thinks me an embarrassment, as well?'

'I don't know what he thinks, but he's a good man to work for.'

'He is.' Don ground out his second cigarette and stood up. 'Tess, I wish I could talk to you. Say the things I want to say—'

'Too late, Dad.'

'Aye.' For some moments, he stood looking at her. 'Tell you what I'll do – I'll walk along to the pottery and see if I can see your mother there. She'll no' want me here when she gets back.'

'Will she want you at the pottery?'

'I'll be discreet.' He put on his jacket that had been hanging on the back of his chair. 'Maybe I'll see Nola as well, eh?'

Tess shrugged. 'You might.'

'Anyway, I'm glad I've seen you, Tess.' Don's voice wavered a little. 'It'll be something to remember.'

She hesitated. 'You're no' thinking o' coming back, are you?'

He shook his head. 'I canna come back, I'm in too deep. In fact, I'm going to ask your ma for a divorce. It's what Val wants, and I think it'd be right.'

'I see.' Tess's lip trembled. 'I never thought you were coming back anyway.'

'Would you have wanted me to?'

'I don't know.' She put her hands to her eyes to hold back the tears, but they came just the same, and her father taking her in his arms again, soothed her and kissed her brow.

'I wish to God I could come back,' he said in a whisper. 'But I've made ma bed and I'll have to lie on it. That's what they say, eh? It's what your ma will say, I ken that.' As he released her and she stood with her handkerchief to her eyes, he tried to smile. 'Don't make the wrong decisions, Tess, eh? Be careful.'

'Oh, I'll be careful,' she sobbed. 'You've taught me to be that.'

Chapter Fifty

When Rena came back with Nola from the pottery, Tess was waiting, strung on wires with nerves.

'Did you see him, Ma? Did you see Dad?'

'Aye, I saw him.' Rena took off her felt hat and smoothed her permed hair with a slightly shaking hand.

'So did I see him,' murmured Nola, whose eyelids were red. 'Got the shock of ma life, when he came seeking me.'

'He'd already seen me,' Rena said curtly. 'We didn't talk long.'

'What did you say, Ma?' asked Tess. 'About the divorce?'

'How d'you know about the divorce then? When did you see your dad?'

'Here, at the house.' Tess, spreading the tablecloth and setting out cutlery, was careful not to say why she had been at the house. 'He'd let himself in. Still has his key.'

'Has he indeed?' Rena sat down heavily and put her hand to her face, which was pale and shiny. 'If I'd known that, I'd have asked for it back.'

'But what did you tell him, Ma? Did you say yes?'

'Aye, I did. Why not? I said, if you can afford a divorce, Don, you can have it. I'm no' interested in hanging on to you, and that's the truth.'

'He must have been pleased you agreed,' Nola commented.

'It's that girl who wants it,' said Tess. 'I don't think Dad does.'

Her mother gave her a long hard stare. 'Did he tell you that?'

'He said he wished to God he could come back.'

Rena turned her eyes on Nola. 'Well. What do you make o' that?'

'I don't know what to make of it, Ma. If he wants to come back, why on earth's he asking for a divorce?'

Rena leaped to her feet and began taking pans from the cupboard, crashing them onto the cooker, sending lids flying.

'He doesn't want to come back!' she cried over her shoulder. 'He'd have said that to please Tess. That's the way he is, always has been. Says anything.'

'Ma, I don't think that's true,' Tess retorted. 'I got the impression he knew he'd made a mistake. I'm sure he does regret leaving us.'

'Well, if he does, there's nothing I'm going to do about it.' Rena shook her head. 'He's made his bed and he can lie on it.'

'He said you'd say that.' Tess blew her nose. 'He said that very thing.'

Her mother gave her another long, considering look, then shrugged. 'Come on, you girls, who's going to give me a hand with this tea?'

A dark cloud hung over the meal, which all three women were glad to finish. No one put it into words, but seeing Don Gillespie again had hit them hard. For Tess, already confused by the day's events, the meeting with her father had proved so emotional, she only wanted to blank it out; as she would have liked to blank out the sight of those kisses between Erika and Toby Dene. There was little chance of that.

While the sisters stacked up the dishes and began the washing up, Rena put on lipstick at the kitchen mirror and

227

announced that she was going with Vera to her weekly whist drive.

'You're still going?' asked Nola.

'And why shouldn't I?'

'Thought you might be too upset.'

'Upset? What gives you that idea? Your dad's got no power to upset me now, Nola.' Rena's newly bright lips set in a thin, hard line. 'He lost that long ago.'

'Well, have a good time then.'

Rena nodded and was putting on her jacket when a light tap sounded at the kitchen door. On the threshold stood Erika.

Oh no, thought Tess, she's in her black again. And wearing her ma's necklace as well. Oh, I canna face her. Why is she here?

'Mrs Gillespie, might I have a word?' asked Erika, her English sounding more accented than usual. 'I hope I am not interrupting?'

In a black sweater and long black skirt, her mother's pendant hanging on her breast, she appeared to have returned to the early days of mourning. Gone was the relaxed, confident girl they'd been seeing lately; back was the waif. But she's got Toby, thought Tess. She needn't be wearing black.

'No, no, pet, that's all right,' said Rena, drawing her into the kitchen. 'What can I do for you?'

Erika's eyes went to Nola, standing with a tea towel in her hand, and then to Tess, who immediately looked away.

'Mrs Gillespie, I am so sorry, but I wish to give notice on my room. I should like to leave next week.'

'Notice? What are you talking about, Erika?' Rena was smiling, though baffled. 'You canna leave here, pet. This is your home. You've been here since you were a bairn.'

'I know, and I am so sad.' Erika was twisting her hands together. 'I cannot tell you how sad. This is my home, you are right, but now I have to leave. I am sorry.'

'But why, Erika? Why? Where are going? Back to Austria?'

228

'Oh no. Only across the city. Someone has found me a room near the university.'

'But I canna understand – why d'you want to go? There must be a reason. You've always been happy here, eh?'

'Very happy.' Erika's voice thickened with emotion. 'I must tell the truth. I do not want to go, but I think it would be best. That is all I can say.'

Rena, looking for help to Tess, saw the expression on her daughter's face and turned back with furrowed brow to Erika.

'Is this something to do with Tess? Have you two had a falling out? Och, that's a piece o' nonsense. You don't leave home because o' that. Come on now, let's sort this out—'

But Erika was already on her way. 'I will see you later, Mrs Gillespie. I will settle up and leave on Saturday. Goodnight, goodnight.'

And she was gone, leaving Rena and Nola staring at Tess, whose face was now scarlet.

'Is it to do with you, Tess?' her mother demanded. 'What have you done then, that Erika wants to leave us?'

'You should've asked Erika what she's done!' cried Tess, stung. 'She's been seeing Toby Dene for weeks and never told me!'

'Seeing? You mean going out with him?' Rena's eyes were glinting. 'I canna believe it. Are you sure?'

'She's a lovely girl,' Nola murmured. 'I thought he was taken with her.'

'But he was Tess's young man. Erika'd never go out with him.'

'Wouldn't she?' asked Tess. 'Well, they're in love.'

'In love? No.' Rena shook her head. 'They don't even know each other, eh?'

'Ma, you saw him at the hospital. You saw him at the funeral. Wasn't he always around Erika? So kind, everybody said.' Tess laughed shortly. 'Yes, very kind.'

'Tess, don't be bitter,' Nola said softly. 'These things happen.'

'His excuse, too.'

'Well, folk do fall in love. It's hard, I know. But you canna blame them, eh?'

'If she'd only told me!' Tess cried stormily. 'But she kept it secret. She let me think everything was just as usual, and all the time she was seeing him.'

'Because she didn't want to hurt you. Tess, you can understand that. She would've told you, in time.'

'You're very understanding of Erika, Nola,' Rena said slowly. 'I agree with Tess. She's in the wrong. She should've made it clear right from the start. I'm glad she's given notice. How could she ever have stayed here with that fellow calling?'

When Rena had finally departed for her whist dive, Tess looked moodily at her sister.

'Never thought you'd take Erika's part instead o' mine, Nola.'

'I'm no' taking her part. I'm just saying I can understand why she didn't want to tell you.'

'I canna forgive her, that's the thing.'

'Should've thought it'd be Toby Dene you wouldn't forgive.'

'He doesn't care for me, but Erika's ma friend. Well, I thought she was.'

'She's still your friend, Tess. When you get to see things straight again, you'll see that.' Nola put her arm round her sister. 'Poor old Tess, you've taken a hammering today, eh? With Dad, an' all.'

'I do feel sort o' bruised. Wouldn't mind a cigarette, if you've got one.'

'Oh, Tess!' Nola clicked her teeth, but took out her cigarettes anyway. 'How did you think Dad was looking then?'

'Older. And sadder.'

'Aye, I thought the same. Getting mixed up with that young woman's done him no good at all. Serve him right, eh?'

230

But neither of Don's daughters took any pleasure in his downfall, if that was what it was.

'You know, when I was on the sands today, I'm sure I saw Mr Seton's dog,' Tess remarked, after a silence. 'But no' with Mr Beith.'

'Who, then?'

'Some other fellow. Didn't know him.'

'Was he a chauffeur?'

Tess drew on her cigarette. 'Couldn't say. I was in such a state, I wasn't taking anything in really. Only, I did think I saw Honey.'

'Must've been somebody standing in for Mr Beith then.'

'Must've been. Oh Nola, I'm so weary!' Tess sighed. 'But if I go to bed early, I'll never sleep.'

'Why don't we go to the pictures then?'

'Wouldn't feel right, going to the pictures.'

'Why ever not?'

'Well, everything's so sad, eh? We've seen Dad, and he's no' coming back, and Erika's let me down—'

'There's a Gene Kelly film I think we'd like. *Singin' in the Rain*. If we go now, we'll get the last showing.'

'OK. Let's try it.' Moving slowly, as though she really was bruised, Tess got up from her chair and put out her cigarette. 'It'll be better than staying here, feeling sorry for maself.'

'That's the ticket. Always used to cheer ouselves up, going to the flicks, didn't we?' Nola grinned. 'Sometimes wish I was back in the box office, you ken. Happy days, eh?'

The sisters ran up the kitchen stairs and left the house for the cinema, arm in arm.

Chapter Fifty-One

A week later, Erika departed. She had kept out of everyone's way until the end, when she paid what she owed Rena and thanked her for all that she'd done, all that she'd been to her mother and herself over the years.

'I shall never forget your kindness to us, Mrs Gillespie,' she said, bravely meeting Rena's gaze. 'Not just when Mutti was ill, but from the very beginning, when we first arrived. You made us feel at home, and I can't tell you how wonderful that was for people like us.'

Rena, for once, was at a loss what to say. She had been so fond of Mrs Lange and young Erika had been almost like another daughter to her. Now Mrs Lange was dead, this sad young girl was departing, and though Rena had been disappointed in her and had even said she should go, she felt a great wrenching sadness at the thought she would probably never see her again. A link with a part of her own life had been broken, and after she'd written out a receipt for Erika's last rent and put it into her hand, she burst into tears.

'Och, what a fool, eh?' She blew her nose. 'It's just that I canna believe you're going, Erika.'

'I know, I know, I can hardly believe it myself.' Erika threw her arms round Rena. 'Things have happened that I never wanted, but I know I should go. I will keep in touch though, if you want me to.'

'Aye, that'd be nice. Now, do you want any help with your luggage? We can give you a hand, you ken.'

'No, no,' Erika said hastily. 'Thank you, no, I can manage. I have a taxi due in half an hour.'

'At least, it doesn't look as though that Toby Dene is coming here for Erika,' Rena told Tess, who had been keeping out of the way in the front room while Erika talked to her mother.

'That's a relief,' muttered Tess.

'So why don't you go up and say a few words to Erika then? Come on now, be forgiving.'

Tess, who had been looking pale and strained for the entire week, said nothing.

'It's true, she should've told you what was going on, and she's been a fool, anyway, to let that young fella sweep her off her feet, but she's that upset, Tess. It'd make all the difference if you spoke to her.'

'All right, Ma.' Tess's voice was low. 'I'll speak to her.'

Erika, still wearing black, was standing in the centre of the room that had been her mother's and, more recently, her own. All their belongings had been cleared away. Some packed into a trunk that had been sent to the new address; some into suitcases now at Erika's feet, with no vestige of Mrs Lange's sweet personality remaining. No cushions, pictures or coffee pot. No photograph of Anton Lange, Erika's father, or snapshots of Erika as a great-eyed school-girl. Nothing but the figure of Erika herself, standing so still, survived to remind Tess of what once had been.

The two young women faced each other, their eyes wary, yet Erika was beginning to smile.

'Oh Tess, you came,' she said softly. 'I'm very glad. I didn't want to go without seeing you.'

'Thought I'd say goodbye,' Tess murmured. 'Though I don't know why you're going. I mean, I never meant you to.'

'I hurt you, Tess, and I'm sorry. It's best I should go.'

'You did hurt me, I canna deny it, but maybe I should've tried to understand.' Tess sighed. 'It was just such a shock, you ken, finding out about you and Toby. I suppose I couldn't take it. And then you'd never told me.'

Erika pressed Tess's hand. 'I should have told you, I see that now, and I'm sorry.'

'You were trying to protect me.' Tess shook her head. 'Thing was, you couldn't. Once you and Toby'd fallen in love, I had to know.'

After an awkward silence, Erika said quietly, 'We never wanted to fall in love. In fact, we fought against it for a time.'

'Seems a funny thing, no' to want love.'

'But it's come too soon, you see. We have our careers to think about. I am applying to medical school next year, and Toby is in the middle of his studies.'

'No room for love then?' asked Tess.

She knew it wasn't true, and from the light in Erika's eyes, so did she.

'Must be nearly time for your taxi.' Tess bent to pick up one of the suitcases. 'I'll take this down for you.'

'Oh Tess, is this goodbye then?' Erika's face was suddenly anguished. 'But we can meet sometimes, can't we? I'll still be working at Meldrum's, you know.'

Tess hesitated. 'Let's see how things go, eh?'

Erika lowered her eyes. 'Well, I've left my address with your mother. If you want to, you can get in touch.'

'OK. Want a last look round?'

'A last look round.' Erika swallowed hard. 'Yes, I'll take a last look round.'

'See you downstairs then.' Tess, knowing that Erika was now thinking of her mother, left her to herself in the room that had been her home for so many years, and now was empty of more than possessions.

Just before the taxi was due Rena had come up from the

kitchen to say goodbye, and Nola had come running from the High Street where she'd been shopping on her afternoon off.

'Caught you!' she cried, giving Erika a hug. 'Now, you take care, eh? And don't forget where we live.'

'Nola, you're very kind. You've always been very kind to me.'

'Even when I was like your big sister?' Nola smiled and stepped back as it was Rena's turn to kiss Erika's cheek, and then Tess, who was presenting herself as very calm, very matter of fact, but who was looking rather woebegone all the same.

'Tess, you will keep Heidi?' asked Erika.

'Heidi? Ma doll? Yes, why shouldn't I?'

Erika smiled uncertainly. 'I thought you might want to throw her away. You haven't thrown her away, have you?'

'No, of course not.' Tess, who, in her lowest moods, had thought of it, laughed at the very idea. 'I'll keep her in memory of our good times, eh?'

'You make it sound as though I'm going a long way away.'

'Well, you are, aren't you?' Tess held Erika close and let her go. 'Goodbye then, and good luck.'

'Here's the taxi!' cried Nola. 'All the best, Erika.'

'Where to, miss?' asked the driver, stowing away Erika's luggage.

'Seven University Street, please.'

Erika slowly climbed into the taxi, looked back once and was driven away, as the Gillespies watched and waved.

'Seems pretty upset to be going,' observed Nola when the taxi had disappeared into traffic. 'End of an era for her, eh?'

'Us too,' said her mother. 'First her ma gone, now Erika. I canna believe it. But at least we were all nice and friendly at the last. You did well, Tess.'

'You did,' Nola agreed. 'Have you forgiven her then?'

'I suppose so. I think she made a mistake, but she didn't mean to hurt me.'

'Took your laddie though,' Rena murmured. 'Now, I'd never have thought she'd do that.'

'Wasn't mine, was he?' Tess turned away. 'Och, it's cold. Let's go in.'

Chapter Fifty-Two

Rena had decided to have a television set after all. It was true, she liked going to the pictures, but you couldn't go to the pictures every night, whereas the telly was on every evening and had the news, and shows, and cookery, and that sort of thing. And then there was the Coronation coming next year. It'd be nice to have a set for that.

'You could hire one at first,' Nola suggested. 'That's what Clark's done.'

'Aye, and so has Vera. Seemingly, these tellies have a tube that's awful dear if it goes wrong. Maybe it'd be safer to hire then, and the stores have got some good offers.'

On the following Saturday afternoon, Tess was asked if she'd like to go with her mother and Nola to look at the sets, but she said she'd rather walk on the sands, get some fresh air.

'All alone?' asked Nola.

Tess shrugged. 'I don't mind being alone.'

She did some window shopping first, carefully avoiding Mr Meldrum's shop, for though she'd parted on good terms with Erika, she didn't really want to see her. She missed her, or more accurately, missed their old friendship, but still didn't want to see her. Or Toby Dene, of course. Luckily, he was no longer in Porty.

On that chill autumn afternoon, there were very few

people on the beach and she could walk where she liked, looking far ahead, her hands in her pockets, her hair as usual blowing free.

Suddenly she saw Honey, who came bounding up, waving her great sandy tail, and when Tess raised her eyes from patting her, she found a stranger looking down on her. It was the man she had seen with Honey before, the one who wasn't Mr Beith, although she could see now that he was wearing a dark suit like Mr Beith's, and a peaked cap. A chauffeur then? Mr Seton's chauffeur? But where was Mr Beith?

She straightened herself and gave a small nod as the man politely said, 'Good afternoon.'

'You're with Honey?' Tess asked, as Honey herself moved off on an interesting trail across the sand.

'Yes, I'm with Honey.' He smiled and touched his cap. 'I'm Rob MacNair. Chauffeur to Mr Seton.'

'What's happened to Mr Beith?'

'You knew him? He's retired.'

'I never heard that.' Tess pushed her hair back from her face. 'Yes, I knew him. I often saw him out with Honey.' She looked back along the beach. 'I live past the power station, at the top of the King George Road. My name's Tess Gillespie.'

'I'm very pleased to meet you.'

Rob MacNair put out his hand and after a moment's hesitation Tess shook it. Talking to a stranger – maybe she shouldn't be. Rena had always said not to, though Porty was safe enough. Perhaps the chauffeur guessed what was going through her mind for he said he must catch Honey, she was running too far ahead. Yet he still lingered, looking at Tess as she looked at him.

He was a tall man, with dark-blue eyes under level brows. When he took off his cap, she saw that there was a touch of copper in his light-brown hair, but nobody would have called him 'Ginger'. Probably nobody would ever have called him anything he didn't like, for there was

238

something very strong about him – in the way he held himself, in the set of his jaw. Not the sort, perhaps, who would want to be a chauffeur, but then maybe he just liked driving the Daimler. She wouldn't have minded driving that herself.

'Well, better get on,' he said after a moment, and replaced his cap. 'Nice to have met you, Miss Gillespie.'

They exchanged smiles and after a moment he left her, whistling to Honey, and she watched him go. It was hard to guess his age but she put him in his late twenties. Had he a wife, she wondered, waiting for him in the chauffeur's quarters at Pax House?

Somehow she didn't think so; he didn't have the look of a married man to her. Turning up one of the ways that led from the sands to the town, she laughed at herself. As though she knew what made a man look married!

'Did you get one?' she asked her mother when she got home. 'A telly?'

'Aye, we rented one,' Rena told her. 'It's coming on Monday.'

'Ah, I was looking forward to seeing it tonight.'

'Well, you'll have to be patient.' Rena, smiling sunnily, seemed pleased with herself. 'Got good terms, didn't we, Nola? I think it'll no' break the bank and will be nice to have.'

'Did you have a good walk?' Nola asked Tess. 'You've lovely rosy cheeks.'

'Aye, it was grand on the beach. Tell you who I saw? The new chauffeur from Pax House.'

'New chauffeur?' Nola stared and Rena frowned.

'Why, what's happened to Mr Beith?' she asked.

'He's retired. He was beginning to look a bit elderly, Ma.'

'Fancy us no' hearing though!'

'Fancy you no' hearing, Ma.' Nola smiled. 'Missed that on the Porty telegraph, eh? What's this new fellow like then, Tess?'

'Seems nice. Youngish. Well, late twenties.'

'Youngish? I like your cheek! I'm no' far off the late twenties maself.'

'And how did you get to speak to him?' asked Rena.

'Oh, you ken how it is. Honey ran up and then he came up and just passed the time o' day. Said his name was Rob MacNair.'

'Have to be careful, you ken, getting into conversation with strangers.'

'I knew you'd say that, but he'll no' be a stranger long, will he? If he's come to live at Pax House?'

'Sounds like he's no' a stranger to you anyway,' murmured Nola, but Tess refused to rise to her teasing and no more was said.

Later though, Tess thought of the chauffeur again. She had said he seemed nice, but perhaps 'nice' had been the wrong word. Made him sound less strong. But then how did she know if he was strong or weak? And did it matter? If she saw him again, it would only be to speak to in passing, as one did to people walking on the sands.

Chapter Fifty-Three

Tess did see Rob MacNair again. It was on Sunday afternoon two weeks later, when she and Nola were walking
briskly down the promenade eating what would probably be
their last ice-cream before the winter set in, while back at
home Rena sat, charmed, before her new television set.

'Is it no' a marvel?' she had asked as usual before they
went out. 'How they'd ever invent such a thing?'

'Don't get carried away, Ma,' Nola told her. 'There's
life outside the telly, you ken.'

'Aye, and sometimes it's nice to forget it,' Rena
retorted.

'I'm glad Ma's so pleased with her telly,' Tess
murmured as they bought their ices. 'She needs to be
cheered up.'

'And she was doing so well till Dad turned up and asked
for that divorce,' said Nola. 'Since then, not another cheep
out of him. Och, once it's all settled she'll be herself again.'

They reached Pax House, and of course paused to look
in at the gates, then Tess stiffened. A tall figure in uniform
had appeared at the front door, with Honey and an elderly
man.

'Let's move on,' she said hastily, anxious not to be seen
looking like a child with an ice-cream cornet.

'That'll be Mr Seton,' Nola whispered. 'And is that the
new chauffeur?'

'Yes, but let's go, eh?'

Rob MacNair had seen them, however, and touched his cap before giving his arm to his employer, who was leaning on a stick, while Honey circled round wagging her tail. Tess, managing to smile in acknowledgement, pushed Nola forward by the elbow, so that they could be on their way by the time Rob and Mr Seton had reached the promenade. It seemed they were going for a walk for there was no car in evidence, and when Tess looked back she saw Mr Seton gingerly approaching the steps to the beach while still holding Rob's arm.

'Honestly, Tess, what's the rush?' asked Nola. 'We might have had a word with them. I've always wanted to meet Mr Seton.'

'He'll no' want to see us, Nola.'

'I've got the feeling the chauffeur might.'

'Well, I don't want to see anybody when I'm eating this ice-cream. Why ever did we buy ices? It's too cold for ice-cream anyway.'

Nola gave her sister a thoughtful glance. 'Mr MacNair is quite good looking, isn't he? Is he married?'

'I've no idea. And don't care.'

'Oh Tess, you promised me you wouldn't pass up your chances if any came along!'

'I don't remember promising anything.' Tess, having finished her ice-cream, wiped her sticky fingers on her handkerchief and quickly replaced her gloves, for the late autumn day was bleak. 'I wish you wouldn't always tease me, Nola. You were the same about Toby Dene, and it's just hurtful, that's all.'

'I'm sorry, Tess.' Nola took her arm. 'I don't mean to upset you, and I'm no' really teasing. I only want you to have your chance for happiness.'

'I'm all right as I am and you must admit, trying to match me up with a fellow I don't even know is a bit ridiculous.'

Nola laughed ruefully. 'Put me down as your crackpot

sister, eh? All right, I promise, no more matchmaking.'

'Unless I find somebody for you.'

'Oh no.' Nola's laughter died. 'I'm like you. I'm all right as I am.'

Rob MacNair's name cropped up again, however, when they were having Sunday tea. Rena, passing her soda scones, said she'd been talking to Mr Seton's housekeeper, who of course knew all about the new chauffeur.

'Met Miss Turner at the butcher's. She's Mrs Fleck's niece, you ken – a very nice, sensible woman, an' all. Usually gets her orders delivered, but she was picking up some extra chops – always does well with the rations, of course—'

'Ma, what did she say about the new chauffeur, then?' asked Nola.

'Well, she said he was a very pleasant laddie. Seemingly, he comes from over Haddington way, where his dad was a farmer, but his parents are dead now. His brother's got the farm, but Miss Turner says Mr MacNair'd never want to do farming. Och no, he's too fond o' cars!' Rena laughed. 'Like you, Tess.'

'All right, I like cars. Nothing wrong with that. Was Mr MacNair in the army?'

'Yes, with the King's Own Scottish Borderers. Told Miss Turner he'd enjoyed it. Well, being a bachelor, he'd nobody at home to worry about.' Rena's face darkened. 'Not that everybody worried about the folk back home.'

Nola and Tess looked at their plates without speaking. Rena poured more tea.

'Never heard another thing from your dad, you ken. Does he want a divorce, or doesn't he?'

'I expect the lawyers are taking their time, Ma, sending the documents, or something,' said Nola.

'Well, it's him paying for them, no' me, and I hope he's happy.'

'And you think I should get involved with somebody

243

again?' Tess asked her sister when their mother had retired to watch a programme of hymns on the television, and they were washing the tea things. 'Be made miserable like Ma?'

'She's no' always miserable. She's bounced back well until now.'

'Let's hope she bounces back again then. I feel so angry with Dad, no' getting in touch.'

Some days later, a letter arrived for Rena from Don. He was very sorry he'd troubled her but Valerie had said not to bother about the divorce. It would be a lot of expense and a long-drawn-out business, so they'd leave it for now. He sent his regards to them all.

'Regards!' cried Rena. 'I'd give him regards!'

But it seemed to her daughters that she was happier now that she knew where she was again. She hadn't wanted Don back, but at the same time had not wanted all the difficulties of a divorce in her life, never having been one for washing dirty linen in public. Now they could keep the status quo and get back to things being nice and peaceful.

'What a relief,' sighed Nola. 'I think I'll leave ma life as it is too. For the present anyway.'

'That goes for me too,' said Tess.

Chapter Fifty-Four

Tess made no conscious decision to avoid Rob MacNair, but during the next few weeks did not go back to the sands. It was, after all, late November and not good weather, and then she had her Christmas shopping to do whenever she had free time.

So she argued, quite satisfactorily and in straightforward fashion, to herself, until she saw Rob again one Saturday afternoon in Logie's. She had been idly looking around, not planning on buying anything for Logie's prices were beyond her, when she came face to face with him in the middle of Perfumery. And then nothing seemed straightforward any more.

Of all the places to see him though! A tall man, hatless and wearing a dark raincoat, marooned in Logie's, a place about as different in spirit from Porty beach as it was possible to be. And how lost he looked! Tess almost smiled. It seemed likely that the atmosphere of sophisticated Logie's had sapped his strength more easily than his enemies had managed to do during the war.

'Mr MacNair,' she said quietly, wondering if he would recognise her. 'This is a surprise.'

'Miss Gillespie!' His dark-blue eyes lit up; he recognised her all right. 'Ah, you're a lifebelt to a drowning man. I'm trying to find a present for ma sister-in-law. You wouldn't be able to help me, would you?'

'I could try. But I don't know what she'd like.'

'She runs the farm with ma brother, beyond Haddington. Works hard, doesn't get many pretty things. They've invited me for Christmas and I want to get her something nice.'

'Well, I'm sure we can find her something special, but this shop is awful dear, you ken. Do you no' think you might be better off trying at John Johnson's, or somewhere like that?'

'I don't know one damn' thing about Edinburgh shops,' he confessed. 'You think I'd do better somewhere else?'

'I think you could get better value for money.'

'I don't like to ask you – I mean, it's a bit of a cheek, eh? Taking up your time? But would you go with me to this other shop?'

'I'd be glad to, Mr MacNair.'

'Rob, please.'

'Well, you know ma name is Tess. Teresa, really, but everyone calls me Tess.'

'Tess,' he repeated softly. 'I hadn't forgotten.'

'J.J.'s is just over on the North Bridge,' she told him, when they left Logie's and were battling through the crowds of shoppers on the pavements. 'No' very far.'

'Maybe I can give you a cup of tea there?'

'That'd be kind. There's a nice orchestra plays in the tea room.'

'That's for us then.'

He did not take her arm as they crossed from the east end of Princes Street and made for the North Bridge, but she was very much aware of him walking beside her. Aware too that his gaze was often upon her, though she didn't return it. He was attracted to her, she knew it, and tried to pretend to herself she felt no attraction towards him. It would be a terrible thing to get involved again. To risk more heartache, just when she'd finally become free of love.

When they reached the vast department store of John Johnson's, usually known as J.J.'s, Rob put his hand to his brow and said he already felt tired.

'These places, Tess, they knock the stuffing out of me. Can we go for tea now?'

'No, we get the present first. Then we have tea.'

'Slave driver!'

'Cheer up, it won't take long. You were in the perfumery department at Logie's. Were you thinking of scent for your sister-in-law?'

'Well, Katie'd never buy anything like that for herself, and I think she'd like it.'

'You could get her a nice box, with scent and hand cream, and bath stuff all together, eh? They've got plenty to choose from here.'

'You choose, eh?' Rob took out his wallet. 'I'll just pay.'

When they had settled on a prettily packed box from the cosmetics counter, and the assistant had given them a carrier for it, Tess smiled approvingly at Rob.

'Now we can have our reward. All we have to do is find a table in the tea room.'

'I'll find a table,' he said confidently.

Sure enough, he did. He's the type, thought Tess, to get what he wants, and was not surprised when the queue at the tea room seemed to melt away and a waitress was soon showing them them to a table, and a window table – at that. As the little orchestra played its selections from *Annie Get your Gun* in the background, and Tess poured the tea that had speedily arrived, she put her thoughts into words.

'Am I right, Rob, you're the sort to get what you want?'

'Me? No!' He selected a cake from the stand on the table. 'What makes you say that?'

'I'm no' sure. There's just something about you, I suppose.'

'I'm flattered.' He gave a short laugh. 'Haven't got ma own business, have I? That's something I want. Haven't been lucky in love.'

'I'm really surprised to hear that.'

'Flattering me again, Tess?' His dark-blue eyes were steady. 'Och, it was just one o' those things. A girl I met in the war – found somebody else.'

'Same thing happened to me,' Tess said quietly. 'The man I cared for – fell in love with ma friend.'

'Tess, I'm sorry.' Rob stretched out his hand and covered hers. 'Has it put you off? Caring, I mean, for anyone else?'

'Yes. Yes, it has.'

'Did me, for a while.' His warm, strong hand caressed hers. 'But not now.'

Tess gently removed her hand from his. 'I don't want to be hurt again.'

'You have to believe you won't be.'

'You can never be sure.'

'No, you have to take a chance.' Rob pushed his cup across the table. 'May I have some more tea, please?'

As Tess poured it, he watched her carefully.

'Sometimes you can be pretty sure, though, that you'll be all right.'

'Maybe.'

When they left the department store, it was already dark. Lights were on in all the shops and strung across the North Bridge, from where the view across the city to the castle on its rock was dramatic.

'May I take you home, Tess?' asked Rob.

'Oh yes, we can get the tram.'

'I was thinking, maybe we needn't go straight back. We could go to a film perhaps?'

Tess hesitated. 'I'm expected back. I'm sorry.'

'You've got something planned?' As she said nothing, he sighed. 'Or you just don't want to come?'

'I do! But – well – maybe we could make it another time.'

'All right, I understand. We'll get the tram.'

248

'You're no' mad at me?'

He grinned in the lighted dusk. 'I'd never be mad at you, Tess. I'm disappointed, that's all.'

'I don't like disappointing you.'

'Never mind about it. Come on, let's go back.'

On the tram to Portobello, leaning close to Rob's firm shoulder, Tess remembered travelling with Toby Dene, and of how he'd joked about the Snow Queen and her icy heart, and of how they'd laughed together. It occurred to her that Toby was very boyish compared with Rob, who was so much the man she couldn't imagine his ever joking about Hans Andersen stories. What of it? That was the way he was. Maybe that was the way she wanted him to be.

'You haven't told me what you do,' Rob suddenly remarked. 'I mean, where d'you work?'

'At Todd's Garage.'

'Todd's Garage?'

'In the office.'

'Ah.' He smiled. 'I was going to say, couldn't see you repairing the cars.'

'I'd quite like to repair cars as a matter of fact.'

'Would you?' Now his smile was indulgent. 'Girls aren't usually interested in what's under the bonnet.'

'We're no' all the same, you ken. Girls, I mean.'

'Of course not.' He took her hand and held it. 'I apologise.'

'Ma father used to work at Todd's.' Tess looked down at their clasped hands. 'He left us a long time ago. Ma and me, and Nola, ma sister – we don't see him now.'

'That must've been hard.'

'We don't talk about it.'

They swayed together as the tram took a corner and were silent for a time, until Rob told her that he too had worked in a garage before he was called up and after he was demobbed. He had wanted to get as much experience as possible, because one fine day he definitely wanted to start a business involving cars. He wasn't sure yet what sort of busines it would be. Might be repairs, might be driving.

'That's why you went to work for Mr Seton?' asked Tess. 'To get the driving experience?'

'Yes, though I'd already driven for a chap in Haddingon. When he went down to England, I applied for the job at Pax House. Smashing Daimler there, Tess. It's a post-war model, you ken. Mr Seton replaced the old one when I started working for him.' Rob gave a happy sigh. 'I really love that car.'

'I've only seen it in the distance. Will you show it to me some time?'

'Sure I will. If it was mine, I'd take you out in it.' He smiled wryly. 'But of course it's Mr Seton's.'

'Mr Seton's no' so well, is he?'

'He's not. I have to do a lot for him, but he's a good chap. Been very kind to me.'

They had reached their stop and left the tram, walking now arm in arm, and enduring the cold wind blowing in from the Forth.

'This is where I stay,' Tess said nervously at the steps to Number One. 'Fine view of the power station, you'll notice.'

'Aye, I've noticed. Walked up the King George Road one day with Honey. The road to the sands, Mr Seton said it was called in the old days.'

'You came up ma road?'

'Thought I might have seen you. Remember, you told me where you lived.' Rob shrugged as he looked down at her. 'Given maself away, haven't I? Let you know I wanted to see you again?'

'I'm the one to be flattered now,' Tess said, trying to laugh.

'But you don't mind? No, don't answer that.' Rob took a step or two away. 'Look, I'd better be getting back. No' far to go, have I?'

'Rob – wait!' Tess kissed him on the cheek. 'I'm sorry

250

about tonight. I should've said yes. But if you want to, I'd like to go out with you again.'

'Like to?' He swept her into his arms and kissed her hard and strong. 'Tess, just tell me when.'

Chapter Fifty-Five

They went to the pictures the following Saturday, holding hands in the back row, and spooning up ice-cream from cardboard tubs in the intermission. Tess told Rob they were like the young folk she used to see as a child, when her sister let her have free seats at the cinema where she worked.

'Nola was in the box office, you ken. She always said it was OK for me and ma friend to go in for nothing, but we were always scared we'd be in trouble.'

'And you saw all the young lovers in the back seats? Dare say they'd think me an old man.'

'Why, how old are you then?'

'Twenty-eight.'

'And I'm twenty.'

'Only twenty?' Rob gave a sigh. 'No' too young for me, are you?'

'Too young?' Tess laughed. 'Some o' thae kids I used to see would call me getting on.'

Rob laughed with her and squeezed her hand. 'Tell me about your sister with the pretty name. Was she the one I saw with you outside Pax House?'

'Yes, that was Nola. It's Finola, really, an Irish name. Ma gran had some Irish cousins, and Nola was called after one o' them. She's a few years older than me, but we get on very well.'

'There's just the two of you?'

Tess told him of Rickie, who had died when he was little, and Rob shook his head in sympathy. What could be worse than the death of a child? Still, Tess had her sister. Was Nola married?

'She's separated.' Tess gave a little shrug. 'We seem to be an unlucky family, eh?'

The lights were dimming, the curtains were parting from the screen, but Rob, taking Tess's hand again, whispered urgently,

'Don't say that, Tess. Don't say you're unlucky.'

She made no reply, keeping her eyes straight ahead as Rob kept his on her, and as the opening titles of the second film began to roll up on the screen, wondered if she could believe him.

When they kissed again, many times, outside the door to Number One, the pleasure was intense, yet bittersweet, for she knew she was moving into his power and would be vulnerable as she had been before. Yet when he asked if they could walk on the sands next day, as Mr Seton didn't need him till evening, she immediately agreed. Maybe she should have drawn back, taken more care, but there'd have been no point. She'd drawn back the week before and had simply ended up seeing Rob again, for the truth was, she wanted to see him. Wanted to be with him with a longing that consumed her more completely than she had ever thought possible.

She didn't tell her mother that, of course, or Nola, and if they saw something in her face after she'd left Rob and run into the house, they were strangely understanding and made no effort to interrogate her on her evening out. Her mother did say that she would like to meet Mr MacNair some time, but Tess said it was far too soon to think of that.

'Just as you like then,' Rena said 'Nae bother. Now, do you want to watch the telly for a bit, or have your cocoa?'

'Oh, I'll just have ma cocoa and get to ma bed, I think.'

'Me too,' said Nola.

'What's got into you?' asked Tess, when she and her sister were upstairs. 'Where's all the teasing about Rob MacNair?'

'I did say I'd give it a rest, didn't I?'

'I was sure you and Ma would go on at me about him, because I've been out with him.'

'We want you to be happy, Tess, that's why we didn't say anything,' Nola told her seriously. 'We don't want to spoil things.'

'Who says there's anything to spoil?'

'Come on, Tess, you're no' being straight. This Rob MacNair is special, I can tell. Are you are seeing him again?'

'Yes, he's asked me, and I said yes.'

'That's good, you're showing a bit o' sense at last.' Nola smiled widely. 'But bring him in to see us some time, eh?'

'I'll see how things go,' said Tess.

Chapter Fifty-Six

They were to meet at the end of the road to the sands at half-past two. Tess, dressed in dark winter coat, scarlet scarf and matching beret, was there on time, but not before Rob, who was already waiting. A thin winter sun showed the copper in his hair, for he was out of uniform and wore no cap. When he moved to greet her, accompanied by a joyous Honey, she thought how young he seemed that day, and how handsome. Perhaps he was happy? Hadn't Erika said once that happiness made people good looking?

Oh, I hope he's happy, being with me, thought Tess.

'No cap?' was all she asked though, for she'd been suddenly seized by nerves. This afternoon should be no different from any other at this time on Porty beach. Just a winter walk on heavy sand, a look to the Forth and the wide sky, then a rush for home to get out of the cold. Yet, the way she felt meeting Rob, she knew it would not be like that. No, something would happen, but she didn't know what.

'Have to wear a cap so often, I don't wear one if I needn't,' he told her, taking her hands. She wore gloves, he didn't, yet she imagined she could still feel the warmth of his hands.

'I don't see what's wrong with wearing a cap,' she murmured.

'My cap's a private service cap. That's what's wrong with it.'

'Don't you like working for Mr Seton? I thought you said he'd been very good to you.'

'So he has, but he's still the master.' Rob shrugged. 'I don't want a master, I don't want to be in service. As I said, I want ma own business.'

'I can understand that.'

'Aye. But that's enough about me.' He took her arm. 'Haven't come out with you to talk about me. What'd you like to do then?'

'Aren't we just going to walk on the beach?'

He looked down the length of the sands where other people were braving the wind, and shook his head.

'Wish we could be on our own, Tess. There are too many folk here. Eyes everywhere.'

That was true. Even had the beach been empty, there would have been eyes from people on the promenade, or at the windows of the houses. Or they'd have thought there'd be eyes, which was the same thing.

'What I need is ma own car,' Rob muttered. 'I daresay Mr Seton'd lend me the Daimler if I asked him, but I never have. Like I said, it's his car, no' mine.'

'I'm saving for a car,' Tess told him as they began to walk slowly along the beach, watching Honey chasing some mysterious scent. 'I passed ma test first time, you ken.'

'Did you?' He looked down at her and smiled. 'That was excellent, Tess. First time, eh? Who taught you?'

'Fellow I know at Todd's. He was really good.'

'Should have been me who taught you. This fellow – is he an admirer?'

'No, he's getting over an unhappy love affair.'

'Didn't stop him taking you driving.'

Tess stared. 'We're just friends, Rob.'

'You think I'm jealous?' He gave a rueful grin. 'I know I've no right to be.'

'I don't even spend time with Luke now. I've finished ma driving lessons.'

'Sorry.' He pressed her hand. 'Look, we canna talk here,

256

the wind's too strong. Shall we go up to the promenade?'

'It'll be windy up there too. And there won't be anything open, it's Sunday.'

Rob laughed. 'Good job we've got each other, eh? Come on, we can always sit in a shelter. Honey! Honey! Come on, girl!'

'Oh, not there, Rob!' Tess cried, halting at the shelter they had reached, which was where she had sat with Toby and heard him say he didn't want her love.

'Why, what's wrong with it?' he asked curiously, but as she met his dark-blue eyes, she only shrugged and smiled.

'Nothing, if it's empty.'

'You can see it is.'

'Well then, it's OK.'

It was an effort at first to enter the glass-walled shelter, but as she and Rob sat close together, with Honey panting at their feet, it was a relief to find the image of Toby fading. Real-life Rob had ousted him; she should have realised that he would.

'There, we're out of the wind anyway,' said Rob. 'Quite pleasant really.' He turned his head. 'See Pax House? It's just a step or two away.'

'Ma favourite house,' Tess told him. 'When I was little I used to think I'd like to live there. 'Of course, I only saw the outside.'

Rob's smile was gentle. 'One day I'll take you inside. I'll introduce you to Mr Seton.'

'Rob, you wouldn't!'

'Aye, why not? I'm sure he'd like to meet you. After all, I'm going to show you his Daimler. Why not see his house and meet him too?'

'I canna believe it,' she said, laughing lightly, as outside their glass shelter the mist began to roll in from the water, and the light began to fade. 'You seem to be able to open all the magic doors.'

'You like being with me though?' he asked softly. 'Even without the magic doors?'

257

'Yes. Yes, I do.'

'I think we get on well, eh?'

She nodded, looking deep into his eyes.

'Haven't known each other all that long, but I think about you a lot.' He smiled cautiously, as though he wasn't sure how she'd take his words. 'From the first time we met, to tell you the truth.'

'When we talked on the sands?'

'Before that. Weeks ago now. Perhaps you don't remember seeing me? I walked past you with Honey. You looked so lost.'

Tess bit her lip. She knew how she must have looked that day.

'Lost,' Rob repeated. 'But so lovely. I wished I could see you again. I wished I could get to know you.'

'Well, you did.'

'Yes, I was lucky. Still am lucky, because you're here with me now.'

'It's nice of you to say that.'

'Nice? Selfish, maybe. I'm thinking maself lucky, but how do you feel, Tess? Do you want to keep on seeing me?'

'Rob, you know I do.'

'Even if it means taking a risk?'

She was silent, the colour rising to her brow. Don't make the wrong decisions, her father had said. Right or wrong, she knew what she wanted.

'The risk wouldn't be just for you, Tess. I've been hurt, too.'

'I'd never hurt you, Rob!' she cried passionately.

'If we kept on seeing each other, the risk'd be there though, for both of us.' He touched her face gently. 'You did say people could never be sure.'

'And you said they had to take a chance.'

'Well, shall we take the chance then?'

'Do you want to?' she asked huskily.

'Aye. More than anything.'

258

For a long time she looked at him, her eyes in the dusk glittering, before she put her arms about him and held him close.

'So do I, Rob,' she whispered against his face.

They clung together, kissing, for so long that Honey looked up uneasily, then laid her great head on Rob's foot, which made him laugh and finally draw apart from Tess to soothe Mr Seton's dog.

'The mist's coming in fast,' he murmured when he let Honey go. 'Better get you home, Tess, before you're chilled to the bone.'

'You wouldn't like to come in for a minute, would you?' she asked, taking a sudden decision. 'Meet Ma and Nola?'

'What, today?' He looked taken aback.

'Just to say hello. It wouldn't mean anything.'

'I'm no' saying I don't want to see them – but would they want to see me?'

'They've said so.'

He looked across at Honey waiting impatiently on the promenade. 'We've got Honey.'

'They wouldn't mind Honey.'

'OK then, if you're sure it'll be all right.'

'We'll only be having a cup of tea; of course it'll be all right.'

Arm in arm, they walked out into the mist, while Honey, relieved to be on the move again, barked approvingly and hurried on ahead.

259

Chapter Fifty-Seven

Tess, with astonishing confidence, had told Rob it would be all right just to drop in for tea at her home. When they reached Number One, however, she wasn't so sure. Maybe she should have prepared her mother? It was true she might have then created a huge tea which they didn't want, but as it was she might be thrown into confusion because she hadn't 'a thing in the house', and might not present her best side. Och, too late now to be worrying. They were already on the doorstep.

'Ma!' cried Tess, drawing Rob into the hall, which Honey was already investigating. 'I've brought someone to see you. Nola, are you there?'

'They'll be in the kitchen,' she murmured in an aside to Rob, but of course she'd forgotten about the television and the new lease of life it had given the front room.

Out from that room came Rena, wearing her Sunday dress of dark-blue wool, and beyond her they could see the televison, flickering, and Nola in a pink twinset and pleated skirt, smiling from her seat by the fire.

'Tess!' cried Rena, her eyes sharpening as they went over Rob. 'Why, you've never brought Mr MacNair?'

'I'm afraid she has, Mrs Gillespie,' he said quickly. 'And a rather wet dog.'

'Nae bother, nae bother. Nola, turn off the telly will you? Tess, you'd better introduce us.'

Clearing her throat, Tess performed the introductions, and everyone shook hands and murmured politely, as Honey, looking about this interesting new place, thumped her tail on Rena's faded carpet.

'Just want a cup of tea, Ma, no need to panic,' Tess finished. 'Thing is, Honey here's got sand on her paws. Shall I just take her down to the kitchen and give her a rub?'

'Let's all go down to the kitchen,' Nola suggested. 'We can have tea there; it'll be more convenient. If you don't mind, Rob?'

'Mind about being in a kitchen?' he asked with a grin. 'Suits me fine.'

'I'll just put the guard in front o' the fire then,' said Rena. 'Since I got the telly, I've been lighting a fire in here, you ken, even if it is awful dear. Now, let's away downstairs and I'll see what I've got in ma cake tins.'

Tess, helping to set the table while Rob dried Honey with an old towel, was heaving sighs of relief that everything seemed to be working out well. Her mother was looking nice and being very pleasant, especially as she'd been able to produce a Madeira cake, and Nola was chatting easily as she always did. There was no feeling that Rob was on trial. Even when they sat down to tea, the conversation was general. At least at first.

Rob asked Nola what work she did and she told him she painted pots at the Harebell Pottery.

'Need talent for that, eh?'

'Well, they train you if you're keen. But I'm no' one of the real designers at the moment.'

'You'd like to be?'

'I aim to be. For now, I paint somebody else's patterns on the teapots.'

'And I put on the handles,' Rena said with a laugh.

'I'm sure you're both very talented,' Rob told them gallantly.

'Och, no' me!' Rena laughed again. 'Nola, now, she's a cut above we folk in the handlers' shop, but we all do our best.' She gave Rob more tea. 'Of course, I'm only part time anyway. Tess'll have told you, I let rooms – I've plenty to do here.'

'You've a lovely house, Mrs Gillespie.'

'Thank you. It's nice enough, even if it's no' exactly Pax House, eh? How d'you like working for Mr Seton then?'

'He's a very good employer. Kind and considerate.'

'So you'll likely stay with driving?'

Tess and Nola exchanged glances. Here it comes, their looks said – Ma's interrogation. She had clearly changed her mind about keeping quiet.

Rob was unflustered. 'I enjoy driving, but I'd really like to have ma own business. Something to do with cars.'

'You're like our Tess. She's one for cars.' Rena leaned forward, fixing Rob with her narrow blue eyes. 'Gave up a good job at Appleton's Accountants, you ken, to work in a garage! Would you credit it?'

'Ma,' groaned Tess. 'Don't go on.'

'I can understand the attraction.' Rob smiled across at Tess.

'Well, I did hear from Miss Turner that you weren't interested in farming,' said Rena. 'Your dad's place is out Haddington way, I believe? I'm sorry you lost your folks, Rob, but you've got your brother, eh?'

'Yes, we're quite close. Gordon's married with two wee boys. He took on the farm as tenant when Dad died a couple of years ago.' Rob looked down at his plate. 'My mother died when I was in the army. Always worried about me, but she was the one to go.'

There was a sympathetic silence, broken by Rob himself rising from the table.

'I've really enjoyed meeting you, Mrs Gillespie – Nola – but I'm afraid I should be going now. I have to take Mr Seton into Edinburgh.' He inclined his head politely. 'Thanks very much for the tea.'

'We've enjoyed meeting you too, Rob,' said Rena.

'We have,' put in Nola. 'Perhaps we'll see you again?'

'I hope so.' Rob looked down at Honey, slurping water from the bowl Rena had given her. 'Come on, girl, we've got to go.'

'Tess, see Rob out,' said Rena. 'We'll clear away.'

After goodbyes and smiles and last handshakes, Tess, with a wonderful sense of relief, led the way to the front door, where she swung round to face Rob and went into his arms.

'Don't worry,' she whispered. 'The tenants are all out. No one'll see.'

'Who's worrying?' They kissed for a long blissful moment, before Rob said against Tess's face, 'I think they liked me, your mother and Nola.'

'They did. I could tell. You didn't mind Ma asking a few questions?'

'No, of course not. I expected more.' He gently touched Tess's cheek. 'I'm sure she sees me as prospective son-in-law, you ken.'

Tess stood very still. 'She'd probably say we've only known each other five minutes.'

'I think she's seen through me though. She knows what I want.'

'Ma knows most things.'

'What you want, too?'

Tess laughed nervously. 'I expect so.'

'Tell me then.'

'I have told you. I said I wanted us to keep on seeing each other.'

'That's right. That'll be enough. For now.'

She searched his face, so open, so clear for her to read, and wanted desperately to speak, but said nothing.

'See me again soon?' he asked softly.

'When?'

'Tuesday evening? I don't think I'm needed.'

'Where shall we go?'

'Cinema? Shall I call for you at seven?'

'I'll be waiting.'

263

Tess opened the front door and watched Rob run lightly down the steps, followed by Honey. He looked back, raising his hand to her, then vanished into the rags of mist still mixing with the darkness.

I'm so lucky, thought Tess. Who'd ever have thought I'd be so lucky? And for a moment she wanted to run after Rob and hold him, tell him what was in her heart, but she only closed the door.

'What a nice young man!' cried Rena, when Tess dazedly appeared in the kitchen. 'I'm glad you brought him in, Tess.'

'You liked him, Ma?'

'I did. So did Nola.

'I can see the attraction, Tess,' said Nola. 'A genuine sort o' fella, eh?'

'Of course, it's very early days,' said Rena. 'I mean, you've only known each other five minutes.'

Tess gave a smile. 'Bit longer than that, Ma.'

'But I think he really cares for you. I wouldn't be surprised if—'

'If what, Ma?'

'Why, if you two make a go of it.'

'That's looking ahead,' said Tess, her voice trembling. 'I have to be careful.'

'No' too careful,' Nola told her. 'Don't let him slip through your fingers, Tess.'

'He'll no' do that,' Rena declared.

'How do you know?' asked Tess.

'I can tell. Trust me.'

Suddenly, Tess felt she was trusting everybody.

Chapter Fifty-Eight

Rena was right, as usual, for so anxious was Rob not to slip through Tess's fingers, or to let her slip through his, that by January they were engaged and a date in April had been booked for the wedding.

For Tess it was all one amazing dream; she couldn't believe any of it was happening. Even when she had Rob's grandmother's ring on her finger, it didn't seem real, and when she looked at it and touched the small diamonds in their old-fashioned setting, she quite expected it to vanish like fairy gold. It remained where it was, though, as the love for her was always there in Rob's eyes whenever she looked at him.

'Very nice ring, eh?' commented Rena. 'Must have had a bit o' money in Rob's family then?'

Yes, there had been money, Rob told them. His mother's family had owned large farms, but there'd been disastrous seasons, debts and eventual bankruptcy.

'No money now,' he'd said with a rueful grin. 'Just a few bits and pieces and some furniture. Gordon got the furniture and Mother's engagement ring for Katie, and I got Gran's ring. For ma future wife.' He gave a melting look at Tess, who blushed, as Rena and Nola sighed and agreed afterwards that they'd never known such a pair of love-birds. Ah, but it was nice, eh, to see Tess so happy?

*

The strange state of happiness continued, with Tess sometimes thinking she was getting used to it, and then falling into a dream again. There were no doubts, however, no anxieties about the future. She had long ago learned to tell the difference between what she'd imagined to be love from Toby, and the real love that came to her from Rob. One was the fairy gold she'd feared her ring to be – the other gold itself, solid and true. She need never worry about trusting Rob.

Her only worry, in fact, was one she shared with him, which was how to get through the weeks to their wedding. Their love was so strong, so passionate, it seemed hard that they should have to wait for the ceremony at the kirk before they could go to bed together. Plenty of folk didn't wait, of course, and Tess, who had never considered making love with Toby, discovered she could have been one of them.

In his rooms over the garage at Pax House, when they emerged from one of their long embraces, she once whispered against Rob's face,

'We are engaged, you ken.'

'So?' he asked, smoothing back her tangled hair.

'Well – we could – if you liked—' She looked back at his bed in the room he always kept scrupulously neat. 'Honestly, Rob, do I have to spell it out?'

'No, sweetheart, I'm there before you. Think I don't want to jump the gun? It's in ma mind all the time. But I'm no' risking it. You're too precious.'

'Rob, that's a piece o' nonsense! Think I'm going to break or something?'

'No, no. But you might regret it afterwards. You might change your mind, and I canna risk that.'

'Why would I change ma mind? It'd just be part of loving you.'

'I feel the same, but you're very young and vulnerable, Tess, and I just want everything to be right for you. For us. So I'm prepared to wait. God knows how, but I'll manage.' He laughed a little. 'Maybe we'd better no' stay

266

here on our own though. No point making things more difficult for maself.'

That particular day there'd been as usual a few knowing looks from Miss Turner, the housekeeper, and the two elderly maids, Hattie Laidlaw and Ailsa Wright, when Tess and Rob finally reappeared, but the young folk were courting, eh? It was just what was expected, that they should want a bit of time together, and of course Tess had to look around Rob's rooms over the garage – she would be sharing them very soon.

Tess had been thrilled when Rob first took her to Pax House. He'd promised he would, but it had seemed another part of her on-going dream when they actually walked through the gates and round the drive to the back door. Rob had apologised for not being able to take her in the front door, like a 'proper visitor', but she'd laughed and said she didn't mind which way she went in, as long as she could see the inside of her favourite house.

They'd had another look at the Daimler first, because Tess always took every chance to see the magnificent limousine, so beautifully cared for by Rob. He'd never let her help him clean it, and had only once given her a drive in it, but she didn't mind. She knew he had something of a bee in his bonnet about not owning the car himself, and had told him that one day they'd have a car of their own and she'd drive it too. He'd smiled agreement, but of course any car they owned wouldn't be like the Daimler. That was for the Mr Setons of this world, not to say royalty.

Having sat in the back seat of the limousine and waved her hand pretending to be the Queen, Tess had become serious and stepped out to follow Rob into the house.

Mr Seton had been away that first day, but Rob had introduced her to Miss Turner and the maids, Ailsa and Hattie, who all made a great fuss of her, and said they knew her mother, and hoped Rena was well. It was clear that they adored Rob, who was the only male servant in the house, now that Mr Seton's valet had retired, and of course the only young person anyway. They were fascinated by his love affair and future wedding, and now that they had met Tess were fascinated by her too.

After Hattie had made them all a cup of tea, the portly but energetic Miss Turner showed Tess round the house, which was as beautiful as she'd imagined. There was a central hall with a curving staircase to the upper floors. There were two elegant reception rooms, filled with light from long windows facing the Forth. There were flowers and photographs in silver frames, ornamental vases and lovingly polished furniture. Everything was in perfect order, and when Tess congratulated Miss Turner she modestly inclined her head.

'We do our best, dear, we do our best. Mr Seton is very good to us, and it's only fair we should do what we can, eh? Specially as he's on his own, Mrs Seton being long gone, and Miss Annabel – that's Mrs Vesey, you ken – married and in America.'

'She doesn't come over?' asked Tess.

'Och, now and again. Only now and again.'

If I'd the chance to come to Pax House, I'd no' be able to stay away, thought Tess.

When she finally met Mr Seton, she found him charming. A silver-haired old gentleman with a young man's brightness, who made her feel very special and who won her heart by praising Rob.

After the retirement of his valet, Rob had done a great deal for him, Mr Seton explained, much more than just driving the car, and now he was to be married, Mr Seton wanted to wish him, and Tess, all the very best for their future happiness. When they came back from honeymoon, they must discuss plans for extending Rob's quarters; make it into a proper flat. Would they like that? Would they! With the current shortage of accommodation in Edinburgh, they couldn't believe their luck.

*

268

Tess, afterwards, couldn't get over Mr Seton's kindness.

'And to think you complained because he was your master, Rob! If you have an employer at all you couldn't do better than him.'

'Och, I know that,' Rob retorted. 'It's just that I'd rather be ma own boss. No' have to be grateful.'

'Well, I'm grateful that he's going to extend your quarters, Rob. We could do with a proper flat.'

'Aye, we've things to be grateful for.' Rob's expression was hard to read. 'Earlier on he gave me our wedding present cheque. Said he was sorry he hadn't a proper present, but he thought a cheque would be useful.'

'Rob, you never said!'

'I've no' looked at it yet, but I know how much it's for, because he told me.'

'How much then?' Tess put her hand to her mouth. 'Oh, that sounds awful, eh? Just wanting to know how much. Oh, I feel so bad.'

'It's natural to want to know. That's why he told me.' Rob gave a grin. 'He's given us two hundred pounds.'

'Two hundred pounds?' Tess's eyes were enormous. 'Why, Rob, that's wonderful!' She kissed him quickly. 'You'll no' mind feeling grateful for that, eh?'

'I'll no' mind.' His return of her kiss was joyous. 'It's like I said, we've a lot to be grateful for, but it's no' just money.'

'Think I don't know that?' asked Tess softly.

Chapter Fifty-Nine

Tess and Rob were to be married at the local kirk on the first Saturday in April. All the papers and newsreels were full of the plans for the Queen's coronation, but these of course were as nothing in the minds of the Gillespies, compared with the plans for Tess's wedding.

To please her mother she had agreed to a white wedding, and when Rena had dug down into her savings and bought her a white lace dress at J.J.'s, Tess added it to the dream world that already contained Rob, his grandmother's ring, and Mr Seton's two hundred pounds.

'I never thought I could look like this,' she whispered to her mother and Nola when she tried on the dress and saw how it fitted her slender figure so perfectly, and made her seem quite beautiful rather than just pretty. 'Oh, Ma, thank you!'

'Well, I'd have done the same for you, Nola,' said Rena, dashing away a tear or two. 'But you were so set on the register office wedding. You did look lovely anyway.'

'You did, Nola,' Tess added sincerely. 'And you're going to look lovely as ma matron of honour, as well.'

'Oh, Lord, has it come to this?' sighed Nola. 'Matron of honour? Makes me feel I should step up ma diet right away.'

When the dress had been taken away to be packed in clouds of tissue paper, Tess treated her mother and sister to coffee in J.J.'s restaurant.

'Ma, what about Dad?' she asked, when she'd found the courage.

'What about him?'

'Well, should I tell him I'm getting married?'

Rena stirred brown sugar into her coffee. 'That's up to you.'

'Yes, but what do you think? I don't want to send him an invitation, but maybe I should just tell him about the wedding.'

'I think you should,' said Nola.

'And then he might come,' said Rena. 'He came to yours.'

'I don't think he'll come from down south. Tell him anyway, Tess. If you want to.'

But Tess didn't know what she wanted to do, and in the end did nothing. After all, her dad had forfeited the right to be told anything, hadn't he? It wouldn't do to have him turning up and looking on, embarrassing everybody. At the same time she had a heavy heart for a few days, thinking, maybe she should have let him know. How difficult it all was!

There was Erika to think about as well. Erika, whose words sometimes came back to Tess as the arrangements for her wedding went ahead.

'Talking of white weddings, Tess, perhaps you will have one when the time comes, and please your mother.'

How bitter she herself had been, Tess remembered. How scornfully she'd dismissed Erika's suggestion and had said she'd never marry because she could never trust anyone. Yet here she was, trusting and marrying and planning to wear white. And Erika didn't know.

On her last afternoon of work at the garage before the wedding, Mr Todd laid on a little party for Tess, at which she was presented with a stainless steel teapot and hot water jug on a matching tray, and was hugged by everybody and wished all the best. Mabel Dixon had come in specially,

271

and brought sandwiches and a cake, and Rob, who'd become a popular visitor to the garage, arrived in time to give Tess a kiss as she accepted their wedding present, which was of course loudly applauded.

'Aye, she's a grand lassie,' Mr Todd told Rob afterwards. 'You're a lucky fella, Rob. Just hope she'll stay on with us after she's wed.'

'She wants to do that, Mr Todd.'

'Aye, but married woman canna be sure what they'll do.' Mr Todd shook his head. 'You ken what the poet says, eh? "The best-laid schemes o' mice and men gang aft-agley."'

'I know what's in your mind,' Rob said with a grin. 'But we're no' planning a family straight away. Tess'll be coming back.'

'And you'll be staying on at Pax House, eh? Any time you feel like bringing the Daimler in, we'd give it our best, you ken.'

'I'll do what I can, Mr Todd. Leave it with me.'

There was much ribald laughter as Rob and Tess took their leave, with Norrie making comments about the honeymoon and Mabel shutting him up, and Luke smiling a special farewell, although he was to be a guest at the wedding and would see them then.

Tess had worried a little that Rob might have said something about her driving lessons when he'd first met Luke, but if he'd remembered his little fit of jealousy, he'd given no sign. In fact, he and Luke seemed to get on well, which had particularly pleased Tess, Luke being such a good friend.

As they walked up the High Street, Rob, carrying the wedding present in its box, said he wasn't surprised that Tess had been happy working at Todd's.

'Couldn't find a nicer bunch o' guys, eh?'

'You couldn't. But it was really working with cars that appealed to me, Rob.'

He smiled fondly. 'Even though you don't actually work with any? It's no job for a woman, Tess.'

'Oh, don't say that, Rob! I thought you were pleased we had the same interest.'

'Of course I'm pleased. But I'd have loved you anyway, even if you'd only liked knitting.'

'Knitting!'

'Women aren't the same as men. Why should they be?'

'But I could be a help to you, Rob. I mean, if you ever started your own business.'

'Sure, you could.' He pressed her hand. 'And I'd be grateful. Only thing is, me starting ma own business is as far away as China.'

'It'll come one day, if we work for it.' Tess suddenly halted. 'Rob, would you mind going on to Ma's with our present, and I'll see you there? I just want to pop into the chemist's here.'

Rob's eyes went to the name above the door of the chemist's shop. John Meldrum.

'Isn't that where that Austrian girl works?' he asked quietly. 'The one who used to be your friend? Why d'you want to see her?'

'I've never told her I'm getting married. Haven't seen her for months.'

'I don't think you should see her. I don't want old troubles being stirred up.'

'I want to see her,' Tess said stubbornly. 'You go ahead and wait for me at Ma's.'

'I could come in with you.'

'No, better not. I'll only be a few minutes.'

After gazing at her for a moment or two, Rob finally nodded and walked away, and Tess, taking a deep breath, opened the door of the shop.

She hadn't crossed the threshold since that terrible day when she'd seen Toby with Erika, and even now the sound of the shop bell made her feel cold inside. But then she saw Erika standing behind the counter, looking cool and poised in her white coat, and had to move forward, because even if she felt like it, she could hardly turn and run away.

273

'Tess!' cried Erika, her face changing, losing its look of confidence, as her dark eyes filled with memory. 'Oh, it's been so long!'

'Miss, where's ma prescription?' an elderly man wheezed from a chair. 'MacGill's the name.'

'Mr Meldrum's getting it for you, Mr MacGill, he won't be a moment.' Erika swiftly came round the counter and put out her hand to Tess, who after a moment took it, then let it go.

'Tess, how are you? Oh, I've thought about you so often! Why do we never meet?'

'You don't live in Porty now, Erika. Where would we meet?'

'I thought you might have come to the shop.'

Tess looked away. 'You're still here then? No' away to medical school?'

'In the autumn. I've been accepted.'

'Hope all goes well for you.'

Erika's eyes were searching Tess's face. 'You're looking lovely, Tess. Lovely and happy. Has something happened?'

'Aye, I'm getting married. This Saturday, in fact.'

The colour rose to Erika's brow. 'Married? Oh, Tess, that's the best news I've heard in a long time. Oh, I'm so pleased for you!' She flung her arms around the unresponsive Tess. 'Do I know him? Tell me about him.'

'His name's Rob MacNair. He's the chauffeur at Pax House. Took over when Mr Beith retired.'

'I knew Mr Beith had gone. He used to come in here, told us he was moving to the Borders. Oh, but this is such wonderful news, Tess, I'm so glad you came in to tell me.'

Tess, swallowing hard, made one of her sudden decisions. 'If you'd like to come on Saturday, Erika, you'd be very welcome.'

'No, no. Thank you, but no.' The colour faded from Erika's cheeks. 'It would be better not. But I shall be thinking of you. And wishing you every happiness. Every happiness, Tess!'

'You're still seeing Toby?' asked Tess, moving towards the door.

'Yes.' Erika lowered her eyes. 'He has been very helpful to me. Also, Simon.'

'Perhaps you'd tell Toby about the wedding?'

'Oh, I will. He'll be so happy for you.'

Of course he'll be happy, he's off the hook, Tess wanted to say, but bit back the words and was glad she had. This was a moment of reconciliation; she would not spoil it with bitterness. At the same time it now warmed her very pleasantly to think that Toby Dene should know someone else wanted her, someone else loved her. She put her hand on the latch of the door.

'Goodbye, Erika. Take care, and I'll wish you all the best.'

'Tess Gillespie, is that you?' boomed Mr Meldrum's voice across the shop. He had been in the process of handing Mr MacGill his medicine when his eye had caught Tess. 'Now, we haven't seen you in here for far too long. Not been going to Boot's, have you?'

'Haven't been going anywhere, Mr Meldrum.' Tess found a smile. 'Goodbye, then. Goodbye, Erika. Good luck.'

'Goodbye, Tess, goodbye.' Erika's eyes were filmed with tears she had not shed. 'And thank you – for coming.'

'Feel better now?' Rob asked, when Tess arrived back home.

'Yes, I do. I saw her and I told her, about you and me, and she was very nice. Wished us luck. I wished her luck, too. She's going to medical school in the autumn.'

'So that's a chapter closed, is it?'

'Well and truly closed.'

'And now we only have to look forward to our wedding?' They were standing alone in the kitchen and Rob looked round to make sure Rena wasn't tapping down the stairs before he took Tess in his arms. 'Honeymoon, I should say.'

'Hey, I'm looking forward to the wedding!' cried Tess, laughing.

'Ah well, didn't I just say women aren't the same as men? But I think you'll enjoy the honeymoon, too.'

'I'll no' even bother to answer that,' said Tess.

Chapter Sixty

Tess had thought that the wedding would be another part of her dream, everything a little misty, a little blurred. But it wasn't like that at all. From the minute she saw Rob waiting for her at the end of the aisle, looking so anxious in his dark suit with carnation buttonhole, all was clear-cut and in full technicolour. This was her day and she knew she was going to enjoy it.

When she and Rob came out of the kirk after the ceremony, to smile at the photographer and dodge the confetti, it did come to her mind that her father might somehow be there. Of course he wasn't. How could he be? There was no Clark Walters around this time to tell him his daughter was getting married.

But as Rob reverently helped her into the wedding car, she thought she saw, in the distance, the great dark eyes of Erika. When she looked again, however, after smiling with Rob at the children still throwing rose petals, the girl she'd thought was Erika was gone.

She'd been worried that her mother was spending too much on this wedding of hers, for there'd not only been her dress to pay for, but also the reception at one of the larger cafés in Porty, with dancing afterwards to a three-piece band.

'Honestly, Ma, is it worth it?' Tess had asked. 'I don't want you to spend so much on me.'

'Worth every penny,' Rena had told her. She was just so relieved that Tess had found the right man, someone she could rely on and be happy with, she'd have been willing to spend all she'd got to celebrate. But in fact she wasn't doing that. She'd her rents and her wages from the pottery, and a bit put by, so she wasn't putting herself on the bread line.

'And then your Rob offered to help, you ken,' she added, and smiled at Tess's widened eyes. 'I told him I could manage, but he ended up paying for the band.'

'He never told me,' said Tess.

'Aye, well, that's the sort he is. Now if Clark Walters had done anything like that, all Porty'd have known.' Rena shook her head. 'You've been the lucky one, Tess, no' poor Nola.'

Nola, however, didn't regard herself as one needing sympathy. She was as plump as ever – the latest diet hadn't worked – but so blonde, so pretty, so full of life, she had most of the male guests queuing up to dance with her and was having a wonderful time, she told Tess.

'Och, that Ginger Moffat, he's got two left feet, eh? But we had a good crack about the old days.'

'I did tell you he likes to be called Luke now,' Tess pointed out, but Nola only laughed.

'I told him he was Ginger when I knew him at school and Ginger he'd always be, and he said that was fine.'

'Fancy,' said Tess.

'Aye, but that brother o' Rob's – Gordon – he's a dream dancer. I could've danced with him for ever, only I'd have had his Katie after me, eh? But she's sweet, Tess, isn't she? I think you two'll get on well.

That was true, thought Tess. Katie MacNair, tall and angular, with a mass of thick black hair, was a good-natured, selfless sort of girl, and the days Tess had spent with her and her wee boys, Hamish and Andy, at the farm near Haddington, had been very pleasant. Tess liked

278

Gordon, too, though of course he wasn't nearly as good looking as Rob. Very faithful, though, according to Katie. Never looked at another woman, and it was her guess Rob would be the same.

Ma's right, Tess decided. I'm lucky. But then she didn't need her mother to tell her that.

The time came for the newly-weds to leave, say goodbye to the guests, and make a run for it to the car Rob had hired to take them to a seaside village beyond Dunbar, where they'd taken a cottage in order to be completely on their own.

'No jokes at breakfast from other guests,' said Rob. 'No funny looks.'

'Only thing is, I'll have to cook the breakfast,' said Tess. 'Will I get it right?'

'Don't worry, sweetheart, we won't be worrying about food.'

For a long time on the drive from Edinburgh, Tess kept thinking of her mother's tearful, yet smiling, face at the last farewell, and Nola, who'd hugged her hard and shed a few tears too. It looked as though Nola's own marriage was well and truly over, but that hadn't stopped her from telling Tess she knew it would be different for her.

'It didn't work out for me, but I know it will for you,' she'd whispered as Luke, looking suddenly sad, waited his turn for a final peck on Tess's cheek. And then the maids from Pax House had come up crying, 'Goood luck, Tess, good luck, Rob!' and thrown confetti with abandon.

Of course Mr Seton had not attended – they hadn't expected that he would – but he had sent a telegram, read out by Gordon, giving his best wishes for their future happiness and saying he looked forward to welcoming them home to Pax House.

'Still canna believe I'll be going back there,' Tess murmured.

'Back where?' asked Rob.

'Pax House, of course.'

'Tess, we're just starting our honeymoon and you're thinking of going home?'

She looked at his fine profile, at his strong hands on the wheel, and the curve of his mouth as he smiled, and felt a quick rush of love.

'No,' she said, with passionate truth. 'I wasn't thinking that at all.'

Chapter Sixty-One

Tess managed what cooking she did at the cottage very well, but it was true, she and Rob didn't care much about food. All their time was devoted to each other, getting to know each other's bodies, enjoying the pleasure of uninhibited love-making that was to them completely new.

Sometimes they would surface, to wander on the lonely shores beyond the little fishing village, or they would walk back to watch the boats coming in with the catch, and maybe have a word or two with the locals. They knew that they were known as the 'newly-weds', but no one bothered them, or made remarks. All was peaceful and tranquil until they returned to the cottage, when they would create their own storm, before slowly dressing again and perhaps driving into Dunbar for a meal.

'Got to eat sometimes, I suppose,' said Rob. 'As long as we don't waste too much time on it.'

'What a blessing it is to have the cottage,' sighed Tess. 'Imagine being in a guest house and worrying every time the bed creaked!'

'Now there's another difference between men and women.' Rob laughed and reached for her hand. 'I never give a damn whether the bed creaks or not.'

On their last morning, when Tess was making breakfast, someone came to their door. It was Mrs Fairlie, the woman who ran the village post office and held the key to the cottage.

'Oh, Mr MacNair, I've a telegram for you,' she told Rob, who'd cheerfully answered her knock.

'Telegram?' He paled a little.

'Aye.' She handed him the small orange envelope and stood with her hair blowing around her woollen hat as he opened it. 'Any answer?' Her eyes were kind.

'Oh, Rob, it isn't Ma, is it?' Tess cried fearfully.

He handed her the telegram. 'No, it's from Pax House. I'm afraid – it's bad news.'

'Bad news?' Her heart plummeted, as her eyes went over the pasted words of the telegram. 'Regret inform you Mr Seton passed away yesterday Stop Please come if can Stop Turner.'

'No! Oh, no!' She raised her eyes to Rob. 'Oh, not Mr Seton! I canna believe it.'

'Any answer?' Mrs Fairlie quietly asked again.

'No answer, thank you.' said Rob. 'We're leaving now. I'll drop the key in at the shop before we go.'

'I canna believe it either,' he muttered, driving fast to Edinburgh. 'I mean, he was all right when we left.'

'He was very frail, Rob.' Tess was sitting hunched in the passenger seat, her face stricken. It was almost too much to bear, to think of Mr Seton's dying while they had been so happy on their honeymoon. A light going out while theirs shone so brightly. And he'd been so kind.

'He'd been so kind to us,' she said aloud.

'Aye. I feel worse than ever now, complaining about him.'

'They'll be in a state at Pax House.'

'They will.'

Rob drove for some time in silence, then suddenly glanced at Tess and back to the road.

'You realise this is going to affect us, Tess?'

'You mean your job? Yes, I know.'

'No' just ma job. Our home as well. We've nowhere to live now.'

Tess stared ahead unseeingly. Nowhere to live. When she had been going to live at Pax House. Nowhere to live. She couldn't take it in.

'There's always Ma's,' she said, after another silence.

'Might have to move away to get another job.'

'Leave Porty?'

'Well, I don't know, do I? I don't know what's going to happen.'

'Strange, isn't it?' She laid her hand on his knee. 'One minute we're up in the clouds, the next – where?'

'Still in the clouds, is what I say. If we've got each other, doesn't matter where we go, does it?'

'No. Oh, that's true.'

But wherever they went, one thing was for sure, it wouldn't be Pax House.

Chapter Sixty-Two

Tears flowed when they arrived back, as the housekeeper and the maids gathered them into their arms, while Honey whimpered in the background.

'Oh, Rob, it's such a godsend to have you back,' exclaimed Miss Turner. 'Just to have you to lean on in all this misery. Oh, poor Mr Seton! It's been so awful, I canna tell you.'

'But you poor young things, having to come back from your honeymoon.' Ailsa put a damp face against Tess's. 'We didn't know what to do, whether to let you know, or wait.'

'We thought you'd want to know as soon as possible,' said Hattie. 'Now you'll want a cup o' tea, eh?'

'What happened then?' asked Rob, as Tess sank into a chair at the kitchen table and Honey came up to be comforted. 'Was it his heart?'

'Aye, a coronary,' Miss Turner told him. 'He was taken bad in the early hours of the morning. He rang the bell and when I got there I could see he was in terrible pain. I called the ambulance straight away. I thought, it's the hospital we need, no' the doctor, and when the fellows came, they said I'd done the right thing.'

'Was he able to speak at all?'

'He just said his daughter's name, and I told him I'd send for her immediately. Then he closed his eyes.' Miss

Turner's eyes filled with tears again. 'He died in the ambulance.'

'We've no' been able to do much with Honey,' said Ailsa after a silence. 'She's been roaming the house looking for him, and crying like a bairn.'

'She'll be better now Rob's back,' murmured Hattie.

'We all will,' sighed Miss Turner.

When they'd drunk the tea and put their luggage in Rob's room, Tess telephoned her mother to give her the news, while Rob said he would see what he could do to be useful. Until Mr Seton's daughter arrived, however, it was not possible to do very much; all the arrangements must be hers. No doubt she would let them know as soon as possible what their future would be, but it seemed pretty certain that the staff would be moving on.

'The poor things,' murmured Tess of Miss Turner and the maids. 'They're losing their home too, and Hattie and Ailsa aren't so young. What will they do?'

Rob shook his head and said nothing. He knew no more than Tess, what any of them would do.

It was a relief when Annabel Vesey and her husband arrived by air from the States to make the necessary decisions and take the weight from the shoulders of the staff, who'd wanted to help but had not had the power. Though both were struggling with the shock of grief, they were as considerate as Mr Seton himself had always been, and had booked in at the Caledonian Hotel 'to make things easier', as they put it.

'Aye, Miss Annabel was always thoughtful,' sighed Miss Turner. 'Now if she'd been staying on, we'd have had no worries, eh?'

'Thing is, she isn't,' said Hattie.

Annabel Vesey, in her forties, was slim and fair and dressed in elegant mourning, while George, her husband, a grey-haired New Englander, was a capable and efficient businessman. Making arrangements appeared to be second nature to them both, and within a few days the lawyers had been seen, instructions given and the funeral organised. As the funeral was to be a big affair, caterers had been engaged, and all the staff needed to do was to prepare their mourning outfits and order a wreath.

'I still canna believe it,' Hattie sobbed on the day of the funeral. 'It's all happened too fast. Seems like one day Mr Seton's here, the next he's being buried. How can you get used to that?'

'It was the will of the Lord, that he should be taken quickly.' Miss Turner replied, adjusting her black hat. 'We should be glad he didn't suffer long.'

'At least I'll have something to do,' muttered Rob, who was driving the staff to the church in the Daimler. 'Canna bear standing around doing nothing.'

'When it's all over, d'you think Miss Annabel will tell us what's going to happen to us?' asked Ailsa. 'Mebbe I shouldnae ask, eh?'

'Not now,' said Miss Turner. 'There's a time and a place for everything.'

The funeral service, held in the Episcopalian church, was unfamiliar to the kirk goers in the congregation, but considered very beautiful and an appropriate send-off for the true gentleman that was Mr Seton. After the committal in the churchyard, most mourners returned to Pax House for the elaborate buffet provided by the caterers.

There was the usual relaxed atmosphere that follows a funeral, with even Miss Annabel being seen to smile with friends, while Miss Turner and the maids hurried about, checking on what the caterers were doing to their kitchen. Honey lay under people's feet, not wagging her tail, but seeming not to mind being patted and consoled.

'All over,' Rob murmured to Tess as they stood together, with plates of smoked salmon and glasses of white wine. 'This is the end, eh? Our life here is over.'

'Mine never began,' said Tess.

'Ah, I'm sorry, sweetheart. I know how much it meant to you, to be coming to Pax House.'

'It's like you said, as long as we're together it doesn't matter where we are.' She drank some wine, shuddering a little at its dryness. 'I said I'd look in on Ma tomorrow afternoon. She thought she shouldn't come to the funeral, not knowing Mr Seton personally, but I know she'll want to hear all about it.'

'Fine,' said Rob, watching Mr Seton's daughter move among the mourners with practised ease. 'I have an idea Mrs Vesey will be giving us some news tomorrow.'

Chapter Sixty-Three

'What a thing, eh?' murmured Rena, plying Tess with tea and shortbread the following afternoon. 'There you were, all set, and now everything's changed and you don't know where you are.'

'That's life,' said Nola, who'd come back early from her shift at the pottery specially to see Tess. 'But it seems hard.'

'Rob'll find something else,' Tess said bravely. 'There'll be no difficulty there. Only thing is, we might have to move away.'

'Move away?' cried Rena. 'Where?'

'Well, wherever he finds the right job.'

'Surely he can find something in Edinburgh?' asked Nola. 'Plenty o' rich folk wanting chauffeurs there, I'd have thought.'

Tess shrugged. 'We'll have to see. But we'll no' be living in Pax House anyway.' Her lip trembled. 'And Mr Seton was going to make us a proper flat, you ken. We were going to discuss plans when we got back from honeymoon.'

'Poor lassie,' her mother said, patting her hand. 'It's a shame.'

'I shouldn't be complaining. Think of Mr Seton. Everything's over for him.'

'Aye, that's true.' Rena shook her head sadly, then

jumped a little and raised her hand. 'Listen, was that the door?'

'Tess?' came Rob's voice. 'Are you there? Tess?'

'Of course I'm here,' Tess answered, rising. 'Whatever's the matter, Rob?'

He stood in the doorway, his cap on the back of his head, his cheeks reddened with the wind, his eyes fixed only on Tess.

'Can you come out for a minute, Tess?'

'Want a cup of tea, Rob?' asked Rena, raising her eyebrows, and he hastily took off his cap and came to kiss her cheek.

'Sorry, Ma. Should mind ma manners, eh? Hello, Nola, how are you? No thanks, I won't have tea, just wanted to speak to Tess. We'll be back in a minute, promise.

'I'll get ma coat,' said Tess.

'Whatever was all that about?' asked Rena, as the newly-weds ran up the stairs and out of the front door.

'Rob's got news,' said Nola. 'That's obvious.'

'Good news, do you think?'

'Have the feeling it is. But he said he'd be back in a minute.'

Tess and Rob were walking down the road to the sands, their arms wound together, their eyes constantly meeting.

'What is it, Rob?' asked Tess. 'What have you heard? Has Mrs Vesey said something?'

'Aye.' They'd reached the beach and were turning to walk with their backs to the wind. 'She called us together this afternoon. Said she'd seen the lawyers and knew what was in the will and wanted to tell us about it.'

'The will? I never thought about the will.'

'That's because you're a very sweet girl, Tess. I'm pretty sure the rest of us were thinking about it, though I didn't think there'd be much point for me. I hadn't worked for Mr Seton all that long and he'd already given me a wedding present.' Rob tightened Tess's hand on his arm. 'I honestly didn't think I'd be in it.'

'And were you?' asked Tess, catching her breath.

'I was.' Rob smiled down at her. 'Tess, he's left me the Daimler.'

'Rob!'

'Aye. And another two hundred pounds. I'm – well – I don't know what I am. So sad he's gone, yet so over the moon for maself. I mean – the car. The Daimler.' Rob released her for a moment, swept off his cap and put back his head to look up at the clouds scudding across the April sky. 'Tess, it's mine!'

He replaced his cap and looked down at her again.

'Well, ours. Because what's mine is yours.'

She leaned against him, speechless, and he put back her curly hair and kissed her.

'I'll tell you about the others. Miss Turner got three hundred pounds, she being the senior one, and Hattie and Ailsa got two hundred each, same as me.'

'Oh, they'll be so happy!'

'They are. Happy and relieved. Something for the savings, even if they're out of a job. Mrs Vesey said she would be selling the house, but not immediately, so they can stay on till they find something else.'

'And so can we, Rob?'

'No' for long. We've got other plans.'

'What other plans?'

'Can't you guess? I'm going to start ma own business. I've got the Daimler, I've got a bit of money, and I'm going to open up for chauffeur-driven hire. Tess, it'll be perfect. Perfect!' He held her arms. 'Don't you agree?'

'Of course I do! It's what you've always wanted. And I can help you, can't I?'

'You can, you can do the books, make appointments – we'll be a team. I've already thought of the name. MacNair's Chauffeur Services. What do you think?'

'I suppose there'll be no chance of me driving the car?' she asked, smiling, as though it was a joke.

He laughed and she knew it was. 'I'd never ask you to do that, Tess. But we'll be building up towards a second car and second driver as soon as we can. I'll look round for somebody good. Oh, Tess, is it wrong to feel so happy, even though Mr Seton's gone? I feel bad, you ken, because I canna help it.'

'It isn't wrong,' she said firmly. 'He wanted you to have that car. He probably knew what you'd use it for, and I think he'd be pleased for you. I do, honestly.'

'I'd like to think so.' Rob took a deep breath. 'Well, shall we go and tell your ma and Nola?'

'They'll be so happy for us.' Tess's eyes were glistening. 'Specially if we can stay in Porty.'

'Oh, we'll stay in Porty, or pretty close. I'm going to start looking for premises, soon as I can.'

'And where will we live, Rob? We'll have to find somwhere when Pax House is sold.'

'We will, but it'll have to be to rent and something small. I'm going to need all the money we've got for the business.'

'Ma might fit us in, just to begin with, if one of the tenants moves out.'

'That'd be grand, except that—'

'Except what?'

'I've said we'd take Honey.'

'Honey?' Tess gave a cry. 'Oh, Rob, I'd forgotten her! Poor dog, she's lost her home, just like the rest of us. Of course we'll have to take her.'

'What about your mother?'

'She won't mind, I'm sure she won't. It'll only be temporary anyway. I've nothing against Ma, but I think I'll be looking for ma own place.'

'We'll have our own place, Tess, and it'll be a good one, don't you worry. I'm ambitious!'

They clung together for a long shared moment of joy, then Tess pulled away.

'Come on, let's go and tell ma folks about the plans.'

291

'About the Daimler,' Rob said seriously. 'Everything hinges on that.'

'The Daimler,' she repeated.

They linked arms and turned to walk up the road from the sands, silent now, their minds filled with the future and the man who had given it to them, who was himself already part of the past.

PART FOUR

Chapter Sixty-Four

Sputnik? On a chill October morning in 1957, Tess, only half listening to the wireless, wondered if she'd heard the word aright.

'Sputnik?' she repeated to Rob, as she settled her two-year-old daughter, Karen, into her chair and gave her a bowl of cereal. 'What's that then?'

'It's a Russian satellite,' he answered, trying to listen to the announcer over Karen's sudden wail as she dropped her spoon. 'It's a man-made satellite orbiting the earth. Would you credit it? They've bloody well done it!'

'Language, Rob,' murmured Tess. 'Karen picks up every word you say, you ken.'

'Aye, sorry. But it's no' every day the space age starts.' He laughed and began to eat his cornflakes. 'I'd heard the Russians were close to sending something up, but I never thought they'd beat the Americans. What next, eh? A man up there? Wish it could be me.'

'You've enough to do down here.' Tess gave Karen another spoon and took out a frying pan. 'Want some bacon, Rob?'

'I've no' much time. Got to take Honey out, then get to the hotel to pick up the Americans.' He looked fondly to where Honey, having heard her name, was sitting bolt upright in her basket. Poor Honey, he thought. Still handsome, but growing old. Didn't run any more. 'Unless you took her out, Tess?'

'I suppose I could, if you're pushed.'

'Good, I'll have the bacon, then.'

The MacNairs were in the kitchen of their small flat over the converted garage that housed their Daimlers. It had taken them two years to find suitable premises. Two years of trying to run MacNair's Chauffeur Services from a warehouse at the other end of town while living at Rena's house, which had been so difficult they'd felt at times like giving up the whole idea.

It hadn't helped when unplanned Karen was born and Tess had had to cope with a baby while still doing her work for Rob. Even though both she and Rob adored their copper-haired daughter from the moment of her arrival, and even though Rena did what she could to help out, things hadn't been easy.

'Dark hours before the dawn,' Rena would say. 'Things'll get better.'

And she'd been right. Suddenly, the dawn arrived.

First, they found their ideal premises in Grey Lane, off the High Street, with ground-floor space for cars and a small office, and a four-roomed flat above. Then, Rob began to take on more clients. He was able to borrow extra money to buy a second Daimler and to employ an assistant, Ewan Beale, to drive it, while Tess paid Polly Wight, whose children were at school, to help look after Karen.

Yes, life was good, not only for Tess and Rob, but for people in general. The war was receding into history; rationing was finally over; there were plenty of jobs. True, young people seemed to be set on annoying their elders with their 'rocking n' rolling' and trying to sing like Elvis Presley. And true, there was still a cold war with Russia, and Britain had had to retreat from a little skirmish with Egypt over the Suez Canal. But world peace was holding, that was the thing, and prosperity seemed to be on the horizon.

Tess, being Labour, didn't like the Tory Prime Minister,

Harold MacMillan, but he did seem to be the type to get things done, and Rob said he admired him. Which was to be expected. Even in the early days of their marriage, Tess had teased him about turning into a Tory and capitalist, and he'd admitted it.

'Makes sense to be a capitalist, when you've got your own business.'

'Still wear your chauffeur's cap that you used to say you didn't like.'

'Ah, but it's a different cap from the one I wore for Mr Seton, Tess. This one I wear as ma own choice, and the clients are part of ma business. I'm no' in service any more.'

'The business is called Chauffeur Services, Rob.'

'Provides a service, Tess. There's the difference.'

She'd shrugged. 'If you say so. As long as you let me drive the cars sometimes, and do a bit of maintenance, I'm happy anyway.'

'Well, I do let you help out with maintenance now, don't I? And drive the cars.'

'Never for a client.'

'Ah, come on, Tess!' Rob had smiled his indulgent smile. 'Imagine what thae rich Americans'd feel, if you rolled up to take 'em to the Highlands, or wherever!'

'They'd be thrilled. American women can do anything, I've heard.'

Rob, however, had not been convinced, and Tess, who knew how far she could go with him, had not pressed him further. It was therefore he, and more recently Ewan, who were waved off on trips to the beauty spots of Scotland, or golfing tournaments, or special occasion dinners, or whatever the clients wanted, and it was Tess who did the accounts and made the bookings and tried not to mind. One of these days, though, she would dream, one of these days things might be different.

On the morning they'd heard about the Russian Satellite

orbiting the earth, Tess said she'd like to stop and think about it, because she knew it was amazing, but she just hadn't the time. By nine o'clock she liked to be downstairs in her little office, ready to take bookings, with the flat tidied up and Karen ready for Polly's arrival. So if she'd to take Honey out first, she'd better get on, and so had Rob, as he had to be on time to collect Mr and Mrs Dwight Winthrop for their trip to Loch Lomond and the Trossachs. This was to cover two days and would be very lucrative, while Ewan's trip to the Borders would bring in a good return too, which was why Rob was humming cheerfully as he adjusted his cap at the kitchen mirror.

'That Ewan at the door?' he called to Tess. 'What's he want, coming up here then?'

'Soon find out,' Tess replied, as she opened the flat door and smiled at Rob's assistant driver, the thin, lantern-jawed, Ewan Beale. 'Hello, Ewan. Want to speak to Rob?'

'Aye, if you don't mind, Mrs MacNair,' Ewan muttered. Though he called his boss Rob, he called his boss's wife Mrs MacNair. That was Ewan for you. Very formal, very polite, but close as an oyster. An oyster that was looking just a little apprehensive as he came into the kitchen, taking off his cap.

'Mind if I have a word, Rob?' he asked, turning the cap in his fingers.

'Have to be sharp, Ewan. I'm away in five minutes.'

'I'll come to the point. Thing is, I'm wanting to put in ma notice. I'm sorry, but you'll have to be finding yourself another driver.'

Chapter Sixty-Five

Rob's face had turned dark red; his eyes were bright with anger.

'What the hell are you talking about, Ewan? Putting in your notice? What for?'

'It's ma brother in Dundee, Rob. He's starting a taxi firm, wants me to go in with him.'

'For more money, I suppose?'

'He's family. Money's got nothing to do with it. I've no complaints about what you pay me, Rob.'

'What does Cora think about going to Dundee?' Tess asked, as Rob continued to stare angrily at Ewan.

'Says she's quite happy, Mrs MacNair,' Ewan told her. 'I'd never've said I'd go if Cora wasnae keen.'

'Obviously you've discussed this with your wife,' Rob snapped. 'Couldn't you have discussed it with me? It's going to be pretty inconvenient, you departing like this, Ewan. We've bookings lined up, you ken.'

Ewan's long face was now expressionless. 'Aye, I ken that. But I'm willing to work till the end o' the month. That'll give you time to find another driver.'

Rob, his colour fading as his anger subsided, nodded.

'Well, that'll be a help all right,' he said grudgingly. 'We'll advertise as soon as possible. Tess, could you see to that?'

'Don't forget, I could drive if necessary,' she said

without smiling, to let the men see she meant it. 'Just until you find somebody, Rob.'

But Ewan, who always looked shocked if he saw her at the wheel of one of the cars, or with a spanner in her hand, said quickly, 'No need for that, Mrs MacNair, I'll no' leave Rob in the lurch.'

'Thanks, Ewan, I appreciate that.' Rob glanced at his watch. 'Look, we'd better get on our way. Sorry if I was a bit touchy just then – you caught me by surprise, that's all. Tess, come down with me, eh? I'll just get ma bag.'

Tess, with Karen in her arms, descended the stairs from the flat to the garage below, where the cars stood waiting. It always gave her heart a lift to see the two handsome limousines, and to know that they were Rob's, and therefore hers. Long ago, she remembered laughing with her mother over the idea that she would ever have a car like Mr Seton's. Well, it hadn't been such a joke after all, even if as yet she didn't actually drive Rob's clients around in the Daimlers.

'Oh, Rob,' she murmured, as he put his bag in the boot of the car and settled himself in the driving seat.

'What?'

'Nothing. Take care, that's all.' She bent to kiss his cheek and let Karen kiss him too, smiling as the little girl's plump hand ran down his face.

'Bye, Dad.'

'Bye, pet. Take care of Mammie then.'

Ewan had opened the garage doors and was now smoothly backing out, not smiling a goodbye because he never did, but Rob was also on his way, taking one hand off the wheel to wave to Karen, calling to Tess not to forget the adverts for the papers.

'See you tomorrow evening!' she cried, but he had already deftly turned the car out and driven away.

'Hello Tess!' cried Polly Wight, hurrying in from the street. 'No' late, am I? It's thae kids, eh? I'd rather scrub a hundred floors, than get 'em off to school, I'm telling you!'

'And I believe you,' Tess answered, laughing, 'I can see how it's going to be with Karen.'

'Och, no, she's a sweetie.' Polly, still as blonde and youthful looking as when she'd lived at Number One, closed the garage doors, then took Karen from Tess and began to climb the stairs to the flat. 'Lassies are always easier than boys – till they grow up.'

'Would you mind just listening for any early phone calls?' asked Tess, putting on her coat. 'I have to take Honey out. I'll no' be long.'

'Nae bother, Tess. Take as long as you like and I'll have a cup o' coffee ready for you when you get back.'

'You're the sweetie,' said Tess, taking down Honey's lead and bracing herself for the dog's excitement. 'Karen, you be a good girl for Polly now, till Mammie gets back.'

'Me come, Mammie?'

'No, pet, your pushchair sticks in the sand and I want to give Honey a run on the beach.'

'A run?' echoed Polly. 'Poor old thing then. It's a long time since she had a run, eh?'

'She's fine,' Tess said quickly. 'Just a bit stiff, with lying down. Come on, Honey, let's away to the sands.'

Chapter Sixty-Six

The sands were close. Only a short walk down Grey Lane and there you were, on the promenade and facing the sea. That was one advantage of the site of MacNair's. Another was the proximity to King George Road and Rena's house, which were just a little further on, past the swimming pool and the power station. Tess liked to call in to see her mother when she had the time – and Nola, of course, who was still in her bedsit.

Rena, now approaching fifty and not above having a bit of a 'touch-up' for her greying hair, seemed quite content with her life, as far as Tess could tell. She rarely mentioned Don, who had made no more contact, but was always full of her own plans, and was as Nola described it, 'soft as butter' with wee Karen.

'Aye, that lassie's transformed ma life,' Rena declared. 'Even if she has got a name nobody's ever heard of.'

'Ma, it's a very popular name and very pretty too,' Tess told her, but Rena only pointed out that there'd never been a Karen in their family and everybody knew you should choose family names if you could. Ah, but the little girl herself was the sweetest bairn in the world, and Rena's only grandchild, and therefore to be indulged.

'Only grandchild, *so far*,' she would say, with meaning. 'Next one'll be a laddie, eh? Karen would like a brother.'

And Ma, remembering Rickie, would like a grandson,

302

thought Tess, but would still murmur that there was plenty of time, at which Rena would shake her head and say you could never be sure of that.

'No good looking at me for bairns,' said Nola, and of course it was true she'd never been able to have a child when she and Clark were married. That, of course, might have been Clark's fault, but who would know when there'd been no one to replace him in Nola's life? In fact, they were still only separated and not divorced.

'So, why don't you get divorced?' Tess had asked out of her mother's hearing.

Nola had shrugged. 'Just haven't got round to it. Neither of us has met anyone we want to divorce for, I suppose.'

'I think Ma's afraid you're leaving the door open.'

'What do you mean?'

'Well, to take Clark back some time.'

Nola's eyes flashed. 'That's ridiculous. I'll never go back to Clark.'

'Are you sure?'

'Quite sure. To tell you the truth, I'm more interested in ma work than anything else. I'm a proper designer now, you ken. If the Harebell ever folds, I'd no' mind starting up on ma own, if I could manage it.'

'Why ever would the pottery fold, Nola? It's doing well.'

'Tess, lesson number one is that any business can fold any time.'

'Oh, don't say it,' cried Tess.

Before she took Honey onto the sands, Tess made herself depressed by walking along to take another quick look at Pax House. Why did she do it? What was the point? The awful changes that had come over the house she loved were not likely to have been reversed since the last time she saw it, which was only a week ago.

'Och, you're like a lost soul, haunting that place,' Rob would tell her. 'I know it's a shame it's gone down the way it has, but there's nothing you can do. Best leave it alone.'

'I only look at it,' sighed Tess. 'The way I used to do when I was little.'

The decline of Pax House had begun after the people who bought it from Annabel Vesey tried to turn it into a guesthouse. When planning permission was refused, they let it to a variety of families and students, carrying out only the minimum of maintenance, meanwhile removing themselves to Glasgow.

It didn't take long for the house to change. Within weeks it had lost its air of pristine splendour and had begun to take on the look of a rundown boarding house, with weeds flourishing in the gravel of the drive, and curtains sagging at the windows no one ever cleaned. Unpruned roses crept over the façade, as great dandelions rose in what had been the lawn, and the once elegant gates that had been the main entrance to the property no longer closed.

Standing before those collapsing gates, Tess could only feel relief that Mr Seton was no longer around to see his house in its present state, and that Miss Turner and the maids had moved away and need not weep. Only Tess herself wept inwardly and was glad to turn aside.

'Come on, Honey,' she murmured. 'We've seen enough, eh?'

But the Labrador knew her old home and was whining and straining on her leash – it was all Tess could do to haul her along to the sands. Even chasing after her ball brought none of the usual joy, but then chasing was something that did not come easily to Honey any more.

'She has rheumatism in her back legs,' the vet had explained. 'Can't do much to help, I'm afraid. And she is eighty-four, remember, in terms of human age.'

Eighty-four? Tess couldn't bear to think what Honey's age might mean. Couldn't bear to think that the dear dog, that had been a part of her life for so many years, might one day be a part of it no longer.

'Oh, Honey!' she cried now, as Honey came back, panting hard, and laid her ball at Tess's feet. 'Oh, that'll

304

do for now, eh?' Tess hugged her close. 'No more running for today.'

'What's up, Tess?' she heard a voice say, and scrambled to her feet to find Luke Moffat taking off his cap and smiling down at her. It seemed to her that he was taller than ever.

'Luke, where did you spring from?' She shook his hand with pleasure. 'You taking a day off?'

'No, I've been delivering a car to a fellow down Joppa way. I was walking back when I spotted you from the promenade, and your poor old dog.' He bent to pat Honey's head. 'No' too fit, eh?'

'She's all right. Just out of breath.'

'Well, you're looking grand anyway, Tess. Never put on an ounce. Where's the wean, then?'

'Polly Wight's looking after her for me.' Tess bent to put Honey on her lead. 'And I'd better get back, I have to answer the phone, you ken.'

'I'll walk with you. Long time since we met, eh? Was it Norrie's wedding?'

'Must have been. I don't get into Todd's much these days. It's usually Rob who takes the cars in for servicing.'

'You're a big miss, Tess,' Luke said quietly. 'That lady who got your job, she's nice enough, but, och, she's no' the same as you.'

Tess smiled self-consciously, and as they left the sands, glanced covertly up at Luke's broad, freckled face.

'Wedding bells for Norrie. How about you, Luke?'

'Safety in numbers. I take girls out, but I don't get involved.'

Tess hesitated. 'Luke, you can be happy again, you know. Even if you were hurt once.'

'Och, I never think o' Lorna these days, Tess. I've just no' met Miss Right, that's all.

'Well, keep looking, is my advice. I can really recommend marriage.'

'It's grand you're so happy,' said Luke, putting on his

cap and taking Honey's lead as they crossed the promenade.

At the doors to the garage, with its handsome sign for 'MacNair's Chauffeur Services', Luke said it had been grand talking to Tess again, and would she remember him to Rob? Nodding towards the sign, he asked after the business and hoped it was going well.

'It's fine, except we need a new driver. Ewan Beal's going to work for his brother in Dundee.'

'Ewan Beal, old misery guts.' Luke laughed. 'He'll be no great loss, eh?'

'He's a good driver. Very reliable. Rob's pretty upset he's going, as a matter of fact, but we're putting adverts in the papers today. Hoping for the best.'

'That right?'

Luke and Tess stood looking at each other.

'You happy at Todd's still?' asked Tess casually.

'Aye. But I've been there a hell of a long time.'

'You wouldn't like a change?'

'Driving, you mean?' Luke shook his head. 'Och, no, I canna do the fancy stuff, Tess.'

'What fancy stuff? You just have to be a good driver, which you are. You drive like Rob. Like a dream.'

'Wouldn't say that.' Luke gave an embarrassed laugh. 'Always say I can spin a car on a sixpence, but a lot o' guys can do that. Canna see me in a chauffeur's cap though.'

'Well, think about it. The adverts'll be in the evening papers. If you want to apply, give Rob a ring.'

'All right, I will. I mean, I'll think about it.'

Luke touched his cap and walked away, looking back once to smile, and Tess, entering by a side door, found herself feeling quite cheered at the thought of his replacing Ewan Beal. Of course, there was no guarantee that he would even apply for the job, or that Rob would give it to him if he did, but something told her that Luke was interested and that Rob would be glad to take on someone he knew and could trust.

She decided that as soon as she'd had her coffee, she'd phone in the adverts to the papers.

307

Chapter Sixty-Seven

Luke started work for MacNair's at the beginning of November. His had been the best application from the several that Rob received, no doubt of that. Not only was he an excellent and experienced driver, he was also a trained mechanic who would be particularly useful on the maintenance side. Yet Rob had initially hesitated over taking him.

'I don't see the difficulty,' Tess had commented with some impatience. 'Luke's obviously the best for the job and we already know him; that's worth a lot.'

'Aye, but I'm no' sure about him, all the same. I just canna see him with the clients.'

'Why ever not? He'd be as good as Ewan, probably better.'

'Ewan's on the dour side, but very polite. And sort of negative, if you see what I mean. He's always seemed just part of the car, no' somebody that stands out.'

'You think Luke'd do that?'

'Well, he is pretty big, Tess. And has that red hair.'

'There's nothing wrong with red hair,' Tess retorted, thinking, except on Valerie Arnold. 'Anyway, Luke'll be wearing his cap. And if he's big and strong looking, the clients might like that. Might feel safer.'

'Aye, maybe.' Rob had run a hand through his hair and sighed. 'OK, we'll give him a try then.'

'I'm sure you're doing the right thing,' said Tess.

At first, Luke was very nervous. Not where driving was concerned, but over having to talk to the folk who hired him.

'I'm OK if I just have to drive 'em from A to B,' he told Tess. 'Where I get worked up is when they want me to tell 'em about the countryside and that sort o' thing. I'm no good at that.'

'They canna expect you to talk too much when you're driving. As long as you can answer questions on the route, you'll be OK.'

'How do I answer the questions though? I mean, where do I find the information?'

'I've got notes on all the areas already. I'll go through them with you.'

'Would you, Tess? That'd be grand. I'd be so grateful.'

'And with the winter coming on, we don't get so many people just wanting tours. They mainly want to go to conferences, or hotels, or entertainments, so that'll be easier.' Tess grinned. 'And by next spring, you'll be an expert on the routes anyway. I guarantee it.'

'Don't know what I'd do without you, Tess.'

'Well, you taught me once. Now it's ma turn to teach you.'

'You seem to be spending a lot of time with Luke,' Rob observed to Tess in her office some days later.

'I'm just helping him with local knowledge. So's he can answer clients' questions.'

'Should've thought he could mug that up himself, rather than bother you.'

'You know I've got files on all the things folk like to know about.'

Rob twirled one of Tess's pencils between his fingers. 'Doesn't he have a girlfriend?'

'He told me he went out with plenty of girls.'

'Time he settled on one then. He's too old for that sort of thing.'

'He's only thirty-one.'

'As I say, time he was wed.'

'Better no' say any more, he's just back,' Tess said coolly, looking out from her office to where Luke was expertly bringing in the second Daimler. 'I think he does very well, Rob.'

'I've never said he wasn't an excellent driver.' Rob inclined his head as Luke stepped out of the car, waved and grinned, and took off his cap. 'All well, Luke?'

'Fine, thanks. I've just taken ma chap back to his hotel. He's booked to go back to Perth for another meeting tomorrow.'

'Didn't ask you too many questions, I hope?'

Luke's eyes flickered. 'Didn't ask any. Studied balance sheets all the way, far as I could see.'

'Here's Nola!' Tess said hurriedly. 'We're going out to get Ma's Christmas present. You remember you said you'd man the phone for me, Rob?'

Nola, in a scarlet winter coat and matching hat, looked colourful enough to be on a Christmas card herself, as she stepped through the open garage doors and waved to Tess and Rob. But then her gaze went to Luke, leaning against his car, all six feet four of him, and her eyes sparkled.

'Hello Ginger!' she cried. 'Long time, no see!'

When the sisters had chosen the new Hoover they were clubbing together to give Rena for Christmas, Tess said they might just have time to snatch a cup of tea at Brodie's. Rob, in addition to manning the phone, had agreed to look after Karen when Polly went home, which meant Tess wasn't in a desperate hurry to get back.

'Can always do with a cup of tea,' said Nola. 'Spending money's so exhausting, eh?'

'Think Ma will like it? The Hoover?'

'You know Ma. She'll probably say her old one's still

310

OK and why did we go spending all our cash, etcetera, etcetera. Truth is, her old one sounds like a Lancaster bomber taking off – it's ready to break down any minute.'

'She'll no' hurt our feelings, Nola. She'll say she's pleased, anyway.'

'Aye, I'm only joking.' Nola poured the tea when it came and gave a reminiscent smile. 'Listen, I'd forgotten you had Ginger Moffat working for you now. It was really nice seeing him again.'

'You did seem to have plenty to say to each other,' said Tess, remembering how quickly Luke had straightened up when Nola went over to see him, and how long they'd stood chatting, while Rob fetched Karen and her selection of toys to be deployed around the office.

'Haven't seen him in years, you ken, but we just seemed like old friends.'

'Well, you are old friends. You went to school together.'

'So he knows exactly how old I am. Help!'

'He's the same age as you.'

'Och, men can be any old age and nobody gives a damn.' Nola lit a cigarette. 'Wonder why he's never married.'

'Safety in numbers, as you used to say about me. He's been out with a lot of girls.'

'Has he?' Nola's eyes narrowed. 'Well, we'll have to see how we get on then.'

'How do you mean?'

'He's got ma phone number.'

'Nola! He asked for that just now?'

'No, I gave it to him. Now don't look like that, Tess, all matchmakery. It doesn't mean anything.'

Tess wondered, doesn't it? Whether it meant anything or not, she was looking forward to telling Rob.

That evening, when Nola was washing her stockings in the bathroom, Rena came looking for her.

'Phone for you, Nola.'

'Who is it, Ma?'

311

'Luke Moffat.' Rena's eyes were bright with interest.

'Well, well.' Nola dried her hands, smiling. 'I'll be down in a jiffy.'

She ran lightly downstairs, followed by her mother, and picked up the phone.

Chapter Sixty-Eight

On Christmas morning, Rena assured her girls that she did indeed like her new Hoover, and to prove it vacuumed the house from top to bottom on Boxing Day. Even so her best present, as she confided to everyone, was Nola's romance with Luke Moffat. Aye, the poor girl had found happiness at last, and with a fine, sensible young man, known to them all – his family, too. Was it no' wonderful, the way things could work out?

'Honestly, Ma, I don't know what you're on about,' Nola told her. 'You're happy enough without a man in your life. It wouldn't have been the end of the world if I didn't have one either.'

'Nola, stop fooling now. It's true I'm happy as I am, but you're young, you've got your life before you, and don't tell me you want to live like a nun.'

Nola lowered her eyes then laughed. 'OK, I am glad I've found Luke, but I just don't think all women need men. We're all brought up to believe we've got to get married or we'll be failures, and that's what I think is wrong.'

'Maybe, but don't forget the bairns, Nola. Most women want 'em. I think you do too. And if you marry Luke, you might be lucky, eh?'

'Maybe, but I'm no' free to marry Luke.'

'You get on to Clark then,' said Rena shortly. 'I'd say it was about time you fixed up a divorce.'

And that was true, for on a snowy night in January, when Rena was out with Vera at the pictures, Nola and Luke became lovers. Nola's idea, of course. Dear Luke would never have suggested it – they weren't married, were they?

'Oh, come on, Ginger!' she had cried, leading him up to her bedsitter on the second floor. 'We're grown ups, right? We can do what we like.'

'Nola—' His great figure had hovered at the door of the attractive room she had arranged to suit herself, with pictures, pretty curtains and matching coverlet on the double bed. 'This is no' right, you ken. I mean—'

'You don't know what you mean.' She went to him and put her arms around him. 'You love me, don't you?'

'Oh God, I do.' He held her close. 'But how can we be wed? You're no' free.'

'I will be free. I'm going to get in touch with Clark.'

'He might cause problems.'

'The marriage is over. He knows that.' Nola began to loosen Luke's tie. 'But why are we standing talking? Ginger, we're wasting time.'

They undressed quickly, with Nola suddenly losing her matter-of-factness and becoming as excited and as shaky as Luke as they moved to her bed.

'Am I no' lucky?' she whispered. 'This room Ma gave me just happens to have a double bed. How'd we have managed in a single?'

'We'd have managed,' he answered hoarsely. 'No more talking, Nola, eh?'

Later, sitting fully dressed in the front room, waiting for Rena's return as though the world hadn't changed, hadn't blown up around them, Luke asked Nola when she would be getting in touch with Clark.

'Tomorrow,' she answered firmly, but he thought he could detect a little nervousness under her confidence. He'd noticed before that any mention of Clark seemed to bring that out in her. Five years they'd been separated, and she still seemed to feel guilty about leaving him, though from what Luke had heard of Clark, he'd certainly deserved to be left.

'Canna wait,' he whispered, against her face, 'to get the go-ahead.'

'Come on, we don't need it,' she said with a smile.

'Yes, we do. Think I just want to go to bed with you when your mother's out at the pictures?'

She put her fingers over his lips. 'Don't worry, we'll sort something out. There's the door. Ma's back.'

'Och, that wind's sharp!' cried Rena, taking off her winter boots in the hall. 'Have you two kept the fire up?'

'Sure,' said Luke, hastily throwing on coal. 'Enjoy the picture, Mrs Gillespie?'

'Wasn't bad, just one o' thae musicals, you ken. Nola, shall we put on the kettle?'

'This kitchen's about as warm as the street,' Nola complained, shivering, as she took down the tea caddy. 'Look, you can see ma breath!'

'No' surprising, as you've let the range die down,' said Rena, opening the door of the old range and rattling the poker in the bars. 'What've you been up to then?' She looked up and gave a sudden smile. 'As if I didn't know.'

'Ma, what are you talking about?'

'Well, I'm no Sherlock Holmes, but if I see a girl wearing her jumper back to front when it was on straight before, I think I can make a good guess about what's been going on.'

'Oh,' said Nola, turning red.

'No' need to worry, pet.' Rena put her arm round Nola's shoulders. 'You deserve a bit o' happiness, and if you and Luke canna get married yet, what's it to me if you don't want to wait.'

'You don't mind, Ma?'

'That's what I'm saying. After all, Nola, you're old enough to know what you're doing. Just take care, eh?'

315

Nola threw her arms around her mother and they stood quietly for a moment or two, until the kettle began to splutter and Nola dived to make the tea.

Chapter Sixty-Nine

The good news was that Clark said on the phone that he too wanted a divorce. The bad news was that he wanted to come up and discuss it.

'No need to do that,' Nola said hurriedly. 'We can let the lawyers deal with it.'

'It'll be no trouble, Nola. Obviously, we'll have things to decide. And I'd like to see you anyway.'

'You want to come and stay?'

'No, I'll come up by the early train. Go back the same day. Day after tomorrow suit?'

'Fine. Where'll we meet then?'

'The North British, for lunch?'

'Be serious, Clark!'

'I am serious. My business is doing very well – I'd like to give you lunch.'

'Well, I'm no' going to a smart place like the North British. Make it that pub we used to go to in the West End. Smithy's.'

'OK. One o'clock?'

'One o'clock.'

'Now, what's he playing at?' Nola asked Tess later. 'Why's he coming up to Edinburgh? He needn't.'

'He says he wants to see you. I think that's only natural. You'll have plenty to discuss.'

'We could have done it all through the lawyers.' Nola drew on a cigarette. 'I don't trust him, Tess. He says he wants the divorce, but I bet he doesn't.'

'Did you tell him about Luke?'

'Yes, I said I wanted to marry again. He didn't say if he'd found anybody.'

'You've been separated a long time, I'm sure he's reconciled to losing you, Nola.'

'I hope so.' Nola shook her head. 'Because he lost me a long time ago.'

He'd put on weight. That was the first thing she noticed when they met in the pub crowded with West End office workers, smoking and chattering, while the wireless blared out rock and roll. Yes, his face had filled out so much, he'd lost his old Clark Gable look, yet still had the smile, still had the charm.

'Nola, you look smashing,' he told her, rising from the table he'd found near a window. 'Never change, do you?'

'No' slimmer, that's for sure.'

'How about me? You can tell I'm living the good life.' He laughed. 'Not strictly true. It's my mother's cooking. Keeps inviting me for meals.'

Nola asked after his mother and his family. Clark asked after Rena and Tess. It was all very polite, very civilised. When Clark had fetched drinks and sandwiches from the bar, Nola made an effort to move things forward the way she wanted.

'P'raps we'd better get on with what we came to say, Clark.'

'Not so easy here, is it?'

'I did say no' to come.'

'I told you, I wanted to see you.' Clark set down his ham sandwich. 'One last time.'

'We'll be meeting again, I expect.'

'I mean, while we're still married.'

Nola sighed. 'You are happy about the divorce, Clark? I

318

mean, you're no' going to make difficulties?'

'Have I ever been a difficult chap?'

'No, but this is a very difficult time. Everybody says so.'

'I know you've found somebody you want to marry, and I suppose it's time I did too.'

'Oh, I wish you could! I wish you could find someone to make you happy.'

'And what if she finds everything wrong with me, the way you did? You never did make any sense, you know.'

He hasn't changed, she thought. He will never change. He still couldn't see why he should. Maybe someone else could live with that, but thank God she didn't have to any more.

'Let's talk about the divorce,' she said quietly.

She'd taken a day off from the pottery so was able to see him off at Waverley, still unsure of his real intentions, but relieved that on the surface, at least, he'd been co-operative.

'Tell me about this guy you've met,' he murmured, as they waited for his train. 'He'll not be like me, I suppose?'

'He's very quiet.'

'Not like me at all then.' He laughed. 'Just hope he makes you happy, Nola.'

'Thank you.' She leaned forward and kissed his cheek. 'And thanks for being so helpful.'

'Why d'you never trust me?' The platform lights glowed dimly on his face that seemed suddenly blank, suddenly strange, without its charm. His voice was soft, persuasive, though he was no longer trying to persuade. 'I'd always want to help you, Nola.'

She opened her mouth, wanting to find something to say, when a hissing and steaming announced the arrival of the train south, and she stepped back.

'We'll be in touch,' she called, as Clark picked up his bag. But he dropped it again and took her in his arms, holding her tight.

'Goodbye, Nola,' he whispered. '"Ae fond kiss, and

then we sever ..." Isn't that what your poet says?'

He kissed her lightly, took up his bag again and climbed onto the train.

'Imagine you quoting Burns,' she murmured at the open door to the corridor. 'You can always surprise me, Clark.'

'I tell you, you don't know me at all.'

Other passengers were boarding, he stepped aside, waved and shouted, 'Don't wait!'

But she did wait until the train moved away, as though she wanted to see him really leave, and then she turned away herself and Luke's face came suddenly, gladly, into her mind.

Oh, Ginger, she thought, life's going to be so much easier with you!

That evening, before Luke arrived, Nola rang Tess to tell her the good news that all had gone smoothly with Clark's visit.

'Seemed strange really, he was so nice. I'm still wondering if he'll come up with some spanner to throw into the works.'

'Nola, why don't you trust him?'

'Funny you should say that – he asked me the same thing. And I couldn't really say. Maybe I'm just too scared to believe things are going well.'

'Luke's so happy, you ken. If you could see him at work these days – he's just one big smile. Isn't that right, Rob? Isn't Luke over the moon?'

'Happy as a sandboy,' said Rob.

'Rob says he's as happy as a sandboy – whatever that means,' Tess told Nola and was still smiling as she rang off.

'I'm happy too,' she said to Rob. 'Just thinking of Nola and Luke.'

'Nola's well shot of Clark Walters, from all accounts.' Rob yawned, and opened one of his road maps. 'Suppose I'd better check the route for ma trip north tomorrow.'

'Thank goodness it's no' snowing.'

'Aye, that's a relief. I should be back by about eleven.'

'You could always stay overnight if necessary.'

'Like to get back if I can.' He came to Tess and kissed her on the lips. 'It's lonely in hotel rooms.'

Chapter Seventy

Early in February Tess took a booking from two business-men for a drive to Glasgow where they would be attending a meeting, followed by a company dinner at one of the main hotels. Rob had taken them to the same event the year before and was pleased to be asked to drive them again. It was a long day for him and involved a certain amount of hanging around, but that didn't matter – the money was good.

On the morning of the trip, Tess looked out from the garage doors and was relieved to see that the day, though bitterly cold, was fine.

'I dread the snow,' she murmured to Luke, who was giving his car a last polish before leaving to take an elderly lady to relatives in the Borders. 'Not for maself, I never mind the weather, but for you folk. Always worse, eh, thinking about other folk?'

'Black ice is worse than snow,' commented Luke. 'And have you ever tried to get through freezing rain? I remember once when ma whole car frosted up around me like a wedding cake – couldn't see a damn thing!'

'Talking of wedding cakes – canna wait to be eating yours,' Tess said, laughing, and Luke gave a seraphic smile.

'Canna wait maself, though I ken fine it'll be a long wait.'

'You'll get there in the end,' said Tess, as Rob came running down the stairs with Karen.

'All set, Luke?'

'That's right. Reckon I'll be back from Kelso before you.'

'Aye, it'll be midnight for me or even later.' Rob handed Karen over to Tess. 'Don't wait up, sweetheart. These dinners can go on for ever.'

'Why don't the clients stay overnight?'

'Want to get home, like me.'

Tess, with the wriggling Karen who was not allowed to get down until the cars had departed, waved, as first Luke, and then Rob, departed.

'Bye bye, Dad,' sang Karen, as Tess finally set her down and closed the garage doors.

'Bye bye, Dad,' echoed Tess. 'Come on then, let's go and see Honey and wait for Polly.'

'Dad come back soon?'

'Not very soon, pet, you'll be in your bed by the time he comes home.'

'See him in the morning?'

'In the morning,' said Tess, and held Karen's hand as they climbed the stairs.

After successfully filling in his time while his clients, John Henderson and Stuart Mason attended their meeting, Rob collected them and drove them to the hotel where their company dinner was to take place. Both had already changed into dinner jackets and were anxious that Rob should have a good meal himself, even offering him a hefty tip for it, but he told them it would all go on the bill. Yes, he did know a place to eat, and would be back to pick them up at half past eleven.

'Sorry it's so late,' said John Henderson, who like Stuart Mason, was fortyish, fit and confident. 'You know what these things are like.'

'Yes, sir.' Rob grinned. He should do, he thought, he'd

323

taken enough guys to dinners and waited around for them. Just as long as they weren't sick in his Daimler, he didn't mind what time he got home. 'No need to worry.'

As his clients moved to the bar, joining a gaggle of men looking identical to themselves, Rob braved the bleak winter evening to find the café he always patronised, and ordered steak, chips and tomatoes. Thank God the days of rationing were past, he thought, and bought an evening paper to see what was on the pictures.

By half past eleven, he was back at the hotel, having sat through a quite unmemorable film and afterwards listened to the wireless in his car. Elvis Presley. You couldn't get away from the fella. Rob had shaken his head in wonder. Give him Bing Crosby any day of the week!

He'd hoped to find his clients waiting, but there was no sign of them in the foyer, and a yawning receptionist told him that the company dinner was not yet over.

'They're still on the speeches,' he added. 'They pay the speakers a fortune, so they want their money's worth.'

'Hell,' muttered Rob. 'Mind if I wait here?'

'You're welcome.'

It was well after midnight before a stream of men in high spirits began to appear from the private room where the dinner had been held, and John Henderson sought out Rob.

'Mr MacNair, I really must apologise.' He ran his hand through his hair and coughed. 'Never thought it'd go on so long.'

'That's all right, sir.' Rob's eyes were busily going over faces. 'Is Mr Mason with you?'

'No.' Mr Henderson gave a shamefaced smile. 'To tell you the truth, he's had a bit too much of the old vino and we've had to book in at the hotel for the night. I'm afraid we won't be coming back with you to Edinburgh.'

Rob, poker-faced, said nothing.

'I couldn't feel worse about this,' Henderson went on. 'You might have gone home hours ago.'

'These things happen, sir. And you didn't know where to find me.'

'Well, look, you must let us get you a room here. You won't want to drive back now, will you?'

'Thanks all the same, but it's no distance, and I should really get home. I've an early start tomorrow.' Rob hesitated. 'In fact, I won't be able to collect you in the morning.'

'That's all right.' Harrison tried another smile. 'We should be sober enough to get the train tomorrow. Charge us for the round trip, though. We don't want you to be out of pocket.'

Nor do I want to be out of pocket, thought Rob, making his way to the public telephone in the foyer, where he put through a call to Tess and told her he'd be home even later than expected.

'You're still in Glasgow?' she cried. 'Oh, Rob, what's gone wrong?'

'Don't ask.' He laughed. 'You just get your sleep and I'll be home as soon as I can.'

'Take care then.'

'Always do. See you soon, sweetheart.'

Outside the hotel, the night wind cut like a knife, and a steely rain was beginning to fall, glittering on the Daimler's roof in the lights of the car park. Rob, shivering, was thankful to get into the driving seat and start the engine, be out of the cold and on his way home at last. With a car like his, he wasn't really worried whatever the weather threw at him, but if that rain was going to turn to sleet or snow, he'd still prefer to be out of it. At least, at that time of night, there would be very little traffic.

He knew the Edinburgh road so well, he felt he could have driven it blindfold, and the Daimler, unimpeded by other cars, was going like a dream. In fact, he began to think as he covered the miles, that his whole journey was a little like a dream anyway. One of those dreams where you

325

journey on and on, past silent houses and sleeping towns, and you finally realise you are the only person left alive in the whole world, or at least the only person awake.

His neck gave a jerk, his head flew back and he knew that for a split second he had been asleep. Asleep. Oh God, he should stop. Stop at once. But if he stopped, he might sleep till morning and he couldn't risk that. After all, he was on the home stretch, he'd be all right to keep going if he reduced his speed, turned off the heater and opened the window for fresh air. That should do the trick.

At first he felt better, breathing in the cold air, but then realised he was getting soaked from the sleeting rain blowing in, and that his hands on the wheel were almost numb. He closed the window and turned up the heater; just for a little while, he told himself, till he thawed out. Pretty soon, he'd be seeing the lights of Edinburgh, but for now all was dark. There was just himself and the car, moving slowly through the night. Himself and the car, then nothing at all, until ahead of him the whole road seemed lit by tremendous radiance. A great circle of light that dazzled and dazzled, until he and his car hit it, when it disappeared. And so did he.

Chapter Seventy-One

It was some hours later that two police officers, one a woman, gently told Tess that her husband had been involved in an accident. They took her up to her own kitchen and made her tea. They told her she wasn't to worry, Mr MacNair had been injured in a collision, but he was all right, he was alive. He'd been taken to the Royal Infirmary. Did she need help with arrangements to go and see him?

She said yes, then no, then shook her head, sitting at the table, a cup of scarcely tasted tea in front of her, while Honey whined at her feet and Karen slept in her cot. Every part of her wanted to run. Just run and run, across Edinburgh to the hospital, to Rob, her own darling, who wasn't dead, thank God, only injured. But how badly?

'How bad is he?' she whispered. 'Can you tell me?'

'He has a head injury, but the doctors aren't saying it's serious. We're no' sure about the other driver. He's in the Royal too.'

The other driver. Tess's eyes widened in horror. She hadn't even thought of anyone else. Something cold seemed to trickle down her spine.

'He's no' dead?' she cried.

'No, no, Mrs MacNair,' the policewoman said soothingly. 'No one's dead. They've been lucky. Now, is there anybody we can ask to come and give you a hand?'

'Thank you, thank you very much, there's a friend coming in anyway to help with ma little girl. I can go to the hospital soon as she comes. And then there's ma mother, but I'd better phone her maself – she'll be in a state, if you say you're the police.' Tess stood up, putting her hand to her brow. 'She'll come, she'll help me. We'll go to the Royal together.'

'You're sure you'll be all right then, Mrs MacNair?'

'Yes, I'm fine. Thank you again, you've been very kind.'

'We saw from his identification that Mr MacNair is a chauffeur,' the policeman said at her door. 'A very experienced driver then?'

'Very experienced,' Tess said quickly. 'A wonderful driver. He's never had an accident.'

'And driving a Daimler.' Both police officers shook their heads, and said again she wasn't to worry. Then they saw themselves out.

Afterwards, Tess wondered how she'd got through those first terrible moments when she was alone and had to make her phone calls and decide what to do, all the time thinking of Rob. But folk did get through things, didn't they? From somewhere came the strength. You kept going because you had to, otherwise you collapsed.

But her mother was soon rushing in to take her into her arms, followed by Nola and Luke, who said he would drive Tess to the infirmary.

'To hell with the bookings!' he cried, his hair aflame against his grey face. 'Nola, can you look in the diary and cancel the bookings?'

'The bookings,' Tess said in a daze. 'I'd forgotten about them.'

'Don't worry, leave them to me,' Nola told her. 'I'm no' going in to work this morning.'

'Nor me,' cried Rena. 'I'll come with you to the hospital, Tess.'

'Anybody home?' cried Polly, bouncing up the stairs, then turning pale when she saw the faces looking at her. 'Why, whatever's happened?'

At the hospital, only Tess was allowed to see Rob and then only for a few minutes. He had recovered consciousness, but was suffering from concussion symptoms and a possible fracture of the skull, caused by his head hitting the car windscreen.

'Don't worry,' the doctor told Tess, seeing the look on her face when he used the word fracture. 'It may be only a linear fracture, nothing serious. X-rays will show just what damage has been done and whether there's any internal bleeding. I think myself that the signs are good. Your husband's been lucky.'

Lucky? He didn't seem particularly lucky when Tess looked down at him, lying with his eyes closed in his side ward. He was so still. So pale. His face was as white as the bandages round his head. It was true, though, that he was lucky, because he was alive. Whatever had happened, whatever he'd done, he was alive. And that was all that mattered. Absolutely all.

'Rob?' she whispered, sinking to her knees by his bed. 'Rob, it's me, Tess.'

His eyes opened, and in their dark-blue depths, something flickered.

'Oh, Rob—'

In tears, she reached out to hold his hand, but after a few moments, during which Rob made no sign that he knew her, the nurse said she should go. Mr MacNair might be much better tomorrow.

Outside, in the corridor, Tess stood very still. She was trying to think why that strange phrase had come into her mind when she'd first looked down at Rob.

'Whatever had happened, whatever he'd done.'

329

Why should Rob be the one to have done something wrong? Nobody had said whose fault the accident had been. Perhaps it was the other driver's fault; perhaps no-one's.

Why should she, of all people, blame her husband?

I'm not blaming him! she cried inwardly.

But she couldn't forget the look on the policeman's face when he had commented on Rob's being a chauffeur. 'A very experienced driver, then?' As though he had been surprised.

Chapter Seventy-Two

The name of the other driver was Mark Andrews, a commercial traveller who'd been travelling home to Glasgow after some days on the road. As he admitted, he'd stopped off on the evening of the accident for a few drinks with pals in Edinburgh, and on continuing his journey had decided to pull in to the side of the road to sleep.

'Oh, God,' groaned Rob. 'He was sleeping?'

He turned his face away from Luke, who was sitting by his bed, and bit his lips, trying to gain some self-control. Although it had been established that he was suffering only from a minor fracture of the skull, he felt so sick and weak he could have burst into tears in front of the sympathetic Luke.

'Seems so.' Luke shifted uneasily on a chair that was too small for him. 'He'd left his lights on, thought he'd be OK.'

Rob moved his bandaged head on his pillow. He didn't speak.

'Look, he's no' been badly hurt,' Luke said awkwardly. 'Cracked ribs and a punctured lung. They say he'll be fine.'

'Lucky is the word,' muttered Rob.

'Well, it's true, Rob. If he'd no' been stationary and you'd been doing a normal speed, things would've been different.'

'So, I should be grateful. Well, I am grateful that that fella's alive. But what's going to happen to me?'

Luke cleared his throat. 'You've no' seen the police yet?'

'They're interviewing me tomorrow.'

'Just tell 'em the truth, Rob, it's all you can do.'

'Luke, they already know it.' Rob's voice was turning faint. 'I fell asleep at the wheel. I crossed the road. They'll charge me, you ken. They'll have to.'

'You don't know that, Rob.'

'Aye, I do. And it'll be the end o' me.' Again, Rob turned his face away. 'Think you'd better go, Luke.'

'Rob, if there's anything I can do—'

The tears finally broke from Rob's eyes and made slow trickles down his cheeks. 'Only put the clock back. Canna do that, can you?'

Tess was waiting in the corridor when Luke finally left Rob, walking like a tired, old man. As soon as she saw him she flew to him, catching at his arm.

'How is he, Luke? The nurse said I couldn't go in till you came out, but he's better today, eh?'

'In a way.'

'What do you mean? They said he was much improved!'

'I mean – well, he's a bit depressed, Tess. You'd better – prepare yourself.'

Her grey eyes, stricken, searched his. 'He's worrying, Luke?'

'Aye.'

They said no more. Tess released Luke's arm and turned turned aside.

'I'll go to him,' she said in a low voice.

He was still handsome, even though so pale, but his profile seemed sharp, his cheeks quite hollow. As she came near him, it seemed to Tess that Rob was still very sick.

'Tess?' He turned his still-bandaged head and tried to smile, but she could see the marks of his tears on his face, and wanted to collapse, weeping, over his bed. Instead, she pulled up the one chair and gently touched her lips to his cheek.

'How are you, Rob?'

'Fine. They're moving me to a main ward tomorrow.'

'That's grand, that's really grand.'

'Have to be interviwed first.' He licked his dry lips. 'By the police.'

'Oh, yes. Well, they'd be sure to want to speak to you, eh?'

'Aye.'

In his eyes that were dark now, rather than blue, she could read everything he wouldn't tell her, everything she already knew.

'The other driver's going to be all right,' she said after a pause. 'Mr Andrews.'

'I heard.'

'That'll help, eh?'

For some time, Rob made no reply. Finally, he said in a voice she could scarcely hear, 'Did you know he was sleeping?'

'Sleeping?'

'In his car.' Suddenly, Rob dragged himself up from his pllow and stared, wild-eyed, at Tess. 'If only that'd been me, Tess!'

'Lie down, Rob, lie still! You shouldn't be upsetting yourself.'

'It should've been me, Tess. I should've been that man! But I kept on. I kept on and I threw everything away. Everything!'

'No' me!' cried Tess and held him fast. 'You've still got me, you've still got Karen, Rob. Think of us!'

At last he grew calmer and Tess wiped his face, kissed him and made him lie back.

'You have us. And you're alive. That's all that matters.'

'Aye,' he whispered. 'That's true, that's true. I'll hang on to that.'

Some days later, however, he was formally charged by the police with dangerous driving.

333

Chapter Seventy-Three

The family at that point moved into limbo. What else could they do? Nothing could be decided, no plans made, until they knew what was to happen to Rob, and they had been informed that his case would not come up for some time. How could he ever get well then, with such a sword hanging by a hair over his poor, shaven head? How could he ever follow the doctors' orders to rest when they finally sent him home? That was a laugh, that was, telling a man waiting for judgement, to rest.

But rest to begin with was vital, the doctors said. Although he appeared to have made a good recovery, Mr MacNair might still have problems. Headaches, perhaps, or nervousness, or depression. On the other hand, he was young and strong and might have no problems at all. At least, not medical problems.

Once Rob was home, everyone rallied round, of course, though there was not a great deal they could do. Gordon came from the farm whenever he could, and Katie brought cream, butter and fresh vegetables to put some weight on Rob's and Tess's bones, for they were both like a couple of spectres, so they were.

'Aye, you're nothing but great eyes, the pair o' you,' Rena would tell Tess in agreement, and take the lid off another stew, or unpack another apple pie, while the neighbours would bring shortbread, or sweeties for poor wee Karen, who couldn't understand why her dad looked so strange and spent so much time lying down.

'I've tried to explain,' Tess sighed to Nola. 'But it's no' easy for a wee lassie to understand, eh? At least Rob seems no different to Honey, except that she keeps waiting for him to take her out, and of course he canna do that yet. Och, it's no' much to worry about at a time like this, but it mounts up in ma mind, even so.'

'Thing is, you've too much to worry about, Tess, and you're trying to do too much. It'll do nobody any good if you crack up.'

'I'm OK, I'm stronger than I look. And everybody's helping anyway. You, Ma, Luke—' Tess shook her head. 'I don't know what I'd do without Luke.'

'Good old Ginger,' Nola said, with a smile. 'Ma hero.'

'Well, he is a hero, Nola. The hours he's putting in, driving that one car! If anybody's doing too much, it's Luke, but he wants to do it for Rob, for the business.'

'Aye, I said the same about cracking up to him as I said to you, but he'll no' listen. Tells me he's even going to work on Rob's car. Is that right?'

'Yes, it's been released to us and Mr Todd's got it. Luke's going round to the garage when he can to give a hand. That's another thing he's doing for Rob.'

'I bet Rob's really grateful he's got Luke, eh?' asked Nola, lighting a cigarette, and after a moment Tess lit one too.

'Oh, yes,' she agreed. 'He really appreciates Luke.'

Rob, enjoying his rest as much as a caged lion might, leaped up from the sofa in the living room when Tess came in later from the kitchen.

'Any post?' he cried.

'No, it's far too late for post now, you ken that.'

She began to straighten the cushions behind his head, trying not to touch the healing wound that glowed red and

335

angry in the fuzz of his newly growing hair. The doctors had said the scar would fade and would scarcely be seen once his hair had completely grown, but there was no doubt that at present he looked strange. His energy was returning though, and when he took her hand, she could almost feel him throbbing, raring to go, longing to get off that sofa and return to work.

'I thought there'd be a second post,' he muttered, still holding her hand. 'You ken what I'm waiting for, eh?'

'News of your case – yes, I know. Well, it hasn't come, and you're no' to worry about it, Rob. Just concentrate on getting well.'

'I am well! I'm fit enough now to get up now and drive Luke's car.'

'Thank God you canna do that,' she said with a shudder.

'You think I canna drive now?'

'I think you're no' well enough to drive.' Tess took her hand from his and sat down near him. 'Nola was just saying how lucky we are to have Luke.'

'Aye.' Rob took a packet of cigarettes from his jacket pocket. 'Will you give me a light, Tess?'

'I wish you wouldn't smoke, Rob. I'm sure the doctors don't approve.'

'I have to have something to get me through the days, or I'll go off ma rocker. What do you think it's like for me, sitting here, worrying about the insurance and everything?' He cleared his throat. 'Waiting for that call to go to court?'

Tess struck a match with a sigh and lit his cigarette for him. 'Luke says he's sure they'll be lenient. You didn't mean to fall asleep.'

'Luke? What the hell does he know about sheriff's courts? I was driving without due care and attention, I admit it. They canna overlook it.'

'Why do you talk of Luke in that way? He's only trying to help.'

'Because I wish I was him, that's why.' Rob drew shakily on his cigarette. 'I wish I was being helpful and

336

doing ma best, instead o' feeling ashamed.'

'Oh Rob, don't!' Tess took his face in her hands, willing him to listen to her. 'There's no need for you to feel ashamed. The men at the hotel had kept you late and you were tired – it's no wonder you fell asleep.'

His eyes on her were dark and empty, as he slowly shook his head.

'Tess, I should have stopped. Like Mr Andrews, I should've pulled over and stopped. He did the right thing, and I went into him because I didn't.'

'He's all right, he's recovered!'

'Aye, and if he hadn't I'd be looking at prison.'

'Rob!'

He slowly swung himself from the sofa and stubbed out his cigarette in an ashtray on the sideboard.

'I'd have deserved it, an' all,' he added quietly.

'He didn't die, you'll no' be going to prison!'

Rob shrugged. 'We don't know what's going to happen to me, do we? See now why I'm ready to go crazy?'

Long weeks passed before Rob's case came to court, by which time his hair had grown and covered his scar and he looked almost his old self. He was certainly much stronger; ready to take up his life again, if allowed. No one dared to face the possibility that that might not happen.

When he had to present himself before the sheriff, all the family went to court, though he had said he'd rather they didn't.

'Now that's a piece o' nonsense, Rob,' Rena told him bluntly. 'Tess has got to be there; she has to know as soon as possible what's going to happen. And if Tess is there, I'll be there.'

He'd shrugged and nodded. There were times when you could argue with Rena, and times when you couldn't, and he knew which was which.

'OK, all of you come,' he said wearily. 'I just wanted to spare you the ordeal.'

'Och, Rob, as though we'd no' want to support you!' She'd kissed his thin cheek. 'Get on with you then. My guess is you'll be walking out o' that court without a stain on your character.'

But Rena wasn't right about that. The sheriff presiding over the court said that although he'd taken into account the defendant's exemplary record and that he needed his licence to run his business, his offence was grave and might have had very serious consequences. Had the other motorist involved been fatally injured, the defendant would have been looking at a custodial sentence. As it was, he, the sheriff, had no choice but to disqualify him from driving for a period of two years and to impose a fine of fifty pounds.

As Rob left the court, accompanied by his lawyer, Tess ran to him and took his hand, but he looked at her as though he didn't know who she was.

Or who he is himself, thought Nola. Oh God, how are they going to get through this?

Chapter Seventy-Four

As soon as they arrived home, Rob went into the bedroom and closed the door. He had not spoken since they'd left the court.

'Rob?' called Tess, tapping on the door. 'Will you let me in?'

He made no answer.

'He's no' locked the door,' said Rena, standing with Karen in her arms. 'Just go on in.'

'I don't like to. I don't think he wants me.'

'He needs somebody,' said Nola. She looked in her bag for a cigarette. 'Just wish Luke was here.'

But Luke was out driving, as he always was, trying to do the work of two.

'He'll be in a state,' Rena murmured, 'when he hears about Rob.'

'We're all in a state.' Nola put her arm round Tess. 'Go on, Tess, go and talk to him. Make him see that what's happened is no' the end o' the world.'

'It is though,' said Tess. 'For him.'

He was sitting by the window, looking out at the spring evening. There was not much of a view of course, just a street, but the sky was still azure blue and the clouds were small. It would be light for hours yet.

'Rob, sweetheart, turn round,' whispered Tess. 'Look at me.'

He did turn round, he did look at her, but his face was so blank, his eyes so dead, it was hardly possible to say that this was Rob. He had become a stranger again and Tess felt her courage fast flowing away as she tried to find the words to reach him.

'Look, it's all right,' she began, but he held up his hand.

'All right? Ma business is finished and you say it's all right?'

'It's no' finished, Rob. How can you say that? You'll get your licence back – this is just a temporary problem.'

'Oh yes? A temporary problem?' Suddenly, his face was animated again, flushed and sweating, but he looked no less strange. 'A temporary problem that's going to kill ma business stone dead? Who's going to want to use a chauffeur service run by a man convicted of dangerous driving? Who's going to ring up and say, "Oh, is that Mr MacNair, the one who's lost his licence? How about driving me to Gleneagles then?" I could laugh ma hat off at you saying that, Tess, if I didn't feel like bawling like a bairn!'

'A lot of the people who call on you, Rob, are strangers to the city. They won't have seen reports of what happened to you. All they'll do is ring up and book Luke.'

'Luke, oh yes, Luke!' Rob's mouth twisted.

'Yes, Luke! That's the point, we've still got Luke. And we've still got two cars. Yours has been repaired, it's as good as new, you know that, and I can drive it. Why not?'

'That's your solution, is it? You driving ma Daimler?'

'Well, I can. There's no reason why I shouldn't share the trips with Luke. He could do overnights with male clients, I could do the rest. Don't tell me I couldn't drive old ladies to the Borders or wherever, Rob, because I know I could!'

'I'm no' having it, Tess. You're no' doing ma work for me.' Rob ran a trembling hand over his brow. 'Don't ask me to say yes to that, just don't ask me!'

'It'd only be temporary,' she pleaded. 'Just till you got

back to work yourself. It'd be a way of keeping the business going, can you no' see that?'

'I see you and Luke running what was mine, that's what I see.' Rob's flush had faded and he was now very pale, drops of sweat standing on his brow, his eyes dark pools. As Tess stared, mystified, he suddenly leaned forward and grasped her wrist. 'It's what he's wanted all along, eh? This precious Luke we canna do without? He's always had his eye on you, and now he's got you and he's got ma business an' all. Think I'm going to stand by and let him take both?'

'What are you talking about?' Tess pulled her wrist from his hold and stood rubbing it, her eyes desperate on his face. 'Luke doesn't care about me, he's engaged to ma sister. They're only waiting for the divorce to come through to be married.'

'He's only engaged to Nola because he canna get you, Tess. And now he sees his chance. He'll be running the business with you, and I'll be doing what? Lying down, resting? Taking the bookings? Think I could stand that? I'd rather die!'

'Rob, it's your accident that's making you talk this way. When you feel better, you'll see that.'

Tess tried to take Rob's hands, but he pulled them away and moved to a chair by the bed where he sank down, turning his face away.

'Will you just go now?' he asked quietly. 'I think I do need to rest.'

'All right,' she said eagerly. 'Why don't you go to bed for a while? I'll bring you your tea and then you'll soon be yourself again.'

'Aye, maybe.'

'I mean it, Rob.' Tess was pulling off his shoes and undoing his tie. 'This business is no' going under because of what's happened. It'll be kept going for you, I promise you, because it's your business and no one else's.'

He lay on the bed, fixing her with his same sombre gaze,

but he made no reply and she stooped to kiss his brow.

'You're exhausted, you ken. You'll see everything differently when you've had some rest.'

She moved quietly to the door and when she looked back, saw that his eyes were closed.

Chapter Seventy-Five

'How is he then?' asked Nola, when Tess joined her in the kitchen where she was washing lettuce. They had decided to have a cold meal that evening, to make things easier after the court case. As though anything could seem easy after the court case, Tess had thought, but she didn't care what she ate anyway.

'He's no' well,' she answered now, not looking at her sister, feeling her cheeks burn at the memory of Rob's accusations. 'Canna cope yet.'

'I'm no' surprised,' said Rena, slicing ham on the bone. 'After all he's been through, to have all of this to worry about, and the fine to pay as well. But I'll help, Tess, I'll see you're all right.'

'We can manage, Ma, but thanks.' Tess poured herself a cup of tea. 'I'll take some of that ham into Rob, though he might be asleep.'

'Why's Dad asleep when I'm awake?' asked Karen. 'It's no' night time yet.'

'He's very tired, pet. He has been ill.'

'Can I go and see him? I won't wake him.'

'Not just now.' Tess kissed her daughter's soft cheek. 'You're going to have your tea.'

'You look as if you should be sleeping yourself,' Nola told Tess when Karen had danced off. 'Listen, what's going to happen? Are you going to try to carry on?'

'Of course they're going to carry on,' cried Rena. 'They've got Luke, eh?'

'We'll have to see,' Tess answered with lowered gaze. 'When Luke comes in, we'll discuss it.

'Och, I canna believe it,' groaned Luke, sitting in front of a plate of ham salad, not touching it. 'No, I canna take it in.'

'Of course you can,' said Nola. 'It's what you expected, eh? It's what we all expected and never wanted to say. Rob did cause an accident, it canna be denied.'

'Aye, but they needn't have banned him for two years. They knew his livelihood was at stake.'

'Maybe they thought he deserved a longer ban then,' said Rena. 'I mean, if he was a professional. Och, you canna tell what's in thae sheriffs' minds. I mean, that other fella was never charged, was he? Even though he'd been drinking?'

'He'd stopped driving.' Luke picked up his knife and fork. 'Must've let him off for that. But how's Rob taking it, Tess? How are you, come to that?'

'I'm all right, thanks.' Again, Tess coloured and had to look down at the table, rather than face Luke's large, concerned eyes. 'But Rob's pretty bad, to be honest.'

'I thought he would be. He thinks that much of his business, eh? And then, he's proud. He'll no' want me doing everything.'

'You'll have to,' Nola said crisply, 'if the business is going to survive.'

Tess hesitated. 'You're forgetting me. I can drive the second car.'

Three pairs of eyes opened wide.

'Tess, you're never thinking o' driving that Daimler!' cried her mother. 'It's too big for you; you'd never handle it!'

'I've already handled it. I can drive it anywhere.'

'Tess, it'd never work out,' Luke said gently. 'I mean – you, driving men around—'

344

'Oh come on, what year are we living in?' cried Nola. 'In the war, women drove men around all the time. I think it's a grand idea, Tess. It'd solve everything.'

'I thought Luke and me could split the drives, so that he takes the ones suitable for him, and I take the ones suitable for me.' Tess passed Luke more bread and butter. 'But Rob doesn't want me to do it.'

'I thought he wouldn't,' said Luke. 'He's never really wanted you to drive the Daimler, Tess.'

'Well, things are different now,' Nola told him. 'He canna afford to lay down the law when he's dependent on Tess, can he?'

'Oh, don't say that, Nola,' said Tess. 'Don't say he's dependent. Think how he'll hate it! He was always so strong.'

'Why can you no' just take on another driver?' asked Rena.

'Because he'd need wages and I wouldn't,' said Tess.

'And it'd be crazy to do that, when there's Tess ready to do the job,' put in Nola. 'You tell Rob it's been decided, Tess. He'll come round to it, you'll see. If it keeps the business going.'

Tess, swallowing hard, said she'd see how he was in the morning.

Lying beside Rob that night, listening to his ragged breathing, she thought back to the times when they'd been happy and made love in this very bed. But they hadn't made love since his accident, and already she was dividing their lives into before that and after that, and thinking that all their happiness had been before and might never come again.

A great sadness filled her being, as she stared into the darkness, for everything had changed so much and so fast it was hard to imagine ever recapturing what they'd once had. Rob himself had changed, become a stranger, and if that was because of his injury and understandable, he was still different even so. All she could do was make herself remember that the two years would pass, that Rob would have his licence back and be himself again. Hang on to that, she told herself. Remember that.

'Tess,' she heard him say. 'Are you awake?'

'Oh, yes, I'm awake.'

'I canna sleep. Just as well. If I sleep, I dream.'

'You have to sleep some time, Rob.'

'Aye.' He laughed harshly in the darkness. 'Being awake's a nightmare anyhow.'

'Rob, it's only going to be two years, then you'll be as you were before. That's no' so long to wait, is it?'

'You don't understand. I've lost everything.'

'You're right, I don't understand.' Her voice trembled. 'You've had a setback, but you've still got me, you've still got Karen, and you're still alive. And you say you've lost everything.'

'I've lost maself, is what I mean.' he said quietly. 'The man I was – he's no' here anymore. It's you who decides what we'll do now, you and Luke. OK, you say there's nothing between you. I believe you, but that doesn't alter the fact that he's doing the work I should be doing, and so are you.'

'Rob, it's only temporary!' she cried. 'Won't you listen to me? It's only for a couple of years!'

'And at the end of that, what?'

'I keep telling you, you'll be the same as you once were.'

'No, Tess.' He pulled himself up against his pillows, breathing fast. 'I'll never be the same. My strength has gone. I'll never be the man I was.'

Chapter Seventy-Six

Now that the court case was over there were various matters to be settled, not least the insurance claims for Rob and Mr Andrews, but when Tess tried to discuss these with Rob he simply said it was her affair now. Nothing to do with him.

'Rob, the business is still yours,' she told him. 'Just because you canna drive doesn't mean you canna run the business.'

'Driving *is* the business, Tess. You're the driver now. I'm leaving everything to you.'

She stared at him, aware that this was not her Rob talking, yet still bewildered by his attitude.

'Look, I've been thinking – if you really don't want me to drive, I won't. I don't want to upset you when you've been ill. We'll hire someone, eh? And hope we can find the cash. The thing is, we do need money—'

'Do you have to keep on bringing that up? I know we're short. I know what damage I've done, OK?' He fixed her with another long, sombre gaze. 'You drive if you want to. Drive as much as you like. If you get any clients to drive, that is. Have you taken any bookings this morning?'

'Yes, there were a few. From Americans.'

Suddenly she felt weary of struggling with him. She decided she would do what she wanted to do and he could accept it or not; it didn't matter any more. He'd put the reins in her hands and she'd hold on to them. First thing tomorrow, she'd see about an outfit – navy jacket, navy trousers. She might even buy a cap. But as Rob left her, walking slowly away with Honey, for he was now well enough to take her on the beach, Tess thought she'd never felt her heart so heavy, her spirits so low. Not, at least, since she'd been married.

It was true that bookings were slightly down in the first weeks after the court case, but gradually they began to pick up and Tess was able to take out her first clients. Some expressed surprise when offered the services of Mrs MacNair instead of Mr MacNair and asked what had happened to him, clearly not having read the papers, but nobody turned her down. One or two older ladies, in fact, said it was rather nice to be driven by another lady, even though Rena said later that she hoped they hadn't objected to Tess's trousers.

'As though they would, Ma!' Nola had exclaimed. 'Tess looks terrific in her trouser suit.'

Which had not been Tess's aim, for she'd hoped to look only professional and, if possible, sexless, especially if she was driving a man, which she only did, as had been decided, for day bookings. Perhaps she was lucky, but the men she drove, who were mostly business executives, did not on the whole try to flirt with her, and if there ever were any attempts of that sort she very politely suggested that they'd like the glass partition closed and firmly closed it anyway.

Everything seemed to be working out well, the only problem being that she saw less of Karen than before. Polly still looked after her in the mornings, but in the afternoons it was Rob instead of Tess who spent time with her. He enjoyed it, he said, and that was good. Tess liked to think that he was getting to know Karen better, and also growing more relaxed, more willing to accept his temporary situation. After all, wasn't he taking the bookings now when he'd sworn he'd rather die?

'Aye, I think he's getting used to things,' Luke told Tess. 'He's more at ease with me anyway.'

'Is he, Luke? I'm glad. If he ever was – you know – a bit difficult – it was only his illness made him like that, you ken.'

'Don't worry, Tess, I understand. I know what Rob's really like. He's a good chap who's had to go through too much.'

One afternoon in June, Tess returned home from Gullane, close to the Forth, where she'd taken two elderly sisters from Morningside who liked to drive out for lunch at one of the hotels. It had been a pleasant outing, for them and for Tess, and she was feeling, if not exactly happy, at least not depressed as she climbed the stairs to the flat, calling to Rob and Karen.

Only Rob answered. He was in the living room smoking a cigarette, and was wearing, Tess noticed with some surprise, his best sportscoat and a collar and tie. He looked as if he was ready to go out. If so, he hadn't mentioned any appointment to her.

'Had a good trip?' he asked, stubbing out his cigarette.

'Yes, it was lovely.' Tess pulled off her cap and unbuttoned her jacket. 'Where's Karen?'

'I took her to your mother's with Honey.'

Tess stared. 'Why? And was Ma back from work?'

'Yes, I waited till she was. I wanted us to have a talk on our own.'

'I see.' Tess was mystified. 'Talk about what?'

Rob hesitated. His eyes on her were full of pain.

'I don't know how to put this, Tess—'

She waited, her heart thumping warning signals. Get on with it, she wanted to scream, just get on with it! But she waited.

'The thing is – I think it's best – if I go away for a bit,' he said at last.

'Go away? Where?'

'Doesn't matter. Down south somewhere.'

349

Down south. Where her father went. Tess, feeling for a chair, sank into it, keeping her gaze on Rob's face.

'Are you leaving me?' she whispered, with dry lips.

'For a time.'

'How long?'

'I have to be on ma own, Tess. I have to be away.'

'You are leaving me.' She was beginning to panic. 'Why, Rob? What have I done? Is there someone else?'

'For God's sake, no! And you haven't done anything. It's me, I'm the one. I've lost all I've ever worked for, and I've no one to blame but maself.'

'Rob, you're depressed by what's happened – anybody would be – but you're learning to live with it. Luke and me, we were just saying how much better you were—'

'I don't want to hear about Luke!' he cried. 'And I'm no better. No better at all. I canna bear the way I'm living now, and I canna make you see that. I used to run everything maself, I was ma own man. Now I'm dependent on you and Luke. Can you no' understand what that's like for me?'

'Oh, Rob,' Tess wailed. 'If only you could see things as they are.'

'I do, I do see things as they are. I see that you don't need me any longer. In fact, you'd be better off without me. That's what I see.'

'And Karen? Would she be better off?'

Rob looked away. 'Aye, she would,' he said in a low voice. 'I'm no good to anyone, the way I am now.'

Tess gave a long strangled sigh. 'This is all due to your illness,' she said tiredly. 'It's your illness that's making you talk this way. The doctors said you might feel low in spirits, but there are things they can do to help. We could go and see them – get some medication—'

He shook his head. 'Never mind the medication, Tess. I don't need it. I've seen the lawyers and I've arranged for you to run the business officially. There should be enough money coming in, but I'll be in touch to see you're OK.' He gave a short laugh. 'You're doing so well though, I

350

don't think you'll have any problems. You and Luke.'

'Rob, I've told you, there's nothing between Luke and me. Why won't you believe me?'

'I do believe you. I've said so. I just canna sit back and watch you both doing ma job, that's all. I've tried and it doesn't work. So I'm away.'

'I canna believe you're doing this.' Tess, dissolving into tears, rose to her feet and stretched out her hands to him. After a moment, he took them.

'It's for the best,' he said softly.

'For you, it seems.'

'I still love you, Tess, and I'm grateful for all you've done for me. I want you to know that. But I'm no' the man you married. That's what you have to accept.'

'You're going for good, aren't you?' she asked, scarcely listening. 'We'll never see you again?'

'That's no' true, Tess. I'm just going – to sort maself out. Find maself, if you like. Try to salvage something from the wreckage.'

'Meantime, I'm supposed to carry on the business and wait for you to come back if you feel like it?' Tess tore her hands from his and dashed the tears from her eyes. 'Well, you go, Rob, if you want to, but I'm no' promising to wait for you.'

'Tess—'

'Why don't you go, if you're going?'

He looked desperately at his watch. 'I'll get ma case. I've a taxi coming.'

'Goodbye then.' She moved swiftly to the door. 'I shan't wait to see you off, Rob. I'm going round to Ma's, to fetch Karen and Honey.'

'Tess, please!' He held out his arms. 'Please – don't let me go like this!'

'You're the one who wants to go,' she said quietly and left him, running down the stairs and out into the street before her resolution weakened and she cravenly begged him to stay.

Chapter Seventy-Seven

Rena said she'd leave a note for Nola and come back with Tess to the flat, for Tess was in no state to be on her own. She knew, Rena added grimly, how Tess was feeling. Nobody better.

'At least, there's no other woman involved, eh?' Her blue eyes sharpened. 'There isn't, is there?'

'No.' Tess glanced out at Karen, who was sitting on Rena's front step, trying to tie a new ribbon round her teddy's neck. 'Rob's no like Dad, Ma.' Tess was keeping her voice down, still watching Karen. 'Dad left you for another woman, but Rob's left me for himself.'

'Aye, he's selfish. Like a lot o' fellas. Of course, he's had that crack on the head. But why leave you?'

Tess, putting on Honey's lead, made no reply.

Back at the flat, they put a meal together, though Tess said she wasn't hungry.

'Aye, but you have to eat,' her mother told her. 'Oh, but when I think o' Rob walking out like that, I'm speechless, Tess. Speechless!'

'I don't know about that, Ma,' Tess said, trying to smile.

'But how could he?' Now it was Rena looking round for Karen, who had slid off her chair to go and play and no one had stopped her. 'How could he leave Karen, eh?'

'I don't know. But Dad left us.'

'She's only a wee bairn though.'

Rena's face was pale and worn; never young looking, she seemed to have aged further since hearing the news about Rob. How he has hurt us all, thought Tess.

'Maybe he won't stay away,' said Rena. 'He might be back before you know it. This is all just a big act.'

'Why would he put on an act?'

'To try to make you include him more. That's what's wrong, eh? He thinks you and Luke are cutting him out.'

'We canna include him any more than we do, Ma. And I don't think he'll be back. I'm no' expecting that at all.'

The telephone rang and it was Nola, wanting to know what was up. Ma had said to ring, so here she was, ringing. As soon as she'd been told the news and rallied from the shock, she said she'd come round.

'I'll just have something to eat and then I'll be with you. Oh God, Tess, what can I say? I canna believe it.'

'Nobody can believe it.'

'Ginger'll no' be back yet?'

'He's due any minute.'

'I don't know what he'll do when he hears.'

Luke was, of course, devastated. It was the last thing he'd expected. He couldn't believe it.

'Nobody can believe it,' Tess said again.

'But I really thought he was getting used to things,' Luke said blankly. 'He seemed to be more himself, eh? Taking the bookings, and that.'

'Seemingly, he's never been himself.'

'I suppose it's the accident that's responsible.'

'Maybe. But it's funny his illness lets him think of himself, and no' me, or Karen.'

Nola hesitated. 'Will you try to get him back, Tess?'

'No, I won't try to get him back.' Tess's eyes suddenly flashed. 'What'd be the point? I canna change anything. He sees Luke and me doing his job and he canna take it. If that's enough to make him go, I say let him go.'

'I don't blame you for being bitter,' Rena sighed. 'But it never does any good.'

'I was let down before,' said Tess evenly. 'And I've been let down again. But I'm no' being bitter. I'm just facing facts. Like you had to do, Ma.'

After a silence, Nola asked in a whisper what Tess would tell Karen. 'The poor bairn, eh?'

'I'll say her dad's had to go away on business. He was often away before.'

Not for good, thought Nola. She put her arms round her sister, trying to wrap her round in sympathy, letting her know she was not alone. Finally, Tess released herself with tears in her eyes and took down Honey's lead.

'I think I'll go out for a bit if that's all right. Just to the beach with Honey.'

'You'd like to be on your own?' asked Nola.

'If you don't mind.'

It was a fine evening as Tess walked with Honey down to the sands, the sky still high and filled with light, the air warm, without a breeze.

Though many holidaymakers would already have made their way back to their boarding houses for tea, the beach was still busy, with children digging and playing ball, and grown-ups gossiping in deckchairs. But the shadows were beginning to lengthen. Soon the grown-ups would get up and fold their chairs, and the children would be called, and perhaps not come. Would have to be hauled up the sands, trailing their spades, crying, looking back at the sea. How often Tess had walked here with Rob, smiling at those scenes! How often they'd walked together, battling against a winter wind, the only figures on the beach apart from those walking their dogs as they were walking Honey.

It had been a winter's day when she and Rob had first spoken of their feelings for each other. They'd moved up to a shelter on the promenade and Tess hadn't wanted to go in, because it reminded her of Toby. But Rob had sent all thoughts of Toby flying from her mind, and she'd been so sure, then, that he was different, he was not the sort to let her down.

A pain attacked her, a quite bad pain, as she and Honey made their way slowly through the lines of deckchairs, the spread-out towels, the fine sandcastles carefully studded with shells. Heartache, she supposed. But then she hadn't expected to escape that, not here on this beach where everywhere she turned she was reminded of Rob.

Rob taking off his cap and smiling down at her, the sun picking out the copper in his brown hair. Rob introducing himself. 'I'm chauffeur to Mr Seton.' Rob, running with Honey. Poor Honey, who was with Tess now and not running any more.

'Ma thinks I'm bitter,' Tess whispered, as she bent down to pat the old dog. 'And Nola thinks I should go and find Rob and bring him back. But I canna do that. He's left me, Honey. That's all that's in ma mind. I have to manage alone now and look after Karen. So we'd better go back, eh?'

Honey, panting, wagged her tail.

'Come on then.' Tess turned to retrace her steps. 'Come on, Honey, let's go home.'

PART FIVE

Chapter Seventy-Eight

It was Karen's fifth birthday – the 9th of March 1960. She was wearing a blue dress with a white collar made by her gran, and her copper-coloured hair was tied in bunches with blue ribbon. Her birthday cake was pink and white, with five candles stuck in sugar roses and her name written in pink icing, and all the family and her five guests from play school had given her presents and cards. Och, what a lucky girl she was then, said her gran.

'This card's from ma dad,' she whispered to her friends, taking one of her cards from the sideboard when the grown-ups were in the kitchen. 'It's got a dog on, see? Like our Honey.'

'Your dog's dead, eh?' asked one of the girls.

'Aye, a long time ago,' Karen said sadly.

'I thought your dad was dead,' said another child. 'I've never seen him.'

'Of course he's no' dead – he sent me ten shillings for ma birthday!' cried Karen. 'He's just working away.'

'Never comes hame, does he?'

'He does, he does! He'll be coming soon.'

'When?'

'Soon.' Karen's face was red and shiny with embarrassment. 'He'll be coming very soon.'

'Everyone to the table!' cried her mother, coming in with plates of sandwiches and sausage rolls. 'Karen, go and give your gran a hand carrying things in.'

'My word, it all looks grand,' whispered Rena to Tess as she surveyed the party table. 'Bairns today have no idea how lucky they are, eh?'

'You mean compared with us in the war?' asked Tess, moving to the kitchen door out of earshot of the girls.

'Aye, but then before the war we'd no money. Everybody was that short o' cash, you canna imagine it.'

'I just want to give Karen all I can,' Tess murmured. 'She's only got me.'

'Thought Rob'd sent her ten bob and a card.'

Tess's face twisted a little. 'Kind of him. Of course, I don't know where he sent it from. I've no' heard from him in months.'

'Karen showed me her card. Had a picture of a Labrador. Does he know about Honey?'

'I wrote when she died.' Tess's voice faltered. 'He sent me a few lines. Felt as bad as me, I think. Ma, will you keep an eye on the girls? I'll just make some tea for you and me.'

In the kitchen, Tess pressed a handkerchief to her eyes for the tears came easily when she remembered Honey. Remembered that awful morning when she'd found the dear old dog sleeping, it seemed, in her basket, and had smiled and said, 'Honey, what's come over you? Still asleep at this time of day?' Only Honey hadn't been asleep.

How Tess had missed Rob's presence, then, when they might have grieved for their old companion together. She hadn't even been sure he'd get her letter, he seemed to move around so much, but a reply had eventually arrived. Now he was – who knew where?

To begin with, he'd written from Birmingham, saying he'd found work at a garage. He'd asked if Tess was managing all right and when she'd gladly told him she was, had not written again, except to send money now and again for Karen's post office savings. New addresses came from Wolverhampton, then Derby, finally Coventry, where he'd taken a job at the Daimler factory, but where he was now Tess had no idea. In fact, she had grown used to not knowing, as she'd grown used to doing without him. Except for such times as when she grieved for Honey.

Och, better get on, she told herself, and filled the kettle. At least Karen had had a card from her dad and a postal order. Whatever her little friends thought, she could say he had not forgotten her.

'Mammie, Gran's going to light the candles!' Karen cried from the door. 'Come and see me blow them out! And Auntie Nola's here.'

Chapter Seventy-Nine

Tea was over, the candles blown out, the cake sliced for the grown-ups, or wrapped in fancy paper for the children to take home. Mothers were arriving, telling their daughters to be sure to thank Mrs MacNair now, for giving them such a lovely time.

'I think it's that good o' you,' one young neighbour whispered to Tess at the door. 'I mean, your man gone and everything, and you still giving your wee girl a party!'

'Nae bother,' Tess answered coolly. 'When do men do anything for parties anyway?'

'Got a point there!'

The young woman laughed as she shepherded her little girl down the stairs, and when the other mothers and children had followed, Tess closed her door with a bang and turned back to her family with scarlet cheeks.

'What's up?' asked Nola, cutting herself another sliver of the cake. 'Somebody said something?'

Now Mrs Luke Moffat, for she and Luke had married six months before when her divorce came through, Nola was looking well in one of the new 'sack' dresses, which she described as a godsend for her figure. No need to worry about a waist when nobody else had one anyway!

Tess, clearing the table, told her that nothing had been said. At least, nothing unusual.

'Take no notice then.' Nola gave her sister an encouraging smile. 'Don't let 'em upset you.'

'Och, folk don't mean any harm. It just annoys me having 'em feel sorry for me, that's all.'

'They don't feel sorry for you, they're envious. I mean – you've done so well. Business is booming, eh?'

Tess smiled. Yes, it was true. It might have been coincidence, but since she'd taken over bookings had risen. In fact, she and Luke were thinking of taking on another car and driver, maybe even branching out into wedding work, which was lucrative. Then there were plans – for the future, of course – of making a proper reception area from the office, where Polly would be working full time now that Karen was soon to start at 'big' school. Nobody could say – and by 'nobody', – Tess meant Rob, that she wasn't running the business well.

'You look like the cat that's swallowed the cream,' Nola observed with a laugh.

'I won't deny I'm pleased with the way things are working out. But I couldn't do anything without Luke, Nola. He works so hard and does so much for the cars, I'd be lost without him.'

'Aye, but he says folk really like you as a driver, Tess. You should take some credit, you ken.'

'I'm just a novelty. Folk aren't used to women chauffeurs. But did Luke tell you we were thinking of going in for another car?'

'He did, and I'm thrilled.' Nola dabbed at her lips with a paper napkin. 'Lovely cake, this.' She hesitated. 'What do you think Rob'll say then?'

'Rob? He's no' here to say anything.'

'But doesn't he get his licence back this summer? He'll surely come home then?'

Tess shrugged. 'Somehow I don't think so. Maybe I don't want him back anyway.'

As Rena came to the table with more tea, Nola was silent.

'Cigarette?' asked Tess, taking out a packet.

363

'Wouldn't say no,' Rena answered, but Nola shook her head.

'I'm giving up. Just in case, you ken. Some say it's bad for a baby if you smoke.'

'No luck yet?' sighed Tess.

'Early days,' said Rena. 'You've only been married six months, Nola.'

'And look how long I was married to Clark.' Nola's expression was downcast, but then she brightened a little. 'Listen, did I tell you he'd found somebody?'

'No!' Tess and Rena had brightened too. They knew how much it would mean to Nola to have Clark truly happy without her. 'Who is it then?'

'She's the daughter of some new pal of his mother's. They met at Bingo. Perfect, eh?'

'Is it no' grand the way things work out?' asked Rena, smiling.

'Grand,' Tess agreed, at which Rena's smile faded and she fumbled with a match to light her cigarette.

'They'll work out for you, too, Tess, I promise you. Rob'll come home, he will.'

'I've just said, maybe I don't want him home,' said Tess, rising to carry plates away from the table. 'Like a piece of this cake for Luke, Nola?'

'Oh, yes please! And could you spare another little bit for me?' Nola exchanged glances with her mother. 'Better no' say any more,' she whispered.

'Said too much anyway,' Rena answered sadly.

It appeared that Nola had left it until last to speak of something that was important to her. She was putting on her coat to leave when she casually mentioned that she might be buying a little studio. A pottery, in fact.

'A what?' cried Tess. 'Nola, whatever are you talking about?'

'Well, you know I said once I'd like to start up as a potter? Well, you've done so well with your business, when

I saw Shona Kay was selling up and retiring, I said to Ma, how about if we have a go?'

'Ma, you never said!'

'Och, it's all talk at the moment. We'd have to get a loan. It'd be risky.'

'No, it wouldn't,' Nola retorted. 'Plenty o' folk get loans to start up businesses. And Ginger and me have no mortage, we're only renting the flat.'

'But where is this place?' asked Tess. 'I mean, is it a proper pottery with all the equipment?'

'It's off the Joppa Road, called the Merlin. Not big, but it's got the kiln and wheel and everything needed and Shona says she makes a living. I'm going to see her tomorrow.' Nola grinned. 'Fingers crossed, eh?'

'Well, I wish you luck,' Tess said blankly. 'I'd no idea you'd got so far with the pottery idea. Or that Ma was interested.'

'Why should I no' be interested?' asked Rena. 'Nola's very talented and I've got some experience. I wouldn't mind trying to make a go of it. We think there's a market for stuff that's less pricey than Harebell's.'

'That's what Shona's been providing,' Nola put in. 'And why shouldn't this place support another pottery anyway? When you think how many we used to have?'

'There'd be a lot to consider before you got going,' Tess said carefully. 'And I don't know that these little studios ever make much.'

'We'd make enough, I guarantee it,' Nola said stoutly. 'Anyway, like Ma says, it's all just talk at the moment. Something to occupy our minds, eh?'

'If you do fall for a baby, Nola, you'll have something to occupy you anyway,' her mother said, with a smile.

'I've no great hopes,' Nola said quietly. 'Ma pottery will have to be ma baby instead.'

It took Tess some time to persuade Karen to wind down after her party and think about going to bed. Oh no, she wouldn't go to bed because that meant her birthday was really over. As long as she stayed up, even though her eyes were closing, it was still the day she'd looked forward to for so long – that was the way she saw it.

'Aye, but all days come to an end, pet,' said Tess, who was so tired she could cheerfully have lain down in Karen's bed and gone to sleep herself. But she wasn't prepared to lose the battle. Karen would go to bed, she would go to sleep. That would be it.

'But I'm sad, Mammie,' sighed Karen, when she was finally in her bed, clutching her teddy and looking reproachfully at Tess over the edge of her sheet. 'Everything's over.'

'You've still got the nice dress Gran made you, and your presents and your cards.'

Karen's grey eyes, so like Tess's, did not waver. 'But ma dad never came, did he?'

'He sent you a lovely card and a postal order.'

'Why does he no' come back though?'

'He's very busy, and he's no' well yet. He canna come home.'

'How can he be busy if he's no' well?'

Tess turned her head away, thinking how true it was that children could always find the flaws in their parents' arguments.

'He does his best,' she said at last. 'And he does remember you, doesn't he?'

Karen seemed unconvinced. 'Some folk think he's dead,' she whispered. 'He's no' dead, is he?'

'No!' Tess held her daughter close. 'He's just, like I said, very busy. You tell your friends that, Karen.'

'I did tell 'em. But they never see him, so how do they know it's true?'

Tess could think of nothing to say. How could she let Karen hope that her father might come home when it was quite possible that he would not? Her own father had never returned to his family, and even though circumstances were different, that was a fact that couldn't be denied. Some men went away and stayed away. Some women, too, Clark Walters might have argued.

As Karen, against her will, began to drift towards sleep, Tess settled her against her pillow and moved quietly from the room, relieved she'd been temporarily let off the hook. But how difficult it was to work out the right things to do or say, and why should Rob have put her into such a situation?

I can never forgive him, she thought, sitting in front of the television. Whatever the reasons for what he did, I'll never forgive him.

After a moment or two she switched on the set and watched various well-dressed people competing in some sort of panel game. It seemed to amuse the studio audience very much, but when it was over she couldn't remember one thing about it.

Chapter Eighty

Some weeks later, on a perfect April morning, Tess arrived at the Northern Park Hotel in the New Town to collect a Mr and Mrs Denison from California. They were a pleasant, middle-aged couple who were spending their trip to Scotland looking up relatives. Tess had already taken them to Dumfries and Glasgow; today it was the turn of Aberfeldy, where they were to have lunch with cousins.

When she had asked the hotel receptionist to inform the Denisons of her arrival, Tess took up a position near the lifts where she knew they would see her and passed the time looking about her. Hotel lobbies, like stations, were fascinating to her. One of the things she liked best about her job was seeing so many different people from so many walks of life, all different from her own.

Nor was she unaware that her own appearance usually caused a certain interest. A slender young woman in a dark trouser suit and a chauffeur's cap set on curly hair – who would she be? She could see that some of the hotel guests here were eyeing her and probably wondering that very thing.

There was a grey-haired man, for instance, who'd been reading a newspaper and now was studying her. A bit of a cheek, she thought, an old fellow like him! Then she saw his hands as he folded his paper and realised that they were young hands. He wasn't old in spite of his hair. In fact –

her mouth suddenly went dry – she knew how old he was, just as she knew his name and everything about him.

'Tess?'

He had left his leather armchair and was coming towards her. 'Tess Gillespie?'

'Tess MacNair,' she answered huskily and looked into Toby Dene's bright brown eyes.

His eyes were the same, his cheerful face was the same; it was only his hair that was different. As thick as ever, but now prematurely silver grey instead of dark brown. It made him seem – she couldn't put her finger on it – someone new? Someone she didn't, after all, know? Yet he was certainly Toby Dene. Dr Dene now, she supposed. And then she remembered Erika.

'Of course, you're married,' Toby was saying, his eyes going over her face, rising to her cap, moving to her suit. 'I remember hearing about it. You haven't changed a bit, you know. Unlike me.' He touched his hair, smiling slightly. 'It's just a family thing, we all go grey early. But I bet you thought I was some old codger, didn't you?'

Stunned, she shook her head.

'But this is wonderful, isn't it? To meet again? Look, won't you sit down? Have coffee with me?'

'I'm waiting for some people. Clients. I run a chauffeur hire business now.'

'Chauffeur hire!' His eyes danced. 'I did notice the cap. And you do the driving? That's amazing. No, maybe not. You were always interested in cars, if I remember rightly.' He ran his hand over his brow. 'But what a bit of luck, to meet like this!'

'Is it?' Tess's eyes were on the lifts. 'What are you doing here anyway? Are you a doctor now?'

'Yes, I am. I've been in Australia for a while.' He grinned. 'Working with the flying doctors, in fact. Thought I'd get the experience. Now I'm back and looking round for a place to start a practice.'

'You're going to be a GP?'

'That's right. Simon and I are going to go into practice together. Probably here in Edinburgh. You remember Simon Maitland?'

'Oh yes.' Her voice was cool. 'But I'm sorry, Toby, I have to go. I see ma clients coming.'

He followed her gaze to the lift door, from which the Denisons, both beautifully dressed and wearing hats, were emerging, and shook his fine head.

'Tess, it would be a shame not to have a talk after all these years. Couldn't we have a drink together when you come back?'

'Why are you being like this?' she asked in a low voice. 'As though we were friends? You know there's no point in us having a drink. Now – I have to go.'

His smile faded and he stepped back. 'Suppose I deserved that,' he said quietly. 'Well, I was pleased to see you anyway.'

Without looking at him again, Tess hurried forward to meet the Denisons.

'Always so punctual, my dear,' Mrs Denison said, observing the retreating Toby. 'I see you were talking to that gentleman there – we saw him at breakfast. Such a handsome man!'

'Very distinguished looking guy,' Mr Denison commented. 'But don't let him steal you from us, Mrs MacNair. If he wants a chauffeur – chauffeuse, I guess I should say – tell him to look elsewhere.'

'Dr Dene doesn't want a chauffeur,' Tess said with a smile. 'He's just someone I used to know a long time ago.'

'He's a doctor? Now I'd have said he was something like that. Trustworthy. Well, shall we make a start? Looks a beautiful day.'

'Can't beat Scotland on a beautiful day,' Mrs Denison said happily as they left the hotel.

It said something for Tess's professionalism that she managed to put Toby Dene from her mind on her drive with the Denisons. It was only when she had deposited them with their relatives and was having a solitary lunch in a small café, that she allowed herself to think again of the face from the past.

'Distinguished,' Mr Denison had said of him. And 'trustworthy.' Trustworthy? Oh, God. Well, she'd thought the same once. And perhaps if she considered the past objectively, he had not actually betrayed her. He had never promised her anything. He had never said he loved her. She had assumed he felt the same as she did.

Drinking a cup of coffee, smoking a cigarette, she reviewed those days when she'd been hurt so badly. It was true, Toby'd been at fault. She'd been so young, so inexperienced, he should have known what would happen when he asked her out. But then he'd been young himself. And he'd never meant to hurt her.

She stubbed out her cigarette and looked at her watch. Time to collect the Denisons. Time to put Toby Dene from her mind again. Yet she hadn't found the trip down memory lane too painful. She'd had another, greater hurt since then, one she didn't care to dwell on, but as she drove to meet the Denisons, it occurred to her that Toby had not asked about her husband. Nor had he mentioned Erika.

'Another lovely day,' said Mrs Denison, as she and her husband alighted from the Daimler outside the hotel. 'And such a pleasure to be driven again by you, my dear.'

'We'll see you next week?' Carter Denison asked, putting the strap of his camera over his shoulder. 'For Robert Burns's Land, right?'

'Burns's Country, dear,' his wife corrected.

'Whatever. Next Tuesday, Mrs MacNair? Same time?'

'Same time, Mr Denison.' Tess slightly bowed her head. 'Mrs Denison.'

As the Denisons disappeared into the revolving doors of the hotel, Tess returned to her driving seat, then gave a start as someone tapped on her window. She wound it down.

'Toby?'

'I was just walking back when I saw the car. Thought I'd catch you.'

'Look – this is silly—'

'No.' His look was serious. 'I'd really like to talk to you, Tess. I've wanted to for years. Just to tell you – well, let's not go into it now. Couldn't we go somewhere for a quick drink?'

'I'm married, Toby. I don't want to have a drink with you.'

'I'm not going to do anything that'd upset your husband. I just want to talk to you.'

As she hesitated, his brown eyes took on a melting look she remembered.

'Please, Tess?'

'All right. Get in then. We can go to one of the other hotels.'

'You drive very well,' he told her as they bowled through the city decked out for spring, with trees in early leaf and daffodils on the Mound. 'And this is a beautiful car. A Daimler. I'm impressed.'

'Ma husband inherited it from his employer. He used to drive for Mr Seton who owned Pax House.'

'Pax House? I remember it. You admired it, didn't you?'

'I did, but it's gone down since Mr Seton died. Let to tenants who don't take care of it.'

'That's a shame.'

She knew he was looking at her and was glad she'd taken off her cap. Didn't want folk to think she was his chauffeur – or, chauffeuse, as Mr Denison put it. But what was she doing anyway, agreeing to go for a drink with him?

'I can't stay long,' she said firmly, as she parked outside a hotel on the outskirts of the city. 'Ma wee girl's being looked after, but I don't want to be late.'

'You have a daughter?' Toby smiled warmly. 'I didn't know! How old is she? Does she look like you?'

'She's just five,' Tess answered, smiling in return. 'No, she doesn't look much like me, though some think her eyes are like mine. Her hair is prettier. Copper coloured.'

'Your hair is pretty,' Toby said gallantly.

'Hers is more like her father's,' said Tess. 'Now, here's the cocktail bar. I'll just have fruit juice, if you don't mind. I never drink when I'm driving. What was it you wanted to talk to me about then?'

Chapter Eighty-One

Toby set down a grapefruit juice for Tess and a whisky for himself on the glass-topped table they'd found in the corner of the bar. He seemed ill at ease, his gaze wandering over the crowd of early drinkers. When his eyes finally rested on Tess, they were full of that contrition she'd seen before and didn't want to see again.

'I just want to say how sorry I am, Tess, for the way I treated you,' he said in a low voice. 'I know I said so at the time—'

'You did,' she said impatiently.

'But it was only as I grew older that I came to see how cruel I was.'

'I wouldn't say cruel. You didn't mean to hurt me.'

'Callous, then. Selfish. Bloody insensitive.' He shook his head. 'It wasn't the way I thought I was. I never imagined I could be like that.'

'There's no need to go over it all again, Toby. It's water under the bridge. Let's forget it.'

'That's strange, isn't it? You've put it out of your mind. I haven't.' He drank some whisky. 'But then, you've married someone who's made you happy.'

Tess looked down at her drink. 'What about Erika?' she asked quietly.

'Erika?' Toby shook his head. 'That was crazy – what we felt. Didn't last. Could never have lasted.'

'Why? Why couldn't it?'

He shrugged. 'I suppose it was just too intense. Sort of thing you can't live with for long. And Erika's real interest turned out not to be me at all. It's medicine. That's what she lives for.'

'You're no' like that?'

'I love my work, but I leave space for other things. Erika doesn't do that. She's been working in a Glasgow hospital since she qualified. Wants to specialize eventually in chest diseases.'

'Because of her mother?' Tess smiled faintly. 'I can understand that.'

Toby suddenly reached across the table and touched her hand. 'You're an understanding sort of person. Think you understand now how I feel?'

'I suppose so. You're a decent sort, Toby. No' really callous.' Tess twirled her empty glass in her fingers. 'Maybe I expected too much. Folk canna love to order.'

'I shouldn't have led you on, Tess. I should have handled everything differently.'

'You were young. And anybody can make a mistake.' Tess glanced at her wristwatch. 'Well, if that's cleared the air for you, I think we'd better go. Thanks for the drink.'

They stood up, looking at each other with sudden self-consciousness.

'Like a lift back to the hotel?' Tess asked, moving away.

'You needn't take me all the way. Just drop me somewhere en route.'

At the corner of a quiet side street, she drew up smoothly and turned to him.

'This OK?'

'Fine.' He gave her one of his ready smiles. 'Thanks, Tess. Thanks for seeing me.'

'That's all right.'

'I wish – I wish I could see you again, in fact, though I know it's not possible.'

'No, it's not.'

'Don't want to upset your husband. You know, you haven't told me much about him.'

'You never asked.'

'Well, what's he like? I don't even know his name.'

'It's Rob.' Tess bit her lip. 'He's – look, I don't want to talk about him. I have to be going.'

'I expect he's a nice, steady chap. Somebody you could depend on. That'd be the sort you'd look for, after what happened with me.' Toby looked seriously into Tess's face. 'Isn't he like that, Tess?'

She turned her head away as her eyes suddenly began to fill with tears. The more she tried to control them, the faster they fell, and as Toby stared, appalled, she dragged a handkerchief from her pocket and for some moments wept into it.

'Tess, what's wrong?' cried Toby. 'Oh God, what is it? What have I said?'

He put his arms around her and she rested against him, still weeping, until gradually she grew calmer and pulled herself away.

'Tess, please tell me what's the matter,' he begged, but she shook her head.

'Sorry about that. I'm better now. There've been – a few problems. Nothing for you to worry about. Would you mind getting out now? I really have to get home.'

Very slowly, he opened the car door and stepped out, looking back with serious eyes. 'You realize I can't leave you like this?'

'I'm sorry, Toby. It was nice seeing you again, but that's got to be it. Goodbye then. And good luck.'

Before he could speak, she had started the engine and was away, the great dark car taking her back into the traffic, then vanishing from his sight.

Chapter Eighty-Two

Tess and Luke were checking their bookings with Polly the following morning.

'This looks like mine,' Luke said cheerfully. 'More Scottish Americans going to Fort William to look up their forebears.' He rubbed his hands together and grinned. 'That should pay well, eh?'

'Certainly should,' Tess answered, swallowing an aspirin with a cup of tea. She'd had so little sleep, she was not surprised to feel a headache coming.

'You OK?' Polly asked her sympathetically.

'Fine, thanks. What have you got lined up for me?'

'Well, there's your lady today – you know about her – going to Loch Katrine again – and a doctor has asked if you'd give him a ring to arrange a trip.'

Tess grew pale. 'Doctor? Do you mean Dr Dene? He asked for me?'

'Aye, that was the name. He's left a number.' Polly's eyes were curious; so were Luke's.

'I'd better give him a ring then.' Tess's smile was strained. 'I'll use the phone upstairs, eh?'

Polly and Luke watched her run up the stairs to the flat, then exchanged glances.

'She didn't ask me for the number,' said Polly after a pause.

'Knows it then,' said Luke.

'What are you playing at, Toby?' Tess asked angrily when she had rung the Northern Park on her private phone. 'You know I canna see you again.'

'Tess, you're in trouble and I want to help. All I'm asking is that you tell me what's wrong.'

'There's no trouble and I don't need any help. You shouldn't have rung me here. I'm no' booking you for a drive.'

'I don't want you to drive me, I've got my own car. Nothing so grand as your Daimler, but I'm looking at flats to rent and you could come with me. It'll be just a friendly outing, nothing more. Let's meet today.'

'I'm busy today.'

'Tomorrow then. I'm not going to let this rest, Tess. I have to know what's wrong – couldn't sleep last night for thinking of you.'

'I didn't sleep either.' Tess put her hand to her aching head. 'Oh God, Toby, you wear me down.'

'Tomorrow. Shall I come round and collect you tomorrow? About eleven?'

'No, no, that wouldn't do. I'll come to the hotel. I'll park somewhere.'

She heard Toby give a long sigh of what might have been relief.

'Thank you, Tess. Till tomorrow then.'

She rang off without saying goodbye.

Yet, after another sleepless night, she was at the hotel the next morning, dressed casually in a tweed jacket and skirt, and shaking with nerves. What was Toby playing at? she'd asked. More to the point, what was she playing at? Going to meet an old love who wanted to know what she didn't want him to know? So why meet him? That was something she didn't want to know herself.

He was waiting for her at the hotel entrance and ran down the steps to meet her.

'Tess! I didn't think you'd come.'

Her eyes slid away. 'I said I would. Where's your car then? I've parked mine.'

'Round the back. It's a Rover.'

'Good cars, Rovers.'

'And you'd know.' He led her round the rear of the hotel to where guests' cars were parked, and opened the door of a well-polished dark saloon. 'How will you feel about being driven by me? I'm not in your class.'

She took her seat next to his, sighing with exasperation. 'You're like ma sister, always teasing.'

'It's just nerves,' he said quietly.

'Nerves?' Her own hands were still trembling.

'I feel bad about making you meet me, Tess. Interfering in your life when I've no right. All I can say is that I was upset the other day seeing you cry. I wanted to do something to help – didn't know what. But if you don't want to talk about things that are nothing to do with me, you could still look at these flats with me, couldn't you?'

How well he talks, she thought. Yet she was sure he was sincere.

'I suppose I could,' she said slowly. 'I've taken today off.' She glanced quickly at his earnest face. 'Had to make up an excuse.'

'I'm sorry.' He put some papers into her hands. 'Those are the particulars of the flats if you'd like to see them. I want something for a base, while I look round for the right property. Just a bachelor's pad, sort of thing.'

'Nice areas,' she commented. 'The Grange – the New Town – these rents are no' cheap.'

'I'm not planning to rent for very long, and I'm doing some locum work anyway – that should pay the bills.'

He would always be able to pay his bills, wouldn't he? As he drove away, she remembered how she'd always thought he'd never needed to struggle. That was nothing to hold against him, of course; it was just part of what had made him what he was. She was not badly off herself these

379

days, but she knew what it was to be short of money; there was the difference between her and him.

It was an interesting morning, collecting keys, being shown round properties by estate agents. In spite of their nerves, Tess and Toby both enjoyed it – Tess especially, because there was something very pleasant about looking at houses you weren't buying. She quite threw herself into the hunt, and in the end Toby said she'd been 'jolly helpful'.

'I'm not sure, but I think I'm going to go for that mews flat off Queen Street,' he told her when they'd left the last agent with promises to get in touch. 'It's pricey, but has all I want. What do you think?'

'I think it'd be perfect for you, Toby. I had a good look round and it's in apple-pie order. You wouldn't have to do a thing.'

'That's for me.' He grinned down at her. 'Now, what about some lunch?'

'That'd be nice, but I think I should go home now.'

His face fell. 'You said you'd taken the day off.'

'Yes, well, I've always got plenty to do.'

'I'd be very disappointed if I had to have lunch alone.'

She gave in. She'd known she would. 'Nowhere grand though.'

'You didn't like those restaurants I used to take you to?'

'I did, but today I just feel like something ordinary. A pub, maybe.'

'Edinburgh pubs aren't geared up for women on the whole.'

'Nola used to like Smithy's in the West End. Women office workers go there quite a lot.'

'Smithy's it shall be then.'

Over their drinks and sandwiches in the crowded bar, they felt more relaxed. Tess asked about Simon and Toby told her she'd been wrong about him. He hadn't chosen to go up the hospital ladder. Like Toby himself, he wanted to be

380

in general practice which was why they were going into partnership together. At present he was in the south, leaving it to Toby to find a property.

'Should work out for you,' Tess commented.

'You mean, with his money?' Toby shrugged. 'I think I can arrange capital myself, but yes, it'll be no drawback having Simon involved. Let's not talk about him though. Tell me about your family.'

'Ma's OK. She's living her own life, she's happy. Nola's divorced and remarried. To a chap who works with me, as a matter of fact. They're happy too.'

'That's good, I'm pleased to hear it. Pity about Nola's divorce, of course, but these things happen.'

'In our family anyway,' Tess muttered. 'Divorce, separation – seem to be part of our lives.'

Toby looked at her thoughtfully, then said he'd get coffee from the bar.

'Listen,' she said quickly. 'It's silly to be here like this with you and no' tell you about Rob.'

'Tess, you needn't. I should never have asked you.'

'I want to tell you though.' She lowered her eyes from his intent gaze. 'It's sad, you ken. Sad for all of us.'

'Are you sure you want me to know?'

'I'm sure.'

He glanced at the people around them.

'Shall we not bother with coffee then? You won't want to talk here.'

'We could walk a bit maybe? Pick up the car later?

'I'll just settle up.'

Chapter Eighty-Three

After the smoke and noise of the pub, it was a relief to be
in the fresh air and walking through the elegant streets of
the West End. This was mainly Victorian Edinburgh, built
on a large scale for the well-to-do, even including a cathedral that had been begun in the 1870s and only finished in
1917.

'Did you know two ladies paid for that?' Tess asked, as
they looked up at the vast pile of Saint Mary's. 'The Misses
Walker. Imagine having enough money to build a cathedral!'

'People with money don't build cathedrals any more.'
Toby took Tess's arm and led her to a nearby bench.
'Come on,' he urged gently. 'Talk to me.'

It made it easier to talk because he was such a good
listener. His special talent, wasn't it? Listening? Tess
remembered it from the old days. Remembered telling him
about her father's desertion, just as now she told him of
Rob's. And all that went before. Her marriage and the
death of Mr Seton; the founding of MacNair's Chauffeur
Services; the accident on the Glasgow road that had
changed their lives for ever.

Toby listened without interruption, his strangely silver
head bent, his eyes on her face serious with interest and
understanding. Only at the end, when she turned to him,

did he press her hand for a moment before letting it go.

'So you see, Rob's left me,' she said quietly. 'No' for another woman. Sometimes I think I might've understood it better if there had been someone else.'

'No, he told you why he had to go. He couldn't live the way you wanted him to live.'

'It wasn't me who told him how to live, Toby! He lost his licence, but all he had to do was put up with things until he got it back, and he wouldn't do it.'

'From the sound of it, he couldn't, Tess. He'd had a head injury, remember. Even when a person recovers, he's sometimes got problems. The hospital doctors warned him, didn't they?'

'He wouldn't listen to warnings.'

'Another symptom, perhaps.' Toby again pressed her hand. 'I'm sorry, Tess. You've had a very difficult time. No one could have expected you to do more than you did.'

'Why do I get the feeling you think I should have done?' she asked stonily. 'I tried ma best, Toby. I had to hold the business together, but I told Rob it was only temporary. All he had to do was wait.'

'My poor Tess – he couldn't see that.'

'So you think it was all right for him to walk out? Leave Karen? Leave me?'

'No, I think it was crazy. But then as I say, he wasn't seeing straight at the time.' Toby hesitated. 'What's odd is that he hasn't come back. I should've thought he'd have come out of his depression by now and come home to you. The fact that he hasn't is strange.'

'Ma dad never came back,' said Tess.

'But then he started a new life with someone else, didn't he?'

Tess looked bleakly into Toby's eyes. 'How do I know that hasn't happened with Rob?'

'You said yourself there was no other woman when he went away.'

'That was then.'

383

Toby for the first time seemed at a loss what to say.

'If you don't know the facts, there's nothing you can do,' he said at last.

'All I know is that I'm on ma own, just as ma mother's on her own. Maybe it's better that way.'

'You said the story was sad, Tess. Sad for all of you. That includes Rob.'

'You keep taking his part,' she said darkly. 'I don't know why.'

'I'm sorry, I don't mean to. It's my training, I suppose. I try to understand what makes people do what they do.'

Tess's face cleared a little. 'I'm sorry, too, then. What I said – that was childish, eh?'

'There's nothing childish about you, Tess. You've grown up.'

'I've had to.'

When he had driven her back to collect her own car, he put his hand lightly on her arm as she took the driving seat.

'This has been a good day, Tess. Shall I see you again? You could help me look at more properties.'

'I thought you'd decided on a flat?'

'I'm looking for something suitable for our practice, remember. I told you Simon's leaving it to me.'

She gave him a long, direct look. 'Toby, why do you want to see me? I mean, what's the point?'

'Does there have to be a point to meet a friend?'

'We canna really be friends. You know that.'

'No, I don't know it.' He bent his head to look into her face as she moved his hand from her arm. 'Things went wrong for us, it's true, but you've been in my mind for years.'

'You told me. Because you felt guilty.'

'It was more than that. I realized it when I saw you again in the hotel, looking the same – so beautiful – yet so much more composed – so confident. You'd changed, but you were still the Tess I remembered. I knew I had to speak to you.' He put his hand over hers on the wheel. 'Now we've spent some time together, I know we can be friends again, Tess. That's all I'm asking – to meet as friends.'

'You know ma situation, Toby.'

'I know your husband's left you. Whatever the reason, he's not here. I think you've had a hard time without him, and I want to make your life pleasanter.' Toby straightened up. 'That's all I'm offering, Tess.'

She sighed, drumming her fingers on the wheel. 'I don't know, Toby – I really don't know what to say.'

'Shall I just give you a ring then?'

'On ma house number. It's in the book.'

'I'll find it.'

As she started the engine he raised his hand, then stood back, watching her drive away from him as he had watched before.

Chapter Eighty-Four

It wasn't possible for Tess to help Toby look for a property. As she explained to him, spring and summer were the busiest times for MacNair's Chauffeur Services; she really couldn't afford days off. Their meetings, if they met at all, would have to be in the evenings.

'If we meet?' he had echoed. 'It's agreed that we meet. And evenings are fine by me. I don't do locum work every night. How about Friday of this week?'

'All right, Friday then,' said Tess. 'If I don't have to be late back from a drive.'

With some apprehension, she booked Polly's sister instead of her mother to babysit for Karen, and met Toby at the King's Theatre to see a play.

It was all very decorous. They sat together in the old plush seats of the stalls. They had coffee in the interval and discussed the play. They did not hold hands. Afterwards, they went for a drink, then Toby drove Tess home, looking with interest at the outside of her business premises, but of course was not invited in.

'You see, that was all very painless, wasn't it?' he asked, smiling, and brushed her cheek so faintly with his lips, it could not have been called a kiss. 'You enjoyed it, didn't you?'

'Yes, I did,' she answered frankly. It was a long time since she'd been out to anything that could be called entertainment. When she came to think about it, all she'd done recently was work.

'I get the keys to the flat next week. Want to come round to see me installed?'

'I'm no' sure about that.'

'I thought you might bring your little girl. I'd very much like to see her – I don't suppose you'll be asking me into your home.'

'Karen?' Tess's eyes widened. 'Well – I might manage Saturday afternoon. I try to keep that free.'

'Perfect. I'll buy some little cakes.'

'I'll bring the cakes,' said Tess. 'I know what Karen likes.'

It seemed that what Karen liked was Dr Dene. She took to him instantly, recognizing that here was a grown-up to be added to her list of admirers, and she was of course right. Toby took her by the hand and showed her all round the flat, letting her look at his leather-backed brushes, put her small feet into his large polished shoes, smell his shaving soap, peer into the cartons of books he had not unpacked. Finally, he gave her five lovely new shillings for her moneybox and they came back to his little sitting room, where Tess had set out tea and home-made chocolate cake, and they sat together as though they were a family.

'Mammie, isn't this nice?' asked Karen, looking from Tess to Toby with her beautiful grey eyes. 'Why have we no' been here before?'

'Well, Dr Dene has just moved in, pet, that's why.'

'So are you a new friend of Mammie's,' Karen asked Toby.

'I'm an old friend,' Toby told her. 'And I've been working in Australia. Have you heard of Australia? It's so big, some of the doctors have to visit the sick people in aeroplanes.'

'Aeroplanes!' She was charmed, and began to zoom around the flat with her arms stretched out, calling to Tess that she was a doctor visiting sick people. She might be a doctor when she grew up. Or else a nurse. Nurses had prettier clothes.

'I bet she'll be anything she wants to be,' Toby laughed as he and Tess carried the tea things into his minute kitchen. 'What a character, Tess. And what a beauty. She is like you, you know. I see it clearly.'

Tess, smiling, was beginning to run water at the sink to wash the cups when Toby suddenly put his hands on her shoulders and turned her round to face him.

'What a fool Rob is,' he said in a low voice. 'Almost as big a fool as me.'

Their eyes, meeting, were huge and tragic, and it seemed they would have stayed where they were without moving, just looking, and trembling, if Karen's voice from the next room had not forced them apart.

'I'd better go,' Tess whispered.

'Tess, you will see me again?'

She did not answer, but her eyes were riveted on his.

'Mammie, where can I put ma money?' the little voice from the next room came again.

'Come and say thank you to Dr Dene, Karen.' Tess had torn her gaze from Toby's and had averted her face, though she knew his eyes were still on her. 'We're going home now.'

'Now?' The little girl's face twisted. 'Mammie, I don't want to go. Dr Dene said we could walk in the gardens. Why have we got to go?'

'We'll go to the gardens another time,' Tess said hurriedly. 'Goodbye Toby, and thanks.'

'I'll come down with you.'

'No need—'

'I'm coming.'

In the cobbled mews lane, where horses had once been led to their stables, Tess and Toby faced each other again at Tess's Daimler.

'I'll be in touch,' said Tess, opening the door for Karen.

'No, let's arrange a meeting now.'

'I haven't got ma diary.'

'Next Friday,' he said firmly. 'I'll call for you.'

'I don't think—'

'Seven o'clock.' He looked in at Karen and smiled and waved. 'Next time, we'll go to the gardens!'

'Next time, the gardens!' cried Karen waving back, but Toby had already turned into his door. This time he did not watch Tess driving away.

Chapter Eighty-Five

Back at home, Tess had just garaged the Daimler when she heard voices and looked up to see her mother accompanied by Nola and Luke arriving at the open door.

'Guess what, we've got the pottery!' cried Nola. 'It's champagne time, only we haven't bought it yet.'

'Need the cash for the payments,' said Luke, but he was smiling. 'I could bring in some beer.'

'Oh no, was it the closing date today? Oh, I should've rung you!'

Tess, filled with compunction, put her hand to her brow. She'd been so absorbed in her own affairs she'd quite forgotten all about her sister's battle to buy the little pottery. There'd been problems securing the loan and problems in putting in an offer, but the lawyers had fixed a closing date for sealed bids that morning, and obviously Nola's must have been successful.

'But you got it? Nola, that's grand. Ma, I'm so plesed for you!'

'Tried to phone you this afternoon, Tess, but you weren't in,' said Rena. 'I've got some news an' all, but I wouldn't say it was so good.' She picked up Karen and hugged her. 'Have you been out, pet? Where've you been then?'

'To Dr Dene's!' cried Karen triumphantly.

Upstairs, in Tess's living room, Karen ran off to put the

five shillings Toby had given her into her moneybox, while the grown-ups stood around, avoiding one another's eyes.

'Well, if you're no' offering, Tess,' Rena said, after some moments, 'I'm going to put the kettle on.'

'Of course I'll make you tea,' Tess retorted. 'But what's your news then, Ma?'

'What's yours?' asked Rena. 'Who's Dr Dene? He's no' who I think he is, is he?'

'Don't let's spoil things, Ma,' said Nola. 'What's it to us who Dr Dene is?'

'He's Toby Dene,' Tess said levelly. 'Yes, he's come back. He wants to set up as a GP in Edinburgh.'

'And got in touch with you?' asked Rena. 'Oh, my God! To think you'd have anything to do with him after the way he treated you.'

'I met him by chance. He's changed, Ma. He's quite different. Very kind, very friendly—'

'And you took Karen to his flat? I canna believe it.'

'We had a cup of tea and a piece of chocolate cake!' Tess cried. 'What's it got to do with you? I've been on ma own since Rob walked out, I've been let down by folk I care for, and if one says he's sorry and wants to make it up, why shouldn't I let him?'

'Why indeed?' asked Nola. She put her arm round her sister's shoulder. 'Tess is right, Ma. None of this has anything to do with us. If she wants to go out with somebody, why shouldn't she? Rob canna blame her – he's no' here.'

'I'm no' saying she shouldn't go out, and Rob's got no rights, that's for sure. But why him? Why Toby Dene?' Rena looked at Tess, shaking her head. 'I'm sorry if I spoke out o' turn, Tess, it's only that I worry you'll be hurt again, you ken. You canna blame me for thinking that.'

'I know, Ma, I know. But I'm no' going to get hurt again, you've no need to worry. Now, why don't you tell me your news then? If it isn't good, how bad is it?'

Rena shrugged. 'Well, what would you say? Your dad's

391

coming up again. Wants to see me next week. Thursday, in fact, if it's convenient. Would you credit it? After all these years, him turning up again?'

'What do you think he wants?' asked Nola.

'A divorce, I expect. That's what he wanted before. Och, I'll find out soon enough.'

'Did anybody ever put that kettle on?' asked Luke. 'Or should I go out and get the beer?'

'I'll make the tea,' said Tess hastily. 'And then I want to hear all about the pottery. Going to change the name, Nola?'

'You bet. It's going to be Finola's!' Nola smiled. 'Might as well get some use out o' ma proper name.'

As soon as her family had left her, Tess found her thoughts returning to Toby Dene, as she'd known they would. Even the excitement of the pottery purchase, or the news that her dad was turning up again, had not been enough to knock those moments in Toby's kitchen from the forefront of her mind.

She knew that if Karen hadn't been there, they would have kissed. She knew, too, that that was what she'd wanted. To kiss and be kissed, to make love even. It was years since she and Rob had made love. Had sex, as folk called it nowadays. But Toby Dene wasn't Rob. Even to think of making love with him was playing with fire, and Tess was afraid of getting burned. She decided she would not see him again.

Chapter Eighty-Six

It was two o'clock when Don Gillespie arrived at Rena's door, which she opened to his first knock. At first she thought he looked older, his curly hair being thick with grey, but then she took in his trim figure and still soldierly bearing, and decided he'd not worn too badly.

He was wearing a good tweed sports jacket and well-pressed flannels, and as Rena ushered him into the front room she wondered if he could be trying to impress her. Didn't seem likely, yet she'd taken trouble herself to look her best. Maybe they were both out to prove something – who knew what?

'I use this room a lot nowadays,' she told him, as he sat down and looked around at the familiar surroundings. 'I've got the telly in here, you ken.'

'Very nice.' His grey eyes rested on her. 'You're looking well, Rena. Still got your fair hair.'

She flushed a little, thinking he might be letting her know he could tell her hair was dyed, but then she dismissed the thought. That sort of spite wasn't Don's style.

'Can I get you some tea or coffee?' she asked politely.

'No, thanks. I had some at the boarding house. I've booked in along the prom.'

'A cigarette then?'

'Take one o' mine.' He lit both their cigarettes with his lighter and they relaxed a little as they smoked.

'You've had a long journey, Don,' Rena said. 'What's it all about? You've no' been in touch for years, so I suppose you're after something.'

It was his turn to flush, the colour rising high to his tanned brow.

'I'd have been in touch if you'd wanted it, Rena.'

'Last I heard you'd changed your mind about a divorce. Have you changed your mind back again?'

He looked for a long time at his cigarette. 'The fact is, Val's left me.'

Rena's eyes flickered. 'Oh yes?'

'It was some years ago. No' very long after I came up here that time, in fact.'

'When you said she wanted a divorce?'

'Aye. To begin with, she did. She asked me to come up and ask you, but when you agreed and I told her we could be married – I don't know – she went off it.' Don sighed heavily. 'Told me she'd changed her mind. Said she wanted to go.'

'And did she go on her own?'

'I thought so.' He put out his cigarette. 'Turned out there was someone else.'

Rena's face was expressionless, but he knew, of course, what she was thinking. *Now you know what it's like, don't you? Hurts, eh? Don't expect me to feel sorry for you.*

'Why are you telling me?' she asked. 'It's of no interest to me, what your Val does.'

'It might be.'

She raised her eyebrows.

'If – if there was any chance you wanted to take me back.'

'So that's what this trip's for! You want to come back? Because your young woman's left you, you think of me?' Rena shook her head, smiling. 'Sorry, Don. It's no' possible. I'm happy as I am. I don't want you back.'

'Rena, think about it. Please don't just say no.' Don was leaning forward, his face still dark red, his eyes glistening

394

with intensity. 'Look, I know I hurt you badly, but God knows I regret it. There isn't a day of ma life that I don't regret leaving you and the girls. I must have been crazy – out o' ma mind. But there was no going back. You told me I'd made ma bed and I had to lie on it.'

'Aye, I did. Still true, Don.'

'But Val's gone now, Rena, and I'm glad she's gone. I'm shot of her, and I can think about living again. It's taken me all this time to get the courage to speak to you, but we're no' old, you and me, we could still have a future together, see our girls and Tess's bairn—'

'I already see our girls and Tess's bairn,' Rena said calmly. 'I've ma own future to look forward to, and it doesn't include you. I'm sorry, Don, but that's the way it is.'

'Are you telling me you're happy? On your own?'

'I've just said, I've the girls, I've ma wee grand-daughter. And a new job, an' all. Nola and me are going to start a pottery. She's married again, you ken, but she wants to run her own business, and I'm going in with her. There's no place for you in our lives, Don.'

He ran his hand over his face. 'Nola told me she was getting wed again. Sent me a card. And Tess told me about her wee girl and her man's chauffeur business. They want me, Rena, even if you don't.'

'Did Tess tell you her man had walked out? Had an accident and couldn't cope. She's doing the driving now.'

'What, little Tess?' Don's colour had drained and he looked suddenly older. 'Rena, I wouldn't mind that tea now, if you've a mind to make it.'

'Never let it be said I wouldn't make somebody a cup o' tea. Even you, Don. Come on downstairs.'

He didn't stay long after he'd had the tea. There was no point. He knew that because he knew Rena. She would not be persuaded now, and deep down perhaps he realised he had no right to persuade her anyway.

When he stood up to go, they were both probably relieved. A long time ago they'd shared happiness and pleasure in love; now they were as far apart as strangers, and their meeting was a strain. Still, Don said he'd like to see the girls. Their girls. All they had now in common.

'Oh yes, they're expecting you,' Rena told him as they went up the stairs. 'They'll both be at Tess's place this evening. You'll be able to see Karen an' all, but ring Tess before you go.'

'Can you give me the number?'

She scribbled it on a scrap of paper from a drawer in the hallstand and handed it to him. 'Listen, Don, I want you to know I'm no' bitter about what you did, and I hope things go well for you, but what I say is this – you've got your life and I've got mine. I don't see 'em coming together.'

'You're right,' he said heavily. 'You were always right, Rena. Will you shake hands?'

'Aye, I'd no' mind.'

Their hands touched for a second or two, then Rena kissed him lightly on the cheek.

'Goodbye, Don.'

'Goodbye, Rena.'

He gave a long, last look round the hall of the house that had once been his home, then he opened the front door and went out. He did not look back. He was pretty sure Rena wouldn't have been watching anyway.

Chapter Eighty-Seven

They were all nervous meeting up again – Don, his daughters, even Karen, who sensed the tension in the air. But Don had had the forethought to bring Karen a present, a doll dressed as a nurse, complete with cape and bag containing miniature bandages, and she was so charmed the ice melted. Everyone relaxed.

'Oh look, Mammie, look at her wee bag!' cried Karen. 'Look at her cape and her dress, and everything!'

'Aren't you a lucky girl,' said Tess. 'Say thank you to your grandad then.'

Karen, smiling radiantly, thanked the strange man who had appeared in her life, and immediately set about examining her doll, while Don watched with fascination.

'You've done just the right thing, Dad,' Nola told him. 'Couldn't have pleased Karen more.'

'I always remember you lassies with your dolls.' He took a sip of the beer Tess had given him. 'Did you no' have one called Alice, Nola?'

'That was mine, Dad,' said Tess. 'I've still got her. Nola's was called Gloria.'

'Tess washed her and she fell apart.' Nola laughed, her eyes on her father. 'I'd some other dolls too, but they've all gone.'

'Happy days, when you were little,' Don murmured. 'They never come back.'

'Well, there's grandchildren,' said Tess.

'I'm no' likely to see Karen very often.'

Whose fault is that? his daughters wanted to ask, but let the moment pass.

'That was a grand Daimler down there,' Don remarked, after a pause. 'I was very impressed with your whole place, Tess. The garage, the office, the lot. And to think you do the driving! You're a chip off the old block, eh?'

'Nola's Luke shares the driving, but he's no' back yet. He's been a tower of strength since – since Rob's accident.'

Don made no comment. Tess had told him what had happened, but it was too painful for him to speculate on why her man should have left her. Too near the bone and he didn't like to think of it.

'The business is doing well though?' he asked at last. 'Seems you're thriving.'

'We are. In fact, we're going to take on a new driver. Luke's just found a car for us – an Armstrong–Siddely. Should be perfect.'

'A new driver? Have you found one?'

'We're going to advertise.'

Don drained his beer and wiped his lips. He looked thoughtfully at Tess. 'I wouldn't mind doing some driving for you.'

Tess and Nola exchanged glances.

'You couldn't do that, Dad, they want someone permanent,' Nola said quickly.

'I could be permanent.'

'Dad, what are you saying?' Tess had gone rather pale. 'You'd come back here?'

'Aye. I'd no' mind.'

'With Valerie?' asked Nola curtly.

'She's left me.'

Again, Nola and Tess looked at each other.

'Does Ma know?' asked Nola.

'I came up here to tell her. I asked her—' He sighed heavily. 'Well, you can guess what I asked her. She turned me down.

Thought I just wanted to come home because Val had gone, but that's no' true. I've wanted to come home for years.'

'Didn't do much about it,' said Nola.

He shook his head. 'I couldn't. I was trapped. I'd trapped maself, you might say. Anyway, your ma doesn't want me, but I'd no' mind being back in Porty. Able to see you girls and wee Karen here. Able to help you, Tess.' He gave her a long pleading look. 'What do you say?'

Tess looked down at her hands on her lap. 'I don't think it'd be a good idea, Dad, for you to work for me. I don't think Ma'd be happy.'

'She needn't see me. It's you girls I want to see. You're ma family.'

'She's always in and out of this place, she'd see you all the time. It just wouldn't work.'

'Nola – what do you think?' Don asked urgently.

'I'm sorry, Dad, I'll have to agree with Tess. It wouldn't work.'

'I could get another job. Live in Edinburgh, maybe. I'd still be able to see you.'

'Dad,' Nola said gently, 'it's too late.'

He left them soon afterwards. Said he wouldn't wait for Luke, though he'd have liked to meet him. Remembered his dad – Georgie Moffat. Nice fellow.

His daughters hugged him and Karen kissed him. He said he'd keep in touch and went slowly down the stairs to the street.

'I could walk back with you to the guesthouse,' offered Nola, but he shook his head. He'd just look round Porty for a while to say goodbye.

'Funny, you make one mistake,' he murmured, not looking at his girls. 'One bloody mistake, and it ruins your whole life. Take care then.'

'And you,' they called as he left them, marching away as though on parade, to make his farewells to Porty and all that mattered to him.

399

'Oh God,' Nola murmured, as she and Tess returned to the flat. 'Don't you feel terrible?'

Tess's throat was choked with tears. 'You think I did the right thing, Nola? I couldn't let him drive for me, could I?'

'No, it was a crazy idea.' Nola blew her nose. 'He canna come back and he knows it.'

'Would you like some coffee or anything?'

'If there's any o' that beer you got Dad, I'll have that. I feel like some alcohol.'

'Auntie Nola, will you help me get ma nurse's dress back on?' asked Karen. 'I got it off and now it'll no' go on.'

'Dear, oh dear, have you undressed the poor nurse?' Nola, half laughing, half crying, began the struggle to get the doll's dress back over her head, while Karen watched intently.

'Where's Grandad gone then? Is he no' coming to live here?'

'No, pet, he lives somewhere else.'

'I think he's nice. I wish I could see him again. He looks like Dr Dene, doesn't he, Mammie? He's got the same colour hair.'

Chapter Eighty-Eight

It was Friday. Seven o'clock. The time Toby had said he would come to collect Tess. Driving home late after a tiring journey back from Fife, she was praying he wouldn't be waiting for her. He shouldn't be. She'd sent him a note telling him she didn't think they should meet again, she hoped he'd understand. But as she drove up to her garage doors, there he was.

'Oh, Toby.' She stepped out of her car, swinging her keys. 'Didn't you get ma note?'

'Yes, I got your note.' He wasn't smiling. 'Obviously I ignored it.'

'I meant what I said.'

'Give me your keys. I'll open the doors for you.'

She drove into the garage, switched off her engine, and gave a long, troubled sigh as he slid into the passener seat next to her.

'We arranged to meet this evening, Tess.'

'You arranged to meet.'

'When I got here and your babysitter told me you weren't in, I thought you'd gone out deliberately. I couldn't believe it. But then she said you'd been delayed.'

'The queues for the ferry were worse than usual. Canna wait for them to build that new road bridge.'

'Poor Tess.' Toby took her hand. 'You work so hard. Why won't you let me take you out sometimes?' He lowered his voice. 'Are you afraid of me?'

'Do you blame me?'

'Things are different now. We're different people from those two kids we used to be.'

'Some things don't change.' She withdrew her hand from his. 'Besides, I'm no' free.'

'You don't owe Rob anything, Tess.'

'You once tried to find excuses for what he did.'

'Not excuses, reasons. I never said he could blame you if someone else came into your life.'

'If I let someone into ma life, you mean.'

'If you let me into your life,' he said softly. 'I'm already there, I think. In your heart, you know it's happening. I'm falling in love with you.' He held her gently and for the first time in many years, they kissed. And the kiss was sweet.

'Why don't you stop fighting, Tess?' he whispered against her face. 'Admit you feel the same? You do, don't you? All that early feeling for me's coming back. That's why you tried not to see me, because you were afraid it'd all be the same as last time, but it won't be. It won't be, Tess, because, as I say, we're different people. I'm different.' His voice was strained and earnest; he seemed desperate to convince her. 'Can't you see that? Can't you see that you can trust me now?'

'Toby, I think I can.' She leaned against him, suddenly luxuriating in the sensation of being loved again; it had been so long since she'd felt that. So long since someone had wanted her. 'But it's no' easy for me. I've got ma responsibilities. I have to be careful.'

'We needn't rush things.' He stroked her hair, then kissed her again, still gently, as though he too were being careful. 'We'll just go out together, have meals, see shows. Be friends, if you like, till you're sure. All I ask is that you keep on seeing me and don't send me any more notes.'

She laughed at that and the mood lightened. They left the car and kissed and held each other until Tess said she had to go in as she hadn't seen Karen all day.

'I'm sorry, I'm being selfish. You go in to her.' Toby released her and stood, smiling faintly, as he looked around the shadowy garage, where Tess's car was parked, and next to it, Luke's. 'I'll always remember this place. Who'd have thought it could be so romantic?'

'Me!' she cried promptly. 'I've always thought garages were romantic.'

'Ah, Tess, you're wonderful. When can I see you again?'

They arranged that he would telephone, then Tess let him out of the garage and he lingeringly took his leave.

'I'm closing the doors,' she warned him. 'I have to lock them.'

'All right, all right, I'm going.'

He kissed his hand to her and she gave a last smile as she closed and locked the doors.

Karen was in her nightie, and Polly's sister, Maureen, in her jacket, all ready to go, when Tess let herself into her flat and began long apologies for her lateness. Maureen was very understanding.

'Aye, that ferry over the Forth, it's a nightmare, eh? Won't it be grand when we get the bridge?'

'Canna come too soon for me,' said Tess, hugging Karen. 'Have you been a good girl for Maureen then? I'm sorry I'm so late.'

'But, Mammie, where were you? We heard the car come back ages ago. Ages and ages ago.'

'Aye, she was all set to go down to you,' Maureen told Tess from the door. 'But I said she was in her nightie and was to wait here. Were you in the office then?'

'That's right.' Tess smiled stiffly, thinking, Oh God, she might have seen us, Karen might have seen us. Liking Dr Dene was one thing for her daughter; seeing him kissing her mother would have been quite another.

'I was doing ma paperwork, you ken,' she added, and Maureen nodded.

'Always a lot o' that. Did you see the fellow who came seeking you then?'

'What fellow?'

'Nice looking man. Silver hair, but no' that old. He never gave his name.'

'It was Dr Dene, Mammie!' cried Karen. 'I was playing with Nursie when I heard him. I was going to find him, but he'd gone.'

'Oh, yes, Dr Dene,' Tess said lightly. 'No, I didn't see him.'

What had she got herself into? Telling lies to Maureen. For no reason.

Tess, changing into shirt and slacks after Maureen had gone, felt weighed down by her own strange glibness. What was it to Maureen if Tess met someone who wasn't her husband? Even her family knew she was seeing Toby Dene. Yet there was an atmosphere of secrecy about the relationship that cheapened it and made it seem wrong. Made her feel she should ask herself if it was, in fact, wrong.

'You don't owe Rob anything,' Toby had said. And hadn't she herself told Rob she wasn't promising to wait for him? Why should she lose the chance of a new love, for a man who had left her?

But then, the new love was an old love, and had its own dangers.

'Can't you see that you can trust me now?' Toby had asked.

She didn't know. She still wasn't sure. But when she was alone again, with Karen in bed and her modest supper in front of her, she suddenly gave herself up again to the pleasure of being loved. That was something Toby had given her and she was grateful. Whether it would last, or not, she had it now, and if it was not like her to live for the moment, well, perhaps it was true, she was different from her old self. Just as Toby declared he was different from his old self. So perhaps she could trust him, after all.

Chapter Eighty-Nine

It was a busy summer. Tess and Luke were looking for a third driver for the Armstrong-Siddely. Toby was still looking at properties for a surgery. Nola and Rena were renovating their little pottery, while still working at the Harebell.

'No point in giving up our wages till we're ready,' said Rena. 'And Nola wants to get pieces ready for our grand opening.' She laughed. 'Whenever that'll be!'

Tess, who had seen the pottery and thought it sweet but very small, worried that there wouldn't be enough profit in it for her mother. Nola had Luke's earnings to help her out, but Rena only had her modest rents, which she'd always been able to supplement with her wages.

'Are you sure you'll be able to manage, Ma?' she asked, but Rena told her to stop her nagging. When had she ever needed a lot o' money?

'Everybody needs money, Ma, and you're always trying to help us out and leaving yourself short. Once you and Nola are on your own, you'll have to be more careful.'

'Careful? What a cheek! Who's more careful than me? You're the one who's splashing out with another car, an' all. When are you going to find this new driver then?'

'We're having to advertise again. Luke didn't think the ones who applied were right for us. I'd have liked a woman, but no luck there.'

'I suppose you've no' thought—'

'What?'

'Well, will it no' soon be time for Rob to get his licence back? If he came home, you'd no' need a third driver.'

Tess bit her lip. 'Who knows what Rob'll do?'

'Aye, you canna tell. Best get on with your interviews then.'

At least her mother had not mentioned Toby Dene, thought Tess, for which she was deeply grateful.

Of course, she was seeing him. Throughout those summer weeks, they met whenever they could, sometimes having a meal together, sometimes going to the theatre or a film, sometimes taking Toby's car and driving through the evening light to walk on a beach that was not Portobello's.

Tess felt guilty leaving Karen so often, and paid out large sums to different babysitters so that it wasn't obvious to any one of them that she was going out so much and always with the same person. Karen herself seemed to like seeing different faces anyway, and Tess had promised her that when she got the new driver, she'd be free to spend much more time with her as soon as she broke up from school. But Karen had not forgotten that Dr Dene had said he'd take her to the Queen Street gardens near his flat, so when were they going?

'Karen can look round the gardens any time, and come to my flat,' said Toby. 'What's the difficulty?'

'I don't want her to get too used to you.'

'What's that supposed to mean? You still don't trust me?'

'No. It's just – well, I have to make sure she's isn't upset. Supposing we were to stop seeing each other, for instance—'

'You still think that'll happen? Is that why you don't come to my flat yourself?'

'You did say we shouldn't rush things.'

He looked at her ruefully, then kissed her with a passion he did not usually show. 'I'm beginning to wish we could put a spurt on then. Couldn't we make things official?'

'You mean what, exactly?'

'I mean, you should ask Rob for a divorce.'

Tess stared, completely taken aback. Ask Rob for a divorce? She hadn't considered it. Yet for many people it would have been the obvious step, and perhaps only fair to Toby. How long was she going to keep him dangling?

'I'll have to see if he comes home,' Tess said slowly. 'When he gets his licence back.'

'Oh God, is that likely?' Toby grasped her strongly, his face, above hers, stricken. 'I'd quite given up believing he'd come home.'

'I don't think he will,' said Tess.

He didn't. The days passed and there was no sign from him. Tess and Luke finally gave the job of third driver to Aaron Smith, Norrie's younger brother, a less outgoing personality than Norrie himself, and a good, careful driver, vetted by Luke.

'I think we're in the clear,' Toby told Tess. 'Wherever Rob is, he's not coming back.'

'You said that was strange, didn't you? You said you'd have expected him to have come back by now.'

'I did say that, but we just don't know, do we? Let's not think about him now.' Toby's eyes were at their brightest. 'Let's think about you and me. I want you to come and look at a place I've found. A very special place.'

'A house for your surgery?' she asked with interest. 'Where?'

'Not far from your garage. Not far from the sands.'

'Oh, stop teasing and tell me, Toby!'

'Well then, it's on the promenade.' He held her at arm's length, laughing. 'Tess, it's Pax House.'

407

Chapter Ninety

The young man from the lawyers brought the keys. Thinnish, slightly balding, he stepped out of his car into the humid August weather and greeted them with a pleasant smile.

'Dr Dene? Good afternoon. Hope I haven't kept you waiting?'

'Not at all, we've just arrived.'

Toby shook hands and introduced Tess. It was only a few minutes after two, the time of the appointment, but they had, in fact, been waiting a while because Tess had been so desperate to get to the house and go inside.

'Take it easy,' Toby had told her fondly, as she paced up and down, not sparing a glance at the nearby crowded beach, gazing only at the house they'd come to see, the house she'd never thought to visit again. And one that might be hers.

That was the unbelievable part. She wouldn't just be working there; if she married Toby, it would be her home. Simon was only going to have a consulting room; he wouldn't be living in the house. It would be hers and Toby's. Always assuming someone else didn't bid more than the two doctors could afford, but Toby was confident they could beat any opposition.

'Very fine, isn't it?' asked young Mr Stimson, gazing blandly up at the elegant, unwashed, windows. 'Needs a little attention, of course—'

Toby and Tess exchanged glances.

'But nothing that will cost too much, I think you'll find. And of course it has wonderful views.'

'Better out of season, I should think,' said Toby. 'The beach is pretty close.'

'Perhaps, but a sea view is always a bonus.'

'Such a lot to do though. Might put people off.'

'Depends how much they want it.' Mr Stimson was ushering them through the gates and up the overgrown drive. 'If you like the house, I'd advise you to ask your solicitor to declare interest as soon as possible, so that we can arrange a closing date for offers.'

'Our offer will be a good one.'

Mr Stimson smiled. 'In that case, you could be lucky. Now – let's try this key.'

The house was a shell. A finely proportioned, beautiful shell. Everything had been removed – rugs, furniture, curtains, even light fittings – but Toby, striding over the echoing floors, called to Tess that that was good. You could see the rooms better. See what they might become. It was plain that he was already visualizing how they would look when he moved in.

'This is the drawing room?' he asked, checking his sheet of particulars in one of the fine rooms at the front of the house. 'It's splendid. I'd be tempted to keep this for myself, but it would make an excellent waiting room. Don't you agree, Tess?'

'What?'

She was standing at the long windows, looking out to the Forth. When she turned he saw that she was very pale.

'I'm sorry, Toby, I didn't hear what you said.'

It was because of the other voices in her head that she hadn't heard what he'd said. So many voices, murmuring, whispering. Whose voices? She knew them all.

'Pax means peace, you know ... I've only seen the outside ... one day I'll take you inside ... introduce you to Mr Seton ... Rob, you wouldn't ... we do our best, dear, and it's only fair we should ... Mr Seton is very good to us ... Rob's done a lot for me, Miss Gillespie ... it's not just a question of driving the motor.'

'Could I have a look at the garage?' she asked the lawyer hurriedly.

'The garage?' He seemed astonished.

'Mrs MacNair's interested in garages,' Toby said with a smile.

'I'm sure I have the key – we go out from the staff quarters, I believe.'

'Through the lobby at the end of the kitchen,' Tess told him. 'I used to know this house.'

'That's most interesting, Mrs MacNair. When was that then?'

'A long time ago.'

Like the garage itself, the stairs up to what had been the chauffeur's room were covered in papers and packing straw, which Tess pushed aside with the toe of her shoe as she climbed towards the door.

'You all right, Mrs MacNair?' Mr Stimson called, mystified, from below.

'Yes thanks, as long as this door's no' locked.'

'The interior doors are all open, but I can come up if you like—'

'No, you're right, it's open.' Her hand on the doorknob, Tess looked down at him. 'Maybe Dr Dene would like some help? I'll just look round here.'

As soon as she heard the lawyer's steps retreating, Tess moved slowly into Rob's old room. It was empty, of course, its little window so covered in grime, even the summer daylight was scarcely filtering through. But she didn't need light for her memories. Herself and Rob, arms clasped, bodies touching, mouths meeting. So happy.

She shouldn't have come, she thought. It was too hard, too painful.

But she had wanted to come. To come up here to Rob's old room. Ever since she'd stepped into Pax House, she'd known she would. She'd known she would come looking for her old love, looking for him. Rob was everywhere in this house, she felt his presence in every room, but no more so than here, where they'd kissed and caressed and looked forward to bliss.

She hadn't wanted to wait for the bliss and smiled now, as she remembered her young self attempting to be so sophisticated.

Honestly, Rob, do I have to spell it out?

But he had been so serious, so careful for her.

No, sweetheart, I'm there before you ... imagine I don't want to jump the gun? I think about it all the time, but I'm no' risking it, you're too precious.

Yes, she'd been precious to him and he to her. They'd had happiness based on the sort of love and trust she'd never expected to find, and as time went by had never expected to lose. Where had it all gone wrong?

Well, of course, she knew where it had all gone wrong. After the accident, Rob had changed. Become envious of her and jealous of Luke; sick at heart over his own failings. As she paced the little room that had been his, Tess knew that all those charges were true. Yet there'd been failings on her part, too. She'd only seen the symptoms and been resentful; she hadn't tried to look beyond, to reach the man who was suffering. Even Toby had tried to understand. Why hadn't she?

She should never have let Rob go. She should, at least, have gone after him. Brought him back, so that they could sort things out, maybe get help from the doctors.

Was it too late?

There were footsteps on the stairs. She didn't even wonder whose they might be. All that mattered as she stood transfixed was that she knew now what she wanted. Pax House had told her. Pax House, where she would never

live, but would always be special to her, because she and
Rob had been so happy here long ago. Pax House, that had
made her see she must fight with all the strength she could
command to find that same happiness with Rob again.

Chapter Ninety-One

'Tess, what's going on?' It was Toby at the door, gazing in at her with a strange, anxious expression. 'What are you doing here?'

She shrugged and smiled. 'Just looking around.'

'Why here, for God's sake? There's nothing to see.'

As he continued to stare at her, she saw the understanding swim into his eyes. 'Ah, I get it. We're over the garage, aren't we? Was this Rob's room?'

She didn't need to reply; the colour was flooding her face. Toby went to her and took her by the hand.

'Come on then, Tess. There's no point in staying here, is there?'

'Where d'you want me to go?'

'Well, to look round the rest of the house. You'd like to, wouldn't you?'

'I know the house, Toby.'

'But I don't and you're here with me. I thought we'd look round together.'

'I think – I think I'd like some fresh air. I'll wait for you outside, shall I?'

He continued to study her. 'Are you feeling all right? I noticed before, you were very pale.'

'I'm OK. Just need some air.'

She knew he was worried, afraid that something was wrong, but there was nothing she could do, no way she could reassure him. They left Rob's room together, Toby carefully closing the door, Tess not taking a last look for fear he would read her face. They made their way back through the house to the entrance hall.

'Ready to go?' Mr Stimson asked brightly, appearing from the drawing room. 'Actually, someone else is due in five minutes.'

'Yes thanks, I think I've seen all I need.' Toby briefly shook his head at Tess, who was looking surprised. 'Thank you so much for your time, Mr Stimson. I like the house and I'll be in touch.'

'Why didn't you finish looking round?' asked Tess, as they walked through the wilderness that was the garden of Pax House. 'I never meant you to miss out because of me.'

'I couldn't concentrate. I wanted to talk to you.' Toby opened the crazily hanging gates. 'Something's happened, hasn't it?'

As she opened her mouth to reply, he put his hand against her lips. 'Please don't say no.'

'I wasn't going to.'

He heaved a long sigh. 'And I was hoping you might. Shall we walk? Find somewhere to sit?'

They couldn't get away from the crowds, of course, but when they finally found an empty seat facing the beach, somehow it helped, seeing all those people without cares, or appearing to be without cares. All those dads digging and children paddling and mothers looking in purses for money for ice-cream. Made them see there was still a world of normality, even if they were, for the moment, not a part of it.

'Happy days,' Toby muttered. 'We used to go to Bamburgh before the war.'

'We never went anywhere but here.'

'Nothing wrong with Porty. Tell me what happened, Tess.'

*

414

Even as she was stumbling through her thoughts and decisions, she knew that she had no need to be telling him anything at all. He'd known from the moment he'd found her in her husband's old room that she'd changed her mind. That was the way he was. Intelligent. And also a lover. Lovers never needed words.

'So you've forgiven him,' he murmured when her voice had died away. 'He's left you and you're going after him.'

'I never said I was going after him.'

'But you are, aren't you?'

'Maybe I should.'

'You were afraid once of what you might find.'

She drew in her breath. 'I'll have to take that risk.'

'Sorry, I shouldn't have mentioned it.' For some time, Toby watched the seagulls wheeling and crying. 'Put it down to misery.'

Tess winced and caught at his hand. 'Toby, I'm sorry. I'm the last person to want to hurt anybody—'

'Maybe you are. So maybe I won't say you've got your revenge then.'

She dropped his hand as though it burnt her own. 'You think I'm doing this for revenge?'

'No.' He sighed. 'No, I don't. I'm just being rotten again. You've a good heart, Tess, I know you'd never want to hurt me. Truth is, I think I always knew, deep down, that you still loved your husband, but I wouldn't let myself believe it.' He laughed a little. 'There's arrogance for you. You'd loved me once, why not again?'

'I do care for you, Toby. And I always will.'

He leaped to his feet. 'That's my cue to go, I think. When people start talking about caring, instead of loving, you know just what they mean. I'm going back to my car now, Tess. I'll say goodbye.'

'Wait, I'll go with you.'

She had to run to keep up with him. He was striding ahead, deliberately not waiting, but when they reached his car, parked in a side street, he turned and looked at her with desolate eyes.

'I don't think we've much more to say, Tess. Let's not draw this thing out.'

'But what are you going to do?'

'Do?'

'Well, will you be putting in an offer? For Pax House?'

'Oh no, I won't be putting in an offer. Pax House was for you.'

Her head drooped and her eyes filled with tears. She couldn't speak.

'He must be quite something, this Rob of yours,' Toby said coolly. 'When you think what you've given up for him.'

She looked away to the end of the street, where the light had the special quality that comes from the closeness of the sea. If she stared hard enough, she thought, she might stop crying.

'Maybe you're right, Toby, we don't have anything else to say.'

'Goodbye, then.' He opened his car door and eased himself into the driving seat. 'Tell Karen I'm sorry we never went to the gardens. Or maybe you'd rather not speak of me?'

'I'll tell her you had to go away.'

'Better not. She'll think that's what all men do.'

Toby gave Tess one last long look, then started his engine and slowly moved off. It was the first time she'd watched him leave her, though she knew he'd often watched her, and even though she wanted him to go, she couldn't help feeling the sadness of their farewell. What he'd said of her was true of him: he had a good heart, and there had been a time after they'd met again – a very short time – when she'd thought she might find happiness with him. But she knew now where her happiness lay and it was not with Toby. They would probably not see each other again.

416

Chapter Ninety-Two

Three days later Tess was in Coventry. She had left Karen with her mother, turning a deaf ear to Rena's protestations that she was just crazy, so she was, to go after a man who should have come to her; had put Rob's last address in her bag and simply taken off. 'Like a rocket,' Rena had muttered. 'Aye, and you'll come down with the stick!'

Well, maybe she would. Maybe she'd get nowhere and have to come home alone. All she knew was that she had to try to find Rob. Had to see him and make the offer to start again. Had to salvage what she could of her marriage that had once meant so much. And, oh God, still did.

So now she was where Rob had been, and might still be; walking Coventry's new streets and recalling all she'd heard of its devastation by enemy bombers during the war. As a child she could remember Rena listening to the wireless and shaking her head in sorrow. Oh the poor city, eh? Practically destroyed, because its car firms had been turned into armament factories. And the beautiful old cathedral had gone as well. That was war for you.

Back in 1940, it had probably been hard to believe that the city would ever rise again from the ashes, but here it was, replanned and rebuilt, with new streets, squares, shops and even a new cathedral almost finished, ready to replace the old. Tess, hurriedly sightseeing, marvelled, and thought of Rob.

As he walked these streets where she walked now, had he taken courage from what could be done to recover from terrible damage? Had there been any sort of message here for him? It was impossible to say. Pointless really, even to speculate. As she booked into a little guest house and asked directions to the last address he had given her, she knew he had become such a stranger to her she couldn't possibly know what was in his mind.

'That street's near the Daimler factory,' Mr Craddock, the owner of the guest house informed her. 'Well, Jaguar, I should say now, seeing as they've bought it. Same difference. They'll still be making the Daimlers.'

'Folk'll always want Daimlers,' Tess said confidently.

He looked at her a little curiously, perhaps wondering what she would know about Daimlers, but he made no comment, only told her which bus to take down the Radford Road.

'Just tell the conductor you want to be off at that street. It's near the railway and the factory – you'll have no trouble finding it. Nice little terrace houses, as I recall. Will you be back for high tea, Mrs MacNair?'

'Oh, yes,' she promised.

As though she could even think of eating! In her room, she put on lipstick with a trembling hand and prepared to set out for the bus.

The little house where Rob might or might not be staying was one of a row of brick-built houses, neatly kept up, but darkened by time and proximity to the railway running to its right. Ahead was a car park and beyond that the factory buildings that made up the huge Daimler plant. For some moments, Tess gazed across at them, picturing Rob working there, wondering if she would see him.

At the thought of meeting him again after so long, her throat was dry and her palms damp, and it came into her mind that there was always the bus back to town. She didn't have to knock on this door, did she?

She knocked anyway.

'Yes?' asked a short, dark-haired woman with round brown, bird-like eyes. She wore a dark-blue cotton dress and had an apron over her arm, as though she'd just taken it off before answering the door.

'I'm sorry to bother you,' said Tess, speaking quickly in her nervousness, 'but, is there a Mr MacNair living here?'

'There was. I'm afraid you've just missed him.'

'He's left?'

'Moved on, only yesterday.'

'Oh.' Tess felt her energy draining from her. Yesterday. It seemed too cruel. 'He was a lodger here?'

'One of 'em – I've three. My name's Mrs Wynne. What a shame you were just too late then. You're his wife, aren't you?'

Tess stared. 'How did you know?'

The woman smiled. 'I've dusted your photo often enough, my dear. And your little girl's. Mr MacNair kept 'em by his bed. Told me once who you were.'

Colour flooded Tess's face. Rob had their photographs by his bed? He must care then. He must still love them surely? She felt quite light-headed with relief and joy, and then, as the landlady's bright gaze didn't move from her face, embarrassed.

'Don't worry,' Mrs Wynne said, lowering her voice. 'He never told me anything else. I never knew why he was on his own, but I felt that sorry for him. Such a nice man. Though sometimes so low in spirits.'

'Was he?' asked Tess faintly.

'Oh yes. You could see he had something on his mind. He did tell me once that he might not stay long, because he liked to be on the move, but he was with me a good while in the end.'

'Did he leave a forwarding address?'

'I'm afraid not. Said he might send one when he was settled. I'm wondering if he's gone looking for something new. He's been doing evening classes – something to do

419

with business methods, I believe.'

'Evening classes?' Tess was mystified.

'Maybe he just wanted a change?'

'Maybe. Thank you very much anyway, Mrs Wynne. You've been very kind.'

At the despondent note in Tess's voice, Mrs Wynne's brown eyes softened.

'Would you like to come in for a minute, Mrs MacNair? My lads'll be in soon, but I could make you a cup of tea, if you don't mind being in the kitchen.'

Tess, who could now smell something good cooking in the background, thanked Mrs Wynne for her offer, but said she wouldn't trouble her. She'd better get back to her guest house. In truth, she had no desire to see where Rob had lived when he was no longer there.

'All right, dear, just as you like, but I'll wish you the best of luck.' Mrs Wynne put out a small, worn hand for Tess to shake. 'I do hope things work out for you. I'm sure they will. I mean, look at us in Coventry. Who'd have thought, when we were bombed, that we'd ever be like we are today, with our cathedral coming back to us and all? Keep your spirits up, Mrs MacNair.'

Chapter Ninety-Three

It wasn't so easy to do that. Arriving back at Waverley the following afternoon, Tess felt bowed down with failure. It was true, there'd been a ray of brightness in the shadows when she'd heard about Rob's keeping the photographs, but how much did that mean after all? He was on the move again, which meant she'd even less hope than before of finding him. And what was all that about evening classes? He might be anywhere by now, trying for some new job – Land's End, or John o'Groats. She was beginning to feel she would never see him again.

She did see another face she knew though, as she moved through the crowd of travellers. A very attractive face it was, too, with high cheekbones and expressive dark eyes. A face from the past.

'Erika!' she cried, and the elegant young woman came to a halt.

'Tess?'

They eyed each other warily for a second or two, then hugged strongly, as though there'd never been anything but friendship between them.

'Tess, I haven't seen you for so long,' Erika cried. 'How are you? You're looking well.'

How can she say that? thought Tess, who knew she looked tired and dispirited, and distinctly crumpled after the long hours in the train.

'No' as well as you, I think.'

'Nonsense!'

But Erika, in a narrow-skirted grey suit and white blouse, with her dark hair expertly cut and her ears pierced for little pearls, looked beautiful, intelligent and completely in control. Yes, a professional woman, one dedicated to her work, as Toby had said. But why the pierced ears? Erika was not just interested in work perhaps? Or was her care for her appearance only to please herself?

'It is so wonderful to meet again,' Erika was saying. 'Have you time for coffee?'

'Oh, I don't think—'

'Please, Tess, don't say no. It would be so lovely to talk. I've just been to a meeting, I'm going back to Glasgow, but there are plenty of trains to Glasgow.' Erika's eyes were pleading with such anxiety, Tess shrugged, and agreed.

'As long as we don't take too long. I have to get back to ma little girl.'

'You have a little girl? Oh, Tess, I didn't even know. Oh, I should have known!'

'We haven't kept in touch. How could you have known?' Tess took Erika's thin arm. 'Come on, let's no' waste time.'

They went to a little café outside the station rather than the buffet, which always brought back unhappy memories for Tess. Erika ordered her usual strong black coffee, and Tess chose café au lait. With sugar.

'I feel I need it,' she said, half smiling.

'You've been travelling?'

'I – went to see somebody in England. Warwickshire.'

'How nice.' Drinking her coffee, her eyes on Tess, Erika had lost some of her poise. 'I can't tell you how pleased I am to see you,' she murmured. 'I think of you so often, you know. I think always of the past.'

'I met someone from the past no' very long ago,' Tess answered casually. 'Toby Dene.'

A pale pink flush rose to Erika's cheekbones. 'Toby? I haven't seen him for a while.'

'He's planning to set up as a GP in Edinburgh with Simon Maitland.'

'He did say once he'd like to do that. How did you come to meet him then?'

'We have a chauffeur hire car business now. I do some of the driving and Toby was at the hotel where I collected ma clients.'

'You drive as a chauffeur, Tess? That's wonderful. So expert! I remember though, you were always interested in cars.' Erika's eyes slid away. 'But tell me, how did you and Toby get on? Were you friends again?'

'You could say that.'

'I'm glad. Very glad, Tess. You know how awful I felt when we – when Toby and I – upset you.'

'I made too much of it.' Tess looked carefully into her empty coffee cup. 'Erika, I should have apologised to you a long time ago.'

'Tess, you did. But there was no need. I was the one who upset you.'

'Aye, but did I make you understand I just got things wrong? I knew you'd never meant to hurt me. Look, shall we say no more about it?' Tess raised her eyes. 'But I was really sorry in the end, that things didn't work out for you and Toby.'

'He told you?'

'Yes. He said you only cared about your work.'

Erika's eyes flashed. 'Now that is not true! I did love Toby very much, but it didn't last. It was the same for him, I believe. Our love burnt itself out. Naturally, I turned to my work.'

'I think he would like to see you again, Erika.'

'There would be no point in seeing him.'

Tess hesitated. 'He's rented a flat. I could give you his phone number.'

Erika pushed aside her coffee cup. 'What's this about,

Tess? Why are you trying to make me see Toby?'

'I'm no' trying to make you do anything, Erika. I just feel he'd like to hear from you again. He's – he's in low spirits at the moment.' Tess glanced at her watch. 'Think I'd better be going. It's been grand meeting again, eh?'

'But we haven't really talked about you, Tess, or your family. I mean, your mother and Nola, and your little girl. I'd love to hear about your little girl. I don't even know her name.'

'Everyone's fine. And ma daughter's called Karen. She's five.'

'Couldn't we meet again? We were good friends once.' Erika took a card and a pen from her bag. 'Look, I'll give you my phone number. What about yours?'

'We're in the book.'

'Right. Well – if you like – I could take Toby's.'

Tess, making no comment, took out her diary and watched as Erika copied Toby's number into a notebook.

'I might give him a ring sometime,' she said smoothly. 'If he's feeling low.'

'Better make it soon, in case he decides to go south.'

'Why would he do that?'

'Mightn't get what he wants here.' Tess put out her hand. 'I'll say goodbye, Erika. Maybe we'll meet again one day.'

'Oh, I hope so.' Outside the café, Erika caught at Tess's arm. 'Please remember me to your mother, and to Nola.'

'I will.'

Watching her walk swiftly away to catch the next Glasgow train, Tess was possessed by a slight feeling of guilt. She hadn't been exactly straight with Erika. Hadn't said that Rob had left her, or that Toby had professed new love for her.

But it was too soon for confidences, she reassured herself. Erika had been her friend, and was still, but the friendship had lapsed; the time for heart to hearts was not quite yet.

As she ran to catch her bus to Porty, Tess thought about Erika's taking Toby's phone number. Would anything come of that? How strange it was the way the wheel turned. At one time, the idea of Erika's ringing Toby would have been enough to plunge her into despair. Now, it filled her with sweet relief.

The trams had gone in 1956, but Tess missed them still. She was just being sentimental, of course, for the bus was more comfortable and made the same journey. Still, a good many local folk were unhappy about the loss of their trams. Just one more change, wasn't it, eh? There'd been so many changes, not all for the better.

Tess, clutching her overnight bag, left the bus at the stop close to Number One. No changes there. The power station was still sending out its smoke. The traffic was still roaring by. And from the not-too-distant beach came the cries and laughter of the holidaymakers.

She should go in at once, she knew, to collect Karen who would be waiting, but she hesitated, bracing herself for her mother's questions.

'So he wasn't there?' Ma would say. 'It was all a waste of time?'

I'll tell her he keeps our photos by his bed, thought Tess. Then she'll know it wasn't a waste of time.

Her eyes wandered down the road to the sands, which for a moment seemed quiet. Only one figure was approaching and that was a man's. In the warmth of the summer evening, he was casually dressed, in loose jacket and flannels and open-necked shirt, and as he came nearer, Tess suddenly became very still.

It seemed as though the world had stopped turning. Everything was hushed, even the noise from the beach, as though something important was about to happen and everyone was waiting. But it was only Tess who was waiting. Waiting to be sure, though she was already sure in her heart.

'Rob!' she cried as he came towards her, and as she ran to him and his arms closed around her, the noise came back and the world started again, but neither of them knew.

Chapter Ninety-Four

He looked so well; that was what surprised her. She'd been picturing him as he'd been after his accident, pale and strange, his eyes shadowed. But he was bronzed. He stood tall and strong, his eyes clear and blue. He was more than just well.

'Rob!' She held him at arm's length, studying his face in the evening sunlight. 'You've come back.'

'I have.'

'I don't mean you're here. I mean, you're—'

'Better,' he said simply. 'Yes, I'm maself again.'

'Why did you stay away then? Rob, why did you?'

He gathered her back into his arms. 'Canna talk here. Let's go home, eh?' He looked beyond her to the top of the road. 'Is that your case there, Tess? Have you been away?'

'I've been looking for you. I've been to your lodgings in Coventry.'

'You went to ma lodgings? You met Mrs Wynne?'

'I did. She told me you kept our photos by your bed.'

'Did you think I wouldn't?'

'I didn't even know you'd taken our photos with you.'

'Oh, Tess!' He gave a shaky laugh. 'But that's the strangest thing, eh? You went down there, and I came up here. Can you believe it?'

'Rob, we have to go.' She began to draw him gently up the road towards her mother's house. 'We have to go to Ma's. Karen's waiting for me.'

'Karen? Wee Karen? Oh, God. I'm no' sure I can face her.' He put his hand to his brow. 'I've been a crazy man, Tess, just crazy, that's all I can say, and I know it's no excuse.'

'Come on,' she said softly. 'Karen will be so happy when she sees you.'

'And your ma? What's she going to be?'

'Never mind about Ma. We're your family, Karen and me. We want you back. Why d'you think I went seeking you? It was to bring you home.' Tess's voice trembled. 'But you came yourself. You came yourself, Rob. That's what I'll always remember.'

There were tears in their eyes as they stood together, their mouths meeting in a long heartfelt kiss that each knew sealed the homecoming. They hadn't kissed in that way since before Rob's accident. There had been many times when Tess had thought they would never kiss again, never know love again. What was happening seemed a dream.

'I don't deserve you,' Rob murmured. 'Still here, waiting for me. Tess, you're a saint.'

'No,' she said quickly. 'No, I'm not. Don't say it. Look, let's go to Ma's. Get it over with.'

'Aye, that'll be best. I'll take your case.'

For the first time, Tess wondered where Rob's own case might be; he appeared to have come up from the sands with only the clothes he was wearing. But now was not the time to go into that. Now was the time to face Ma.

When Rob came walking into the kitchen, clasping Tess's hand, Rena's face turned white.

'Oh my God, Tess, you've found him!' she cried, putting her arm round Karen. 'I canna believe it! Karen, here's your dad, come home!'

'I didn't find him,' Tess told her. 'He came back himself. I saw him on the road outside, coming up from the sands.'

'Hallo, Mrs Gillespie.' Rob, not daring to look at his

428

little daughter, was bravely trying to meet Rena's eyes. 'I'm sorry if it's a shock, seeing me again like this.'

'It's a shock all right.' Still hanging on to the bemused Karen, Rena's tone was cool. 'Where'd you come from then?'

'From Coventry yesterday. I've been working at the Daimler factory. Today, I've just been walking.' He laughed a little. 'Trying to find the courage to go home.'

'Put me down, Gran, put me down!' Karen, wriggling from Rena's arms, ran to Rob and looked up into his face. 'Are you ma dad?' she demanded.

'I am, pet.' As he brought himself down to Karen's level, he finally looked into her wondering eyes.

'So it's true, you're no' dead?'

He blinked a little, then laughed, and gently took her into his arms. 'I'm no' dead. Here, you can tell, feel ma hands. Nice and warm, eh?

'Mammie said you weren't dead, but some girls I know said you were.'

'Well, now you can tell 'em I'm alive.' For a moment, he held her aloft, then set her down. 'I'm home and I'm going to stay.'

'Have you brought me a present?'

'Karen!' cried Tess.

'He might have,' Karen retorted. 'Grandad gave me Nursie. Dad, would you like to see ma nurse doll? She's got her own case.'

'Yes, go and find your doll, Karen,' Rena said sharply. 'I want to talk to your dad.'

'We're going home, Ma,' said Tess. 'That's where we want to be.'

'You'll be having your tea first. I've got it all ready. Why, you've been travelling all day.' Rena glanced at Rob. 'You'd better have something too, Rob.'

'Thank you.' He drew Karen to him again. 'I have got something for you, pet, but I'll have to get it for you tomorrow. It's at the place where I'm staying.'

'And where's that?' asked Rena, as Karen skipped away to fetch her doll.

'Guest house off Brighton Place. I was lucky to get in. Seems Porty's bursting at the seams, and then there's the Festival on as well.'

'Imagine booking in at a guest house!' cried Tess. 'Whatever were you thinking of, Rob?'

'He was thinking you might no' want him home,' snapped Rena. 'And he was right to think that, an' all. After what he's put you through, Tess.'

'Rob's been ill, Ma. He wasn't himself when he left me.'

'Still managed to think of himself, though, didn't he?'

Rena moved to the sink to fill the kettle, while Rob looked at Tess and Tess lowered her eyes.

'You've every right to think badly of me, Mrs Gillespie,' Rob said heavily. 'You couldn't blame me more than I blame maself.'

She took a checked cloth from the dresser drawer and shook it fiercely over the table. 'I've just the table to set, and then we'll be ready. It's all cold, you ken – I wasn't sure what time you'd be back.'

'Ma, I did say—' Tess began, but Rob shook his head at her.

'Tess looks as if she could do with her tea, Mrs Gillespie. I could get something where I'm staying, though, if you'd rather I didn't stay.'

'Och, don't talk so daft! Sit down both of you, and I'll call Karen. She'll be away to your attic, Tess, for her doll – thinks it's grand up there.'

Rob suddenly moved to put his hand on Rena's arm. 'Mrs Gillespie, I want to tell you that I feel terrible about what I did, but if Tess'll have me back, I'm going to do everything I can to make it up to her and ma wee girl. That's a promise.'

'You know I want you back, Rob,' said Tess. 'I want to make a fresh start.'

430

'Aye, well that's up to you,' Rena told her. 'It's no' for me to interfere between man and wife. If you want to forgive Rob, Tess, you forgive him. I'll say no more.'

'Ma, you forgave Dad in the end.'

'Never took him back though.'

Rob dropped his hand to his side. 'Perhaps I should go. Tess, I'll see you back at the flat.'

'No!' She ran to him. 'We'll go together.'

'Dad, here's ma Nursie!' cried Karen, hurrying in with her doll. 'Want to see her case? It's got all wee bandages and sticking plaster.'

'It's grand, pet, just the thing, eh?'

'I can show you ma other dolls when we go home. When we've had our tea.' Karen suddenly looked a little anxious. 'Dad, are you having your tea with Gran?'

Rena, her eyes on her grandaughter's face, gave a short sigh.

'Aye, he is,' she said with sudden decision. 'Come on, then, Rob. Here's your place.' She briefly laid her hand on his shoulder. 'Tess is right, we'll all make a fresh start, eh?'

'Thanks, Ma,' whispered Tess, as she passed the plates of cold beef and ham.

Rena brushed that aside. 'Be sure and phone Nola after your tea. She'll be knocked all of a heap, Luke an' all. You know they're married now, Rob? Nola and Luke?'

'No, I didn't know that.'

'I'm sure I told you,' said Tess.

'Never got the letter.'

'Well, you were always on the move, eh?' asked Rena. 'Like one o' thae nomads.'

'What's a nomad?' asked Karen.

'Folk who move around,' Rob told her. 'But that's no' me, because I'm home and I'm going to stay.'

Karen put her small hand in his. 'For always?'

'For always.'

She looked at him with her mother's grey eyes and made

431

no reply, so whether or not she believed him, he had no idea. But she did leave her hand in his, which was a comfort to him.

Chapter Ninety-Five

There was a bad moment when they first arrived home, because Honey wasn't there. Rob's gaze went straight to the corner where her basket had always been, and for a moment he couldn't speak.

'It's all right, Dad,' Karen said, swinging on his hand. 'It's all right, don't cry.'

'I'm no' crying, pet.'

She wasn't convinced, but took him to see her toys, which she was sure would cheer him up, while Tess sighed and said she didn't see them ever getting Karen to bed that night. Eventually though she wearied, and consented to try to go to sleep if her dad would read to her first.

'Six stories on the trot,' he whispered to Tess, after he'd tiptoed from Karen's little room. 'Do I get some sort of reward?'

They went to bed. In spite of all the long tragic years since they'd made love, there was no strangeness in it. Only, when their bodies met again, such rightness and bliss, it was as if they'd never been apart.

Afterwards, Tess lay close to Rob's side, while he smoked a cigarette and she cried, 'Shame!'

'Och, no,' Rob murmured. 'Everybody knows the best cigarette is after sex. And I want everything to be the best tonight, because I'm so happy. Sunshine after cloud, eh?

And you canna appreciate the sunshine if you've never known the cloud.'

'Poor Rob, you've known the cloud,' Tess murmured.

'Aye, and so have you.' He was silent for a time, then stubbed out his cigarette in the ashtray by the bed. 'Thought I'd come out of it if I went away, you ken. But I took it with me. Never seemed as though it'd go.'

He stared into the summer darkness as Tess ran her fingers over his chest, then he reached for her hand and kissed it.

'One morning, you ken, it just went. I woke up and felt different. Felt free. And all the world was in colours again. Tess, you've no idea what that was like.'

'Why didn't you come home then, Rob? When you were better?'

'Felt too ashamed.' He sat up and swung himself to the edge of the bed. 'The other side of feeling better was that I could see straight again.' He glanced back at Tess. 'Could see just how bloody selfish I'd been, leaving you. Leaving Karen. Minding about you driving and me not. Minding about Luke. OK, I was maybe crazy at the time. How could I ask you to take me back again after all that?

'You weren't yourself, Rob.'

'Aye, but I did leave you. And I left ma daughter. I'll never forgive maself for that.'

'But you came back,' she said softly. 'You came back to us.'

'Finally found the nerve. Finally knew I'd have to try. See what you thought.'

'Now you know what I think.' Tess slipped out of bed and put on her white cotton nightie. 'I'll make some tea, shall I?'

'Coffee, please. I've become a coffee man since I went away.' Rob was turning things over in the chest of drawers. 'Is my old dressing gown still around, Tess? I think I left it here.'

'Back of the door.'

He smiled. 'No' thrown out?'

'I didn't throw anything of yours out, Rob.'

'Ah, Tess, that tells me a lot.'

They held each other again, their faces cheek to cheek, then Tess released herself.

'Don't say you won't forgive yourself, Rob. You were ill when you did what you did. And everybody's got something they regret.'

He followed her to the kitchen, watching as she began to make the coffee. 'What have you got to regret then, Tess?'

His voice was so tender, so full of love, she almost lost her resolution. After all, some said it wasn't always best for husbands and wives to be completely honest with each other. But if she didn't tell Rob about her relationship with Toby Dene, there would always be that secret between them, known to her and not to him, and the trust they depended on would not be there.

'When you stayed away, I thought you didn't love me,' she said in a low voice, setting out the coffee cups with trembling hands. 'And someone from the past came back.'

'Someone from the past?'

How quickly his voice had changed. All softness gone. But not the love? Surely not the love? So quickly?

'Who?' he asked hoarsely.

'You remember, I told you about him. His name is Toby Dene, he's a doctor.'

'The one who let you down? And you took up with him again?'

'To begin with, it was only friendship—'

'To begin with? And then what?' His voice was shaking. 'Tess, you didn't sleep with him?'

'No, never!'

'What happened then?'

'He wanted me to marry him if I could be free. He was going to buy Pax House—'

'Pax House?' Rob's face was white. He tried to drink his coffee, but set down the cup untasted. 'Toby Dene was

435

going to buy Pax House for you? Oh, Tess, I canna take this in. I thought you loved me—'

'I do love you. That's why I told Toby I couldn't see him again. When he took me round Pax House, all I could think of was you. All I wanted to do was find you. You'd left me and I didn't even know if you still loved me, but I knew I had to be with you again.'

Very gently, Tess touched Rob's cheek. 'You see how it was, Rob? I never loved Toby. I'm no' even sure if he really loved me. I think we were just lonely folk, needing someone. Only Toby wasn't the one for me.'

Rob bent his head and she saw the faint scar that would always be there in his copper-brown hair. 'Oh God, Tess, what can I say? I was to blame for all that, no' you. If I'd never left you, you'd never have needed anybody.'

He raised his head as the thought came to him. 'And you gave up Pax House for me? Did you, Tess? You gave it up for me?'

'What's a house, Rob?'

'But if you hadn't given it up, I might have come back and found you there with this Dene fellow, mightn't I?'

'No, that would never have happened.'

He breathed a long desperate sigh. 'I was lucky then, eh? Lucky to have you.' He put his arms around her and for some moments they stayed quietly together.

'Oh, Tess, why the hell did I ever mind about you driving?' Rob whispered as they drew apart. 'I'm proud of you driving and taking on the business. I'm proud of you, and I'm grateful to Luke. Tomorrow, you might tell me how things have been going. But I'll no' be interfering, I can promise you that.'

'There'll be no question of interfering,' she told him, kissing him. 'It's your business, Rob.'

'No,' he corrected her quietly. 'It's our business, Tess.'

Chapter Ninety-Six

First thing in the morning, before breakfast, Rob was down in the garage looking at the cars.

'Hey, Tess,' he called, coming back up the stairs to the flat, 'what's that Armstrong-Siddely down there? When did you buy that?'

'No' so long ago.' She looked at him a little apprehensively as she set the table. 'We decided we could do with another car. And another driver.'

She had lain awake half the night, worrying what Rob might say about the changes she had made. 'It's our business,' he had said, but did he really mean he was going to share it with her now? He looked so fit and well, so much the old Rob, she couldn't imagine his simply accepting her decisions. 'I'll no' be interfering.' That was another thing he'd said. But surely he would want his say?

'Another driver?' he repeated.

'Aaron Smith. Younger brother of Norrie, who works at Todd's. Luke said he would be first rate.'

'And Luke chose the Armstrong-Siddely?'

'Yes, he checked it very carefully.'

Rob smiled and put his arm round Tess's shoulders.

'Don't look so worried. I meant what I said yesterday. I trust you and I trust Luke. If you folks decided we needed a third car and driver, that's fine by me.'

Tess gave a relieved smile and moved to fill the kettle.

'Like coffee for breakfast?'

'Oh, tea'll do, if you're making it.' Rob sat down at the table and looked up at the clock. 'Luke should be arriving any minute, eh? And this new guy I'd like to meet. What about you, Tess? Are you driving today?'

'No' today. I wasn't sure I'd be back from Coventry.' She hesitated a moment. 'Rob, before Karen appears, perhaps we'd better discuss the driving problem.'

'What driving problem?'

'Well, now you're back and you've got your licence, I won't be needed so much, will I? I was thinking, we might move into doing weddings. I could p'raps drive for them at weekends?'

Rob shook cereal into a bowl and added milk and sugar. 'I don't think we can get involved with weddings just at the moment, Tess. You'll still be needed as a chauffeur.'

'But you're back, Rob. You've got your licence.'

'I've got ma licence, but I won't be driving.'

Tess raised her eyebrows. 'I don't understand. What do you mean, you won't be driving?'

'I should've told you yesterday.' He ate some cornflakes, crunching very deliberately, wishing, as Tess could tell, he might put off saying whatever it was he had to say. 'Didn't want to spoil what we had.'

'Spoil?'

'Thing is, Tess, I'm better, I'm maself again. Except I canna drive.'

She sat with her hands tightly wound together and waited. Waited for Rob to put down his spoon and talk. But there was sweat on his brow and he was finding it hard to look at her; seemed it was easier just to carry on eating cornflakes.

'Rob,' she said at last. 'You'll have to explain.'

'Sounds such a piece of nonsense.' His eyes reluctantly met hers. 'I mean, I can work with cars, I can travel in cars – in the passenger seat – but I canna drive one. It's what they call a block. A psychological block.'

'Because of the accident?'

'Aye. Every time I try to drive a car, I think I'm going to kill a man.' He shrugged and pushed his cereal bowl away from him. 'So I don't try to drive.'

'Rob, you didn't kill anybody. It's just another effect of the accident.' Tess leaped up and went to him, taking his face in her hands, holding his gaze with her own. 'You can get treatment. There's folk can help you.'

'So the doctor said. But I'm no' sure how they can.' Rob gently put her aside and stood up. 'Shall we make that tea?'

'Oh, yes. And toast. Would you like toast? I've no bacon.'

'Toast'll be fine.' Rob folded his arms across his chest and stared sombrely at Tess. 'You'll have guessed this was another reason for me no' coming back? '

'Because you couldn't drive? Why, Rob, that's nonsense!'

'Is it? There was I, making Daimlers. How could I tell you I couldn't drive one?'

'But you knew I'd have understood.'

'Aye, I did. Deep down. But it was the same old thing with me. Pride got in the way.'

Under her great anxious eyes, he gave a tired shrug.

'Didn't want you to see ma weakness.'

She was silent for some moments, still searching his face. 'You did come back,' she whispered at last. 'Why? Did something happen?'

'Nothing dramatic.' He put his hands on her shoulders, meeting her eyes with a long steady gaze. 'I suppose I just – saw the light.'

'Tell me.'

'Well, I was in ma room at the lodgings one night. I was thinking about the future, wondering what'd become of me. Then I looked at your photograph, and wee Karen's, and I thought, what the hell am I doing here? Why am I keeping us all apart?' He tried to laugh. 'It was crazy, eh? Just for the sake of no' losing face, I was giving up everything that mattered to me in the world. That was when I knew I had to see you. Had to come back. And take ma chance.'

'If you hadn't come back, I'd have found you,' Tess said unsteadily. 'Seems strange. We both had the same idea. To be together again.'

'I should've had the idea before then. Blame me, Tess, for wasting so much time.'

'Let's no' talk of blame.'

They kissed gently, then passionately, until Rob let Tess go and sat down abruptly at the table.

'Point is, Tess, we have to face facts. I'm no' much good to you, am I? No better off than when I lost ma licence, to be honest.'

She stared down at him, her face flushing.

'How can you say that? You're better and you've got your licence, everything's different.' She put slices of bread into the toaster. 'This is just a temporary setback. You'll get over it. We'll work on it together.'

Rob, scarcely listening, rested his cheek on his hand and stared into space. 'I'm sick o' working with cars and no' driving 'em, Tess. I took a bookkeeping course in Coventry. Thought I might get some office work.'

'Office work? Heavens, that's no' for you. Look, you have to be positive. Make up your mind you're going to get back to driving for MacNair's Chauffeur Services. Because that's your job.'

'I know what ma job is,' he said quietly. 'You'll have to believe me. I canna do it.'

The way he looked, the way he spoke, turned a knife in Tess's heart.

'Here's your toast,' she whispered, and turned her head at the sound of steps on the stairs. 'Oh, God, I think this must be Nola.'

'We've no' come for breakfast!' cried Nola, bursting in with Luke quietly following. 'We just want to welcome Rob home. Oh, Rob, it's so good to see you!' She flung her arms around him as he stood up and kissed his cheek. 'And you're looking so well. Quite your old self!'

440

'You're looking grand yourself,' Rob murmured.

'As plump as ever.'

'As pretty as ever. And I hear congratulations are in order. I mean, to you two on your marriage. Rob's eyes went to Luke and he put out his hand. 'Luke, belated good wishes, eh?'

'Thanks, Rob.' Luke, visibly relieved at Rob's welcome, warmly shook his hand. 'It's grand to have you back – just grand.'

'Grand to be back. And I want to tell you I'm grateful for all you've done, Luke. Helping to carry on the business, supporting Tess – couldn't have done without you.'

'That's all right,' Luke muttered, colouring. 'I was just doing ma job.'

'A pretty good job, I'd say.' Rob cleared his throat. 'We'll have a talk later, eh?'

'Luke, why don't you and Nola have some tea?' Tess asked, setting out more cups. 'Come on, sit down.'

'Just for a minute then. I'm due out in half an hour.' Luke glanced at Rob. 'And I expect you'll be wanting to meet Aaron, eh? It was OK, wasn't it? Taking him on?'

'Sure, if he was needed.'

'But now you're back—'

'As I say, we'll talk later. Have your tea, Luke.'

'Did you tell Rob about the pottery, Tess?' asked Nola, helping herself to one of Rob's slices of toast.

'I'm sorry, Nola, I'm afraid it slipped ma mind.'

'Slipped your mind? It's all that's in mine. We're hoping to open soon. Shall I cut some more bread?'

'Is ma dad still here?' asked Karen, standing in the doorway.

'Of course I'm still here.' Rob went to her and lifted her up, looking into her face and laughing, then lowering her to the floor. 'But I'm going out now to fetch your present. I think you'll like it.'

As she danced around him, demanding to know what it was, he put his finger to his lips. 'Ssh. It's a secret. Tell you what, if you get ready and eat your breakfast like a good girl, I'll take you with me. Would you like that?'

As Karen flew away to find what she wanted to wear, Rob grinned across at Tess and Nola.

'It's a nurse's outfit,' he whispered. 'I think I've got the right size.'

'Oh, Rob, you're a genius!' cried Nola. 'And you didn't even know Dad had given her a wee nurse dolly!'

'You're right, I'm a genius. Let's see what madam's up to, then.'

As he left the kitchen, Nola exchanged glances with Tess.

'Oh, Tess, he seems so happy,' she murmured. 'It's just as I said, he's his old self again.'

Tess smiled and nodded and buttered toast, but the knife was still in her heart. A man who lived for driving suddenly couldn't drive. How could he be his old self? Rob was like a jigsaw that had been painfully put together, but was still missing one piece. The vital piece – for him. And where to begin looking for it was something Tess couldn't even imagine.

Chapter Ninety-Seven

The truth had to come out, of course. It wasn't long before everyone connected with him had been told that Rob MacNair of MacNair's Chauffeur Services could no longer drive. His licence had been returned to him. He'd paid his dues, but it seemed his punishment wasn't over. The man whose driving was so smooth, so elegant, it could only be described as a thing of beauty, had become a bystander. Forced to watch, while others handled his Daimler and drove the clients that should have been his.

Nobody could understand. Rena, for instance, simply couldn't accept that a big strong fellow like Rob should not be able to get in a car and drive. What was to stop him?

Nola, Katie and Gordon, though unwilling to say so, were of the same opinion, and Aaron Smith said it was like falling off a bike or a horse, eh? You straight away had to get back on again, and even if Rob had missed doing that, he shouldn't just be giving up, should he?

Polly Wight, the neighbours, the workers at Todd's, all agreed on that, and even Luke, the most sympathetic of men, confessed himself mystified. Why could Rob no' make himself do it? He'd been through the war, so he was brave enough. There seemed no reason why he shouldn't overcome this last hurdle.

'There's nothing reasonable about it,' sighed Tess. 'It's a block. It's what they call a phobia. Like when somebody's scared o' spiders, you ken.'

'I canna understand that either,' said Luke. 'But what can we do?'

Tess gave a desolate shake of the head. She didn't know what they could do. In spite of her own great longing to help, the one time she'd driven Rob out into the country, he'd refused even to try to drive them home. He didn't want her to see him getting into a panic, was all he would say.

'And that's what he does, you see, Luke, he gets into a panic. He sweats and canna breathe. His heart starts hammering and he says he sometimes nearly passes out.'

'Maybe I could help though? I could drive him somewhere, sort o' get him used to the car again?'

'That's kind of you, but I don't think you'd have any more luck than me. I think we'll just have to hope that the doctors come up with ideas. He's being sent to see someone at the hospital.'

The person Rob saw at the hospital was a middle-aged woman named Mrs Forsyth. She told him she was neither a doctor nor nor a psychiatrist, but a therapist, who would try to help him to lose his fear of driving by repeatedly facing what had caused it. What she was doing was fairly new, but she had had success with other patients and was confident that she would have the same with him. If success did come, she added, it would come quickly. Rob didn't ask what would happen if success didn't come at all.

Though he had no great hopes that her treatment would work, he liked and trusted Mrs Forsyth, who was efficient and practical. If anyone could help him, he thought, she could.

With her, he went through every aspect of his accident, reliving that terrible night, seeing again the lights of Mark Andrews's car, feeling the impact as he hit it. Over and over again, he endured and faced his experiences, until Mrs Forsyth declared him ready to spend time with his Daimler

– the one he had been driving at the time of the accident.

'I'm no' sure I can do that,' he told her frankly.

'Oh yes, you can, Rob. Have someone with you and very quietly approach the driving seat. Open the driver's door. And sit inside.'

Her eyes on him were steady, even though she could see the drops of sweat already forming on his brow.

'Try it,' she said gently. 'If it doesn't work, you can try again. And then again.'

Two nights later, Tess, almost as nervous as he, went down with Rob to the garage and advanced upon Mr Seton's Daimler. Luke had driven it during the day and cleaned it when he brought it back, but now he had gone home, and there were just the two of them facing it.

'It's so beautiful,' Rob,' Tess whispered. 'Your favourite car, eh?'

'Aye, it was always ma favourite.'

'Seems a shame never to be in it.'

'Aye.'

She took his hand and felt it trembling. 'How about opening the door then?'

He was very pale and sweating hard. 'Give me the keys,' he said hoarsely

When she put the keys in his hand, he opened the driver's door and stood looking in at the seat he'd taken so many, many times before.

'Rob, get in,' said Tess.

'I canna, Tess. Ma heart's pounding. I canna breathe.'

'You can, Rob, you can. Just think of me. Think of Karen. Think of driving Karen.'

'Karen,' he whispered, and stepped into the car.

As soon as she saw him in position in the driving seat, Tess ran round to the passenger's side and moved in next to him.

'Well done, Rob, well done. You're in. You're in the driving seat. Have you got the keys? Put them in the ignition.'

'No, don't ask me, Tess. Just don't ask me.'

But though he was breathing fast, as though he'd climbed a mountain, he was making no move to get out of his seat, and Tess, taking courage, reached across and lifted his hand that still held the keys.

'Now – ignition. Is this no' like learning to drive all over again? Bet it was easy as pie for you, eh? Rob, put the car key in the ignition.'

Like some sort of automaton, he obeyed. He put in the key, he turned it, and the splendid engine roared into life.

'Tess!' he shouted. 'Oh, God, Tess!'

'It's all right, you've done it, Rob, you've done it.' Tears were misting Tess's eyes. 'Switch off now, switch off.'

They were both trembling when he'd turned off the engine and their eyes were meeting, filled with something like awe.

'I canna believe it,' Rob said softly. 'Tess, I canna believe it. This is more than Mrs Forsyth expected. She never thought I'd get to turn on the engine.'

Tess clung to him, not trusting herself to speak, and he smoothed back her hair from her brow and kissed her.

'Tess, will you do something for me?'

'Anything, sweetheart.'

'Open the garage doors.'

A few minutes later, the great car was gliding slowly from the garage with Rob at the wheel, ashen-faced, shaking like a learner on his first trip, hands firmly fixed at the ten-to-two position, but driving. Oh God, driving.

'Oh God, I'm driving,' he cried to Tess. 'I feel I'm going to take off. I feel I'm flying!'

'We canna go far, Rob, we've left Karen in her bed.'

'Just round the block then, just round the block. Oh, look, it's a grand evening. No' dark yet, which is just as well, as I canna remember how to work the lights. Tess, let's go back and get Karen, eh?'

446

'Get her out of bed?'

'Come on, she'll no' be asleep. And this is a special occasion. I'll drive back and you go in and get her, eh?'

'Oh, Rob, if you think it's all right.'

'It's all right, Tess.'

It was, they were always to say, the best drive of their lives. The three of them in the car. Karen, wrapped in a blanket on the back seat, over the moon at the excitement of it all. Tess, looking misty eyed at Rob's profile. And Rob himself, gradually relaxing, gradually becoming the driver he had always been, as the beautiful car responded to his touch and they swept through the streets of Porty like royalty.

'I'll never forget this night,' Tess murmured.

'Nor me!' Rob said with feeling.

But back in the garage, when Tess took the sleepy Karen out of the car, Rob seemed loth to leave his seat.

'I'm afraid, Tess. Supposing, next time, it all goes wrong again?'

'It won't, Rob, it won't. You've cracked it. You've won. Come on now, let's get Karen back to bed.'

'I'll just switch on the engine again, eh? Just to make sure I can?'

'All right.' She stood smiling over the top of Karen's head. 'If it'll make you happy.'

He turned on the engine, listened as it came to life, then switched it off again and sat for a moment, running his hands up and down the wheel, lost in dreamland, as Tess told him, laughing.

'Come on,' she said again. 'I want you to carry Karen.'

'Sorry.' He slowly left the car and locked the door. 'Give her to me, Tess.'

'You're keeping the keys?' she asked lightly.

'I'm keeping the keys.'

*

447

When they'd put Karen back to bed, Rob said he had a bottle of wine he'd been meaning to open on his return. That had been cause for celebration, but this was another. At least, he hoped it was.

'Stop worrying, Rob,' Tess told him. 'You're all right now. You've made the breakthrough, that's all that matters.'

'Aye, I know, and Mrs Forsyth said if her treatment worked, it'd be quick. But I've waited so long, you ken, I still canna believe I can drive again.'

'Think of us in that car with you, Karen and me. You know you can drive, Rob.'

'That's true.' He gave a relieved smile. 'Yes, I'm OK. I know I am. And I'll no' lose ma driving now.'

'We should have a celebration,' said Tess. 'Give everybody the news that you're really better.'

'No, no celebration. Tell folks, aye. But I don't want a celebration. I don't deserve it.'

Tess began to speak, but he quickly kissed her lips.

'Maybe just for the two of us, eh? I wouldn't say no to that.'

'Nor me. Let's open the wine then.'

They drank their wine, they made love, and afterwards, Rob said he was going to send Mrs Forsyth some flowers. He owed her a lot.

'She didn't tell me anything I didn't know, but I needed her to make me face what I had to do. I'll always be grateful.'

'You should send flowers to yourself, an' all, Rob. You found the will to get into that driving seat.'

'Couldn't have done it without Mrs Forsyth, or you, Tess. I mean it. You were with me, you got me through.'

One time, she knew, he would never have been willing to admit his dependency, but this was a different Rob before her now, with a different kind of courage. Now, he knew that there were times when he needed help just like everybody else, and he was ready to take it – from Mrs Forsyth, or herself. She loved him for it.

'So, when can I expect some flowers then?' she asked smiling.

'Flowers are no' enough for you.'

'I'll settle for them as long as I've got you.'

'You'll always have me.'

They embraced quickly, to put from their minds the time when she had not had him, then Rob lay back and stretched.

'Expect I'll be too excited to sleep tonight.'

'What about tomorrow?' asked Tess.

'What about it?'

'Well, will you be taking on some of the driving? Will you be – you know – sorting out – who does what?'

He hesitated. 'You bet I'll want to be driving, but I think I'll need a bit of time to get used to things first. Have to be very sure of maself before I drive clients.'

'That's true, but I don't think it'll take you long to get to that stage, Rob.'

He touched her cheek. 'You're no' worrying, are you?'

'It's just, there's Aaron – and me. I wouldn't mind being part-time – I'd like to spend more time with Karen – but Aaron needs the work.'

'Sweetheart, nobody's going to get the sack. We've big plans, haven't we? Big plans for expansion. Weddings, as you say, or I'm even thinking we might branch out into self-drive hire.'

'Self-drive? That's something new for you.'

'Well, I'm looking ahead, of course. We have to keep our options open. You heard that Jaguar has just bought Daimler? There might be changes in the cars. Might no' be so many limousines.'

'There'll always be folk wanting limousines, Rob. And you'll always be wanting to drive them.'

'That's true.' He kissed her. 'I'm just talking of plans.'

'And you're right, they're big plans.'

'We'll be making them together.'

'Together.'

Tess said no more before she fell asleep, breathing quietly and regularly against Rob's chest, as he lay awake, looking into the darkness, seeing a bright future, thanking his lucky stars.

Chapter Ninety-Eight

When all the excitement over Rob's return to driving had died down, Nola and Rena announced their own news. Finola's Pottery was to have its grand opening the following Saturday. Adverts had already gone out and it would be open house from eleven until four o'clock, everybody welcome. Especially the public. It was hoped they'd be buying.

'I'll be buying,' said Tess. 'Why, I'm sure we'll all be buying.'

'Aye, the family will be kind, maybe,' said Nola. 'But we've got to attract strangers.'

'Come on, your things are lovely. You'll attract buyers, all right.'

'What do you think of ma teapots?' Rena asked anxiously. 'All thae years o' sticking on handles, I thought, why should I no' make the whole thing?' She shivered. 'But I'm that nervous now, I canna tell you. If anybody buys one o' ma pots and the handle falls off, what'll I do?'

'Nothing's going to fall off, Ma,' Nola said crisply. 'Have a bit o' confidence, eh? It's no' like you to be nervous.'

'Things are different, now I'm – ahem – an artist.'

Rena laughed and her girls laughed with her, marvelling at the way she had taken to her new interest and glad that she looked so well on it. Had she even put on a little weight? She looked younger anyway.

'Och, we'll have a grand opening,' Nola told Tess. 'Even if Ginger's too scared to appear. Aye, he's made sure he's got a drive on the day.'

'Well, Rob's manning the phone, but he's promised to look in,' said Tess. 'Polly's coming too. I tell you, we're all supporting Finola's!'

'And afterwards, you're all coming back to Number One for your tea,' Rena reminded them. 'I'll have everything ready before I go out, nae bother.'

'All that and making teapots too,' sighed Nola. 'Ma. I don't know what we'd do without you.'

Tess, joining a crowd of Porty folk looking round Finola's on the opening day, declared herself impressed by the pieces on display. Even her mother's teapots were pretty and well made, but Nola's things were really stylish and imaginative.

Of course, she'd seen some of her sister's work already; Nola had been showing her bowls, vases, platters, and jugs for some time. Here, though, displayed in the showroom, Tess felt she was truly appreciating them for the first time. Not only was Nola a professional, she was also, as Rena had jokingly described herself, an artist.

'I'm so proud of Nola,' Tess whispered to Rob. 'Did you ever think I'd have such a clever sister?'

'I did, as a matter of fact. When she first told me what she did at Harebell's, I knew it'd take talent.' Rob picked up one of Rena's teapots. 'But look at this your ma's done, eh? You should be proud of her, too.'

'I am.' Tess hesitated. 'Rob, you are getting on better with Ma these days, aren't you?'

'Aye, I think so. I think she's forgiven me. And I appreciate it.' He looked at his watch. 'I'd better go, Tess. Where's Karen? I'll say goodbye to her.'

'She's helping Ma at the till.'

'Helping?' asked Rob with a grin.

'Taking off price tags, having a wonderful time.'

Rob swiftly kissed Tess's cheek. 'See you later at Number One then.'

'I'm going to look for Nola.'

Nola was at her wheel, her face flushed, her blue eyes shining, as she demonstrated to a crowd of onlookers how she centred the clay and then shaped it as she wanted, her hands working so smoothly, so deftly, their movements seemed to be having a hypnotic effect on the watchers.

'Och, you make it look that easy,' sighed Vera MacFee, her eyes a little glassy. 'But I'd niver be able to do it in a month o' Sundays!'

'Practice is all it needs,' Nola answered cheerfully. 'You should see Ma, Vera. She's a natural. Now, I'll just stop ma wheel a minute and show you folks the kiln. It's electric, you ken, but you can get gas. Everybody's always interested in ma baking, eh?'

'Is she no' in her element?' Rena, suddenly appearing, whispered in Tess's ear. 'She's really happy, eh?'

'She is, Ma. It's grand to see.'

'Think it's just the pottery though?'

Tess stared. 'Why, what else?'

'I'm no' sure.' Rena pursed her lips. 'Just lately I've thought she's got that look, you ken.'

'What look?'

'Och, you ken fine what look.' Rena lowered her voice. 'Think she could be expecting?'

Tess shook her head, laughing. 'Ma, you're hopeless. Talk about wishful thinking! You know what Nola always says – the pottery's her baby.'

'Aye, but she might find she's got another one. It'd be just like the thing, eh? For a babby to wait till she starts up in business? But I'll be here to help.' Rena nodded with satisfaction. 'She'll no' have to worry.'

'Aren't you supposed to be on the till?' asked Tess, still amused. 'And where's Karen?'

'I've got Polly standing in. Still, I'd better get back. Be sure and buy something, Tess.'

'One o' your teapots, I promise.'

Tess was debating which teapot to buy, and which of Nola's vases, when she felt a light touch on her arm and a familiar voice spoke her name. When she spun round, she saw Erika.

Trying to keep out of the way of the customers, they moved into a corner of the showroom, Tess still surprised at having met up with Erika again, Erika herself quite calm. Hadn't Tess expected her to come? Nola had put adverts in all the local papers, and of course, Erika had wanted to see Nola's work, and Rena's too.

'It's so beautiful,' she said earnestly. 'So talented. I must confess myself astonished.' She blushed a little. 'No, that sounds rude, but I had no idea they could do such work.'

'Neither had I,' Tess told her. 'Ma's things are really good, I think she's done well, but Nola's – they're amazing. I just hope she'll be successful.'

'Oh, she will be, she must be! I am going to buy this bowl that is like a peacock's feather. See how the colours move togther, blue and green, and seem to shimmer?'

'I think I'll go for one o' her vases.' Tess looked away self-consciously. 'How are things with you then? Did you phone Toby?'

'Yes, I did, in the end.' Erika too was self-conscious. 'He seemed surprised to hear from me.'

'I'm sure he was pleased.'

'Well, we met for dinner. But you were right, he is not staying in Scotland. He thinks he'd be better off down south. Simon agrees.'

'I see.' Tess was still looking away. 'But I'm sure he'll get in touch with you again, before he goes.'

'Perhaps.' Eria shrugged. 'But we have our own lives to live. Tell me about yourself, Tess. Is all well with you? Is your family here?'

'I'm sorry, Rob isn't, but come and meet ma daughter, Karen. She's with Ma at the till, helping to sell things, if you can believe it.'

'I should so like to see Mrs Gillespie again.' Erika looked down into the swirling colours of Nola's bowl. 'She was always so very kind to Mutti and me. And, of course, I want to meet your little girl.'

It was four o'clock and the pottery was closing. Rena, still keyed up with excitement, said they'd done really well, sold far more than they'd ever thought. She hadn't had time to total up the cash, she'd to hurry along home, but she already knew it was enough to get them off to a splendid start.

'We've done well, Nola,' she said seriously. 'I ken fine it'll no' always be like this, but folk did like our stuff, eh? I think we can keep this place going as well as Shona Kay.'

'I agree,' said Nola. 'Ma, I'm proud o' you.'

'It's you I'm proud of. Did you see Erika Lange? Came and had a word with me, bought that lovely blue-green bowl you made. She was really singing your praises, I can tell you.'

'I did see her. She was very sweet.' Nola shook her head. 'Funny to think of her as a doctor.'

'Aye, and smart as paint.' Rena's voice trembled a little. 'Poor Herta would've been that proud.' She put on her coat and tied a scarf over her hair she'd had newly set in beehive style for the opening. 'Well, let's away. It's a good job you've got your car, Nola. We'd no' be wanting to walk all the way to Number One, eh?'

'It's been a long day,' Nola admitted, as she locked the door of the pottery. 'But satisfying.'

'Aye, it's been grand. No' too tired, are you?'

'Me? No, I feel wonderful. How about you?'

'The same, the same.'

But Rena gave Tess a meaningful look, as though to say, Well, she feels wonderful, couldn't that be a sign? And

Tess, smiling to herself, called to Karen to come.

'We're going to Gran's now?' asked Karen.

'Aye, we're all going for our tea.'

'Will Dad be there?'

'Of course he will.'

Oh, ma poor wee girl, thought Tess, as she and Karen squeezed into the back seat of Nola's little Austin. Always asking where Rob was; always checking that he had not gone away. She would do that for a long time, perhaps, and would always be vulnerable. As all children were vulnerable, at the mercy of their parents' mistakes.

Rob felt bad, Tess knew he did; knew he wanted only to make it up to Karen for leaving her. But all he and Tess could do was to love her and make sure her little world was safe again. One day, maybe, she might come to understand.

Chapter Ninety-Nine

As soon as Nola pulled up outside Rena's house, Tess gave a quite unnecessary sigh of relief. Rob was already there, on the steps with Luke, and waving.

'There you are,' she said to Karen. 'There's your dad, see?'

Karen leaped out of the car and flew to him; he lifted her up and swung her round, while Luke, shamefacedly, asked Nola how the day had gone.

'Good crowd, eh? Sold plenty o' pots?'

'It was very, very successful,' she told him, kissing him. 'We sold loads, and if you'd no' been such a great jessie, you'd have seen for yourself.'

'Och, I was just that nervous for you. Anyway, I'd to do a drive. Got back early though. Aaron's still out.'

'He's a good lad, Luke,' said Rob, setting down Karen, but still holding her hand. 'You did well to find him.'

'So different from Norrie,' Tess murmured. 'What a tease, eh? I never knew what he was going to come out with next.'

'Now why are we all standing here?' asked Rena. 'Come away in, and I'll get started. Vera and Phil will be round in a minute, and Polly and Kennie. I'd have asked some o' the students down, just to give 'em a good meal, but these days they'd die o' boredom if they'd to spend time with us old folk, eh?'

'Hey, who are you calling old?' asked Nola.

'Well, you're no' twenty any more, pet.'

'Sweet and twenty – canna even remember being that.'

'I remember,' said Tess. 'It was the year the war ended. You were still twenty that time you went out dancing on VE Night.'

'Fancy you remembering.' Nola sighed, and felt for Luke's hand. 'All too long ago, eh?'

'Aye, well, you sit down and rest yourself,' said her mother, shepherding everyone into her front sitting room. 'Tess'll help me. Rob, I've some Christmas sherry in that sideboard. Will you pour it out when the others come?'

'I wish I'd put on ma nurse's outfit for this party,' said Karen. 'I'd have looked special.'

'You look special, anyway,' said Rob. 'Now, shall we go down to the kitchen and find you some lemonade?'

When the meal was well on its way to being ready, Tess ran upstairs to join the guests for a quick sherry and was buttonholed by Nola.

'What's all this about me resting?' she whispered, lighting a cigarette. 'Ma seems to think I've suddenly become an invalid.'

Tess's face broke into smiles. 'No, she thinks you're expecting,' she whispered back.

'She what?' Nola gave a loud laugh, then coughed as people turned to stare. 'Whatever gave her that idea?'

'She says you've got the look.'

'What look?'

'The look folk have when they're expecting.'

'I may be overweight, but no' that overweight!'

'It's your face, she's meaning. Has a different look, for some reason.'

'Och, what an old wives' tale. I don't look any different.'

'It's no' true then?'

'No' as far as I know. Wish it was.'

458

'You're no' late, or anything?'

'Well, a bit, but that's nothing to get excited about.'

'Still, you never know.' Tess finished her sherry. 'Supposing Ma's right?'

Nola looked at the cigarette between her fingers. 'You knew I'd started smoking again? I thought, what's the point of me giving up, nothing's ever going to happen. And now, you've got me thinking—' She paused, then shook her head. 'No, it's impossible. Ma's wrong.'

'Aye, but if she isn't?'

'I tell you it's all nonsense. It'd be wonderful if it wasn't, but I've waited too long.' Nola smiled briefly. 'No harm in putting this out though.' Reaching for one of her mother's ashtrays, she stubbed out her cigarette.

'I'd say, no harm at all,' said Tess, pressing her sister's hand. 'Now, I'd better go back and help Ma with the food. Are you hungry?'

'Starving.'

'H'm. That's a good sign.'

'Tess – no teasing.'

'Only joking. Anyway, I seem to remember you used to be the one for teasing.'

'When I was sweet and twenty? Like I say, a long time ago.'

Rena's splendid high tea was almost over, and she was jumping up to take away plates, when the doorknocker sounded.

'I'll go,' said Rob, leaping to his feet. 'It'll be Gordon.'

'Is that who you've been waiting for?' asked Tess. 'I saw you looking at your watch.'

'Yes, I've been expecting him. He's late.'

'Why, he could've had his tea with us!' Rena exclaimed. 'Why'd you no' say he was coming over from Haddington?' To Vera and the others who didn't know, she explained that Gordon was Rob's brother, the one that had the farm.

'I'll bring him down,' Rob called over his shoulder from the door. 'No, you canna come up, Karen. You stay where you are. I won't be a minute.'

'There's something going on,' Rena declared. 'Rob's being very secretive, eh?'

'Why, how could he be secretive with Gordon?' asked Nola. 'He's as open as the day.' She smiled reminiscently. 'Lovely dancer, an' all.'

'Better than me, I suppose,' sighed Luke. 'Wouldn't be difficult.'

'You're the only one I want to dance with,' she told him in a whisper, and he smiled and covered her hand with his.

'I want to see Uncle Gordon!' cried Karen. 'Where is he?'

'He's coming.' Tess was listening intently. 'And I think something else is coming, too.'

'What, Mammie? What's coming?'

'Aye, what?' asked Rena.

'Oh, my Lord!' cried Tess, her hands to her mouth, as Rob appeared at the kitchen door, followed by Gordon. 'It's Honey!'

Chapter One Hundred

Of course, it wasn't Honey that was slippering and sliding into the kitchen on a lead held by Rob, but just another golden puppy that was very like her. So like, there were tears in Tess's eyes as she left the table with Karen and stooped to gaze unbelievably at the little dog.

'No, this isn't Honey,' Rob told her, smiling. 'This is Sandy. Gordon's brought him over.'

'Gordon?' Tess kissed his cheek. 'Where did you find him? Oh, he's so lovely. Ma, Nola – come and see!'

Everyone was crowding round, making appreciative noises, as the puppy wagged his tail and made a few squeaks himself, and Gordon explained that he'd come from a kennels near Haddington.

'Rob asked me some time ago to find you a new Labrador, Tess. I got in touch with some breeders I know, put Rob's name down for a puppy and here's the result.' Gordon grinned. 'Sandy. Of course, you can change the name if you like. He's got a kennel name an' all, but that's as long as your arm.'

'No, I think Sandy's grand. Oh, I canna believe it, he's so like Honey. Rob, did you really ask Gordon to find him for me?'

'Aye.' He put his arm round her shoulders. 'I told you, didn't I, that I'd give you something more than flowers?'

'But he's for all of us,' she said softly.

461

'For me as well?' asked Karen, laughing as the puppy tried to lick her hand.

'Like I say, for all of us.'

'When can we take him home?'

'Ma will say as soon as possible, seeing as he's no' trained yet,' said Rob.

'No' trained yet?' cried Rena. 'Och, who cares?'

They didn't leave for home immediately. First, Gordon had to be given coffee and a sandwich, though he said he'd already had a meal. Next, Sandy had to be given a drink, which involved a volley of excited squeaks and yelps, and more water going on the newspapers Rena had laid down than into Sandy himself.

'Poor wee dog!' cried Nola. 'He's no' long left his mother, eh?'

'He'll be fine,' said Gordon. 'He was ready to leave, to go to a good home, of course.'

'Like ours,' said Rob. 'We'd better watch out in case we spoil him.'

'Remembering Honey,' put in Tess.

'Aye, remembering Honey.'

Finally, they were on the outside steps, making farewells to Vera and Phil, to Polly and Kennie, while Gordon opened his car door.

'You're sure you don't want a lift?' he called.

'No thanks, we want to walk,' Rob told him. 'And the basket and dog food's already at the flat, so there's nothing to carry.'

'Except Sandy,' Gordon said with a grin, and thanking Rena again for the coffee and promising to be in touch, drove away.

'Come on, Mammie,' Karen cried impatiently. 'I want to take Sandy on the beach. He's called Sandy, he should see the sands.'

'It'll soon be dark, pet. I think we should go by the promenade.'

'Ah, come on,' said Rob. 'Let him have a sniff of the sea.'

'Wait while I say goodbye, then.'

'Thought you'd said goodbye!' wailed Karen, but Tess wanted to give Nola one last hug and a secret smile.

'Finola's Pottery is going to do really well,' she whispered. 'We're proud of you. And I'll – you know – keep ma fingers crossed.'

'Well and truly crossed,' Nola whispered back, as Tess moved to kiss her mother's cheek.

'Thanks for the meal, Ma, that was grand. I'll pick up ma teapot tomorrow, eh?'

'Just don't ever tell me if the handle falls off,' said Rena, watching as Rob and Karen, with Sandy straining on his lead, waited impatiently at the top of the King George Road. 'Rob's a good lad, Tess. He's made mistakes, you ken, but he loves you. That's the thing, eh?'

'That's the thing, Ma.'

'Take care o' the wee dog then.'

'No need to worry about that.'

Tess smiled and waved goodbye again to Luke and the others at the door, but they were more interested in Sandy's joyous progress down the road to the sands.

'Will you look at the little fella?' asked Kennie Wight indulgently. 'He's got Rob on the run wi' that lead, eh?'

'And wee Karen, too,' said Polly. 'My word, he's going to keep 'em all on the hop, eh?'

'Hey, wait for me!' called Tess, but the tall man and the little girl, running ahead with the golden puppy, were already reaching the sands.

It was lonely down there. They were almost the only people walking under the darkening sky, the sand scudding before the wind, the waves wildly rising. Sandy, released from his lead, had bounded down to inspect the water, but seemed undecided what to do. Should he go in? Should he not?

'Don't let him go in!' cried Tess. 'Rob, bring him up!'

'He's getting covered with sand!' cried Karen.

'Well, that's no' surprising,' said Rob, hurriedly bringing the puppy back up the beach. 'But he's going to be in one terrible mess by the time we get him home, Tess.'

'As Ma says, who cares? You expect a bit o' work with a puppy.'

'Are you pleased with your present?'

'You know I am.'

They stood together, not kissing or embracing, but serenely happy, as Karen raced by, chasing Sandy, who had found some wonderful seaweed to toss around as he went.

'This is where we met,' Tess murmured. 'You were with Honey. I couldn't think who you were.'

'And I wanted to know who you were.'

'I used to come here when you'd gone, remembering you.'

His arms tightened around her. 'Don't, Tess. Don't speak of that. It's all over now.'

'That's why I can talk about it.'

They walked on, their feet dragging in the heavy damp sand.

'Went by Pax House the other day,' Rob said after a companionable silence. 'It's been sold. Saw the notice.'

'I wonder who bought it?' asked Tess.

They both knew who had not.

'No regrets?' Rob asked softly.

'No regrets.'

'I wish I could've bought it for you.'

'I don't. I'll never forget Mr Seton and what he did for us, but the house – it's in the past, Rob. We have to look to the future.'

'Aye, and I think it'll be a good one.' They exchanged a quick kiss for Karen was running towards them. 'And there's part of it, eh?'

'Most important part,' said Tess.

In her mind was the thought that she and Rob should do something about that brother her mother had once talked

464

about for Karen. Or would it be a sister? Either would be welcome. At one time, she had liked to say that there was plenty of time, but not now.

'Dad, Sandy is tired,' Karen was saying breathlessly. 'He's sitting down.'

'Oh, Lord, so he is.' Rob grinned. 'Gordon was right. I'll have to carry him home.'

'It's no' far now,' said Tess. 'But it's really getting dark; we'll have to leave the sands anyway.'

'I hate leaving the sands,' said Karen.

'They'll be there tomorrow, pet.'

'Always be sure of that,' said Rob.

'And other things,' Tess murmured.

'Aye.' He took her meaning and bent his face close to hers. 'Whatever happens, we'll have one another, eh?'

'Dad, Sandy is falling asleep,' called Karen next, and Rob, with a mock groan, hoisted the puppy, flopping like a large soft toy, into his arms.

'Come on, let's away,' he cried, and began to lope towards the promenade, followed by a laughing Karen.

But Tess, lingering, looked back at the beach that was now empty, for they had been the last to leave. The darkness was moving in fast, over the water, over the sands, and she stood for a moment, thinking of tomorrow. She and Karen would be here again, running with the new little dog, and there would be Porty folk about and the whole place filled with light, maybe even sunshine. So many tomorrows, she hoped for, standing there, looking back; so many tomorrows, so much love.

Then, with contented heart, she joined the little girl and the tall man with the golden dog, who were waiting for her under the street lamps of the promenade. And they went home together.

*Watch out
for more
Anne Douglas titles
from
Piatkus!*

GINGER STREET

The Millar family live next door to the Riettis on Ginger Street, a row of Victorian tenements on Edinburgh's south side but their circumstances couldn't be more different. Ruth Millar would like to stay on at school but her father's salary as a grocer's assistant is barely enough to put food on the table, let alone such luxuries as an education. By contrast the Riettis own the local corner shop and a little cafe at the end of Ginger Street.

Ruth's father dreams of one day owning his own business. Meanwhile Ruth secretly dreams of Nicco Rietti. But not only is Nicco older, he is Italian and Catholic, three things which make him out of bounds for Ruth, especially with the threat of war on the horizon . . .

978-0-7499-3383-8

A HIGHLAND ENGAGEMENT

After their parents die, Leslie Mackenzie and her two siblings are taken in by their Auntie Peg. Leslie knows that given the poverty and unemployment in and around Leith, she is lucky to have a roof over her head – albeit her aunt's tenement – and a job to go to. So she can hardly believe her luck when she manages to escape the poverty of Leith and earns a position at the Hotel Grand Forest in the highlands of Scotland.

However, it couldn't be more different from the Edinburgh hotel Leslie is used to working in. The luxury spa hotel is in the highlands of Scotland, in the small village of Glenmar, and caters to the whims of its rich, high society guests. But whilst in many ways it is her dream job, strict rules govern the behaviour of all Grand Forest's employees and staff are forbidden from mixing with guests. But then Leslie meets Christopher Meredith and falls in love . . .

978-0-7499-3501-6

THE EDINBURGH BRIDE

Maeve O'Donavan has arrived in Edinburgh from County Cork, trying to forget her unrequited love for the man who has since married her cousin. However, life in a strange city is at first difficult and Maeve is shocked when she encounters prejudice against her Irish background. When she loses her job as a maid, she is delighted to find a job as an assistant in the wardrobe department of the Queen's Theatre. It's a new and exciting world for Maeve – not least because she finds herself attracted to the brooding Harry Alpin, a theatre lighting man who harbours a desire to act. However, will his prejudiced family ever to be willing to accept an Irish girl as Harry's bride…?

978-0-7499-3850-5